# The Only Poet

# The Only Poet
## *& Short Stories*

# Rebecca West

*Edited and Introduced by*
Antonia Till

Published by VIRAGO PRESS Limited 1992
20–23 Mandela Street, Camden Town, London NW1 0HQ

*A CIP catalogue record for this book is available from the
British Library*

Typeset by Falcon Typographic Art Ltd, Fife, Scotland
Printed in Great Britain by Bookcraft (Bath) Ltd.

# Contents

Thanks are due to Hearst's International Cosmopolitan Magazine for permission to reprint 'The Magician of Pell Street'; to Saturday Evening Post for permission to reprint 'Sideways'; to the New Yorker for permission to reprint 'Parthenope'; to Ladies Home Journal for permission to reprint 'Deliverance'; to Doubleday, Doran & Co. for permission to reprint 'Lucky Boy' from *The World's Best Short Stories of 1930*; to Eyre & Spottiswoode for permission to reprint 'They That Sit in Darkness' from *The Fothergill Omnibus, 1931*; and to Cassell & Company for permission to reprint 'The Second Commandment: Thou Shalt Not Make Any Graven Image' from *The Ten Commandments, Ten Short Novels of Hitler's War Against the Moral Code.*

# *Introduction*

Rebecca West (*née* Cicely Isabel Fairfield) was born on 21 December 1892, and to celebrate and commemorate this centenary Virago, as a coda to its proud record of publishing her work, offers this collection of short stories and incomplete fiction. Several pieces were found among her unpublished papers after her death and, of the others, only one has ever been collected before. They embrace her entire writing career, a career which spanned most of the twentieth century – from the unfinished novel *Adela*, written while she was still in her teens, to the magnificent fragments of a late novel, *The Only Poet*, probably begun in the late 1950s and still being worked on in the late 1970s, a few years before her death in 1983. Here we can trace most of the concerns and preoccupations which engaged a writer for whom emotional and intellectual passion had equal and sometimes troubling primacy. For readers familiar with her work this collection should offer an illuminating and satisfying addition to her body of published fiction, while new readers will find an alluring introduction to her writing.

Rebecca West once provocatively described herself (in *Black Lamb and Grey Falcon*) as a 'typical Englishwoman'. English she was not, having Irish and Scottish ancestry; 'typical' she certainly was not, being something of a phoenix and, occasionally, *monstre sacré*; above all, the range and intensity of her intellectual interests are more akin to those of the European intellectual than those of a 'typical Englishwoman'. Her non-fiction could range from scintillating and contentious journalism and criticism, through a discursive and idiosyncratic essay on aesthetics, *The Strange Necessity* (1928), or an exuberant, compact biography, *St Augustine* (1933), to her majestic mature works, *Black Lamb and Grey Falcon* (1937) and *The Meaning of Treason* (1949). Her fiction has an equally broad compass, starting with the short, psychologically acute *The Return of the Soldier* (1918)

1

and ranging through novels of changing styles and techniques, and short stories light-hearted, grave or satirical, to *The Fountain Overflows* (1956) and its successors, and the intense political thriller, *The Birds Fall Down* (1966). But in all her work, fiction or non-fiction, there are some common themes and elements. One of these is described in *Black Lamb and Grey Falcon*:

> I have never used my writing to make a continuous disclosure of my own personality to others, but to discover for my own edification what I knew about various subjects which I found to be important to me; . . . in consequence I had written a novel about London to find out why I loved it, a life of St Augustine to find out why every phrase I read of his sounds in my ears like the sentence of my doom and the doom of my age, and a novel about rich people to find out why they seemed to me as dangerous as wild boars and pythons.

It is this exhilarating inquisitiveness which gives so much of her work its furious gusto.

Another element which underlies almost all her writing is her temperamental dualism. To many Europeans, heirs to the Judaeo-Christian tradition (in which, as Gnosticism or Catharism, dualism was heresy), it is often an appealing form of moral cosmology, and it permeated Rebecca West's thinking and writing. One of these dualisms is expressed in *The Strange Necessity* (1928) as 'two opposing forces: the will to live and the will to die', and glossed more fully in *Black Lamb and Grey Falcon* (1937):

> Only part of us is sane: only part of us loves pleasure and the longer day of happiness, wants to live to our nineties and die in peace . . . The other half is nearly mad. It prefers the disagreeable to the agreeable, loves pain and its darker night despair, and wants to die in a catastrophe that will set back life to its beginnings and leave nothing of our house save its blackened foundation. Our bright natures fight in us with this yeasty darkness.

Another of these dualisms lies in what she perceived as the polarity of the sexes – what Victoria Glendinning, in her admirable, elegant and comprehensive biography *Rebecca West* (Weidenfeld & Nicolson, 1987), calls 'the dialectics of gender'. For Rebecca West, men and women were fundamentally opposite and, too often, oppositional. She might hope for a fruitful tension, even for reconciliation, but saw more often uncomprehending hostility. In *The Thinking Reed* (1936) Isabelle reflects 'that the difference between men and women is the rock on which civilisation will split before it can reach any goal that could justify its expenditure of effort'. In *Black Lamb and Grey Falcon* West portrays herself as the feminine 'Balloon' while her husband provides the masculine 'Ballast'. The heroines of *Harriet Hume* (1929) and *Sunflower* (1986), despite the fact that both have successful performing careers, are to be read as quintessentially feminine, while the men they love display their masculinity in the public world of action and its sometimes dubious accommodations. These dualities inform even the lightest stories of this collection, and throb like a pulse through *The Only Poet*.

Some years ago Virago was able to acquire a collection of Rebecca West's unpublished work, fiction and non-fiction. All of it was sorted, typed and annotated with affectionate and exemplary scrupulousness by Diana Stainforth, the writer's last secretary. Our gratitude for this knowledgeable and sensitive work, especially on *The Only Poet*, is beyond expression. It was decided, with some reluctance, not to include three of the available complete stories, two of which were found among her papers after her death. 'Encounter' appeared in the *International Literary Annual* of 1958, and looks back to New York in the 1920s. It is very similar in mood and atmosphere to the 'American' stories included here, and has a culminating twist which would be lost on many present-day readers, hinging as it does on the Italian playwright Luigi Pirandello, whose explorations of identity and persona have rather gone out of fashion. It contains an incident which recalls an escapade of the writer's when, with Charlie Chaplin, she broke into a Central Park boathouse to row on the lake at night. Another story, 'Minority Problem', probably written in 1951 and rejected by *Punch* in 1955, is a satire on what she seemed to have perceived as the growing power of a homosexual establishment. Here it is the heterosexual men who identify each other by covert signs, have special meeting places and express profound relief at being able to reveal themselves, at least to their own kind. Victoria Glendinning writes that 'homosexuality in men distressed her because it represented the failure of the sexes to come to any understanding', but assures us that there were many homosexuals among Rebecca West's warm and wide circle of friends. Nevertheless, even a tolerant reader would be likely to conclude that this limp and rancid satire is disappointing when laid beside her other work. The third, 'Edith', was written in the summer of 1982, less than a year before West's death. It is set in a hospital or treatment centre after some unspecified nuclear disaster, and the characters face certain death. But, in spite of this inescapable fate, there lingers – as a palliative, as a sign of human grace – the 'will to live', a fragile hope. The story, evidently in first draft, is, however, incoherent and uncertain, and West herself was deeply dissatisfied with it. When there was so much else to choose from, it seemed perverse and unjust to publish so clearly embryonic a work of art.

*The Only Poet*, which gives its title to this collection, has been placed last, both for chronological decorum and because, fragmentary as it is, it represents Rebecca West at the height of her novelistic powers. Even the tantalizingly little we have shows her piercing intelligence and emotional perspicuity. She was working on it intermittently between the late 1950s and the late 1970s. Although, judging from the 'Outline' she left, there are long sections of the book on which she never embarked, other passages have several workings. The 'real' time of the novel takes place during an evening party attended by Leonora Morton. Now over eighty, she catches sight of the woman who, by the coarseness of her actions, ruined the great love affair of Leonora's life. The core of the novel is centred round this affair and the lovers' meeting ten years later. Rebecca West handles the technical problems

4

of flashback with virtuoso accomplishment, and even in sections where we have only a line or two of dialogue there is a powerful narrative charge. She is capable of holding the reader's attention through long passages of recall or reflection, and the mature artistry and characteristic density of texture which make her so demanding and so rewarding a writer are present here as consummately as they are in her other late novels.

Readers familiar with Rebecca West's life, and with *Sunflower*, will note the painful episode where Leonora is rejected by the rich and powerful man who had seemed to desire her. It echoes West's own sexual humiliation by Max Aitken, Lord Beaverbrook. This painful and inexplicable encounter of the 1920s manifestly continued to rankle with her until the end of her life, a sore to be probed even in her last novel.

It is worth noting that Leonora stands almost alone among Rebecca West's heroines in having no career. As we have observed, even those quintessentially feminine heroines Harriet Hume and Sunflower have vocations, though the rich Isabelle in *The Thinking Reed* seems to see her marriage as her job. The twins of *The Fountain Overflows* and its sequels have an ineluctable destiny as concert pianists. Laura in *The Birds Fall Down*, while too young for a career, seems unlikely to settle for what Rebecca West called 'idiocy', 'from the Greek root meaning private person'. Only the tragic Marion Yaverland of *The Judge* lives the life of 'idiocy', imprisoned by the distorted consequences of love and by a proud shame. In most ways, the destiny of Leonora is happier; she is conscious of 'the very pleasant situation in which she found herself in her old age, widow of a well-loved second husband, with two affectionate and handsome daughters who had married nice men and given her agreeable grandchildren, as well as a world of friends and a pleasant house'. Nevertheless, the loss of her great love, Nicholas, means that 'when the night looked in at any uncurtained window she looked back at it, and saw that when she came to die she would have had nothing out of life'.

In 1934 (in her commentary for *The Modern Rake's Progress*) Rebecca West wrote: 'The two chief ills of life . . . are the loss of love or the approach of death'. This could be the epigraph for *The Only Poet*. At

the end Leonora dies, having spent the evening contemplating the loss
of love. Yet it is difficult to read what exists of the novel without feeling
that Leonora had had something palpably valuable out of life. The
long recall of her love affair leaves us with a sense not of tragedy but
of fulfilment. We are given a rich sense of who Leonora is in the first
part of the novel, which is the most fully worked. It is the portrait
of a distinguished, alertly self-aware and humane woman who – as
we are to see from the flashback section – develops naturally from
her younger self. The section which deals with the affair is far more
fragmentary, deriving mostly from a set of papers marked 'Notes for
Nicholas'. Yet, sketchy though these are, they evoke pungently the
flavour and intensity of sexual passion and erotic intimacy. There
is, perhaps, just a hint of wish-fulfilment here: Nicholas has many of
the traits of the Byronic lover, the Heathcliff, or most pertinently, Mr
Rochester, who leaves so strong an imprint on the bookish schoolgirl.
He is recognizably kissing-cousin to the irresistible Fabrice of Nancy
Mitford's *The Pursuit of Love*, which Rebecca West undoubtedly knew.
All the same, his character is wholly credible, and like the dashing
but sympathetic Richard Yaverland of *The Judge*, he must be ranged in
the gallery of successful male characters portrayed in Rebecca West's
fiction. Our regret that we see too little of him, that there are only
fragments of what promised to be a superb novel, must be tempered
by gratitude that even this much survives.

The first piece in the collection dates from Rebecca West's teens
suggests Diana Stainforth, who is familiar with every development
of her employer's handwriting. The heroine is manifestly an avatar
of the bewitching Ellen Melville in *The Judge* (1922) and, like Ellen,
something of a self-portrait. Adela, who had 'the face of a young
panther', is in her teens already a passionately articulate socialist
and feminist – as Ellen is and the young Cicely Fairfield was –
and, like them, precociously intelligent. All three wince under the
crassness of their more prosperous relations and have, as father,
a 'specialist in disappointment'. Adela's description could serve for
all three: 'not only a beauty[,] she was also that seething whirlpool of

primitive passions, that destructive centre of intellectual unrest, that shy shameless savage, a girl of seventeen'. Prevented from taking up a university scholarship by the miserliness of her mill-owner uncle and by the disconcerting arrival of her wandering feckless father, Adela goes to stay with his patrician relations in the country. There she meets the married man who, it can be conjectured, would have played an important part in the projected plot. Throughout this opening there throbs the sore sense of social displacement which was to afflict West her whole life long. Like the young Cicely Fairfield, both Adela and Ellen live in dire poverty, aware that they are much finer and wiser creatures than the people who look down on them. This soreness runs all through *The Fountain Overflows* (though the narrator despises its expression by the eldest sister, Cordelia), and in the Hertfordshire scenes of *Adela* there is a painful exacerbated atmosphere very similar to the emotion suffusing West's 1960s radio talk 'A Visit to a Godmother'. Adela's kindly, patronizing elder cousin is a bluffer version of the vapid, aristocratic Englishwomen so vengefully portrayed in *The Thinking Reed*. While we might wish for more of this vivid and appealing story, it is unlikely that Ellen Melville would have been created if Adela had achieved complete life. Somehow Rebecca West seems to have needed to re-create her own youth: it is worth remembering that *The Judge* was originally planned as a novel about a judge who has a seizure in a brothel on recognizing the wife of a man he had sentenced to death some time earlier. H.G. Wells, her lover for ten years, voiced his exasperation at West's inability to keep to this structure as she went further and further back in time to develop the character of the murderer's wife, but this exploration seems to have fulfilled some profound creative and personal need.

The next group of stories takes us away from the autobiographical. All were written for American publications and all – like two of the four stories in *The Harsh Voice*, with which they have close affinities – are set in the United States. They explore a world far removed from West's English settings, a world of playboys and speculators and dancers, of precarious money (the 1929 market crash casts a long shadow) and a relative morality. Like *The Thinking Reed* they seem to be written to find out why rich people seem as dangerous as wild boars and pythons. But it is undoubtedly a world West found seductive, partly because of the material deprivations of her youth. This formidable intellectual could, in *The Strange Necessity*, weave an account of 'a sun-gilded autumn day' in Paris during which she had bought a black lace dress and two beautiful hats in elegant salons, and lunched in a room with walls the colour of autumn leaves, into a magisterial critique of *Ulysses* with an examination of Pavlov's *Conditioned Reflexes*, which later uncoils into an extended essay on aesthetics. All her life she was susceptible to the charm and value of such minor arts as couture and jewellery, and alive to female beauty. So these flawed and non-cerebral heroines are seen as having great charm and, almost unwittingly, high moral courage.

In 'The Magician of Pell Street' the beautiful dancer Leonora fears that, at a time of estrangement, she has caused a fatal spell to be cast on the husband she loves 'so much even in those early days that continued possession of him had been necessary to her soul and body'. At last she learns that it is her husband Danny, 'the grave heavy innocence of [whose] large fair head made her think of a chaste lion', who is the true possessor of that instinct which engenders 'good' magic and, by a redemptive gesture, liberates the little Chinese charlatan who is the eponymous magician. 'Sideways' gives us another dancing heroine, 'covered with fame and legend and love – and jewels'. Ruth's 'hair was red-gold and her eyes red-brown and mournful like a fallow deer's, and her skin seemed blanched by moonbeams and a special delicate kind of blood within'. Every action of Ruth's is oblique, sideways, as if 'she didn't want to give anything – even gratitude – away'. However – and this is true of all these frail heroines and strongly reminiscent of Lulah, the apparent gold-digger in 'The Abiding Vision' (the last story in the 1935 collection, *The Harsh Voice*) – 'if anything really important had been turned up, she would have behaved well'. Behave well she does, but so oblique is the grand gesture which crowns her love for and saves her marriage to a comically unprepossessing husband that it manifests itself as flagrantly awful behaviour, giving a high comedic twist to this fairly slight and beglamoured tale. The third dancer, Kay Cunningham in 'Lucky

Boy', is even more similar to Lulah, and disenchantedly aware of her function as a status symbol:

> 'I was what comes after the suits and the studs and the cuff-links and the apartments and the English valets; and he hadn't noticed that I wasn't what a rich man would go after any longer; that I'd been out of fashion for three years. And that wasn't the kind of mistake a rich man would make.'

Like Theodora and Ruth and Lulah she deceives the man she loves to save both him and their love, and Rebecca West implicitly endorses this indirectness and collusiveness. As we have seen, this reflects the dualistic view of 'the dialectics of gender' which finds its fullest expression in the mannerist rococo of *Harriet Hume* (1929) and pervades the posthumously published *Sunflower*. Much of the drama of West's fiction lies in the attempts – or, more often, failures – of men and women to make the required reconciliation, and it is the underlying theme of *The Only Poet*. In these stories such attempts are seen in a comic or tragi-comic light.

'Ruby', while it comes later in the *oeuvre*, has been grouped with these stories because the eponymous character is so patently an older version of their fallible heroines. As the narrator says, 'Sometimes I nearly detest Ruby. She seems to me that stock figure of bad fiction, the golden-hearted courtesan.' 'During the last thirty years she has dropped through destiny like a stone.' The shadowy narrator (three of these stories are recounted by an almost transparently neutral woman) accompanies Ruby to consult a seedily implausible fortune-teller, 'clammy with failure'. But Ruby 'is uniquely good, . . . she performs an act of charity which others cannot achieve'. This redemptive act is almost twin to the one performed by Theodora for the magician of Pell Street. The character of Ruby also has strong affinities with Evelyn in an unfinished short story, 'The Truth of Fiction', found among the writer's papers after her death. Evelyn formerly 'had a golden beauty brighter than any I have seen since, and a matching kindness and generosity'. Her kinship with these heroines is manifest. But 'some deep part of her had made a tryst with disgrace,

9

and she kept it faithfully. Her love affairs were at first spectacular and in the end ridiculous; she was at first extravagant and in the end dishonest; at first she drank a great deal of champagne and in the end, quite simply, she drank.' What she sees as her mortal sin, however, is that though a devout Roman Catholic she seeks through spiritualism the adopted daughter who had died after a bitter estrangement.

Spiritualism, and its fraudulent practices, are the background to the next story, 'They That Sit in Darkness'. Its touching hero, George Manisty, 'had never known any but those who communed with the dead, or who desired to do so'. Son of a father who is a medium and a mother who drinks and contrives 'raps', he finds himself after their death trapped in the deceptions of the successful fraud while longing for his way of life to have truth: 'He was hungry not only for the immortality of his dear ones, but for honour.' When he encounters another medium, 'the most fairylike person he had ever seen', he believes in her powers and 'might have been her husband and her servant if he had not been cursed with this heritage of fraud and trickery'. As in 'The Magician of Pell Street' the supernatural element is redemptive love, but there are strong hints that 'there is in fact a magical transfusion of matter, a sieve-like quality of this world that lets in siftings from eternity'. Certainly in *The Fountain Overflows* we are to take some of the supernatural events which cluster round Rosamund, and Rose's fatal clairvoyance, as being 'true', and Rebecca West was convinced that she had access to the paranormal, even engaging in correspondence with Arthur Koestler. 'The supernatural keeps pounding at my door', she wrote in 1962. Her sense that she was sometimes clairvoyant and the hallucinatory visions to which she was prone during illness seem to have convinced her that the world did indeed have a sieve-like quality. Moreover, just as West's theory of opposing but interdependent polarities of gender is reminiscent of Aristophanes' famous argument in *The Symposium* of Plato, 'They That Sit in Darkness' echoes his allegory of the cave in *The Republic*. But such portentous comparisons should not distract us from the fact that in the main these stories are comedies – that the characters, seen as part of a given social fabric, move through dislocations and discord to a more or less harmonious happy ending.

As war approaches, the mood alters. The tone of 'Madame Sara's Magic Crystal' may be comic, but it is the comedy of bitter lampoon. In the three visits to Yugoslavia which were to form the backbone of the monumental and comprehensive *Black Lamb and Grey Falcon*, Rebecca West conceived an impassioned admiration for that troubled country and its courageous people. In that book she writes: 'it is sometimes very difficult to tell the difference between history and the smell of skunk', and in her view it was the smell of skunk which characterized the Allies' dealings with the rival partisan bands of occupied Yugoslavia. 'Madame Sara's Magic Crystal' purports to be about France, as the fortune-teller reads newspaper stories about various political machinations there, but it can be inferred that the characters of 'Brigadier Prendergast Macwhirter, MP' and 'Major Thomas B. Smith' are slanderous caricatures of Fitzroy MacLean and William Deakin, while the ignominious Marshal Pierrot is manifestly a satire on the character and actions of Tito. After a meeting with a government official Rebecca West agreed to withhold it from publication, 'thus giving guarantee of my willingness to sacrifice myself to the needs of the country', and until now the story has lain with her unpublished work. Its publication at this time has a painful topicality, besides reminding us of the power, penetration and characteristic nonconformism of her political judgements.

The next novella-length short story was written during the Second World War, perhaps just as the tide was turning against Germany but nevertheless in desperate times. 'The Second Commandment: Thou Shalt Not Make Any Graven Image' was commissioned by Armin L. Robinson for an anthology, *The Ten Commandments*, whose subtitle, 'Ten Short Novels of Hitler's War Against the Moral Code', makes it clear that, lofty in its purpose though it was, this is explicitly a work of moral propaganda. Many of the other writers are still renowned, and her inclusion shows how high Rebecca West's international standing was. They include Sigrid Undset, Franz Werfel, Jules Romains, André Maurois and, in a magnificent opening story which uses some of the tone and techniques of *Joseph and His Brethren*, Thomas Mann. Rebecca West's heroine, Elisaveta, is an actress in the Copenhagen State Theatre who, with two courageous and sympathetic playwright friends, finds herself almost involuntarily taking a heroic stand against the German occupying forces. Rebecca West, who had had a brief and unsuccessful acting career herself, had made her heroine Sunflower – the closeness of whose emotional situation to the writer's own was the reason for the novel's posthumous publication – an actress, and seems to have seen acting as an appropriate career for a woman who corresponded to West's idea of femininity yet had a certain self-sufficiency. Not that Elisaveta feels self-sufficient:

> 'I am not a great beauty, I am not a great actress. I am only so-so. It is not fair that I should be asked to take part in great events of history. I could have borne with misfortunes that are like myself, within a moderate compass . . . but all this abduction and killing and tyranny, I cannot stand up to it.'

At a lunch party which has a Last Supper atmosphere, where the 'gaiety of the party had existed inside the terror of the day, enfolded by it', she and her friends are interrupted by a hostile German officer. On his grudging departure the playwright Nils formulates the idea which informs the story's title:

> 'That German . . . said that he and his kind had discovered the way of living that is right for mankind. That means they believe they could draw a picture of God's mind, and another picture of man's mind. What blasphemy! For we know almost nothing . . . that is why it was written in the Tables of the Law, "Thou shalt not make unto thee any graven image or any likeness of anything that is in heaven above, or that is in the water under the earth".'

All three are now set on a course which will lead them to capture, interrogation, even torture, and to a train crammed with Jews destined for a Polish concentration camp. The story is a generous and honourable homage to the extraordinary courage of the many men and women who, overtly or covertly, resisted Nazi occupation. But, for all its loftiness, this is not one of West's most successful works of fiction. It is in fact what elsewhere she described as 'volitional', with a laborious and contrived effect. Sometimes descending into a winsomeness inappropriate to the decorum of the rest, it is recounted in a stilted, vatic tone. She was to employ a very similar tone with great success in *The Birds Fall Down*, but it creaks rather here. The story is never less than interesting though, demonstrating her alertness to the political and emotional cross-currents of European history, and it can be seen as a precursor to her eloquent and analytical reporting of the Nuremberg war trials, and the astonishing explorations of the psychology of treachery in *The Meaning of Treason*. On a lighter note, it furnishes one of those affectionate and vibrant townscapes which are almost additional characters in much of Rebecca West's fiction: the Edinburgh which embraces the first part of *The Judge*, the Kensington whose verdure is *Harriet Hume*'s backdrop, or the urban steppes of south London explored by the young people of *The Fountain Overflows*. Here it is the pretty city of Copenhagen, which West visited in 1935.

In 'Parthenope' we return to the private. It is quite unlike any of her other short stories, though it has something of the atmosphere of *Harriet Hume*. The style, however, is very different. It is told at a double remove, like many classic nineteenth-century stories, ostensibly by the writer. She tells of accompanying her slightly quixotic and 'sideways' Uncle Arthur – who, with his Irishness and perverse honourableness, has something of West's father, Charles Fairfield – to one of those riverside settings which seem so weighted with the pastoral in West's fiction. There they hear someone calling out the unusual name Parthenope, and the narrative dissolves into Uncle Arthur's voice as he recalls the Parthenope he loved but met only at widely separated intervals. There is a powerful atmosphere to this story, whose curious turns would be spoiled if the plot were revealed. A fairy-tale light misleadingly surrounds the seven young women in their soft bright muslins, so like the seven dancing princesses. They recall the 'Ladies Frances, Georgina and Arabella Dudley', irrevocably bound together by a chain of garlands in the whimsical fable recounted by Harriet Hume to her lover. But this is a curdled magic, and the tale has the disquieting effect of one of M.R. James's ghost stories.

'Short Life of a Saint' is another of the unpublished stories found among the writer's papers after her death. Possibly the raw, unmediated personal pain it reveals was the reason it was never published. Maybe it was the memory of the shock and hurt felt by Rebecca West's eldest sister, Letitia or Lettie Fairfield – a response received by the writer with not wholly disingenuous astonishment – when she saw the cruel depiction of herself as Cordelia in *The Fountain Overflows*. For the autobiographical content of this story is insistent and overwhelming. Gerda, the saint of the title, is born in Australia, talented, beautiful and good. She is succeeded by a younger sister, Ellida, before the family return to England. Lettie and the next daughter, Winnie, were born in South Africa before the Fairfields moved back to the British Isles. It was there that Cissie was born and where the story's third daughter, Ursula, is born. Gerda takes anxious – and resented – responsibility for the younger two and, for the highest motives, frustrates their ambitions. When Ursula fails miserably as an actress, as Cissie did, Gerda says, '"Don't you think dear, that you would do better to choose some occupation in which your appearance would not be so important?"' before suggesting that she become a Post Office clerk. According to Rebecca West, this had been Lettie's suggestion for herself. Then 'one day Ursula ran away with a married man'. This is Ayliss who, like Wells, 'had run away with other young women and made them very unhappy'. When Ursula's child is born, Gerda looks after her in the face of the family's estrangement, as Lettie looked after her sister at Anthony's birth. As Gerda's life of self-sacrifice and efforts to correct her sisters' errors continues, it yields her nothing but dissatisfaction. She converts, as Lettie did, to Roman Catholicism, and disapproves of Ursula's Vionnet dresses as drawing too much attention to their wearer. It should be remembered that Lettie, unlike Gerda, had an extremely distinguished professional career as a doctor specializing in public health, and even qualified as a barrister. But Rebecca was never fully to overcome the acrimony and indignation she felt towards her sister, nor her perpetual sense of soreness and exclusion. One of her secretaries saw a piece of paper on which West had written: 'I know I have largely invented my sister Lettie', and Gerda is undoubtedly another version of the ineffable Cordelia. She has similarities, too, with the obdurately self-righteous Alice in 'The Salt of the Earth', one of the stories in *The Harsh Voice*. Yet however frightful Gerda is seen as being, however uncompromising the implicit accusations, there is a flickering ambiguity to the tone: it is possible that here we have a genuine, if unsuccessful, attempt at exploration of and empathy with an alien, uncomprehended, uncomprehending nature – that once again Rebecca West is writing to discover, for her own edification, what she knew about this subject.

'Deliverance', the last short story of the collection, shows Rebecca West at the height of her powers. Within its brief compass it distils many of her central themes. The clearest of these is the strife between the will to live and the will to die. The protagonist, Madame Rémy, is in her sleeping compartment on a train between Rome and Paris, carrying vital intelligence for the man who is both her lover and her spymaster. She learns that travelling on the same train is an assassin with orders to kill her. Again we meet 'the two chief ills of life . . . the loss of love . . . the approach of death'. Her love affair, possibly founded on deception, is going wrong, and her only family connection is bitterly estranged. Like Isabella in *Measure for Measure* she prepares 'to strip myself to death as to a bed/That longing have been sick for'. But the denouement is radiantly life-affirming. Other parallels which suggest themselves are, of course, the highly charged train journey in *The Birds Fall Down*, and that novel's explorations of treachery and deception. Besides these there is the insistence on the primacy of love in a woman's life, and the texture is dense with those warmly, delicately sensuous details which inform so much of Rebecca West's writing, whether light or more serious. It is an adventure story, an oblique love story and a tender portrait of one of those vibrant, self-reliant yet vulnerable women with whom she so readily sympathized. And, as the last of the finished pieces in this collection, it furnishes an appropriate microcosm of the work of this astonishing writer. It shows all the vitality, all the sometimes uncomfortable intelligence, all the delighted sensuousness and all the compelling storytelling which characterize the fiction of Rebecca West.

# Adela

*Diana Stainforth, Rebecca West's secretary, tells us that this is 'an unfinished story of which no more has come to light than the sixty-two corrected manuscript pages . . . The manuscript pages are small and pinned together into three chapters. Adela was found in an envelope with the manuscript of "Indissoluble Matrimony" (published 1914) and the handwriting is very early. It still has the right-slant spikiness of Rebecca West's schoolgirl handwriting and is only just beginning to have the delicate lacy look of her later writing. Furthermore, from the hardness of the nib and the dark-to-light contrast of the ink every couple of lines, it appears to have been written with a dip-pen. These factors alone suggest that "Adela" was written in her mid to late teens.'*

*The only editorial intervention has been the correction of spelling and punctuation.*

## I
## The Kingdom of the Squinting Owl

Beneath the windows of Tom Motley's drawing-room at Boggart Bank lay Saltgreave. In the gathering twilight it was a mass of darkness patched with greasy roofs, a network of narrow alleys overhung by the livid fumes of the factories, a squalid undergrowth of hovels spiked with tall chimneys: a clothed puddle of filth dripping down from the grim hills around where the gaunt instruments of England's wealth stood black against the scarlet sunset. A distant furnace sighed tragically, trains softly rattled away on their mysterious traffics. Slowly, as the sun died majestically on the skyline, the town awoke from her absurd preoccupation with work and began to proclaim the secrets of her heart under the cover of the night. She glowed in warm affection through the little windows of the tenements, vehemently confessed her burning lusts in the undying furnace-flames,

17

innocently confided her chaste passions in the white fervent beam of her electric lights. She pretended to luxury, for the red and green signals on the railway-line that sundered her straightly from North to South gleamed richly like jewels on the ribbon of darkness. Even she began to speak aloud. One heard the happy broken shouts of little boys as they swam their puppies on the only canal that lay like a fat snake under Boggart Bank, and a sensuous waltz refrain travelled sentimentally from the bandstand in some near recreation ground. Now Saltgreave was awake, and she was beautiful.

But Tom Motley's niece, who was sitting in the windowseat, looked down on Saltgreave and caressed her hip and thigh. If fire had leapt down from Heaven and licked up the city and her hundred and sixty thousand inhabitants she would have laughed for joy. Yet if one had looked on her brown eyes, as melting as the wild antelope's, the wide gracious arch of her eyebrows, the smooth waves of her black hair streaked with gold, the delicate droop of her lower lip, one would have judged her mild as the turtle-dove. But Adela was not only a beauty: she was also that seething whirlpool of primitive passions, that destructive centre of intellectual unrest, that shy shameless savage, a girl of seventeen. Hence for various insignificant reasons she would unmoved have seen plague and pestilence stalk down the streets of Saltgreave. For one thing it had no University; no harbour for her young ravenous intellect and her hunger for academic fame. For another, she lived in one of these little houses about whose roofs the chimneys belched their smoke, and her fine beauty felt the murk and grease as an insult. Each morning, when she drowsed in a light sleep shot with dreams of academic victories and adventures in laboratories, she was awakened by the clattering clogs of the halftimes children on their way to the mills: an intolerable reminder of her own poverty as well as theirs. And then – how could human beings have so hopelessly lost all self-respect as to actually submit to squalid slavery just to pile up capital for old Tom Motley! Serfs! Worms!

She turned her back on the window and looked round the drawing-room to see exactly what kind of culture had been bought with Saltgreave's daily crucifixion. It was disordered now, for that morning Tom Motley's only daughter Marie had been married to

Jack Hereford of the Redpuddle Ironworks, and it was only half an hour since the last guest had left the wedding-reception. The air was still so heated that no one had lit the great crystal chandelier whose deep lustres gave the room by daylight the raffish gloom of a bar-saloon at dawn, and only a few silver candlesticks stood among the champagne-glasses on the little tables here and there. Of course Adela knew the room by heart, having been brought there every Sunday after lunch since she was ten. The walls were covered with a blue paper with a broad satin stripe sprigged with pink rosebuds, but sobriety was retained by the draperies of maroon brocade with gold tassels over the fireplace and the screens at the door and by the upholsteries' dull ruby velvet. But she looked past the jungle of mahogany furniture to the end of the room, where on a long table lay Marie's wedding presents. About one gift, the unique, most admired, stood five lighted candles. This was Tom Motley's contribution to the bric-à-brac of his daughter's new home.

Tom Motley had wealth and power. The jewel-chests of Samarkand, the mines of Golconda, the purple bays of Ceylon, would have surrendered their treasure at his bidding. Eager men in London and Paris would have set their youth and genius in search of some new beauty for his gold. At his words wise agents would have hurried through the languors of old Greece and Italy, plucking from the mould the lovely fragments of shattered civilizations. But he had done none of these things. On the contrary, he had spent the morning in Birmingham and paid out thirty golden guineas for a thrice lifesize enamelled green owl, with a jewelled clockface in its stomach and black china eyeballs that squinted inwards to mark the seconds.

To ugliness as such Adela had no objection. Sometimes the hideousness of Saltgreave brought a strange gloomy ecstasy to her bosom by its drab insistence on the mystery and sadness of human life. But this was simply a monument of three stupendous fools: the fool who designed it, the fool of an employer who actually paid that designer money, and Tom Motley who was fool enough to buy it. She cursed it with the naked vocabulary of the adolescent.

But there it stood like a god, its altar lights about it, squinting to mark the passage of old Time.

To possess such luxuries as this had Tom Motley imperilled his immortal soul and ground down the faces of the poor.

Its squinting rubbed on Adela's nerves, and she rose and walked down the room. Round a radiator on the hearthrug sat three of Tom Motley's poor relations, drab women in the most miserable fag end of middle age. In trying to live up to the maroon brocade and the squinting owl they had all assumed accents of frigid gentility, but their backs were the backs of the very poor – bent with toil and bony across the shoulderblades with the ridge of cheap corsets. They looked so pitiful sitting there that Adela hovered about them for a minute, her young heart full of kindliness. But her excursions among the clouds had unjustly gained her a reputation for sullenness, and they looked up at her shrewishly. So she passed on and curled up in a big armchair facing the owl, where she could hear their thin voices rambling on.

'I'm always fit to drop with sick headaches,' complained one in a voice harsh with unhappiness. 'And all night I lie and think till my head bursts what Jack and Cyril had best be put to. Neither of them's been bright at school. Boys are a rare nuisance.'

'All right, Mrs Mahaffy,' said the oldest grimly. 'You're lucky to have your Jack and your Cyril. I've nursed eight up to men, and now they're up and down America from the Argentine to Vancouver, and me left homing alone with my sick headaches.'

'That may be, Mrs Tomlin, but your lot's earning good money. Mine isn't. I wish you had my Gerty to try your hand on. Making thirty shillings a week as a cashier and wants to give it up because she says she feels tired. Fact. Because she feels tired. The doctor calls it a nervous breakdown. Sheer selfishness and affectation I call it.'

'Well, it doesn't matter much what you call it if the girl's going to chuck her thirty shillings anyway,' said Mrs Tomlin, frankly wearying of her neighbour's grief. She turned away with a yawn and prodded the third woman in the ribs with a strong, roughened forefinger. 'What's that you're reading, Catherine?'

'A Sales Catalogue I found in the morning-room,' answered Catherine with a dreadful clockwork sprightliness. 'I like to promise myself my little fineries a long way ahead.' She was a music-teacher in a cathedral city and for thirty-five years had had to practise every kind of conversational coquetry to dissemble her commonness.

'Fancy having the spark at your age to think of fineries,' droned Mrs Mahaffy. 'I always wish in the morning I could give up dressing and go out with a blanket wrapped round my nightgown.'

'Your nightgown, Bella! Well, if it was like this!' simpered Catherine, waving the catalogue at them.

The two matrons' unbrushed uncomely heads met over the pages.

'Lace,' said one.

'Low necks,' said the other.

'I wonder who wears them!' cried Catherine with wheezy brightness. 'Ah well, I suppose all the young married ladies like to look nice on their beds.'

'Ssh!' hissed the matrons and jerked their thumbs towards Adela.

At that moment a young married lady entered the room. She was Mrs Tom Motley's niece, Maud, and twelve months ago had become the scandal of Saltgreave. As a bland, beautiful creature of eighteen – a complicated miracle of firm white flesh informed with rich blood, of acquiescent smiles and receptive glances, of bright masses of black hair and moist red lips, obviously designed by immoral Nature to commit arson among the passions of men – she entered an office as typist. Work of any kind being absolutely repulsive to the miracle, she solved the problem of ways and means by marrying her boss, one Graham Seppel, a pompous dotard well on in his sixties. The scandal was enormous and most enjoyable. There were certain elements in it – common to all May and December marriages – that made it hold its own as the favourite topic in the smoking-room of the Midland for considerably more than nine days: elements that made the sober businessmen of Saltgreave and commercial travellers from the uttermost ends of Britain brothers in free discussion. Of this the miracle was not ignorant, being born all-wise concerning men: but she had calmly gone on becoming more miraculous than ever.

To Adela, possessed by the blind infatuation for beauty common to schoolgirls, she appeared to have reached the high tide of miraculousness. Her smooth face flashed like a jewel in the dim shadows of a wide hat that rose upwards into a whorl of rosy foam; the cumulative effect of innumerable immense feathers of some unbelievable bird. From her proud shoulders hung possibly the most useless and delicious coat ever devised by mortal dressmaker – a floating shred of peach-coloured ninon, obviously worn solely to flatter the eye – and at present she was pretending not to be made like a woman. Her glorious bust swelled forth under a golden breastplate of brocade and thence she became a tube; a sinuous and graceful tube, but quite undeniably a tube. It was quite preposterous to imagine this *article de vertu* existing in Saltgreave at all: certainly those exquisite pale kid shoes would sink on their fantastic high heels deep, deep into the mud of nine out of ten Saltgreave streets. But it was in the tenth street, the clean and desirable one, that Maud now lived. In her ill-gotten prosperity she was so lovely a flower that the decent matrons at the hearth looked like the very refuse of civilization – as dull and ugly and useless as the clinker heaps by the works.

They gazed at her with a kind of melancholy admiration: she really had done pretty well out of a bargain out of which they hadn't made much. She smiled back generously, obviously exclaiming to herself, 'You poor old dears! You do look a quaint crew!' and came over to Adela. As Adela rose she put her fingers to her lips and wheeled up another armchair beside hers, so that they were shielded from the women at the hearth. The miracle was not always polite to her elders.

'Look here, what's this you're worrying about, Adela?' she asked, speaking in a whisper. 'You've been looking like a ghost all day. And now your mother's hanging around Uncle Tom's study door like a frightened mouse – oh, you needn't be afraid, she hasn't got in yet. He's still having a joke or two with old Mr Hereford, so the poor relation's kept waiting on the mat. We Motleys have the manners of the *ancien régime*, I don't think. Well, what's it all about?'

'You see, it's like this.' Maud was a jolly good sort and amazingly beautiful and excitingly grown-up: but at close quarters the sparkle of jewels and the soft swish of the magnificent fabrics reminded Adela that she was secretly a member of the Saltgreave branch of the British Socialist Party and as such ought not to consort with this gilded toy of the capitalist. So she felt shy. 'I've got the Saville Scholarship.'

'Good Lord. I'm glad. What in the wide world is it?'

'It's a scholarship that pays my fees at any University – except Girton and Newnham – for a Science degree.' She turned away her head and stared hatefully at the squinting owl.

'I say, you must be clever.' Maud's eyes beat hardly on the sullen pathetic face. To admit the sway of affection or anything but the power of gold would have been fouling her own nest: for she had been born and nurtured in an atmosphere of barter, and the only achievement of her life so far a purely business deal. But Adela looked to her eyes as if she might be a profitable investment. It was true that she was grim against the drab jocosity of the middle-class world, but so was Saltgreave grim and incapable of frivolity, and there was money enough in Saltgreave. So she asked respectfully: 'What's the trouble?'

'I can't use it.' Like many people of genius she had a neurotic lack of control over her voice: so it crept out weakly and brokenly, while she despised it for its hoarseness. 'You see, I would have to live at Manchester or Leeds or Liverpool: and Mother simply couldn't afford to keep me there. We live on what Mother makes by typewriting and I do a lot of that in my evenings. So Mother couldn't possibly send me the cost of my board and lodging. And she's gone to ask Uncle Tom to lend her some money.'

'Surely the old toad'll do it.' There was nothing romantic about the miracle's conversation. 'If not, drown the mean hound in the canal. And then you come to me. I'll get it out of Graham for you.'

'Maud, I couldn't. Why should he lend it to me? I'm no relation.'

'No. But I'll get it out of him. He can't refuse me anything.' She crossed her knees and smiled at her slippers. 'Nor should he. He can't expect to get something for nothing.'

There was a certain fastidiousness about Adela. She had lived among her mother's kinsmen, the untamed denizens of Saltgreave, since she was ten, but – perhaps because her father was an aristocrat – every now and then they nauseated her. So that with (roughly speaking) about twopence farthing between her and the workhouse and the monumental meanness of Uncle Tom between her and her ambition, she nevertheless looked down upon prosperous Maud from a mighty pinnacle. The passion to buy in the cheapest market and sell in the dearest seemed to her as repulsive and ridiculous as a passion for whisky or beating one's mother-in-law. She made no comment.

'Can't your father's people help you? Your Aunt Olga, I mean. She lives in a swanky style, doesn't she?' Maud went on carelessly.

'She hasn't any money either. Of course they have a big house and a motor and all that, but Aunt Olga's brothers, the Lorikoffs, pay for everything. Really they haven't any money of their own at all.' Her voice drooped in sympathetic remembrance of Aunt Olga's tearful protestations of her poverty. She had not yet grasped the most extraordinary phenomenon of British life: that all people who own motor cars and big houses do so in the teeth of the most abject poverty.

There was a pause. Then Maud's face began to glow with mischief and she giggled fatly. She really was an adorable creature.

'I say, are you on for a joke?'

Adela began to giggle in good fellowship. 'Of course I am!' she said; and squeezed Maud round the waist.

Maud put her mouth to her cousin's ear: 'Go and marry old Mr Hereford!'

Adela's brows met and her body stiffened with disgust. 'Maud, don't be silly.'

'There isn't anything silly about it,' said Maud, practical to the point of obscenity. 'He's only forty-four and he's quite a handsome man if you don't look at the back of his neck. And he's mad on you already. Didn't he sit and talk to you half the afternoon and get you ices and things –'

'Oh, that was just out of kindness,' blurted Adela miserably.

'Rubbish. People never do things out of kindness. If a man's nice to a girl, he obviously wants something out of her.' Adela wriggled, but the bland voice rolled on. 'Don't you see what a joke it would be! Uncle Tom and Aunt Kate and Marie have always been beastly to you because you're poor and your father ran away – now you can pay 'em back! Quite easily, don't you see! If you marry old Mr Hereford you'd get the life interest of a lot of his money anyway when he died and keep Marie and Jack out of it for years – p'raps for ever, because you'll live as long as they will. And then if you had a baby – it would be too funny for words! Because then –'

'Oh, for God's sake stop!' cried Adela. She was wrapped in flame. Adult in the things of the intellect, so wise in everything, and expert in a dozen sciences, she was yet to the things of life a quivering babe. She would have liked to quell this fountain of blasphemous intrigue with some wholesome oaths, but lacked the vocabulary. 'I'd sooner work at the pitbrow as Granny Motley did than mix myself up in any of their dirty lives.'

'But don't you see, you silly child, the lovely thing about this is that you won't have to work at all!'

'But I *like* work!'

'Oh, go on!'

Just then the door opened and a woman wavered on the threshold, a contemptible figure in the crude stream of the unshaded gaslight; thin yet dumpy, with protruding pale blue eyes and a tousled mass of fair hair tarnished with middle age. Her face worked and she checked a ridiculous snorting sound on her lips as she saw the three women huddled round the fire. Adela forgot Maud and sprang to her feet, round-mouthed like a little child.

'Mother! has –'

Mrs Furnival took no notice but went briskly up to the other women. 'We must say goodbye now, I'm afraid. Come away, Adela. I'm glad I've seen you again, Matty. How is Mr Mahaffy?'

'A picture of health except for his feet,' replied Mrs Mahaffy gloomily, 'and they run in his family.'

'Catherine, you'll come and take a cup of tea with me some day before you leave, I hope. Yes, it has been a swell wedding.'

'I suppose you're that proud of your brother,' said Mrs Tomlin. 'We all owe him a lot.'

'I don't see how that can be,' snapped the little woman with a sudden gleam in her dull pale eyes. 'Tom never gave anyone the chance of running up debts that I ever heard of.' She drew Adela forward as though she was a little child of five. 'Say goodbye, dearie.'

Adela, sick with fear, was stuffed too full of sobs to answer one word to the farewell courtesies: she wrung the women's hands roughly and glowered down at the carpet. The women glared malignantly at her, thinking her manner the result of pride of learning. 'None of my girls . . .' she heard as she followed her mother into the hall. Then her mother's arms closed about her and drew her head lovingly but uncomfortably on to her bony bosom.

'My pet! My pet!'

'Oh! Oh!' breathed Adela. 'He won't?'

'Not one penny.'

'Did you tell him I'd pay him back when I'd taken my degree and got a job?'

'I did that, dearie, but to no use. He simply won't lend us a farthing. He says it's absurd for people in our station to think of a University education, and that you may get married, and then all the money would be wasted, and he'll take you on as a typist at the works at a pound a week. Oh, dearie, I know it's a disappointment.'

'The old beast! The old beast!' muttered Adela chokingly. 'How he hates me!'

'Tuts, Adela!' whispered her mother nervously, peering up the staircase, suddenly wrapped up in her old reverence for Tom Motley again. 'You mustn't say such things! And you know you've not always been as polite to your uncle as you might have been.'

'Mother!' Adela shook herself free of the withered arms. The quiet deadly little difference of opinion that would never be settled blew between mother and daughter like a cold wind. The woman who from her birth had had to serve and worship Tom Motley and was too old and broken to learn to hate him now gazed spitefully at the girl to whom Tom Motley was just so much tyrannical fat flesh. Adela steeled her upper lip and said gruffly – 'I'll go and get my hat.'

She ran up two flights of stairs to the bedroom where she had left her hat and coat, banged the door behind her, and flung herself down on the bed. The mean little room with white sheets and the highlights of the gigantic mahogany gleaming so coldly through the gathering darkness seemed a symbol of a mean and drear Eternity. Life was over for her now. If they forbade her to be a scientist they forbade her to live. For this shy creature, so fastidious that she rejected half of life, veiled in the mild melancholies of adolescence, was consumed as if by flame with the passion for work. She was abandoned to it as any nun to prayer: the inkstains on her fingers were her stigmata. Nothing could tempt her to dalliance. The quick winds of spring racing across the wet brown earth stirred in her the desire to be at work in the laboratories. The sight of her own beauty, which she often involuntarily perceived reflected in the wavering mirror of a shop-window or the clumsy compliment of a school-friend, only pleased her because she felt that every addition to her value made her a more worthy workman.

And now she was not to be a workman. Formerly she had feared old age because it would corrupt to nothingness her craftsman gifts – her strong intelligence, the intensity of her perceptions, the fine skill of her hands, her tirelessness. And now Tom Motley the fat, foolish, the buyer of the squinting owl, had usurped the power of age or Death and killed all these things while she was still young and lustful to conquer the earth. And she must live on, although the sight had been turned out of her eyes.

Deep sobs racked her; she buried her face in the quilt and surrendered sickly to the degradation of tears.

They say drowning men see every picture of their past life: to Adela, immersed in the floods of her weeping, came many pictures of the future. 'Now I can't go to the University perhaps I'll become like those women downstairs. There's nothing to keep me from marriage now. Typing in Uncle Tom's works is drudgery that a machine could do – slavery that girls do anything to escape. Maybe I'll marry some horrible common man who won't earn enough for us to live on decently and I'll have lots of children and always be ill and cross. I'll get so dead that I'll go on living with my husband and never think of him. I don't believe Mrs Mahaffy ever thinks of Mr Mahaffy all day until she has to get supper ready for him. And then I'll hate the children. I don't see how you can get fond of your children when you're always so busy having the next one and you have ten. And I couldn't bear to get so ugly. Oh, how filthy marriage is! People crawl into it as if it was a dirty black cave and fling outside their beauty and their health and good-temper and everything that make them valuable! And the pigginess of it!' Marriage as she had seen it in her sordid world – the leering secrecy of young love, the long squalid indignities of maternity endured in stuffy kitchens and mean parlours, the gross companionship of torpid middle-aged people obviously incapable of passion – flashed before her and sent the virgin blood protesting through her veins. 'Oh, Life is *putrid*!'

'And if I don't marry I may get queer like Cousin Catherine who's sixty and never thinks of anything but love and marriage and pretty clothes. And then she has to go on working although she has rheumatism and a weak heart because she hasn't saved enough money to live on. Oh, how filthy, how loathsome Life is!'

In the midst of her meditations she heard steps moving about the landing outside with the leisurely tread of a cow nosing round a byre. With a sudden grasp of self-control she jumped up and rammed on her hat well over her eyes. She was shaking herself into her heavy coat when the door opened and Mrs Tom Motley came in.

Mrs Tom stood by the open door and looked at Adela. She was that most hideous of all living creatures, a British matron of the lower middle classes, and her long, corpulent body with short legs and her small flat head were things to make an artist weep: but such was her shamelessness that she turned her black eyes unwinkingly on Adela's clean perfection. Appalled by her physical uncomeliness and the grim disapproval that hung like a fog over her countenance, Adela involuntarily began to make grimaces. The corners of her mouth twitched down and she bit her lips: she longed to vanish through the earth before she began to foam at the mouth.

Mrs Tom slowly examined the girl's flushed cheeks, all streaked and swollen with tears, and her red lids: and then she ran a bulging eye over the disordered bed and its rumpled quilt.

'One of the dogs must have got in here and lain on the bed,' she pronounced. And added firmly, 'Drat them.'

Adela's gloves had fallen on the floor and she had to grovel for them around Mrs Tom's stiff silken skirts, while Mrs Tom stood quite still, looking down on her with passionless malice. A wild impulse seized Adela to jump up and shout 'Why do you hate me so, you detestable old hag?' But instead she scrambled to her feet and put on her gloves with trembling hands.

'Are you going to stay with your Aunt Olga tomorrow?' asked Mrs Tom suddenly.

Adela dropped her gloves again. 'Yes,' she murmured. Beads of perspiration stood out on her forehead.

'It's very good of them to have you,' said Mrs Tom.

Repartee seethed in Adela and she opened her lips to speak scathingly. Instead she gave forth a hoarse grunt.

'How long are they going to keep you for?'

'A fortnight.'

Mrs Tom hastened to remove any false impression that she was interested in Adela's doings for Adela's sake. 'I only wanted to know because Tom won't keep the place open for you unless you can start working with him when his typist leaves in May.'

Adela shook like a leaf with hate. Slowly she wakened into living flame. Her lips were dry amd twisted with loathing, her face was the face of a young panther. And still Mrs Tom did not fear her. She could not bring herself to pay such a token of respect to anyone so poor as Adela. Then Adela's youth and the violence of her hatred betrayed her. Her self-command crumbled away and she became a beautiful but blubbering child. Snorting back her tears, she broke clumsily from the room and cantered downstairs like a shying colt.

At the first-floor landing she stopped in her wild course, for Uncle Tom's study door was ajar, and stood still for a moment trying to collect herself before going down to her mother. Then with a gasp she retreated up a step, for out of the black shadows had materialized a phantom, a strange being of black rotundities spattered with high-lights. There shone glossily sleek black hair with a gleaming white parting, dazzling collars and cuffs; a scarfpin that surely should have been in the Tower with the Crown Jewels: the bulging eyes that the housemaid must have polished every morning along with the boots: and finally and most blindingly, twenty largish teeth lubricated in a bewildering smile. In other words, it was Mr Hereford.

She had forgotten all about him. The memory of Maud's scandalous behaviour suddenly returned to her and she was almost stunned with confusion. She hung her head and blushed: then, in prim haste, she prepared to step past him.

But the teeth remained steadfast: a fruity voice poured through the darkness like a runnel of oil. 'You haven't been wearin' any flowers all day, Miss Adela. Here's a bunch of carnations – a posy as we boys called it when I was young.' He chuckled rollingly into the depths of himself.

Maud was right. The man was maudlin over her. She looked grimly away from him in contempt. Then a passion gripped her heart so strongly that for a second she was blind. Here was the chance to avenge the blasting of her life. If it was ugly, it was also strong. She was too badly wounded to be fastidious; she grasped it unflinchingly.

She put her hand out and took the carnations: the moment of hesitancy made her gesture the more maidenly and graceful. To show her pleasure at the gift she laid the blossoms to her cheek. 'How cool and fresh they are!' she said shyly, and raised her eyes to his. His gaze grew brighter and moister; she sickened under it but endured it till her cheeks were flaming. Then her feminine instinct told her to play the oldest trick in the world: with a little quiver of modesty she pushed past him and fled trippingly down the stairs, another fond chuckle echoing in her ears.

Mrs Furnival was standing in the hall, huddling a heavy mantle over her poor old shoulders. For a minute Adela stook blinking at her, a little dazed: she suddenly wanted to cry. It was mean of God to allow her no revenge save this dirty intrigue with that fat man. Then she grasped her mother's arm and whirled her out on to the doorstep. And she banged the door behind them so that the squinting owl rocked on its pedestal.


## II


It would be impossible to describe how blackly the shadow of Tom Motley lay across the path of the woman and girl who stood on his doorstep. To the woman Tom seemed like the wrath of the Lord, which strikes suddenly – not to say sneakishly – on man in his deepest afflictions. And she worshipped Tom as she worshipped God, with a certain sense of ill-usage but also with the nervous respect one pays to a well-armed man.

Tom was seven years older than she was, and from the start had used this advantage with the firmness, delicacy and consideration for others characteristic of a steam engine. When she was two years old he had carried her weeping from a game of hop-scotch to watch the backyard for tomcats as prey for his catapult. And when she was fourteen he had carried her off to respectability and broken her heart.

Their father, Steve Motley, lost his job as a cashier of a drapery stores: his old age was revealing an unenthusiastic outlook on work and a frivolity of temper unsuited to modern business methods. So, setting his felt hat at a more rakish angle on his shaggy head, he sought the refuge of all the unwanted and became an insurance agent. Later he sank into the deeper obscurity of a 'commission agent'. And then it was Steve found his vocation. As a family man he was without honour, as a wage-earner a laughing stock; but as an amateur singer of comic songs in bar-parlours he could have no rival. So henceforth his grey beard and Bohemian tweeds were seen disappearing between the swing-doors of the local public houses. And soon he began to accept the maxim current at The Green Man and The Bald-faced Stag, to the effect that a horse whinnies better when he's wet his whistle. So that frequently he returned home long after midnight, yet untired: seemingly his youth had returned to him, for he danced and sang.

Tom Motley decided that this would not do. It brought discredit on his high estate, now that of a traveller for Stokes & Co. Chemical Factory. So he took hideous and immaculate lodgings for Amy and himself with the widow of a Congregational minister. Amy cried her eyes out, but she went: Tom preached reason and morality to her for half a day: and then led her hypnotized to the widow's faultily faultless apartments. She spent the evening in a corner snivelling over a school-book. She loved her father: from him she got that fundamental innocence, that quality Adela could only fumblingly call 'jolliness', which made her attractive in spite of her stupidity and unlovely middle age.

31

So in the morning she stole out and ran round to see if Dad was getting on all right alone.

Inside the door she found her father lying dead. He had reeled in from an orgy early that morning and lost his bearings in the unlighted hall. Somehow he must have tripped and struck his head against the umbrella-stand. There was no pain in his face: only a questioning loneliness, a simple yearning that wrung her heart. In dreams she often saw once more his glazed gentian-blue eyes staring up at her, desiring her yet repudiating her.

And Tom had done it again – killed something that she loved. For the Adela who was hurrying her down the steps and along the greasy pavements was not the same Adela who had started out that morning to the wedding. This was someone sinisterly adult, with eyes too full of sorrow to admit tears: blasted with grief into the grimness of a withered tree. Yet this was the loved flesh she had borne, tortured by Tom Motley.

'Oh, dearie, don't take it so hard!' she cried.

Some lingering strain of the baby in Adela answered her. 'O Mother!' she moaned, 'and only yesterday all the girls congratulated me on getting the University Scholarship.' She thought as she said it that it was insincere – a weak appeal to her mother's sympathies. It was impossible that she, the proud adventurer of knowledge, the haughty claimant of renown, could really see things from this infantile point of view. She lifted her head in disdain. The suddenly her lips trembled and she dissolved into a silent gush of tears.

'Oh, dearie, hush!'

They were going down Boggart Bank into the gaudy High Street. Trams shrieked past them, tweaking sparks of fire from the taut wires above. Vans lumbered by with round yellow headlights. The high electric lamps printed smooth spheres of pellucid light over the wet pavements. The mud flashed back gay reflections. The intolerably bright, unsympathetic world! Unsympathetic yet not unobservant. A couple of squalid matrons clasping armfuls of fried fish to thin shelving bosoms stopped dead and turned fishy eyes on her distress. Adela longed for death.

'Come along, come along!' said Mrs Furnival consolingly. 'Up here.'

A dark alley turned abruptly out of the High Street through the graveyard of a forgotten church. In the shadow of its railings they clung together and abandoned themselves to sorrow. In her sad, loving voice her mother began a rambling monologue of misfortune.

'It's not as if I could help it. . . . But me having nothing but what I make by the typing, and only a hundred came in last year and that I couldn't have done without you . . . . And the price of things goes up every day, and I may die any moment with my heart . . . . I wish, I wish you had a good father . . .'

Her voice sank. An unhappy marriage is merely one of the commonest forms of ill-luck. But Tom Motley had convinced her that as a deserted wife she was practically one of the criminal classes.

'Tom might have lent us the money, he says himself he's worth forty thousand. O, he's a hard man. Ever since you were born I've worked my hardest to bring you up to be good and happy – I've kept you neatly dressed and not let you play with the other children for fear of getting rough. I've worked when I felt fit to drop, and now he comes and spoils it all with his tightfistedness. I haven't done it all for nothing, surely, if there's a God above. I only did it to see you happy because I gave up hoping you'd ever really love me years ago . . . I'm too old and stupid –'

The smell of death rising from the dank ground: the stone crosses gleaming dully through the damp blue twilight: the cracked churchbell asthmatically tolling the hour: the melancholy howl of a hymn within the church: the mother's tired voice, husky with misfortune, had aroused in Adela a sudden distaste for death. Even for the misery in which she had been wallowing a second since. She suddenly thirsted for life and beauty and joy. Visions passed by her: of blue seas sleeping silently at the feet of golden mountains whose white peaks probed the strong blue skies, of wide Eastern plains where flowers danced in a thousand changing hues under the high unchanging heavens. Here in her mother's appeal was an emotion ready to hand; she flung herself on it with the same self-abandonment with which she would have got drunk or given herself up to a man's kisses.

'Mother, I do love you!' she cried softly, clasping her mother to

her. 'I love you more than anything in the world!' She felt sincere:
the beauty of her newly discovered affection for her mother took her
breath away.

'No, no,' murmured Mrs Furnival. 'I know I'm too stupid. I often
try your patience.' Her eyes shone with pleasure.

'Mother, you don't! It's only my way – I'm an ill-tempered beast.'

They kissed with a sudden warm sense of comfort.

'You do believe I love you?' said Adela wistfully.

'Yes, dear!' answered Mrs Furnival: she glowed pathetically. 'And
now let's go home. I've got such a nice bit of boiled pork for
your supper.'

Adela abhorred boiled pork: but Mrs Furnival never could remember that. With a sweet consciousness of abnegation Adela did not
remind her. Instead she squeezed her hand and rubbed against her
like a contented kitten. They walked through the warm wet darkness
hugging their throbbing hearts.

'Mother, dear!' said Adela unsteadily. 'It can't be helped. I can't be
a graduate. Instead I'll try and be a good daughter to you . . .'

'And I'll try and be a good mother . . . we'll try and have a happy
little home.'

They looked away from each other as they approached a glaring
lamp.

Now the alley deviated oddly between the jutting roofs of sordid
houses, shelving deeply in rows of cobbled stones from the heights
of the upper and middle classes into the depression where Saltgreave
kept its poverty and shabby gentility. From this perch one could
see, like a well-proportioned panel painted by a skilful artist,
the opposite slope of Saltgreave rising glowing to the stars. A
wind raced across the valley to Adela's cheek. She felt cool, pure
and altruistic. Drawing deep breaths, she let her spirit aspire:
aimlessly, as one permits a kite to soar. Then a little dribble
of complaint from Mrs Furnival's gaping mouth told her that
her mother was finding difficulty in stepping down the cobbled
stones: like most women of her lowly birth she walked little and
her feet were tender. With a sudden access of glory in life, in
their mutual affection, and in her strength, Adela bent down and

lifted her mother in her arms. The burden was easy: she stepped forward lightly.

'Adela, put me down!' her mother's voice quavered.

'No, Mother, you're quite light.'

The peevish music of a mouth-organ caught her ear, evidently played by some unseen person in the shadow of the alley walls a little further on. It stopped with a sinister suddenness that whipped her nerves taut.

'Adela! Put me down this minute!'

Under a projecting gable she perceived three figures. They looked towards her and whispered furtively.

'But, Mother, it'll hurt your feet if you try to walk.'

The figures came towards her with a rush. It happened with the phantasmic smoothness and quickness of a cinematograph film. She lowered her mother on to her feet, and strode forwards against the attack. Saltgreave's wealth had its waste products – clinker heaps high on each side of the canal: youths such as these lounging at every dark place of the city. Ugly, brutish, passionless save for fitful appetites for vice; inviting the contempt of her sinewy youth for physical reasons alone. Belligerent troglodytes, one might call them.

'Gi' us some coppers.'

'Let us pass.'

'Gi' us some coppers to drink yer 'ealth at the pub.'

'Let us pass.'

The blood began to flow like wine in her veins. Without distress she heard through the growling threats her mother's nervous sobs; they seemed like the orchestra tuning up before the curtain rose on some thrilling episode.

'It ain't no use yer callin' for a copper, 'cos there ain't none for ten minutes' 'ard walkin'.' That was true: and the houses turned only their blank back walls on to the alley. 'Better pike us some coppers quietly, lidy.'

She feigned to struggle with a hacking cough, and writhed unhappily. He waited. She stooped and picked up his left ankle. As he lost his balance and fell full length with a howl, her fist caught his bigger companion under the jaw. Meanly and with skill her foot struck the third full in the stomach. It was against the traditions of English gentlewomen, but it was war, and it was superb. In a second she had caught up her mother again in her arms and was coursing down the alley like a greyhound.

'This – this is what I wanted!' she cried to herself. 'I feel confident now. Tom Motley may refuse me money and Mrs Tom insult me and that confounded green owl squint at me till kingdom come, but all the same I've knocked three loafers flat on their backs for once in my life!'

A sudden turn of the alley brought them into a main street where the high tenements towering from the glowing stratum of squalid little shops and flaring gin-palaces told them that they were in the haunts of civilization. She lowered her mother on to her feet and stood looking round her with an ardent smile. On this first victory of her strength she felt a peculiar infantile ecstasy, such as inflames a small boy who has just bought his first pup. For the first time Saltgreave seemed as romantic as San Francisco, as dusky with adventurous villainies, as prodigal in opportunities for heroism. Her own chivalry in protecting her mother's age and fragility gave her passionate pleasure. For one second she stood silently, breathing in deep breaths of the grand free winds of Saltgreave. Then Mrs Furnival's angry sobs caught her ear.

'Adela!' she squeaked. 'It was all your fault! If you'd only behaved properly –'

'What!'

'Picking me up in your arms like that. . . . They'd think you were mad and would give them anything . . . or drunk perhaps. I wish you wouldn't carry on so queer.'

The romantic city of Saltgreave fell in ruins about Adela's head: it became once more the dungeon of youth. 'I'm sorry . . .' Shyness fell on her terribly like sullenness.

'It's no use your getting cross. And all those great men so strong, they might have killed you. And it's so unladylike you fighting and kicking them . . . and they may be all lying dead . . . and the police coming tomorrow. . . . You always are so queer . . .'

It is terrible to be seventeen. Her heart quaked to see their deep affection turn to nothingness between her own 'queerness' and her mother's fatigued peevishness. But she could produce no sound but an inarticulate growl.

In vexed, unhappy silence they made their way across the road to the crescent in which was their home. Adela walked slouchingly, with her hands deep in her pockets, feeling a fool. She knew that her adventure had been the exploit of a message-boy well-read in penny dreadfuls.

Garibaldi Crescent toppled downhill in a double cascade of lean stucco houses projecting ornate and dirty patios into tiny front gardens choked with shabby laurels: down the middle ran no road but a flagged pathway, from which grew a row of dusty lindens, their haggard charms protected by high iron railings. At this evening hour there was nothing much to notice, except that Mr Spence the joiner had come home drunk rather earlier than usual and was clinging to the pillars of his portico like the pictures of Samson pulling down the hall of the Philistines. The humiliations of poverty rose up from the fetid little street as the odour of stale food stank from the little provision shops round it. Disgusted and unhappy she turned in her loneliness to her angry mother and was about to make some hopeless overture towards peace, when something caught her eye.

'Mother, there's someone standing on our doorstep.'

'If it's Coggs sending that beef I ordered for this morning I'll not take it,' declared Mrs Furnival fretfully. 'We pay prompt and I'm sure –'

'No, it's a visitor. He's tall and he's got a great big beard – *Mother!*'

'Yes, dear.'

In her heart Adela was saying: 'No. I can't stand this. The rest has happened and I've just got to bear it. But this – this is too much.'

And aloud she said: 'It's father come back.' She said it plumply with the insensate bravery of the young.

For one minute Mrs Furnival stood motionless, her mouth gaping hideously. Then the colour left her slack cheeks and she dropped like a broken doll against the railings.

'Mother, don't be silly!' cried Adela, half pathetically, half impatiently.

Digby Furnival ran down the steps and stood looking down on his wife; her bulging purple lips and the tarnished hair straggling down underneath her disordered black bonnet made her an unlovely object.

'For God's sake, Amy,' he said in his fastidious voice, 'don't let's have a scene in the streets.'

Adela felt as if she had suddenly become ten years old again. That delicate voice with its perpetual undernote of offended taste had terrorized her childhood into unnatural quietness. From the moment of her birth she had been warned that any rough word or gesture might bring upon her plebeian mother and herself the appalling spectacle of an aristocrat repelled to tears and shame. She gazed at him hypnotized: and the hypnotism was not strong enough. For she was conscious she did not care whether he was repelled or not.

'Bring her in, child,' said Digby Furnival: and walked back to the house.

'Here, open the door!' called Adela, holding out the latch-key. He opened the door and stood impressively against the darkness, the gaslight shining on his magnificent head.

'Is the poor thing better?' he asked finely.

'Light the gas,' said Adela. She waited till she saw the gas wake in the lobby and the dining-room. Then she shook her mother gently. 'You are looking so funny,' she whispered. 'Father will be vexed.'

That did it. Mrs Furnival clutched at the tattered rags of her self-control and trotted up the steps to the house. Digby drew her in with much tender manliness and led her into the dining-room. Very gently and courteously he made her sit down in the big armchair by the fireplace. She sat there very uncomfortably, for it was too high for her and her short legs dangled in the air; she twisted her bonnet-strings and tried hard to master her sobs and the inconvenient heavings of her bosom. Digby, ignoring her distress in the most gentlemanly way, sat down on the other side of the table and undid his overcoat. Adela hovered uneasily at the end of the table, looking down on them, as one who helplessly witnesses a game of skill between a fool and a knave.

Without fear she watched her father's cold eyes rove round the room. She was quite conscious that a few odd bits of furniture bought in a lump at an auction-sale for twelve pounds, a worn-out carpet presented by Mrs Tom when charity was the only alternative to the dustbin, and a few prints cut out of *The Nation's Pictures* and gummed into rush frames, do not make a dainty home. She saw his gaze waver on the fluted legs of the deal sideboard, but was unshaken. This was his doing. He had gambled away his patrimony in the pursuit of copper-mines, and had left poor silly Amy and her child to face the world and the bailiffs.

She faced his eyes without a tremor: though she was glad she was wearing her best dress. But her mother was pitiable. Even if his return did mean some new burden and degradation, she should face it more pluckily than this.

After a long silence Digby spoke: calmly, pathetically, proudly.

'Amy, I've come home to die.'

'O Digby, don't!' squealed Mrs Furnival and evaporated in a series of sobs and weak, stifled screams. Through which Adela asked bluntly and loudly: 'Is there anything the matter with you?'

'What, my dear?' asked Digby deafishly.

'Have you any particular illness?'

He faced her hardness with a sweet resignation and forgiveness: 'My dear, I am an old man now.'

'Fifty-seven,' said Adela. She said it simply. It might have been an assertion. But there was a fine edge on her voice that made it seem a comment. And his eyes shot stealthily at her, reminding her that he had always hated her as a child.

Quite suddenly Mrs Furnival stopped sobbing, and fixed him with big, stupid, terrified eyes.

'Well, Amy, how have you been getting on?' he asked kindly.

'It is awful this happening on top of all our troubles,' thought Adela, watching her mother for another breakdown. 'How *shall* we get him out of the house!'

But Amy did not answer, so stuffed with tears was she.

'Haven't you anything to say to me, Amy?' he went on, easily.

'This would rouse a worm,' declared Adela to herself. 'Even Mother . . .'

Digby, quite undisconcerted by his reception, turned to her and nodded confidentially. 'Leave us, my dear,' he ordered with quiet dignity.

Adela looked him squarely in the eye and turned to her mother for a sign. Rather to her surprise, her mother nodded too. 'Just a minute, dearie,' she gasped feebly.

Adela was puzzled and displeased. For a minute she frowned from one face to the other, trying to read the situation rightly, and then went out, leaving the door ajar. In the hall she noticed that her father had hung his slouch hat on the umbrella-stand: it flapped in the draught from the still-open front door like a bird of evil portent. She pushed it childishly and sauntered on into the kitchen. A tiny point of gas flickered over the damp-stained wall, the paintless dresser covered with coarse pottery, the messy kitchen-range stacked with pots and pans. She looked bitterly round the poor little room, noticing for the hundredth time that though you may chase poverty out of the sitting-room by the exercise of taste, it will always flaunt itself unashamed in the kitchen. On the table the cold pork was gleaming wetly under a white skin of grease on an enamelled iron plate: she shook her fingers at this symbol of the coarse living to which her father had left her and her mother.

She fumbled about in the larder for something to eat and found an apple. Leaning against the edge of the sink, she nibbled it and watched a couple of cats languidly fighting round the twilight backyard. The sourish taste of the apple refreshed her mouth after all the sweet things she had eaten at the wedding-reception.

The supple declamatory tones of her father's voice and little, shrill, sighing passages from her mother reached her faintly as she munched. Her mind turned over hatefully the depressing picture of him as he sat at their table. She smiled cynically to think that if in the street she had seen this magnificent elderly gentleman with the patriarchal beard and so noble a poise of the head walking so majestically with threadbare overcoat, no waistcoat, and linen frayed at the edges, she might have been sentimentally affected. But he was her father. She knew all about him, so she snarled and bit her apple fiercely. To think of it! He had started out with all the things she lusted for today –

wealth, unbounded opportunities for education, gentle, kind people all about him, surroundings of beauty and comfort. . . . And he ended like this – a horrid messenger of sponging and blackmail to two poor women. What had he made of it? A little swaggering in Society, a little swaggering in the Army – from which he had been cashiered for some forgotten offence – a quarter-century of uneasy swaggering as a stockbroker of uncertain status, a sudden slipping to disgrace that stopped miraculously before the prison doors were reached. The fool! The wastrel!

And, after all, he had looked after himself pretty well. From inquiries conducted by Tom Motley – more out of a desire to humiliate Amy than out of any concern to bring Digby back – they knew that after his flight from his wife and his creditors he had lived for some time on the Mediterranean coast. Yes! While Amy had been clumsily thumping the typewriter and Adela feverishly winning one scholarship after another in her frustrated thirst for fame, both of them physically ill for want of good food and ease and beauty, he had been passing along the white roads beside the purple seas in the quiet, balmy airs.

He needn't ask for pity. This must be the first assault of actual poverty, or he would have been back to pick the bones of their lean fortune. Mother had said as much last night.

How disgusting it must be for her mother to sit and listen to that old vampire. It floated into her mind that one night, long ago, in a moment of unendurable misery, when it seemed they must appeal to Tom Motley or be turned into the streets, her mother had burst into a rambling history of misfortune and outrage that culminated . . .

She looked down on her brown hands and was glad that they were strong to fight and kill – if any man should ever be unfaithful to her vows.

There had been a sudden silence. Someone had closed the sitting-room door: now it was reopened, and Mrs Furnival tottered out. She stood stupidly on the kitchen threshold, blinking about with swollen, bleary eyes.

Adela crept towards her, expecting a whisper.

But she spoke it out boldly.

'He's going to stay.'

'What, Mother?' She grasped her sleeve in fear. Was he really coming back to break up this home, to tear up the tender roots of their happiness, to press them deeper down into the morass of destitution to which he had brought them? 'It can't be!'

But Mrs Furnival did not heed her, as she walked over to the gas-bracket and turned up the flame. 'Let me see,' she mused absently, pulling out a pan, 'did Dad like cold pork? I can't for the life of me think. I don't believe he did. I'll curry it.'

And suddenly there flashed a suspicion into Adela's mind. She stood and watched her mother's preparations till suspicion was certainty. About Mrs Furnival's silly, short-sighted movements there was the happy fussiness of a child getting ready for a dolls' tea-party.

'Mother,' she said slowly, 'you're glad he's come back.'

Mrs Furnival did not hear. But the timid smile on her lips answered for her. After a moment she spoke eagerly.

'So you see it's just as well Tom didn't lend us the money,' she said happily.

'Why?'

'We'll want every penny now and your salary'll come in handy. He says he'll look round and try and get something to do, but he needs a long rest. Yes . . . we'll want your salary, and we'll have to try and get extra work in the evening.'

Impossible, extraordinary mother, who rejoiced in the enslavement of her daughter that she might support in idleness a scoundrel who had outraged her even to the last sin . . .

When Adela heard her mother rejoice in the defeat of her soul, she felt as if she was going to die. Now she knew that she was alone in the Universe, without a soul to love or ask for love. She turned blindly into the lobby, which seemed like the Eternity now promised to her soul – solitary, ugly, cold. She closed her eyes and clung on to the umbrella-stand, mortally afraid of life.

Her mother's voice called her back confidentially.

'Adela.'

'Yes?'

'Come here.'

Amy nodded to her meaningly across the kitchen. 'You'd better wire to Aunt Olga that you can't go to her tomorrow,' she whispered. 'He'll be hurt if you go off like this the very moment he's come back.'

'O Mother,' mumbled Adela, the words sticking to her dry lips. 'I've bought the ticket. You told me it was best to buy an excursion ticket the day before. So I . . .'

'Oh, did you!' said Amy shortly. She was annoyed, but did not grasp it was a lie.

Which Adela justified to herself in the lobby. 'Old people are ghosts . . . or slaves. . . . How could I think we'd love each other – she couldn't. She was a ghost that hadn't anywhere to haunt . . . a slave that had lost its master. Now she's found someone to haunt – now the master's come back . . . I'm quite, quite out of it.'

That subtle voice spoke from the sitting-room. 'Adela, my dear, are you there?'

'Yes.'

'Run out and buy a *Pall Mall Gazette*. Those leaders keep a man's intellect really fit . . .'

The front door banged. A wind had sprung up again and was hustling the mists out of Saltgreave. It smote her on the lips. She straightened up her back. Suddenly, in spite of her life's bankruptcy, she felt ready for all adventures.


## III

So next noon Adela started out to stay with her Aunt Olga at Peartree Green, in South Hertfordshire. She felt a certain wistful yet joyous solemnity about the preparations, as though she was setting out on some dangerous voyage arm in arm with Death. Moved by this sense of an imminent fate, she even packed in her trunk some volumes she particularly valued and the manuscript of an unfinished novel that she hardly valued but was harmlessly proud of, and put into a purse a few sovereigns of prize-money she had laid aside for books for the University. And there was a terror about her – as though life was going to fall away from her and leave her naked.

As the train steamed out of the station she leant out for one more look at her mother: but Amy was gazing up with besotted ecstasy at her husband's face. Adela sank back. Strangely enough, this last symbol of their complete severance did not deal her any sharper pang. Rather, she felt as though, at last, a long-expected freedom had been given into her hands.

It was a cross-country journey and early in the afternoon she had to change. She had been deep in the composition of a letter to her headmistress to explain her resignation of the scholarship, and stepped unprepared out of the stuffy railway carriage into the radiant stillness of a country station. A black-and-tan puppy ran out of the porter's room and began to coquette with her on the instant. She tucked it under one arm and walked along the tidy white platform to a distant seat where she could play with it and munch chocolates unobserved. With the young thing snuffling about her and the gentle sunshine lying warm she felt a pleasure in the mere fact of existence quite new to her.

Overhead the sky arched sharply blue over the pageant of the buoyant white clouds pressing down silence on the plains. All round lay the flat green fields, yellowish with spring, checked out by narrow ditches filled full with the shining floods of March, over which leaned honey-coloured alders and short silver willows. Red cows fed sleekly, and here and there a horse cantered in the pride of the early year. Over all lay the changing pattern of sunlight and cloud shadows. On the far horizon a little red-roofed town battlemented with poplars looked snugly on the hazy marshes. Birds scoured the skies. About the placid landscape there was a strange briskness that stirred the blood.

As Adela sat looking at the scene with the kind of strained attention youth gives to beauty, she thought discontentedly how infinitely more perfect and reasonable is the life of the land than the life of the man. The land followed a cycle, and passed with purpose through the hardship of winter, the gladness of spring, the riot of summer, and the ripe profitable return to leanness of the autumn tide. But the life of man knew no change and no law. Those that were born in the springtime of good fortune could go on, in sinfulness maybe, or fatuity, always enjoying the sunshine and the wet loveliness of the fields, without coming to any harvesting. And those who, like herself, were born in the winter of ill conditions must stay there, impotent to struggle towards the quickening sun and showers. Suddenly, as the sense of her doom struck her, she pushed away the puppy and went to the edge of the platform, and turned her face to the fields. For the rest of her life her beauty and her intelligence would be prisoned blackly in Saltgreave. The years would subdue her to the meanness and ugliness of Saltgreave, and when she came to die she would see the chimney stacks of Saltgreave's soul against the sky. She would probably die of some mean disease such as afflicted her hideous relatives, infected by her poverty and pinching habits of life. Saltgreave was her sphere.

And, as she looked wildly over the fields, she saw that a road crossed the plains to the little town. It ran with sudden narrowings like a twisted staylace.

Somehow, this road fascinated her. It seemed the most desirable thing in the world to walk along by the bent alders in the lively winds: to become for a time a part of the joyful traffic of the plains: to reach at last the quiet streets of that little town, flooded with blue shadow and the sleepy sounds of church bells tolling and dogs barking drowsily. . . . To sit in the coolness of some inn and look out on the hot cobbled stones of the marketplace: to watch the pleasant, kindly folk pass in and out on their sober, leisurely occupations, to hold out a hand and grasp at their kindliness. And in the morning to go forth again to somewhere lovelier and more distant to find pleasanter and kindlier people.

For the first time in her life she felt fully the desire for the open road, that before she had only faintly experienced on clear days at the sight of distant purple moors from the high places of Saltgreave. Her cheeks flamed. Overcome by a passion quite as sharp and fiery as any lust, she turned swiftly to make her way out of the station on to that road.

She stopped dead. While she had been musing over the fields a man and woman had entered the station and now stood a few paces away. They were in riding-costume and had evidently just come from a run of the hounds: the joy of physical exercise glittered from the hard surface of their arrogance. The woman was about thirty-five and not beautiful. But if her face was blunt and sallow and heavy, one felt that her high birth and her wealth would cause bluntness and sallowness and heaviness to be proclaimed as essentials of beauty. And if her bosom was solid and square and her hips overlarge, she had retained a pantechnicon-like weight and impressiveness that did not need the aid of beauty to compel respect. And if her expression was self-consciously obtuse, it was because she disdained the vulgar weapon of intelligence. So although she turned ox-like eyes of contempt on Adela, Adela returned her gaze with reverence and admiration. This woman might be stupid, ungainly and uncomely, but she had the supreme gift, the power of being a bully at the right time and in the right way . . . the power that had kept her class stubbornly sitting on top of all the others in spite of their plaintive agreement that it really shouldn't if it had any sort of a conscience at all. What it had bought for this woman! The delight she must have experienced already that day, riding some fine-blooded horse in the keen wine of the spring air, from some distant wooded place, drowsy with morning mists, into these clear plains. And this was only one day of the year, and each day had its particular delight. There must be something valuable in a class that has secured unto itself such an existence, thought Adela, driven into the worship of success by the bitterness of her own defeat.

Then it struck her that she came of the same stock. If Amy Motley was of Saltgreave, Digby Furnival was born at Ferney Manor, Ashby-à-Court, Warwickshire. And by inheritance she possessed that inconquerable sense of her own rightness and value, that arrogance of mind that had sometimes desolated her by its divergence from the slave-morality inculcated in girls' schools. Now she gloried in it. She determined to face life with insolence. She forgot the open road. She was going on to Peartree Green to live not idly in the luxury of her aunt's home, becoming in each moment of enjoyment more and more the blackguard.

The black-and-tan puppy nuzzled about her feet. She picked it up and hugged it, so that its pink tongue licked her cheek. Its supple sides wriggled over its own ribs: it panted with the excitement of being alive.

As she got into a carriage the man and the woman passed her again.

This time she looked at the man, a slim boy of twenty-five or so, his youth and good looks polished by the fair conditions of his being into the illusion of something precious. Their eyes met. Over his smooth face there flashed an expression of soft, casual voluptuousness. It was not discourteous, it was not evil. It was merely a shameless recognition and response to her beauty, and a comment on it. . . . 'If you and I were lovers, that would be jolly, wouldn't it?'

Adela sulked on the instant and drew back. But as the train moved on the incident soothed her as being another evidence of the immense difference between the dumb dogs of Saltgreave and these proud super-blackguards. In Saltgreave one was ashamed of one's most decent joys, just as one was ashamed of having a baby, even though one was married. The very simplest and most innocent passions of humanity were dissembled. In sunny days one repressed the natural desire to bake like a lizard and walked on the shady side of the road. When gathered in restaurants the inhabitants of Saltgreave maintained a dignified reserve towards their food and showed as much pleasure and gratification as does a single-cylinder machine when fed with paper. Emotion was as suspect as Socialism. . . . But these people, these stiff-necked rulers of the earth, were too proud to be ashamed of anything. Quite frankly and charmingly this man had confessed to a passion that was never named in Saltgreave – the mere observation of which made Adela feel a moral bravo. O splendid, shameless Kings among men!

She was physically exalted by this violent change of attitude towards life when she got out at Peartree Green station. Her cousin Evelyn, waiting for her under the railway bridge, thought she looked a little mad. Her face was burnt with a faint copperish flush of excitement: a lock of her strong black hair, streaked with gold, lay across her broad brow: the cheap long coat she wore hung skimpily about her foalish length of limb. The extreme violence of her mental life showed itself outwardly in the intensity of her expression: just now she smouldered with a fierce contemplative fire. The people of Peartree Green were interested. Porters gaped: the driver of a hay-cart that was creaking over the bridge drew up his horse and glutted his eyes on the strange sight: the stationmaster's baby on its mother's bosom stopped howling to consider the apparition. And Adela went on standing there, looking so lean and lank and so stupidly unconscious of it all. She really didn't look quite normal, thought Evelyn, toning down the first crude expression.

So she came forward to protect Adela by her presence. For she was quality, and the people of Peartree Green would never dare to look impertinently at anybody belonging to quality.

'How do you do, dear?' she said pleasantly, and dropped a kiss lightly on her lips.

The porters ceased to gape, the hay-cart moved again. The stationmaster's baby was hushed.

Adela, always a little dazed by formal kisses, hesitated a minute before she expressed her real regard for Evelyn by wringing her hand. She smiled round the green banks of the railway-cutting and said emphatically, 'How well your wild roses are coming on.' They weren't Evelyn's wild roses, so she gazed at them dispassionately and answered, 'I suppose so. Your train is late. The dog-cart's waiting. You sent your luggage in advance, didn't you?'

The dog-cart outside looked just like a toy with its sleek, motionless horse, the immovable groom with a highlight shining fixedly from his top hat, and the neatness and glitter of the polished wood and brass. It revived in Adela the feeling that life with Aunt Olga was half a fairy-tale and wholly a joke.

As she got into the dog-cart the groom turned round to lift aside a rug. She met his eyes and remembered him. 'How's that baby?' she asked with a leaping directness.

'There's another now,' he answered, 'a boy.' Then Evelyn got in and he cracked his whip.

The lane to Peartree Green, being a true South Hertfordshire lane, climbed a hill and ran straightly along the top of a ridge between two high grass banks sprigged with primroses and surmounted by a hedge breaking into green and here and there splashed with the foam of may-bloom. Every now and then at some sudden rise of the road one looked over the hedge at the purplish elm-tops of some other ridge. For the bland green fields sloped down to broad wet vales, and rose swellingly again to another height, topped with such a lane as this. And on the other side they sank again and rose again, and so on. So that to left and right ridges rose one above the other, each one dimmer and bluer than the last, till they melted into the haven of the horizon.

Adela liked driving through this quiet country that always looked as if it was prepared for a garden-party with Evelyn. Evelyn fitted into it so swell, as was only natural: for she was an aristocrat, one of those who had ordered the countryside from the dawn of Society. For on her father's side she was a Furnival, and the Lorikoffs, her mother's people, were, in spite of their Russian name, of the blood of many noble families. And Evelyn was an aristocratic type. She was an undismayed twenty-nine, not beautiful, but good to look upon and eminently 'right'. Her fairness was quite unradiant, but gave the impression that she was cool like the inside of a rose. There was no beauty about her thin figure itself, for the waist was thick and her hips were too flat, but she looked immensely strong and moved slowly with a deliberate grace. Her face disdained expression, but about her there was a suggestion of reserved force and self-control that often made Adela, with her obsession of shyness and her sudden grasps at emotion, feel a fool.

After a long silence Evelyn asked: 'How's Aunt Amy?' She was so determined not to put herself out for anybody that she did not open her mouth when she spoke, so that her voice drawled through her teeth.

Adela winced. She was aware from the intonation that she should have asked at once how Aunt Olga was. She didn't see why. She was quite certain that Aunt Olga was all right. No one could imagine the lady – who weighed twelve stone and ate everything she liked and rode to hounds – being anything else. Nevertheless she felt guilty. 'Oh, very well – how's Aunt Olga?' she stammered, hating herself for showing so plainly that she had felt the rebuke.

'Has had a touch of bronchitis. Went out to the Stitchington meet when she hadn't really got over a cold in her chest. Came home a wreck.'

'I am sorry.' She forced concern into her voice.

'She's all right again, however.'

Then there fell another silence.

'Been doing well at school?'

'Fairly well. I won the Science Scholarship. But of course I can't use it.'

'That's a pity. It would have been such a nice start for you. I mean, one makes such nice friends. Was it Girton or Newnham?'

In Adela's most fatuous moments she had never thought of the University as a place where one went to make friends. She felt her flesh creep.

'No, nowhere like that. I could have gone with it either to Liverpool or Manchester (that's Victoria University) or Leeds.'

'Oh. Then it doesn't matter so much, does it? They're quite new places, aren't they?'

'They have the loveliest laboratories,' said Adela passionately. A stray sentimentalist passing by would have said that her eyes were the eyes of a childless woman yearning for a babe. But really she was looking down the vista of a laboratory, looking lovingly at the light shining back from the glass jars and the scales, watching enviously the quiet figures of those who were privileged to work there.

'Yes, but it isn't that sort of thing that *lasts*, is it? I mean, at Girton and Newnham there's an atmosphere.'

'I wouldn't waste my money going to an atmosphere. I want to study Science,' snapped Adela, her eyes filling with fierce tears. The next moment she thought: 'I mustn't be cross. Hang it all, I am her guest,' and looked nervously at her. But evidently Evelyn hadn't noticed, for her clear brows were serene. How could she be so obtuse about the thirst for knowledge? It was the only passion Adela knew and to her it was as sacred as religion, they say, is to some people. She pushed back the suspicion that Evelyn was stupid, in view of the conception of aristocracy she had formed that morning, for she was young enough to keep to her conceptions for twenty-four hours together. Of course there were so many physical and social delights at Evelyn's command that it would have been sheer greed in her to lust after knowledge.

'Mother and I have talked very seriously over your prospects for the last month or so,' said Evelyn impressively. 'And we came to a definite conclusion last night.'

'I don't see how you could do that!' exclaimed Adela blankly. 'I didn't know myself that I couldn't use my scholarship till yesterday evening.' She was Adela Furnival, prizeman of the Mary Patience Grammar School (established 1725), and seventeen years and three months, and she objected very strongly to anybody discussing such an important subject as herself without consulting her. She compressed her lips and prepared to speak shrewishly. Then she leapt to her feet and looked around with ecstasy. 'Oh, Evelyn, do let's get out and walk.'

They had left the lane. Peartree Green lay to their left, thrown down on the hilltop like a crumpled handkerchief, rucked up into absurd little hillocks, crossed by deep folds from whose velvet-green depths there flashed the lights of scattered waters. It was sundered in two by a wide avenue of age-old elms, whose green treetops sang slowly in the wind. To the left a billow of orchard blossom raised its snowy crest above a sun-soaked red brick wall and seemed about to break, but always the light breezes beat it back. Facing this across the Green was the village inn, with its balcony blazing with jolly red geraniums, and a great swinging yellow sign of the rising sun, neighboured by an ivy-clad house in whose sleek garden a curate mowed the lawn. Next to it noble Scotch firs guarded the yellow stone front of some great house. And far, far down the straggling of the Green there stood the pear tree that, they said, had given it its name, a whirling pillar of light in the quivering radiance of the sun. It caught the eyes and gave so bold a proclamation of the wonder of the world that the blood leapt in Adela's veins and she laughed in sheer excitement.

'Very well, we'll walk,' said Evelyn indulgently. So they got down and Adela ran up on to the springing turf. She wished she had that black-and-tan puppy to play with now, and reproached herself because she had not given it all the caresses it had asked for when she had had it. Running on a few paces before Evelyn, she walked down the avenue with her head bent back so that she could see the pattern the branches stamped out against the sky. She turned round to cry out on the beauty of the day, and saw on her cousin's face a gentle smile – the kind of smile a voluntary helper would bestow on a Bethnal Green infant enjoying the benefits of the Fresh Air Fund.

She smarted horribly. But the sight of the shining pear tree reminded her that she was right, and she refused to feel snubbed. 'Oh, Evelyn, you are a callous brute!' she cried.

'I dare say it is a change after Saltgreave,' said Evelyn. 'I can't think why you didn't settle down at a place like this instead of going to that abominable place.' She spoke with an air of pained and amused common sense.

'I couldn't have got any Education!' exclaimed Adela.

Evelyn's tone changed to one of pained and amused 'niceness'. 'Perhaps not. But it would have been nicer for your mother, wouldn't it?'

'And how in the wise world could Mother have made money by typewriting in a hole like this!'

'Oh,' said Evelyn. 'She wouldn't have needed to. You can live on very little here. I believe you can get quite a nice cottage in the village for half a crown a week.'

'Indeed you can't,' declared Adela.

'My dear, how can you tell? Rents are very different –'

'I've read it dozens of times in Fabian tracts and things. And anyway there aren't half enough cottages – you told me yourself about the overcrowding –'

'Oh, but I think that is just their lack of fastidiousness –'

Adela wanted to respect Evelyn and did not want to think she was stupid. So she pretended she had not heard it. 'So there aren't any to let. And anyway, in such a snobby place as this it wouldn't have done for you to have pauper relatives herding in a tiny cottage down the village, would it?'

'I only meant somewhere *like* this,' said Evelyn tranquilly. 'Not here, of course. It wouldn't do.'

Adela stopped dead. She wanted to strike Evelyn across the mouth and call her out to a duel with pistols. The implication, blandly delivered in that lazy voice, was that Amy and Adela really ought to huddle their poverty and squalid circumstance out of the way of the delicate into the darkest corner they could find. It was insolent and silly: no one had the right to despise them for their war against penury. Yet this insolence and silliness had the power to strip her of every quality. She felt ugly and sordid and uncouth: she stumbled as she walked. Her passion seemed insurgent yet mean, like a beaten lackey's.

Then the avenue ended and they walked over the long-haired hillocks, nearer and nearer to that shining pear tree. But Adela was blind and deaf with humiliation.

The ground swelled suddenly into a mound, on which she paused, breasting the winds that raced uphill and cooled her cheeks. As Evelyn came up behind her she lowered her head sullenly. Her eyes fell on a little dewpond folded in under the prow of the mound, which the lucid light, streaming down through the smooth surface waters on to the emerald weeds that strove upward to the air, made like a hard jewel graved in its depths with some fine pattern. As she looked and smiled, a young man who sat facing her on the green walls of earth that prisoned this little glory of water smiled back at her and dropped a stone into the pond. The jewel shattered into a thousand fragments that liquefied and changed – the coursing white clouds above, the trembling weed, the oily circles of the rippling – and slowly clarified into the same hard jewel as it began. Adela raised her wide eyes to the young man's face. He too had been watching the pond with delight. He stretched out his hand to a little heap of stones that lay at his side and was picking up another, when Evelyn spoke.

'You have had a busy afternoon, Arnold!'

He rose to his feet and slowly dropped in another stone. 'Oh, one does see Life in Peartree Green!' he laughed. His voice was delicate and sleek, like lovely silk.

They all watched the pond in silence, Evelyn holding her peace with a kind of hard deference to the young man. He stood with his hands on his slim hips, his straight black brows knitted in attention. As soon as he had raised his head she said languidly: 'Well, there is tea. May we go on?'

This time he did not answer her but spoke across to Adela, fixing her eyes for one second before the words came. 'What do you think of it?'

She was a little dazzled by his face. The contrast between his black hair and his smooth white skin was unnatural but quite beautiful. His expressions illuminated his face like the changing lights from a beacon, showing now the right proportioning of his forehead, now the subtle curves of his thin lips, or the fine line of the jaw. There was a sort of boyishness about it, yet the lids were very tired. From the midst of her imaginings about him she heard her voice blurt out strongly: 'If you had been a poor man and poorly dressed, they would have thought you the village idiot!'

He took her meaning, smiled, and said it in literary words. 'Being a rich man, as men go, I can afford to spend the afternoon in the consideration of beauty.'

Out of the tail of her eye she perceived that Evelyn, not understanding what they had said, had come to the conclusion that her pauper cousin had committed a gaucherie, and, compressing her lips with annoyance, was strolling over to Arnold, murmuring, 'Really, I insist on tea.' The young man let her pass him and waited for Adela. It took Evelyn a minute to grasp this, and then she said over her shoulder: 'Oh, I must introduce you two. My cousin Adela – Mr Arnold Neville.'

'But you said your cousin was a schoolgirl!' cried the young man indignantly.

'Well, so she is.'

'She isn't. She's twenty come Michaelmas, and very serious-minded for her age.'

'I'm seventeen,' said Adela, looking at him round-eyed.

'I'm thirty,' answered the young man. Her eyes grew rounder. 'Honour bright. Evelyn, tell her I'm speaking the truth.'

'Of course you are. But do stop talking nonsense. You are a couple of children, you know.'

They had come to the edge of Peartree Green and were at the gate of Button Court where Aunt Olga lived; a modern thing of timbering and roughcast, weighed down by the shadow of immemorial elms and the stark majesty of the Scotch firs. Several of the casement windows had been left open, and even from the roadway one could see the blue curtains dancing in the breeze.

'Oh, how careless!' sighed Evelyn.

'No,' said the young man. 'The flags are flying to welcome our distinguished visitor. Can't you hear harps in the air?'

'No,' said Adela.

'I could have gone on like that ever so much longer if you had only played up!' he exclaimed reprovingly. 'But then I'm good at make-believe.'

Adela looked backward on a family of dolls that through neglect came to a sad end in the dustbin. Through the dimness of the past she saw herself always a serious child, too much absorbed in dreams of knowledge and glory to become bitter, yet too conversant with the drunken habits of Mr Spence next door and the uncleanliness of the Wilkins children over the way ever to gain pleasure from any toy made in man's image. Ambitious infant! whose ambitions had turned out to be as useless as her toys when she emerged from infancy! So she replied sombrely, 'I never was any good at make-believe.'

He turned wide sympathetic eyes on her: recognizing that she had had a disappointment, he pretended it was a tragedy. Adela felt babyishly flattened.

They walked down the broad drive for a few paces: on each side the daffodils flamed like great candles stuck in the grass borders. They they struck off through the belt of trees on the left. Sunlight dropped bright patines through the soft swimming gloom of the shadows on to the mossy floor. It was like a lovely sleep shot with lovely dreams. At the edge of the spinney there was a low wall of golden broom, over which they looked on to a broad lawn confined by a circle of flower-beds gleaming with the pale strong colours of spring. To their left, with its red brick back turned to the trees, stood a summer-house. Its other three sides were open to the sunlight, the tile roof being supported by two brick columns clothed with the light foliage of Rambler Roses. From the point they could only see a corner of its interior: but as they stood there, there rang out the sound of a laugh. A high, clear, well-mannered laugh: it was thrillingly pure, like a Mass sung by boys.

The young man said bitterly: 'That's Madelaine.' And the youth left him: he slouched behind Adela loutishly. He had blurted it under his breath so that when he saw Adela gazing under high brows he flushed and began to swashbuckle again.

They were out on the lawn now, so that they could see that two women and two men sat in the shadow of the summer-house. One of the women, a vast figure in purple, was Aunt Olga. As Adela went up the broad steps leading to the raised brick floor she felt as though they were the steps to a throne. So, knowing herself to be hot and dusty with travel, she presented herself to these cool, leisurely persons in a faint frenzy of shyness.

'How d'ye do, dear. You seem to have felt the journey,' said Aunt Olga. 'But perhaps Evelyn can lend you a hairpin. Yes, on the left of your parting.' She raised her queenly, elephantine body from the depths of the basket-chair and suddenly enveloped Adela. Her firm, fleshy white hands patted Adela over – assaulted her soft hair, flattened her turndown collar, fluffed out the silk bow at her throat, and wrenched round her waist-belt – what time her bluff good-natured clarion voice rang out: 'Curious thing – your mother cares absolutely nothing for her appearance too. My word, I would like to have the looking after you for a few months, eh? There, that's more like a human being, isn't it!'

She drew back and exposed Adela to the world – a strange, mad-looking Adela, her face inflamed with a coppery flush, her eyes blinking and smarting, nauseated to the very core of her being by the insolent touch of those insufferable smooth hands. She felt like some abortion of the slums that had disgraced itself by some inbred lowness in the presence of its benefactors. And she gathered that the men and the women eyeing her thought so too.

'Mrs Neville, this is my little niece Adela.' The woman looked up at her with strong, pale blue eyes and extended a cold long white hand. She was very pretty: her honey-coloured hair rose in all sorts of dainty curls and waves from her high forehead and little ears, and she wore a graceful gown of gathered blue ninon. Seduced by her prettiness and the thought that she must be some relative of the young man, Adela involuntarily smiled into her eyes. For a minute there was no response: then she smiled back with a terrible graciousness. 'And I think you know my brothers, Adela.' The two Lorikoffs were exactly alike, except for the pose of their professions. Mr Arthur Lorikoff, the stockbroker, had anointed himself with a permanent geniality, as though perpetually assuring the earth that he was so immensely rich he need not thieve any man's money. Mr Justice Lorikoff, six months raised to the bench, was all sticky with the glue of dignity that stiffened his upper lip and gummed up his eyes. But otherwise they were exactly alike – handsome and massive as Assyrian bulls, with crisply curling silver hair and a bulge of red fat resting on the top of their dazzling collars. They both greeted Adela with the same good-natured grin of brutal compassion.

Then there was an awkward pause. She stood back sulkily, wondering why on earth these people should feel so acutely the fact that she was poor. Then her eyes fell on the young man, standing with folded arms on the top step: he looked so irresponsible among these solemn wealthy folk. She determined that in this one thing she would not be bullied, so she walked back and sat down in the deck-chair in front of him, beside Aunt Olga.

'Why didn't you come by the through train from Saltgreave to Gortwall? You would have got here for lunch,' said Aunt Olga, pouring out tea. She wore an unchangeable expression of outraged common sense, and she also spoke as though abruptly but kindly interrupting a windy rhetorical flight with a few words of worldly wisdom. Her tone implied that Adela had been been wasting time and money wandering round England in goods-vans since dawn. So Adela said passionately, 'There isn't one.'

'My dear child, it's been running for twenty years.'

'It's off. Because of the trouble in Gortwall.'

'Well, I haven't heard of it.'

'My dear, it may be true,' said Mr Justice Lorikoff from the background, in his rich, fruity voice. 'There is trouble in Gortwall. I understand the men on strike won't allow certain goods to enter the town by rail, and on several occasions have raided the station. Some men have been arrested, I believe – one of them an MP, Robert Langlad. I shall try them at the Assizes next week. A most regrettable strike.'

'Unfortunately it isn't a strike,' said Adela, feeling quite at her ease now that they had begun to talk about *things*. 'It's a lockout, and so the men weren't prepared.'

The young man leapt forward and offered her some cakes. 'Have a macaroon,' he begged with a strange intimate earnestness. 'Do have a macaroon.'

'Why must I have a macaroon?' she asked him in a serious undertone. 'I'd rather have a doughnut.'

'We dine at seven, you know,' remarked Aunt Olga. She had much better had said – 'Don't overeat, child!' because then it might have passed with Adela as an unsuccessful joke.

Then Arthur Lorikoff spoke fatly from the corner. 'I wish to Heaven above that the Unionist Government would get into power again. They'd soon stop these strikes. Shoot the fellows down, that's what they'd do. And serve 'em right.'

'But that would be dreadful!' exclaimed Adela in infantile candour of dismay. 'We should all be murdered in our beds. You can't expect the working classes to be murdered and simply sit down under it.'

'The working classes haven't the spirit of cows!' proclaimed Arthur boisterously.

'But they must have, or they wouldn't annoy you by going on strike!' she insisted. In Saltgreave no three people of Adela's set ever met together without delightedly hurling themselves into debate. On an afternoon like this Mr Purkiss and Miss Ralton and she would have finished off the Minority Report of the Poor Law Commission, the Minimum Wage, and the Disestablishment of the Welsh Church, and then parted reluctantly. So that the blood froze in her veins with amazement as Mrs Neville slowly turned her small graceful head and looked remotely at her. She realized that far better had she dipped her doughnut in her tea and sucked it than said what she had. And she could not understand.

Then Aunt Olga began: 'I tell you what it is, Adela. You and your mother shouldn't live in that dreadful place, whatever you call it, Garibaldi Crescent. Quite half the people look as if they had just come out of prison. And I know you can't help coming in contact with them – I suppose they come in and borrow things and so on. And I suppose they're all of them Socialists and Anarchists, and you pick it up from them. I blame myself very severely for having allowed you and your mother to settle in that abominable town. Bedford was the place.'

'I once bought a dog at Bedford,' began the young man with desperate inconsequence, but Evelyn's lazy voice spoke drowsily from a distant deck-chair.

'Mother, it's only a phase. Mrs Boswell says that ever so many of her helpers are Socialists when they go down to the Bethnal Green Settlement, and then, after a little hard experience of the real poor and their degraded habits, they see that's not the way.' There was evidently a moment's exalted brooding on what the way really was, then she ended kindly, 'Of course it's only a phase.'

Adela was by this time resigned to well-meant insults. But she did wish that Mrs Neville would say something: she was so exquisite and so finely made she must be full of gracious manners. Surely she would say something to smooth this situation over. But she made no motion. Adela noticed, as she watched her wistfully out of the corner of her eye, that the black velvet bow on the breast of her gown fluttered like a floating sea-bird, and she was disappointed. Nobody but rotters breathed so high-up, almost at the collar-bone. Oh, they were all rotters here!

# The Magician of Pell Street

*This story, hitherto uncollected, appeared in* Hearst's International Cosmopolitan, *February 1926.*

M r Staveley, who was sitting on the edge of his wife's bed reading the *Times*, coughed. His wife, Theodora, rolled over and pressed her face against the pillow, and said wildly, 'I want to go back to New York.'

Her husband paid no attention, for he was reading a summary of the year's racing. Presently she sat up and put her fingers round his wrist and jerked it, saying, 'Darling, you coughed.'

He bent his lips to her hand and muttered, his eyes going back to the page, 'I smoke too much.'

She continued to stare at him with enormous eyes. 'Are you sure you aren't getting thinner, Danny dear?'

'As a matter of fact,' he replied cheerfully, 'I am. Lost ten pounds since August. Most remarkable.'

'Ten pounds! *Ten pounds!* Danny, that's dreadful!'

'Nothing to worry about, dear heart. I'm still a pound or two overweight.'

'Truly?'

'Truly, I'm eleven stone two. I ought to be ten stone twelve.'

She believed him, because his voice was touched with that faint solemnity with which he always spoke of physical matters with which he had accurately acquainted himself. He felt that this was a specially respectable form of the truth, free from any dangerous association with ideas.

So she purred contentedly when he gave her shoulder a kindly pat and said:

'Better look after yourself, old girl. You're skinny enough, Lord knows. You can't go talking about anybody else.' For she knew that this was his way, her Danny's way, of paying homage to the beauty of her body; which was not thin at all, but was the body of a dancer, that is shaped to slenderness and roundness by the rhythms to which it perpetually abandons itself, even as the stone on the bed of a stream is worn to smooth contours by the water that flows over it.

She loved him inordinately. She was well content with this country gentleman she had married, even though he had made her give up her career. A ray of sunlight was now lying on his hair, which was neither fair nor dark, and showed it powdered with gold. 'Darling!' she murmured proudly and delightedly, as if this effect was due to some surpassing merit and effort on his part.

But Danny coughed once more. He was coughing much more often than he had done even last week. Roughly speaking, it was about once in a quarter of an hour now. She rolled over again and buried her face in the pillows, covering her ears so that she would not hear him cough, hiding her eyes so that she would not see his dear kind face.

How she loved him!

It is impossible to say why Theodora loved Danny. He was handsome in the standard English way; with clear eyes crinkled up with a special air of seriousness as if to exclude not only the light from the retina but also all disturbing impressions from the brain behind, and the straight nose and firm jaw and good skull of one born of healthy stock who has had all the food and fresh air and exercise he needs from the day of his birth. He was enormously powerful; he was one of those very strong men whose shoulders are slightly bowed, as if they carry their strength in an invisible pack on their backs. But in the physical qualities she adored, of which her art was a perpetual worship, speed and grace, he was conspicuously deficient.

He was not intelligent. Indeed, there were certain respects in which Danny was very nearly an idiot. He was a financial fool. While he had any money he thought he had all money. His estate in Hampshire was haunted as by banshees with land-agents and auditors and professional household managers, wailing at the results of this monstrous supposition; and in New Square, Lincoln's Inn, a family solicitor cried not less continually than do the cherubim and seraphim.

He was a fool about people. When he could not understand what people were doing their proceedings seemed to him without reason or, if they were successful and famous people whom he could not dismiss as idiots, the cloaks for nefarious schemes.

He was not interested in politics.

For the arts he had no use, saving the theatre, which filled the interval between dinner and the time when a man goes to bed. Of the sciences he was unaware.

Nevertheless, Theodora loved him extravagantly. There can, indeed, be no exaggeration of the way she loved him. Not because of the passion between them, for that was the effect and not the cause of their love. When she tried to explain it to her friends, she used to stammer confusedly concerning certain instinctive gifts he had, survivals of powers that most people have had to give up in exchange for the doubtful benefit of being human.

You could not lose Danny in a mist on a Scotch moor. He had that mysterious faculty, the sense of the north. You could blindfold him, walk him a mile in and out and back and forward over broken country and spin him round and round; and after a second's setterish lifting of the head he would point due north. He knew too when the wind was going to change, and the rain going to lift: he could tell when people were coming through the woods long before he could have heard their voices; in the night he would dream distressfully of a horse or a dog, and when he rose and took a lantern and went out to the stables he would find the beast sick as he had feared.

These things gave her infinite happiness to contemplate. Her body was hard with muscles raised by her physical efforts; till she met him she had never in all her life had anything, not a dress, not a day's travel, not a halfpenny, which she had not earned by effort. The effortlessness of these tricks of Danny's, their sheer fortuitousness, rested and delighted her mind. And moreover they were surely signs of contact with something . . . with something.

These confused stammerings usually failed to enlighten her friends, though her constitutional desire to tell the truth made her always embark upon them; but they could follow her when she told them that down there in the country he was extraordinarily, beautifully kind. Up here in London he was not: he was apt to be hard and bullying with waiters and commissionaires, because they seemed to him sharp and knowing like poachers; he was shy and sulky with the men he had to meet who actually liked to live in town because of some jiggery-pokery with politics or what not; he thought London women expected to be talked to too much. It was silly of them really to keep on this flat, he hated it so.

But down in Hampshire she, whose faults were vehemence and asperity, was continually amazed and shamed by the unvarying sweetness of the gaze he turned on life. So long as he was not afraid of people because they were a different sort from him he was prepared to be endlessly, inventively good to them. And if they were ungrateful to him his goodness did not flicker. He would neither say nor do anything that took sides with the malevolence that had been brought against him; merely he would knit his brows so that there was a deep furrow between his kind, empty eyes, that was as touching as the mark of disappointment on a child's face.

That was the dreadfulness of it. Danny would not have done it to her, this awful thing she had done to him, which was making him cough. It was true that the initial cruelty had been his, that he had deserted her there in New York, had left her for two months without a word. But the poor dear had not known what he was doing. He was never himself in a town, and New York is the essence of all towns, the supreme defiance of nature. He simply had not been himself. He simply had not understood.

There were excuses to be made for her too, of course. She had loved him so much even in those early days that continued possession of him had been necessary to her soul and body. Without him she had gone mad; there had been days when her maid had had to lift her out of bed and wash and dress her, because the will had perished in her and she no longer had the initiative to do these things. Without him her body had withered as if some merciless and mistaken surgeon had cut out a vital part.

But even if something had happened to Danny which had had the power to reduce him to the same state, he would never have done what she did. He would not have gone to the magician of Pell Street.

Now she said aloud, gently, desperately, 'Danny, my darling,' and drew the sheet over her face. She lay quite still until she heard the sound of the door opening, and her maid's voice saying:

'Doctor Paulton is here, madam.'

She shot up and stared at the maid for a minute. She had known that it would be awkward explaining to Danny why she had sent for the doctor.

Harshly and abruptly she ordered: 'Show him up. Show him up at once.'

Danny folded up the *Times* and said: 'I suppose I'd better clear out. But I say, old girl, what's the matter?'

She lay back against the pillows, smiled mysteriously, and murmured, 'My old complaint.'

It was thrilling to see how puzzled and distressed he was. 'I say, what's that? I thought you were as strong as a horse. What is your old complaint?' She continued to smile, and he bent low over her. 'What is it? You're rotting? No, you're not! Please, Theo, tell me!'

She smiled even more mysteriously, and murmured even more softly, so that he had to put his ear close to her lips:

'In love with you . . .'

His relief was enormous. He picked her up and held her close to him and kissed her on the mouth, whispering, 'Dearest, don't get cured, will you?'

How she was enraptured by his relief and his kiss and his evident love; but at the feeling through his clothes of his strong heartbeat hers almost failed. If her traffickings with the magician of Pell Street had resulted in the destruction of this beautiful, this clean, this healthy, this innocent being! She began to shiver slightly and cried out:

'Danny, would you mind very much if we went back to New York?'

He started back from her. 'Why are you always saying that just now? You used to hate New York! Why should you want to go back? Theo, have you anything on your mind?'

'What could I have? You know every moment of my life since our marriage. There's nothing. Nothing at all. But I want to go back to New York . . .'

'Good Lord, you're shivering. Theo, you are ill! You're all nerves!'

She was laughing and shaking her head when the maid showed in Doctor Paulton. Then she had to pull herself together. Little Doctor Paulton was a man who had won his way to fame by a combination of extreme cleverness and inquisitiveness. As a penniless young man he had had to give up research work in applied bacteriology, in which he had shown genius, and go into private practice in order to be able to marry the girl he loved. With great rapidity he had fallen out of love with his wife, and being an acquisitive person who hates to make a bad bargain, he had set about seeing what he could get out of this pit of a fashionable practice into which he had fallen.

He satisfied his scientific side in part by becoming a marvellous diagnostician; and as that could not wholly satisfy him, since it was not his natural bent, he made up the balance by cultivating a furious interest in the private lives of his patients. Shamelessly he let it interfere with his medical conscience; he would send a patient to a foreign spa for a treatment she did not need because he had sent another patient there in whom he knew she was interested, and he wanted to see how that affair would work out. His patients preferred to refer these interventions to personal devotion rather than to the plain fact that he was as curious as an idle old woman. And so he prospered exceedingly.

Both these dominant characteristics Theo intended to use. He would find out the cause of Danny's cough, if there was a cause. If there was not, she would fall back on his inquisitiveness.

Danny met him at the door. 'Morning, Paulton. I'm glad you've come. I'm not very pleased with my wife just now. She's –'

But Theo cut in. 'Doctor Paulton, I haven't sent for you for myself at all. I'm perfectly all right. I want you to have a look at my husband.'

Doctor Paulton adjusted his pince-nez, took a look at her, and took a look at Danny; and there followed a moment when he seemed to be inspecting the pattern of the carpet, but was, Theo knew, taking a look at the domestic situation. And Danny was saying: 'Theo, what are you thinking of! I'm as fit as a fiddle!'

'He coughs,' she explained. 'He coughs all the time. He coughs about once every quarter of an hour. At least. And it's getting worse.'

'But, Theo –'

'It really is. Last week it was only once in twenty minutes. I'm sure there's something the matter.'

Danny turned to Doctor Paulton with the air of one sensible male appealing to another. 'Honestly, this is all nonsense. I do cough a bit, but then I smoke too much. But I never was better in my life.'

'Doctor Paulton, you must examine him. Really, there's something wrong.'

She would have gone on longer if, oddly enough, it had not been Doctor Paulton that had been moved by her pleas to insist, but Danny that suddenly capitulated. He gave her a teasing smile and said: 'Well, we'd better get it over. But my wife's fussing. You won't find a thing the matter with me. Shall we go into my dressing-room? So long, old girl. I'll be back in a minute, and Paulton'll tell you that you're a dotty young woman.'

The white door closed behind them. She stared at it, the tears rolling down her cheeks. In a few minutes she would know if what she feared was true; if she was a murderess who had killed something infinitely sweet and good, by what she had done with the magician of Pell Street.


It could never have happened if they had met anywhere but in New York. But then if they had not met in New York they never would have met at all, for Danny did not go to dance clubs or cabarets in London, and he never visited Paris or Monte Carlo; and between these four places her life was then divided. It made her heart contract to think what a mere chance it was that had brought him to the Rigoli, on Broadway, where she was doing a midnight turn. But once this amazing conjunction of the simple and the sophisticated had been effected, how inevitable had been the rest!

She had made her entrance and was standing beside her partner François, bowing to the applause that came from the faces and hands that dimly patterned the darkness surrounding the polished floor; and immediately she saw Danny. He was sitting at a table quite close to her, on the left of the entrance with two women and the Englishman, Freddy Moor – poor, handsome, sodden Freddy, who had come over with some money and had contrived to borrow from long-suffering friends to start life afresh as a bootlegger, and who was being picked clean by bemused members of the New York underworld.

She saw at once that Danny was not like that. The grave, heavy innocence of his large fair head made her think of a chaste lion. She perceived with delight and a determination to alter it as soon as possible, that he was not at all interested in her. His face expressed nothing but a desire to get out of this infernally stuffy hole and go home to bed. This struck her as beautiful and unique. She was infatuated.

She moved out into the middle of the floor, holding François's hand, in the golden circle of the spot-light. Before she had let go François's hand she had resolved to marry Danny. She danced marvellously, and solely for him. A week or two afterwards she had asked him what he had thought of her, and he had replied gravely and without intention to offend, 'I thought you seemed an extraordinarily nice girl to be doing that sort of thing.'

She had danced with François the waltz that many people said was more perfect than anything since Pavlova and Mordkin; and she had never danced it better. But on hearing these fatuities she didn't mind. If he was one of those simple souls to whom dancers seem to be a set of persons who enjoy within certain limitations the power to defy the laws of gravity, and not much to choose between them, well, it was lovely that he should be so.

At the end of her programme, when she and François sat down at one of the tables, she was faced by a dilemma. She was determined to marry Danny. Another look at him between dances had made her soul go down on its knees. She wanted not only to live with him, but to live like him. But she also knew that if she wanted him she had to go after him herself. It is only the feminine man that hunts his mate; the masculine man – and Danny was pure male – had to be hunted.

Obviously she must meet him as soon as possible. She knew one of the women at his table, a certain Laura Ballisten, sometime exhibition dancer and now mistress of a Wall Street broker. She could bow and smile at Laura and then Laura would bring him over to her table. For he was interested in her now. His eyes were set on her face. That would certainly bring her in touch with him, but on the other hand it would give him a false impression of her if he met her first as the friend of a woman like Laura; who, in point of fact, was not a friend of hers. Theodora had always despised her, because she had used her dancing not as an end in itself but as a side-street leading into Wall Street.

But while she sat pondering, the thing happened without any effort on her part. Some friends of Laura's had come over to Freddy's table and were occupying the attention of both her and the other woman; and Freddy came over to congratulate her and brought Danny with him. He slowly sat down beside her, and she began to dig her claws into him. She told him that she was English, too, and complained that she never got back there for more than a few weeks at a time and then but once or twice a year, so limited is the market in England for first-class exhibition dancers. She alleged that she hungered for the English countryside.

He sympathized with her particularly on hearing that she had been in the States for nine years. There was, of course, nowhere

like England. He had come over just for the wedding of his younger
brother, who was at Washington, and had married a Southern girl,
and he had hoped to get back last week, but he had run across poor
Freddy in New York. At that he gave her a long scrutiny, which
she returned steadily, though not without a painful effort; he was
so touchingly good.

Then he told her in undertones that he was trying to get Freddy
home. They were all wrong 'uns, weren't they, the people Freddy was
in with over here? They were just taking his money from him, weren't
they? She nodded gravely, and professed an even greater horror of
Freddy's friends than she really felt. She felt justified in pretending
to him to be better than she was, because she knew that she would
become much better than she was if only she could get him.

And in a week she got him. She and he together settled Freddy's
business and put him on a liner for Southampton with a loan from
Danny in his pocket.

Then they rode together in Central Park. They went out together
through the manicured countryside of Long Island and played golf at
Piping Rock. They impaled bacon and beefsteak on the end of peeled
wands and held them over a camp-fire on a hilltop by the Hudson.
Seven days after they met he asked her to marry him. They agreed
not to marry till they got back to England, for Danny hated New York;
and that they could not do till she had worked off the remaining three
weeks of her contract at the Rigoli. She worked as in a dream, her
trained body carrying on the business, but her mind forever absent.
There was nothing real but Danny.

And in another fortnight she lost him. Danny, who she had thought
was above all things the kind of man who does not leave women, left
her. Two things happened to upset him. First of all he discovered
that Theodora had been married twice before, and that her first
husband had been the iniquitous Joseph, dancer and the husband
of four wives.

He was lunching with her at Sherry's when a dark man, with oily
hair and oily eyes and a body supple as spaghetti, pushed by their
table on his way to the door and, catching sight of Theodora, raised
his eyebrows far too high and bowed extravagantly. She had returned

his bow only a little less extravagantly, and they exchanged a laughing look as if there was some joke between them. Danny, who disliked the look of the fellow, had acidly said as much, and she had grimly replied that there was. She had married him when she was eighteen and divorced him when she was twenty.

This shocked Danny beyond belief. He had been aware that Theodora Dene was only her stage name, that she was really Mrs Marshall, and that her husband had been a Chicago lawyer who had died of influenza; but he had not known that Mr Marshall had had a predecessor. He was revolted to find that this previously unsuspected person was a professional dancer – this particular dancer and the husband of four wives.

And Theo could not right herself with him, chiefly because she was so much in love with him that his censure robbed her of speech and reason and everything else except tears and a sense that he would be angrier still if she shed them in a public place. So she did not tell him – and indeed it would have been difficult to explain such subtleties to Danny – that at eighteen she had never known a gentleman and that consequently Joseph's externals had not revolted her, and that she had mistakenly taken his willingness to stoop from his stardom to marry a gawky little chorus-girl as evidence of a noble and loving nature; that her marriage from the very beginning had been loathsome to her; and that she laughed up at her former husband with that air of sharing a joke because she was too proud to let the man she despised know how he had hurt her.

Instead, she was unfortunately inspired to dilate on the fact that she had reaped some benefits from the experience, because Joseph taught dancing marvellously, all his four wives having emerged from the state of marriage with him as headliners. This, to Danny, who attached no importance whatsoever to dancing, seemed flippant and indecent.

The tears burned behind her eyes because she understood perfectly everything that he was feeling. They ate and drank and talked very little, and went back silently to her hotel; and there, since it was not her lucky day, Schnarakoff the *costumier* was waiting with the frock she had ordered for tonight's new dance. Danny had to be left alone with Schnarakoff, a plump, effeminate person, while she went into the bedroom and tried it on.

Gloomily Danny sat wondering why the woman he loved need have so much to do with that kind of person, until various things, revolving round the central fact that Theo was not pleased with the results of Mr Schnarakoff's industry, began to happen. To Danny it simply appeared that the door opened and Theo shot into the room, in an extremely tawdry dress, and shrieked and screamed insulting phrases at Schnarakoff, at the same time picking up portions of the skirt and the bodice and holding them away from her body to exhibit the defects of the workmanship, so that she exposed her underwear and even her flesh.

He did not realize that it was precisely the tawdriness of the dress about which she was complaining; he did not realize that her temper was entirely justified, since the dress had not been made according to her instructions, and had been delivered too late to allow of any alterations before that evening's performance, he did not realize that she was giving way to her temper because shrieks and screams were literally the only language of remonstrance likely to make the smallest impression on the case-hardened Mr Schnarakoff; and as for exposing herself in front of him, the *costumier* had seen almost every English and American actress of the last twenty years in all possible stages of undress, and a modest woman might as well blush before a bed-post.

Danny failed utterly, in fact, to understand that Theo was being as quietly sensible, as soberly devoted to the maintenance of the workaday world, as he was down in Hampshire when he called an unsatisfactory gamekeeper into the gun-room and gave him a fatherly talking-to. He thought she was mad. He was sure she was undesirable. He got up and went out, and refraining from going back to his hotel in case she telephoned him there, wrote her a letter from a club saying that he was sure they were not suited to one another; and by what seemed to him good luck he found a cabin vacant on the *Olympic*, which sailed the next morning at eight. The best of men do this sort of thing if they are frightened. And Theo was left to tread her path that led her ultimately to the magician of Pell Street.

Doctor Paulton was back in the room. She cried out vehemently, 'Have you found out what's the matter with him?'

He shook his head. 'Haven't finished yet. Come to get a new laryngoscope gadget. Left it in my bag in the hall.'

His glasses twinkled as he repassed through the room, and she realized that her face was wet with tears. Well, she did not mind. She meant to use this inquisitiveness for her own ends, if the worst came to the worst. But she didn't really like him. She wished she hadn't been obliged to have the prying little creature. This was another of the hateful consequences her visit to Chinatown had brought upon her.

The only mitigation of the whole affair was that she had not premeditated that visit. Even though she blamed herself for it more than for anything else she had ever done, even though she was whipping up her sense of guilt to its height as if her torture might serve as an expiation, it still seemed something that had happened to her rather than something she had done.

It had occurred one day about six weeks after she had been deserted. She had risen from her bed frenzied and exhausted, since as always now she had lain for hours in the night moaning, 'Danny, Danny, Danny'. And all the morning she had spent, as she spent most of her days now, walking up and down her room. Sometimes she would pause and clench her right hand and drive it downwards as if she were stabbing him. Then she would sob, and stoop, and open her arms widely and welcomingly, as if a big man were casting himself at her feet for forgiveness, and then, as if she were taking his head to her bosom, she would kiss an invisible mouth. Whereat, because there was nothingness there, she would weep and rage and walk again, and stab again.

About one o'clock the telephone rang. She opened the bedroom door and called to her maid to answer it, but there was only silence, and she remembered that she had sent the maid out shopping. The bell rang and rang. She could not answer it, for just now she was very much afraid of people. They were apt to say, 'You're not looking well,' and since she was a truthful person she always wanted to reply, 'Yes,

I've been jilted.' She felt a coward for not saying it. But on the other hand she could not give Danny away as a jilt. She would still have struck anybody who said anything against him in her presence. The bell continued to ring, till she ran into her bedroom and put on a hat and coat, and went out of the hotel.

She walked about the streets of New York all that day. When nightfall came she was somewhere down on the East Side. She had eaten nothing all day, and she made her way to a delicatessen store she saw across the street.

It was a clean little shop, full of the wholesome sweet-sour smell of newly baked rye bread, and the man behind the counter was a jolly person with twinkling eyes and close black curls that seemed to roll in the same curves as his full, smiling mouth. There were strings of little Hamburg sausages everywhere, even round the cash-register, and she ordered one in a rye roll.

But soon Danny came back to her thoughts, and stretched on the rack of her co-equal love and hate of him, she sat tracing the dark veins on the marble table-top with a taut finger.

There came suddenly a shout of laughter from the back of the shop and an outbreak of dispersed giggles, as if the original great, hearty chunk of laughter had splintered into fragments that had flown all over the room. She looked up and saw that the door into the rear had swung right open, and she could see the jolly storekeeper in his clean white apron sitting at his supper, with his fat young wife beside him and any number of bright-eyed little youngsters swarming round the room. The very newest one of all had crawled to his father's side, unsuspected because his head did not show above the table, and had shot up an acquisitive fist and stolen a whole dill pickle off the plate. He had got his little face right into it before it could be taken away, and he was now full of repentance, wailing and spitting at the nasty, salty greenness.

They were all laughing at him except the mother, who with a lazy smile picked up her baby in her great white arms and let him stand on her cushiony lap, nuzzling his disappointed face against her straight, lustrous black hair, while she raised his petticoat and playfully patted his rounded, bloomy little hindquarters. Her movements were very slow. She was indolent with happiness, creamy with content, as if she knew that so far as any human being can be safe she was safe, since so long as one of this company remained alive she would not be alone.

Theodora put down some money by her plate and hurried out into the street. She looked at her watch and almost whimpered when she saw that there were still some hours to fill in before she need go to the cabaret. There had come on her suddenly a delusion that her face was lined and sallow. When presently she found herself in a broad street where there were clanging street-cars and crowded pavements she felt unable to cope with the noise and the jostling of the people, as if she had all at once grown old.

She began to look down the side-streets for a way of escape, but they showed only a straiter dinginess till she came to one which seemed to have more than the others of light and colour and less of screaming children and waste paper. She had a vague impression that it had an unusually large number of chop-suey restaurants, but she walked along it with her eyes on the pavement, and it was some moments before she realized the special strangeness of the place.

People came slipping past her and she noticed that whereas the people in the streets she had left were moving with haste, these people were moving with speed. She raised her head, and saw that they were all little yellow men. She looked around her and saw that she had come to a part of New York which had been squeezed into queer shapes and painted queer colours by a yellow hand.

There were steps running down to caverns of brightness in the basements. There were little shops that looked like ordinary general stores until on looking closer one saw that there was something alien about every item in the muddle and litter that filled the windows, and that the dusty yellow paper books that hung on lines across them were printed not in our print, and from them came trails of pungency that did not seem to melt away, but rather to remain suspended in the atmosphere, doubtless in the shape of some magic charm.

Everywhere, on the doors and windows, on the sign-boards, there were the Chinese characters, those frenzied yet serene symbols that look like the writings of demons that possess the secret of beauty. Down on the street level these demons were content to cover every inch with their signature, but up above they took even greater liberties with this bit of America, twisting the houses into fantastically jutting gables, painting them scarlet and gold.

Theodora had never been in Chinatown before. It pleased her enormously, with its unfailing queerness of detail. At a street corner she halted before a bill-board covered with long scarlet and white strips blackly inscribed with these Chinese characters.

'I wonder what they are?' she said to herself. And as if she had spoken aloud a silky voice said in her ear:

'Only leal estate advertisements, lady.'

A little yellow man was standing just behind her. She thanked him and walked on till the street ran into another, on which the East had laid its hand with even more changing power. Here the houses rose into high pagodas.

Entranced, she walked along until the sight of the harsh lights of Occidental New York at the end of the street dismayed her and she stopped. She did not in the least want to leave this fantastic place, but she was very tired. She had paused in front of a doorway which had a public look and she peered into its shadows to see what kind of place it might be.

A voice said: 'The lady can go in. It is a joss-house. Velly intelesting. Stlangers are invited.'

A little yellow man was standing at her elbow. He might have been the same one who spoke to her at the bill-board, but she was not sure.

She followed him up the flight of stairs that was within the doorway. The place might or might not have been what he said it was. She was not afraid. She was wearing nothing valuable, for nowadays, tarnished by her sense of rejection, she felt inferior to her bright jewels; and she had in her bag only a hundred dollars or so. And indeed she did not care what happened to her possessions or herself.

It was, however, a place where she was obviously safe. Behind a padded door there was a large dark room, dense with pungency, unlighted save where on a dais at its end there sat the immense image of a goddess. She was in a blue dress with blue rays of painted metal coming from her head, and she meant nothing. It was impossible to say whether her hand was raised to invite or repel, and her smooth, oval face was blank as the kernel of the stone of a fruit. There were benches all over the room on which there sat isolated people who were mere contemplative humps. She could not tell if they were white or yellow. She moved across the floor, which seemed to be furred with aromatic dust, to a seat at the side of the room with its back to a shuttered window, which faintly admitted the lights from the streets in thin bars of brightness.

Nothing happened. She began to see that the goddess had meaning; that if her face was blank as the kernel of the stone of a fruit, the name of that fruit was peace. But peace was a lie. She thought of the different kinds of ill luck she had had with Joseph and Marshall and Danny, and she fell to weeping silently.

The little yellow man was standing in front of her. (Was he the same?) He asked: 'Is there anything the lady would like?'

It seemed a queer offer in a place that was something like a church. 'Anything I would like?'

His hand flashed suddenly into one of the bars of brightness admitted by the slats. In its palm a pyramid of white powder lay on a square of paper. It must be cocaine. Well, why not? She stretched out her hand to take it. But that way was not for her. Just as her body which was hard with years of dancing could not have suddenly become soft and obese because she had wished it, so she could not, though she chose, break her strong habit of decent living. Her hand dropped.

And the yellow hand flashed back into the darkness. She could not have sworn in a court of law that it had ever been there. The silky voice continued: 'A cup of tea?'

At that she nodded. A tray was presently set down beside her and she drank what seemed like hot water pervaded by a smell that seemed at once poignant and tenuous, like wood-smoke. It certainly seemed a queer thing to do in a place that was so like a church. Either nobody or everybody was watching, she was not sure which; in any case she did not care. She felt a little better after that and tried to rest, turning her eyes from the lying goddess of peace and staring into the darkness. But like all darkness it presently began to be painted with portraits of

Danny. She closed her eyes: and saw those same portraits on the inside of her lids. She covered her face with her hands.

The silky voice addressed her. 'There is a magician lives close by. Would the lady like to come and see him?'

Theodora lifted her head. She was the sort of woman who could never resist going to a fortune-teller or clairvoyant and going in a condition of implicit faith. But she was almost too tired to move.

The voice persisted: 'There are no people so good as our people at magic. He is a velly powerful magician. He will tell you evlything you want. He will do evlything you want. He lives quite close to here.'

She dragged herself to her feet. Sitting there in the darkness only meant seeing more and more of Danny. So she followed the little yellow man out of the room, down the stairs, and along the streets. It affected her with a faint flavour of the disagreeable that whereas before he had followed her, now she was following him. She felt in some way degraded. But it would be worth it if this man was good.

The little yellow man stopped at a green doorway and looked up at its top stories as if he himself were afraid. 'Evlyone has heard of the magician of Pell Stleet,' he said solemnly.

It was evidently high up in the building. Well, that made it safe. If she was attacked she could always jump out of the window.

They went up flight after flight of stone stairs, past doors through which escaped those solid, undispersing trails of pungency, and came at last on the top floor to a high, wide black door written over from top to bottom with scarlet Chinese characters. The little yellow man tapped a delicate tattoo. The door swung outward and disclosed a screen of polished wood carved in the likeness of a branchy tree. Down in one corner behind the red-brown leaves there peered the face of a yellow hag, so much less lovely in its substance, even so much less human, than the wood.

The hag made a clicking noise, the trunk split down the middle, the tree swung backwards in two halves, the outer door closed behind them with a sucking noise, and they were in a hall hung with turbulently coloured panels of embroidery. Geese flew against the setting sun, a dragon spat fire and writhed a polychromatic spine up to the ceiling, giant warriors whacked at each other with swords as thick as men. Theo was staring at the setting so intently that she did not know when it was, or where, that the hag and the little yellow man withdrew.

Her mind recorded that all this would be frightening if she had any longer cared what happened to her. The silence throbbed every minute or so, as if someone were very slowly and softly beating on a huge gong with a muffled stick, and every thud seemed to thresh down sleep on her brain. She sank down upon a low stool at the foot of the panels, and her head drooped down lower and lower, till a sound, a silken crepitation, brought her to her feet. Though her mind had abandoned fear, her body was still capable of it.

The panel over which the geese flew in front of the setting sun was being held back by a hand stiff with rings. There leaned out presently into the light a girl. Though her dress was Chinese she was white, a marvellous creature of rose and gold. Her face was insolent with pampering; she held herself stiffly in her incredibly gorgeous coat; at her young uptilted breast she held a baby swaddled richly like a kingly doll. She set a hard appraising stare on Theodora and her clothes, but there was nothing of envy in it. Whatever anybody had, she had as good. But a shadow of fear came over her face, and she backed into the shadow as the panel by which Theodora had been sitting began to roll up like a blind.

Behind was a dimly lighted room, dominated by a great golden Buddha thrice life-size, that sat on a dais at its end. Theodora uttered an exclamation of rage because the room seemed to be empty, and she was sick of all these preparations that led to nothing. She walked with savage, raiding speed towards the dais; and halted suddenly when she perceived that at the feet of the image there sat a cross-legged Chinaman. Till one was close upon him his yellow face and golden robe made him melt into the Buddha.

They faced one another in silence. Behind her rolled down the panel.

'What can I do for you?'

Jeering yet hopefully she asked, 'What *can* you do?'

'Shall I tell you the future?'

'If you can.'

79

A crystal ball ran down his wide sleeve to his lap.

For a space she watched him hungrily. But what could he see that it would be any good for her to know? There might be happiness for the fat wife of a storekeeper, there might be happiness for the kind of white girl who would live with a Chinaman. But for her there could be no happiness, because of the vile cruelty of Danny.

She shrieked: 'Don't tell me my future!'

The crystal ball ran back into his sleeve.

She mounted the dais and stood over him, shaking with sudden frenzy. 'Can you work spells? Can you kill people?'

Blandly he replied: 'Last moon a man died in Peking because of me, here in New York.'

'Can you kill me a man in England?'

'It will cost much money.'

'How much?'

'Ninety-five dollars.'

She found she had ninety-seven dollars with her. Her bag smelled oddly, as if it had been touched by hands steeped in some perfume she had never known. Yet surely it had not been out of her possession.

Slowly he counted the bills. With slowness that tortured her he took a black lacquer box from the shadow of the Buddha, and drew out a silver bowl with a flat rim in which there were stamped deep round depressions. He took out three black candles and stood them in three of the depressions. He gave her three slips of thick, yellowish paper and a red pencil, and said, 'Lite his name. On each of them.'

She knelt down and put the paper on the wooden steps and wrote, 'Danny Staveley,' 'Danny Staveley,' 'Danny Staveley.'

He took them, and then was checked by a thought.

'Is he middle-aged or young?'

'Young for a man,' she said bitterly. 'Thirty-five.'

He pondered for a moment and opened the box again, and took out another candle, and another slip of paper. 'In that case we must do more.'

She wrote the name again. 'Danny Staveley.'

He lighted the four candles, and at each he burned a slip. The greasy fragments of the thick charred paper clung about the wicks and made them flicker. He shook his hand over the candles and from a ring there fell a white powder on each flame. They blazed up green. Outward the charred paper flew, as if it had been blown. The flames died down. Again – surely it could not be from the same ring? – he scattered a powder on them, and they blazed up red. The room became a cavern of shifting glows and shadows, and she thought of how she had dreamed of sitting with Danny by some English fireside in such ruddy light as this. Because of his unreasoning cruelty she was working a spell of hate in this evil place instead of being a kind lover in a quiet home. Her unspent tenderness had soured to a corrosive poison within her; she felt her venom eating into the coats of her soul. All her capacity for love was for ever wasted. And life would not come again.

She thought again of the fat woman in the delicatessen store, and the insolent girl with the richly swaddled doll at her young breast. Since the flames seemed to die she moaned, 'Go on! Go on! Kill him! He has killed me!' Without haste he shook more powder from the inexhaustible ring, and the flames shot up purple. They burned so high this time that they coalesced into a ring of fire that mounted and mounted till the heat scorched her intent face. Then they went out; and the lights in the room went out too; and there was night.

The darkness did not endure for more than a moment. When it was lifted the candles had gone, and the silver bowl, and the lacquer box. Only the magician sat there at the feet of the god. His face was blank with a dismissing blankness. The panel was rolled up again.

As she reached it she turned. 'Is that all?'

'That is all. It will be necessally that at each new moon for twelve months certain things are said to the stars. That shall be done.'

'You are sure he will die?'

'He will die. The doctors will find no fault in him, but he will waste away. And in the thirteenth month he will die.'

She breathed a deep sigh of satisfaction, and went. The wooden screen and the outer door were both open for her departure. She was alone when she got out on the pavement. For the first time since she arrived in Chinatown the little yellow man had deserted her. Suddenly she was not sure if she liked the place. She was sure she did not like

81

the pagoda roofs any more; it seemed as if the houses were grimacing at each other up where they thought they would not be noticed. She was not at all sure if she liked what she had done. Suddenly she began to run, pushing past the little yellow people, and she ran and ran till she found herself out in the avenue where there were street-cars and houses that were ordinary all the way up, and big white people.

If only she had never left that sane, that safe New York! If only she had waited! But how could she know, she who had never said anything in her life she did not mean finally and for ever, that the heart of man is more fluid than water, that it flows uphill as well as downhill, that it strays into fidelity as unaccountably as into infidelity? She could not have imagined anything more unlikely than the happenings of a month later when she had gone over to London with the musical comedy that Al Guggenheim suddenly elected to produce there instead of in New York.

The day after she arrived she arranged to lunch at the Embassy Club with a friend, and she was waiting for her friend downstairs on the big plush sofa beside the bar door; and wishing she had not had to cross the Atlantic because the Englishness of everything, the accents of the people passing by, and their high, fresh colouring, reminded her of English Danny. Someone large and fair came and sat down on the other end of the sofa; and it was Danny.

They faced each other whitely. Theodora closed her eyes and whispered, though she had never before used the words, 'Mary, Mother of God, pity me, pity me!'

And Danny said, 'Oh, Theo! I've just booked my passage back on the *Berengaria* to go and look for you and tell you what a brute I was . . .'

There followed perfect happiness, till about a week after their marriage, when Danny began to cough.

She could not think why Doctor Paulton was taking so long. She rolled over in bed arguing the matter out as she had done a thousand times before. There might be nothing in these things; but on the other hand the astonishing fact that she had got Danny again appeared to indicate that there was something in them. For it still seemed to her, who never reversed a considered judgement, utterly miraculous that he should have come back to her after he had left her, and she was inclined to believe that this miracle might have happened because at the moment of their meeting she had called on Mary the Mother of God.

Her rationalism argued that people would not have constantly used these words throughout the ages if there had not been some practical use in them; and there obviously was, since her recitation of them had led to this inconceivable spectacle of a human being going back on a vigorous decision. If there was good magic there could be bad magic. And why else did Danny cough? Still, there might be nothing in these things; but on the other hand . . .

The argument went round in her mind like a wheel, until she avidly laid hold of the one aspect of the situation which gave her hope. Since the spell had been laid for money it might be lifted for money. If Danny's cough did not stop she must go to New York and buy off the magician of Pell Street. It would be a very difficult business. The raising of the money she would find easy enough, for there were possessions of hers that Danny had never seen, jewels she had bought with her savings to dodge the income tax, and never wore because of her profound indifference to personal decoration. But it was going to be the most difficult thing in the world to get to New York.

She could not go without him. She could not accept a dancing engagement there, for her public appearances seemed to him the most shocking violation of their intimacy. The trip would be expensive, and she was always urging economy on him. He loathed New York. Perhaps he would let her go alone, if she told him all about it. But she could not tell him. No one could expect that of her.

Doctor Paulton came in, with Danny behind him, fixing his tie.

'Nothing at all the matter, Mrs Staveley, I'm glad to say. Your husband's a very fit man.'

'Then why does he cough?'

'Oh, there's a slight chronic inflammation. But that's nothing. I'm sure there isn't anything behind it.'

She stared at him with wide eyes. She heard also another voice: 'The doctors will find no fault with him, but he will waste away. And in the thirteenth month . . .'

'Really, Mrs Staveley, there's nothing to be alarmed about. I expect he's right himself – he probably does smoke too much.'

'But he's smoked ever since he was at Eton. Haven't you, Danny? Why should it suddenly hurt him now?'

'I couldn't say. These things start quite suddenly. I can't find any fault with him.'

She shuddered. That phrase decided her, and she began feverishly: 'Well, that's that. But to tell you the truth I wanted you to have a look at me as well. I don't feel fit. I'm nervous. I'm terribly nervous. I want a change. I want to go back to New York.'

It did not sound convincing, but then she did not mean it to be. She was addressing herself not to Doctor Paulton's reason, but to his twinkling and inquisitive glasses. She was aware that his soul was licking its lips and panting: 'I always thought this marriage couldn't last: Danny Staveley and this neurotic little dancing-girl. Bound to be a crash some time. I wonder who's in New York?' She knew that she had only to continue to press her point, and he would say: 'Let's have a look at your eyes. Yes, you are a bit anaemic, aren't you? I'm not sure if you aren't right. The sea trip would do you good. And the New York air's wonderful. Yes, try a little holiday over there.'

She was just opening her mouth to set this train of events in motion when Danny, setting the bow of his tie in her dressing-table mirror, murmured indolently, 'We could get off any time after next week.'

'What, Danny?'

'I said, we could get off any time after next week. I must go to that dinner they're giving to old Lantry on Friday. After that I'm free.'

She was dumbfounded. She could not speak. The love that welled up in her whenever she saw Danny doing something characteristic, something that marked him off as unique among human beings, suffused her and came to her eyes in tears. One of his moments of divination, she perceived, had come to him now. He knew that she was really, seriously, painfully sick in her soul, and that for some reason this trip to New York was the only medicine that would cure her; and so in spite of what seemed to him the extreme unpleasantness of the enterprise, he had quietly yielded to her. All her manoeuvres with Doctor Paulton had been unnecessary. She was reminded of the first night she ever saw him, when she had tortuously plotted and planned to meet him, and he had simply walked over to her table with his friend. For some reason she felt abashed.

She dropped back on the pillows, and conveyed to Doctor Paulton that that was all she had wanted of him. She longed for him to go. Suddenly she felt equally disgusted with herself and with him. She was ashamed because she had proposed to make use of his prying quality for her own ends.

As soon as she and Danny were alone she said softly, brokenly: 'We'll go on one of those boats with a good swimming-pool. Then it won't be so bad for you, will it?'

He answered mildly: 'It won't be bad at all. I dare say I'll like it. I'll go down this morning and see about cabins.'

The way he was not asking her one question but was simply doing the thing she evidently needed, made her whisper to herself, 'Oh, you darling! You darling!' But the next moment she stiffened with fear. If Danny's intuition had told him a part of the truth, wouldn't it tell him the whole? Wouldn't he know that she was a criminal who had planned his death? She slipped out of bed and ran into the bathroom with her face turned from him.

That dread transfixed Theo with horror again and again during the next few days. It came to her on the deck of the *Berengaria* when it was slowly riding into New York harbour like a great lady, letting the common little wenches of ferry-boats and tugs scuttle out of her way, towards sky-scrapers that stood in the October sunlight like clusters of lilies.

She hardly saw them, for the magician had come between her and all beauty. Her thoughts were intent on the jewel-case she carried in her hand. The diamond and emerald necklace alone ought to buy him off, but if that was not sufficient there was also the string of rubies. But she hoped she would not have to give them to him, for she had tried them on after she had taken them out of the bank, and had found they suited her; so she wanted Danny to see her wearing them.

When the people round her exclaimed at the sky-scrapers she looked at them blankly yet piercingly, considering them as a screen behind which lay Chinatown. It struck her suddenly that though Chinatown certainly existed there, the magician might not. He might have died. He might have gone away. In that case her diamonds and rubies would be worthless. She shuddered; and Danny slipped her hand into his and pressed it. She knew the same alternation of joy and panic. She had a magic-working man, he knew things that were hidden from all, she was frightened, therefore he knew she was frightened! Yes, one could have gloated over it till the end of time, had it not been for the thought that if his divination had torn the outer veils aside it might yet tear another, and see why she was frightened . . .

The double feeling came to her again that night. They were staying at the Vanderpool, and Danny's brother and his Southern wife came to dine with them. Theo might have been very happy. New York had lifted her up, as it always does the stranger, to that glorious stage just before drunkenness, when the mind seems standing transparent and sparkling in a happy world like an ice peak in a sunlit blue sea. Snuffing up the old atmosphere she said in the old slang, 'Yes. New York's all right! It's a good act, it gets a good hand!' and sat back to enjoy herself.

It should have been all right, for Danny seemed very happy at seeing his brother, who was very like him, though of course without that special adorable quality; and the Southern girl was innocently thrilled at meeting anybody who had been so famous as Theodora Dene. They were all getting on tremendously well together, and making plans to go on expeditions together, when Danny coughed.

Then Theo remembered why she had come to New York. She smiled fixedly at the little wife's bloomy smile, and thought desperately: 'When will I be able to get off for an hour or two by myself? They are making plans to go up the Hudson – to go to Westchester County – and so on – and so on. But oh, when will I get away by myself to save Danny?'

She had to take her eyes away from the face of the girl, who had never been desperate, whose husband did not cough. She looked down on her lap, and a kind of darkness came over her.

Through this private night came Danny's voice: 'I'll come out with you tomorrow afternoon, but I don't think Theo ought to. She'd better rest in the afternoon, or at most crawl round looking up her old pals. She's been run down, you know. That's why we came on this trip.'

Again it came, that mixture of delight and fear. Only this time the fear was stronger, for as they exchanged smiles she saw that behind his smile lay misery, just as it lay behind hers. His divination was feeling after her guilt, like a grave hunting-dog dropping its muzzle to its scent, its ears going up as it realizes that here is danger. It would be just, it had been well-trained, it would destroy vermin . . .

But he trusted her. She stayed in bed all the next morning, saying that she had a headache. After luncheon he came in and sat by her for a little. The blinds were down, so that she could see only the kind, heavy stoop of him. He did not talk much, keeping up the pretence of her headache, but he took her hand in his. When the telephone rang and told him that George and Marie were waiting downstairs he bent over her and kissed her very tenderly.

'Goodbye, my dear.'

'Goodbye.'

He said mildly: 'You'll be going out, I suppose.'

Her heart nearly burst, for she saw that he had said that to raise the occasion on to the plane of honesty, no matter what she might do. She answered gravely, 'Yes.'

It was necessary that she should get up at once so that she should find the magician at the first possible moment. But because, just after Danny had closed the door and got into the passage, he had given a short dry cough, she was in such a state that her maid had to dress her. The resemblance of that to another period of her life sent her into a paroxysm of weeping; by her own evil nature she had performed the incredible feat of making the days when she had got Danny, which should have been gloriously happy, into the same Hades as the days when she had not got Danny.

She dressed and put into a bag that locked the diamond and emerald necklace, the rubies, her cheque-book, and also a pearl and sapphire brooch. She would give it to the magician if she had to, even though Danny knew it and might miss it and ask questions and know she lied in answer. She was going to save Danny.

Her nerves were so raw that the jolting of the taxi tortured her. She had forgotten that New York boasts the worst streets of any Western capital, and that it is slower to ride in its choked traffic than to walk. It seemed that forever she looked out of the window and saw the same pale people walking sluggishly on the broad pavements with the small mean shops behind them.

When the taxi stopped and she paid the fare she looked round and then turned back suspiciously to the driver. 'Is this right?'

He was ruder than an English taxi-driver would have been, and kinder. 'Sure! This is Chinatown. You paid me to bring you here, not to doll it up for you. Say, was you looking for somewhere else? This is where you said.'

It did not seem possible that this should be where she had come that night. The lower parts of the houses had that dark, dingy, greasy look, like gravy left in a plate after a graceless meal, that makes squalid New York as squalid as magnificent New York is magnificent. The upper pagoda parts were tawdry as stage scenery dragged out into the daylight. There were Chinese people about, but they looked rather ridiculous in ill-fitting American clothes. There was one little yellow man crossing the road now, who might have been the little man who had picked her up in front of the bill-board that night. As she looked at him he grimaced and a convulsion ran through him, so that he nearly pitched forward on his knees. She knew what that meant; she had seen a chorus-man do it once. It meant cheap, adulterated dope. This was a loathsome place, half a warren of mean vice, half a show got up for tourists. It was impossible that anything which happened here could possibly affect the stainless life that she lived with Danny.

It was in her mind to call the driver to wait and get back into his taxi, when the grimacing yellow man stumbled on the kerb and made as if to lurch against her. She wheeled round and backed against the taxi; and wilted as if she had seen a finger pointing at her in denunciation. For there was the green door. The taxi-driver had brought her to the right place.

She waved dismissal to the taxi-driver, who started up, saying cheerfully, 'One time they bumped off a society dame in that chop-suey over there.'

There was of course a risk in coming here. But to save Danny she must go on.

The door, as on that night, opened at a touch. There seemed to be an unbelievable number of steps. She paused on each landing because her heart beat so. If the magician were dead or gone away there was nothing in the whole world she could do. Up the last flight she ran with her hands covering her face. When she was on the top landing she stayed so, rehearsing what she was going to say. 'I came here six months ago and you laid a spell for me . . . I can give you money . . . Some money, not much . . . . Oh, I can't give you all that . . .' She would of course give all she had. She would go home and get some more things if he made her. But she did hope she would not have to give him those rubies. She wanted Danny to see her wearing those rubies.

And when she opened her eyes it was as she feared. The black door was swinging open and the wooden screen that was carved like a tree was off its hinges and propped up against the door-post. Somebody had begun to take down one of the embroidered panels, so that it hung away from a nail at its corner. The plank floor was bare. Plainly the place was being deserted. The magician was dead or gone away. There was nothing in the whole world she could do.

'Oh, Danny, my Danny!' she moaned. 'What shall I do?'

Desperately, not really expecting anyone to answer, she drummed with her knuckles on the open door. And the breath left her when from behind the panel that hung away there stepped a woman in a Chinese coat. That, indeed, meant little, for though she was white she was not the woman whom Theo had seen before, for she was old and rough-headed, and the coat was grubby. But still she might know.

'Where is he? Where is he?'

The woman opened a wide mouth and spoke in a tongue Theo was used to hearing from dressers: the voice, rich as beef-dripping, of the American-Irish.

'Where's who? Are ye one of Li Po's dubs?'

'I want the magician. Where is he? He isn't dead?'

'Sure he's not dead. It takes a lot to kill these Chinks. But – och, the fool!'

'What's happened to him?'

''Tis a long story!' She leant against the wall and settled down for a gossip. 'He had a white wife, my own cousin's daughter she was, and him the finest traffic-cop in New York but dying before he had time to beat her up the way he should. So she came after me, which no girl should've done, and she had the good luck to catch the eye of Li Po before harm came to her. He went crazy about her and married her all proper, and loved her too much to smoke the pipe. That's how the Chinks keep us white girls if we're too pretty.' She gave a tired old bridle. 'That an' bein' good husbands. And Li Po was the best of the lot. Many's the time I've said to the little fool, "Lily Murphy, you've had the grandest luck."'

That mysterious figure with the richly swaddled baby – one had not thought of her as Lily Murphy . . .

'Well?'

'Well, the little fool's run off with a young fellow, used to be a steward on a liner, and they've gone off to Hollywood to try and get in the pictures!'

'But what's happened to Li Po?'

'Now that's the grand, tarnation foolishness of it! Here he is throwin' up a fine business and goin' off to San Francisco wid the kid to live wid his father's people, though he'd ivry sucker in New York waitin' on his doorstep, beggin' your pardon, you bein' one of 'em. But indade it does no harm me tellin' you, for the poor lad's that down and discouraged he wouldn't have the spirit to deceive you, if you put your money in his hands.'

Theo stared at her. 'Then –'

'Away in and see him yourself. He's sittin' around where he always did. You have a kind face on you, I'm thinkin'. If you maybe wouldn't mind lettin' him make a fool of you it might make the poor lad feel more like himself.'

She stepped back and waved Theo in, hospitably, as one woman asking another to participate in the social pleasures of a family catastrophe, as it might have been to a wake; and said sadly: 'He's a good enough guy. I'm wishin' he would stay right here. He's sendin' me money, for he likes the way I play wid the baby. But they'll be gettin' the money off me, the way I am. And I'll miss the baby. 'Tis a roarin' president of a boy. But away in and see Li Po.'

'But –'

'Go in wid you, you kind woman,' said the rough-headed ruin, and with a shaking hand held back the panel she had passed before.

The room was flooded with daylight now. Three windows gave a view of many roofs. It was a cleanly kept room with a felt flooring and plaster walls. On the dais at the far end was a yellow papier-mâché Buddha, turned away so that one could see the lining of newspapers that had been pasted inside its hollow back. In front of it, in ordinary American clothes, sat a little Chinaman, a sad little Chinaman, who looked so like a sick monkey that she found herself foolishly wishing that Danny was there, because he was so good with sick animals. He was sitting on the black lacquer box he had used for his spells.

He did not look up till she had come right to the steps of the dais. Then he said wearily but politely: 'I am velly solly I cannot do any magic for you today. I have gone out of business. A family beleavement. But there is a good magician, a velly leliable magician, in the next block –'

She choked with tears.

'Oh, your wife's left you! That lovely, lovely girl!'

He made no inquiry as to how she had heard. Only his eyes rolled for a second, as if to marvel at the way that these Occidentals ran up and down the world, even breaking into the quiet landscape of Oriental emotions. Gently he said, as if to soothe her by a matter-of-fact statement of his tragedy, not out of any personal feeling but merely to increase the amount of serenity in the universe: 'She thought she was like Maly Pickford. He thought he was like Ludolph Valentino. The lest seemed to follow.' Then he turned his head away from her and looked out on the roofs.

It was a movement of dismissal, but only from the conversation. She knew he would not mind if she stayed there for a little, so she went and sat down on the corner of the dais, and looked round the

room. This was the place of which she had thought with such terror
for so many months, this the man. Of course it was all a put-up job.
The joss-house. Strangers invited. She'd say they were! The little
tout. No doubt it had not even been real cocaine. And here, in
this room, the hocus-pocus had come to a climax. What a parcel
of tricks it had been! Of course they had taken her bag away from
her while she was nodding under the hypnosis of the throbbing gong,
and then cunningly asked two dollars short of all she had. And the
spell had been the cap of all, when the East had put back its head
and laughed silently at the West for its inability to hold its emotional
liquor like a gentleman, and filled its pockets at the expense of the
lurching Occidental.

That was all it had been. All. There was no magic. Of course there
was no magic. Yet a real power of evil had radiated from that room.
She should have known it was bogus, she, with her experience! Yet
it had endangered her marriage with Danny. It had made her days
poisonous with fear lest her darling should die and should detect her
as the contriver of his death. Nothing that had ever happened to her
before had such power to affect her life. Wasn't that magic?

And wasn't it magic the way Danny knew things? How did he know
a horse or a dog was sick when he could not see it? How could he tell
when you blindfolded him and spun him round, where the north was?
How did he know when she felt fear, though he was stupid and she
had an actress's art to help her conceal it? There was a magic of a
sort, surely.

But now she saw what it was. There was the magic of strong feeling.
When he was in the city Danny could not do any of those queer
things – save those that concerned her. He could only do them in the
country, because he loved it. He gave himself up to the country as one
abandons oneself to a lover. He soaked himself in its manifestations.
His mind never slipped from it to his personal concerns. Therefore
his nerves were sensitive to magnetic waves that others, thinking of
what they would eat or read or wear when they got home, did not
feel; and he could find the north; therefore, too, he could notice a
faint, unwonted quality of melancholy in a whinny or bark when to
the groom a beast seemed well enough, and Danny would be able to

reckon, in the unconscious processes of his primitive mind, when the beast's ailment would declare itself.

And he was wise about her for the same reason, since he loved her as he loved the countryside.

And she had interfered with his magic. She had hated, and hate has its magic too. Lord – how she had hated! It was the venom she had felt in this room that had been magic. Yet honestly she had to admit that in this Danny had not been guiltless. He had left her when he knew that he had made her love him. Yet she perceived suddenly that though Danny was to blame for what she had done in the room, she herself was to blame for the power it had acquired to follow her outside the room.

She had never had any faith in the relationship between men and women. Dolorously she had believed that love was an illusion. She had conceived of love wistfully as an occasion of tenderness and generosity such as she had never dared to indulge in in the world of wolves where she had fought for success. She had expected it to turn out badly. There had been a certain satisfaction mixed with her anguish when it had turned out badly and Danny had left her. That was why she had abandoned herself to it so utterly.

Then, when that satisfaction had been withdrawn by Danny's return, she had searched round for something that would support her convictions by ending this love, and she had found it in this hocus-pocus. Wasn't there a trace of meanness and hardness in the way that she had found what she wanted in something for which she could always lay the ultimate blame on Danny? Wasn't the root of the whole thing a meanness and hardness and vanity in herself? Why had she been so reluctant to believe in love if it wasn't that she had been anxious that the standards of the world of wolves should prevail, since it was there she had succeeded, there she was a star? She had always prided herself that she had kept herself aloof from that world, but it had got her, all right. She was to blame for everything. For now she saw that Danny had been right in leaving her. His divination had told him how utterly she had been spoiled by her life, how incapable she would be of enjoying happiness, how indefatigably she would twist and warp their common existence by her acquired habits of harsh and ugly thinking.

She must go back to him at once and start again.

But on the threshold she thought of the little yellow man, and turned about to see what had happened to him. It seemed possible to her that everybody in the whole universe had in the last moment known the relief of a flashing conviction of sin and seen the path to happiness. But he had not. He was hiding his face in his hands.

How it must hurt! She knew, she knew. There came to her a picture of the golden girl in the Chinese coat. Lovely she had been, but she must have been bad. For since she had run away with the other man so soon after, it could not have been joy in her husband and child that made her so insolent, but simply pride in her material possessions. There must have been disloyalty too. It was a mean little betrayal, in the way she had broken through the network of mystifications that it was her husband's business to weave round his clients, just to have a look at a woman's clothes.

'She'll never get on,' she reflected. 'I've seen her sort before. She'll think of her salary before her work, and she'll try to get on by double-crossing the woman above, and grouse if she's put through it. She'll never go in Hollywood.'

She was like Danny, she knew things! She saw the girl white with new horse-sense, having learned just how much her stock in trade was worth, having learned the value of the little yellow man's kindness, coming back to the green door, coming up the stairs . . .

She crossed the room and stood in front of the man.

'Your wife will come back!' she cried. 'She'll come back to you.' He did not seem to hear, so she drummed on his bowed shoulders. 'She'll come back – down and out! But she'll come back!'

He raised a face that suddenly became happy. He knew she knew. The practitioner of false magic knew the practitioner of real magic. Passion flamed up into his eyes, a merciful passion that overwhelmed all the vengeful conventions of a race, and he said, as if disclosing a plot against the law, 'I will take her to a place where the dishonour of my house is not known.'

Their hands met. She ran from the room, out of the door, down the stairs, into the streets. When she found a taxi, she pulled out her vanity case and rouged and powdered, in case Danny was in when she got back. The lights of the city seemed like a celebration. But he didn't like the place, so she must take him away. Wasn't there tarpon fishing in Florida? Only she would have to tell him about the magician. He would forgive her of course, of course, but it was horrible. Also – he might not forgive her.

When she got in he was there – sitting in an armchair by the window. The lights were not turned on, and she left it so, standing in the twilight behind his chair, nervously pulling off her gloves.

She said: 'Danny, New York isn't what I want. Let's go South. There's tarpon fishing in Florida.'

She saw the great bulk of him shake with silent laughter. 'What is a tarpon?' he asked teasingly. He was always amused by her ignorance of sport.

'Well, something that you'd like!' If she were not ashamed of the confession she had to make, she would have liked to go and sit on the arm of his chair.

He looked out of the window at the sky-scrapers and their hard jewels of light. 'Yes, I'd like the tarpons all right. I don't like this place' – he hesitated – 'the less for what I did to you here.'

'Oh, Danny, never think of that! I want to tell you –'

'But I do think of it. You must have gone through a deuce of a time. You feel things so.' He paused and slowly refilled his pipe. 'You must have prayed that I would die.'

She stiffened. 'Danny! What makes you say that?'

'Well, you must have. You were right too. You're cleverer than I am. You knew what a good thing I was chucking away. And you're a wildcat by nature. Of course you said, "O God, kill Danny for me!"'

It was a pity that she was shivering so. 'But, Danny, that's just what I did. I went this afternoon to see somebody I gave money to for casting a spell. I – I –'

He said, 'I figured out that was what you were doing.'

Though she was still shivering, she went round and sat on the arm

95

of his chair. Indolently he muttered: 'You'd better rest, my dear. Tonight's the night. We're going to Sherry's. And then to that place I saw you first. The Rigoli.'

She whispered, her voice having left her, 'I shall wear my rubies.'

# Sideways

*This story was written for the* Saturday Evening Post, *October 1928, and has never been published in the UK before.*

R uth Waterhouse was born in Syracuse, and when she got into her teens she stayed out late nights. In relating her life story, in her high, faint voice that is nearly a breath, that threatens to die away altogether if she is not believed, she attributes this to the interesting and undeniable fact that the railroad line from Buffalo to New York runs slick through the main street of Syracuse, and that the expresses shook the frame house, where she lived with her old Jewish grandfather, from floor to ceiling. According to her, when she frequented whatever the Great White Way of that town may be, she was but pacing the floor. She longed for her pillow. But alas, because of the heavy trains, that could not be. Her old grandfather was, however, not such a light sleeper, and showed an entire lack of sympathy with her insomnia. In fact he said he would 'learn her' and did. This is the only part of the story I can wholeheartedly believe.

But what Ruth learnt was not what he had expected. Instead she learnt – what seems to be a most difficult piece of knowledge to acquire – how to insert herself into the chorus of a touring musical show. And later on she learnt – what I understand is even more difficult – how to transfer herself from a touring musical show to a musical show in Broadway. And later on she somehow achieved an introduction to Joseph, who is the greatest teacher of dancing that has ever been, and he took her on as his partner. This was extraordinary, for though she had great beauty – her hair was red-gold and her eyes red-brown and mournful like a fallow deer's, and her skin seemed blanched by moonbeams and a special delicate kind of blood within, and her little triangular mouth trembled as if in perpetual control of tears – her feet and legs were the worst things about her. I once asked Joseph why he had done it. And the queer thing was that he couldn't quite say. Finally, thinking it over, he became a little indignant.

'I guess that girl put it over on me!' he said. But it didn't matter. For by that time Ruth had learnt to dance like running water, like wind in standing wheat; and she was covered with fame and legend and love – and jewels.

But all the same, it was interestingly characteristic of Ruth. I had adored her ever since I met her in New York, because I had been lucky enough to uncover her most amusing characteristic the very first time I went to her apartment. Sitting at her dressing-table, she murmured to me over her shoulder, 'Is my hand-glass over there?' She knew perfectly well that it was lying on the divan beside me, but she preferred to put her question like that; for one thing, because if she had asked me outright to pass it to her, she would have had to feel grateful to me for the granted favour, and she didn't want to give anything – even gratitude – away; and for another, because she hated outrightness as a thing in itself. It sounds unlovable, but it was not. For one felt that if any really important issue had been turned up, she would have behaved well; and in the meantime she had the charm of being perfectly true to type.

Not once in all our later acquaintance did I know her to employ direct methods, not once did I know her anything but triumphantly acquisitive. Being with her gave one a feeling that life was a game played on a chequerboard, and that one was only allowed to move diagonally, but that one was winning gloriously. I cannot tell you how pervasive of every department of life her indirectness was. If she really wanted to see you, she arranged to be some place where she knew you were going to be. If she asked you to her house, you could be sure that you had been asked for some purpose relating to a third person – to make the young man she had finished with understand that no longer did she desire to be alone with him, to make the young man who was still rather shy and had to be brought on realize that he need not be alarmed; she did not even want to be alone with him. It gave her dancing its fascination. For as this glowing creature floated in the arms of her partner, who was now the exquisite Diego Caldes, so much more like a polished fingernail than a man ought to be, but nevertheless attractive to the mob, it became apparent that she burned only with fairy flames, that she was cold as any ice maiden; he was not really holding her; at any moment she might slip away from him, from the crowd, from the world. That smile she gave the audience had the quality of a farewell – of a farewell before a long journey – from which she would send no news of safe arrival. She was going away – right away.

It gave her her peculiar power over men, too, I understand. Though I knew nothing of her love affairs, except that there was an endless succession of rich and important men whom she seemed to be assuring first that they could never catch her, and later that though they might have thought they had caught her, they hadn't. And in between there was a stage when new jewels arrived. I know nothing more. Nobody does – not definitely.

The way she told me of her marriage was characteristic. I knew there was something afoot from the way she called me up the very morning she saw my name among the new arrivals in the *Paris Herald* and asked me to come out for luncheon to her new villa at Auteuil. If she had just wanted to see me in the ordinary way, and could have taken her time, she would have turned up somewhere she thought I might be – at my dressmaker's at half-past eleven, at the Ritz for luncheon, at the Ambassadeurs for supper – and then our lives would have softly run side by side for just so long as she pleased. I wondered who it was I was to warn by my presence that his day was over or falsely assure that he might call it a day. I have met some of the most famous men in England and America that way.

But when I got there I could see I was the only guest. Ruth was having her massage very late, which didn't look like a luncheon-party. And as I sat in the upstairs sitting-room which adjoins Ruth's bedroom and listened to the terrific smacks and punches that were going on on the other side of the door, old Mary, the coloured servant who has gone everywhere with Ruth ever since she started on Broadway, brought in a tiny tray with only one cocktail on it. She gave it to me with a queer sly smile in her eyes, as if she knew I was going to hear news and she would give her ears to know what I'd think of them, but was too scared of Ruth to talk to me.

After the six-foot-three Swede had stridden out I went in, and I found Ruth looking as lovely as the dreams you can't quite remember, wrapped in a glistening gold wrap, with her arms clasped behind her head.

'I hate massage,' she murmured.

'It certainly sounds as if it hurt,' I said.

'It isn't that,' she went on; 'but you can't ever tell if it's worth the money, because you don't dare lay off and see if anything happens to you like they say it will if you do.'

I shouted with laughter.

She took no notice. 'Anyway, I shan't ever have it again – after I've finished my contract at the Casino.'

That made me think there must be something up. Every star exhibition dancer has a daily massage. 'What do you mean? Ruth, you aren't giving up dancing? You aren't – why, you aren't going to get married!' She shut her eyes and smiled. She might have been smiling in her sleep. I bent down and shook her. 'Ruth, be a sport! Tell me who it is!'

She opened her eyes, dug her hand under her pillow for her handkerchief and held it above her lips in a curious furtive gesture, as if even when she wanted to speak out she still liked to keep an atmosphere of secretiveness about her, though it had now no meaning.

'I met him here when he came over after the close of the run of *Hollywood Harriet*,' she said faintly.

My heart began to slow down. He was an actor! I hadn't expected that! I didn't think it was very wise in view of Ruth's enormous ambition, her boundless acquisitiveness – an actor couldn't add much to that collection of jewels.

And then it dawned on me who it must be if he had been acting in *Hollywood Harriet*. I had seen it just before I left New York, and the juvenile lead was the awful, the unbelievable Jay McClaughlin, who has been married three times, whose wives afterwards tell such sad stories of having been beaten with vacuum cleaners, radio parts and all sorts of utensils that one would have thought unsuitable as weapons of offence. A handy man about the house in the worst sense of the word.

She continued even more faintly: 'But we aren't getting married till he gets back to New York in the fall, because he has it all fixed up for us to be married in a synagogue in Twenty-eighth Street, where his uncle's the rabbi.' Her voice died away.

My heart stopped. I knew who it was. But it couldn't be! However, it certainly was. Everybody knew that Issy Breitmann, the low comedian of *Hollywood Harriet*, was the nephew of the famous Rabbi Goldwesser of the Twenty-eighth Street Synagogue. And he was, at a generous estimate, five feet in height! He was fat! He was funny! He was fussy! He was the most grotesque partner imaginable for lovely, slender, still Ruth, whom one had seen coming into restaurants with grand dukes and cabinet ministers and other creatures who make a profession of dignity.

I began to stammer, and Ruth closed her eyes and smiled – that smile she used to give her audiences – as if she were going to slip away, far away – go on a very long journey. And I perceived that if I made any of a number of maladroit comments on the marriage that were possible, I would never hear any news from her on that journey. The smile was just on the point of becoming a farewell – a very definite farewell.

I choked my exclamations and immediately afterwards was smitten with the desire to utter an entirely new set. For I remembered that

101

little Issy Breitmann was one of those show folks who are possessed by a deep and extremely vocal passion for the old-fashioned ideals of the home. Continually, he was announcing to the press by article and by interview that it was possible – though, he modestly intimated, few besides himself had proved it so – to live as clean a life in the theatre as in a minister's home. He intimated that he himself, although he longed for the joys of domesticity, had not married because among today's crowd of modern girls who rouge their stockings and roll their lips and powder their cocktails – I may have got this a bit mixed, but one has heard that kind of diatribe so often that one can't keep one's mind on it as one used to – he found no one worthy to be his wife.

Frequently he was photographed in company with his mother, the rabbi's sister, his arm usually stretched towards her in a manner suggestive of a signpost, as if indicating to what pattern the lady who wished to be Mrs Breitmann must conform. That Ruth did not conform to that pattern physically was all to the good. One felt that the strength of Issy's family feeling had led him to exaggerate his aesthetic insensibility. But surely she did not conform to the pattern in other ways that were more important. Not that one definitely knew. But all those jewels –

I looked down at her in wonder and concern. I supposed she had, in her marvellous way, put it over on Issy. But if she had done that by deception, wouldn't he find out? And if she had done it by appealing to his pity and his passion, wouldn't there be a never-ending conflict between his Jewish ideal of womanhood and the compromise she had induced him to make? Mustn't there have been difficulties? Wouldn't there still be difficulties? But Ruth's face forbade me to wonder. The smile had intensified – in another second it might become a farewell. Nobody was even to think of what was happening in the heart of Ruth's life. Her smile became softer, was as sweet a recognition of friendship as I had ever received from her, when I broke into conventional congratulations. That was how she liked life to be conducted – through indirectness, through conventionalities.

But as I went on her smile hardened again. For it had come into my mind that I had often heard that this Issy was a golden-hearted creature apt to weep over widows and orphans and fill their hands with dollar bills and sign away a week's salary to homes for crippled children and the like.

I felt very sure that his talk of domesticity was no bluff, but that he would be kind and good to Ruth all the days of her life, and I said as much. And as I spoke, it crossed my mind and was, I suppose, betrayed in some phrase I used, in some tone of my voice, that a young woman of twenty-six does not marry a man whose sole recommendation is that he would be kind to his wife unless she has had some rather scarring experiences of men who are not good to women. I also seemed to remember that I had heard of Ruth's having been seen about with some man whose charm for women and brutality towards them were well known. I wondered and stumbled and, until I had found the right unintimate words again, saw her smile meditate whether it should not become quite finally farewell. Nobody was even to think of what was happening in Ruth's heart.

She shot suddenly from her bed. 'There's Issy! You go and talk to him while I dress.'

Issy I found to be in his private life rather more of a low comedian and infinitely more of a champion of the domestic virtues than he was in his public life. He was one of those Jews who consist entirely of convex curves that reflect the light. There are Jews who consist entirely of concave curves, who have deep pits round their eyes and under their cheekbones where melancholy lives, and hollow chests inhabited by coughs and lacerating racial memories; he was the exact opposite. From his round little hook nose and his round little cheeks, from his chins, of which he already had three, from each of his short fat fingers and his hard, tight, raven-wing curls, there seemed to shoot forth rays of light and cheerfulness.

This effect of gaiety was increased by his choice of shirt, cravat and socks, which by their remarkable colourings also seemed to emit rays, and by his tendency to break into tap-dancing. While his feet jiggled about all over the parquet floor his little cherry-red mouth explained without cease that the reason he was not joining me in a cocktail was that he had promised his mother never to touch liquor, and that he always kept his word to his mother – and who wouldn't? as she was the best woman in the world. . . . Tap-tap-tap. . . . It was very jolly, like having a plump little bird in a nice little cage singing a hymn to a fine sunny day.

He seemed to be greatly given to expressing amiability by slapping people. He slapped Mary to show that he liked her, and thought Negroes grand people, anyway. He slapped Ruth to show he loved her. He slapped me after Ruth had explained what old friends we were. And when we sat down he slapped his thighs every time a dish was put on or taken off the table, to express all the more generalized forms of amiability he was feeling – gratitude to the cook, to the rest of the staff who supported her in her duties, to the food itself, to the Maker of the cook and the food.

'Has Ruth told you about her and me?' he asked me presently. I said the proper things. 'Well, the very first time I met Miss Ruthie, and she told me about the good home she came from up in Syracuse, I said to myself that this is the girl I've always been waiting for,' he said happily.

I had never thought when Ruth told me about the limiteds and her insomnia that I was getting the story of her home life in Syracuse quite straight, but though plainly the version Issy had learned was quite different, I didn't feel that he had been getting it quite straight either. I stole a look at Ruth, but she was looking quite calmly at the chicken on her plate. I expect she knew she could trust me to carry on the way that Issy would like. And I did. Issy liked me so much that presently, generous and exuberant soul, he was suggesting that I should go with them on a Sunday trip to Deauville.

'We'll have more time if we go by railroad at night,' said Ruth. 'There's a time-table on the bureau behind you, if you'd look up a train.'

He found it, pushed his plate away and began to burrow in its pages as people do who are no good with time-tables.

'Wait a minute. . . . I got it. . . . No, that ain't it. . . . Oh, Lordy, these fool things!'

Presently he tossed it despairingly at me. 'I'm no good at this kind of thing. I've had a secretary ever since I was a kid.'

I found it at once. 'The train's at 9.15, if you can make it that early.'

Ruth put out a cool hand and took the time-table from me. She examined it with some care. I wondered why, when I had already found the only train that would do. When she handed it back to me I noticed that her lips were compressed into a straight line.

Later, Issy had to go out and talk to his chauffeur, and Ruth said to me reflectively, 'He got all balled up over finding that train, didn't he?'

'He did,' I laughed, trying to make a joke of it.

'There wasn't any need for him to get all balled up like that over it. Anybody could have found what he was looking for.'

'Oh, I don't know,' I said. 'Good heavens, Ruth, you aren't judging a man for a little thing like that, are you?'

She didn't deign to answer me. But added, 'He gets terrible balled up with French, too, you know. Can't get the numbers right.'

Her eyes were mysterious. She was following some line of thought which I could not quite grasp. Any more than I could grasp what she was doing when Issy came back, and she chose a moment when he was looking at her with special adoration to unpin a magnificent diamond-and-sapphire brooch she was wearing, secure it again more firmly and say, in her most faint, most high voice, 'I got to have that fixed or maybe I'll lose it.' I would have thought she would have been wiser to say as little as possible about her jewels in front of Issy; indeed, I could see that the very mention of that compromising magnificence diminished the radiation of the little man by ever so many candle power.

But she went on, her voice ever so faint, like the topmost spire of a snow mountain seen by the moonlight: 'I guess I ought to be careful with it, because the sapphire's real. I took it out of an old ring I had and put it in this piece.' She gave a little, tired laugh. 'I guess that's the way all my jewellery is. It looks terribly ritzy, but it's all old stuff mixed up with new – little bits of good things with a lot of fake.'

Issy looked better; he recovered much of his lighthouse quality, but, I thought, not all. At any rate I felt I had best leave them alone at the first moment I could, though I was fairly sure that Issy loved her so much that the last thing he would speak to her about when they were alone was those jewels.

As she went with me to the door, I said to her, 'I've an aunt looking for a villa out here. You don't want to sell this place, do you?'

With a queer passionate emphasis, she exclaimed, 'No!' Then more calmly elaborated it: 'I guess Issy and I will come over to Europe for a vacation every summer, just like we did before, and it's nice to come to a place of your own.' Then her eyes travelled past me to the big square villa that was next door. 'Besides, this place has certain advantages.' She made this remark in the portentous English accent which she acquired in the course of a six weeks' engagement at the Embassy Club in London, which always abashes me, since it is so much more English than the accent I more casually acquired by being born over there.

I fled, feeling there was much in Ruth at the moment that I did not understand. As I passed the big square villa, sounds of 'L'Invitation à la Valse' rang out from one of its windows, played on six pianos at once, and from another a nun dreamed down at the road, and I wondered why Ruth found it an advantage to be next door to a convent school.

As it happened, I never found out the explanation of that, or any other of her oddities, on the trip to Deauville, because my paper ordered me off to Geneva to sit and watch the League of Nations for a bit. I read of their wedding in New York in the papers early that fall, and then along in the new year I read that *Hollywood Harriet* had at last finished its Chicago run. And then, suddenly, one March afternoon, when I was staying at Cap Martin with Sheila and Robin de Cambremer, and we were spending the day in Monte Carlo, I saw Ruth walking across the Casino gardens.

I shrieked, 'Look! Isn't that Ruth Waterhouse?'

They weren't sure. She was wrapped up in a great big coat, and she had a close little hat that hid all that marvellous hair. But I watched her and saw her pause for a millionth of an instant as she passed a climbing plant festooning a palm tree with blossom that the strong winter sunlight of those parts made look as if it were cut out of mauve paper as a decoration at a children's party – the prettiest, most artificial thing. After a step or two she turned back as if she were reversing her promenade for the most businesslike reason – because she had forgotten an appointment with a hairdresser, had left her handbag in a shop. But she slackened her pace as she walked past the flower, cast down her head and looked at it out of the corner of her eye. She had simply wanted to have another look at the thing, but had dissimulated it because of an inveterate disposition to indirectness.

'That's Ruth!' I said, and we all ran up to her.

We did a lot of exclaiming, but she did none. Merely she turned on us a face that was exquisite with contentment, and with unconscious insolence seemed to tell us to be proud because our presence did nothing to disturb, because she did not feel anything about us incongruous with her state of harmony. Obviously, the marriage was going well.

Yes, Issy was with her. They had arrived the day before at Genoa and had come straight along here. They had come over here for a long holiday – they would probably be on the Riviera all spring. Issy was out now with an English house agent looking at villas. And she – she was just out walking.

A bad thing to do, we all agreed, for the day was unendurable, cut by a wind that one could have shaved with. Yes, but she had to walk for an hour. She walked for an hour every day. She'd walked fifty-five minutes now. She had been on her way back to the Hôtel de Paris when we met.

Well, what would she like to do? Should we all go to the Casino and gamble?

She turned her head towards the Casino, looked at it through narrowed eyes and turned her head back again. You have seen your cat make the gesture a thousand times.

'No,' she said, very high and very faint, 'I can't go to the Casino. The air's bad. I can't sit in bad air.'

That surprised me, because in the past Ruth had been an infatuated gambler after her own fashion, which was to make fifty francs' worth of counters last for hour after hour after hour.

Well, should we go on and do what we had been thinking of doing. Which was to send Robin off to his club and go and look at Meuxynol's spring collection of clothes that he was showing in his lovely shop that is just round the corner from the Casino, overlooking the harbour.

Yes. She thought carefully, and decided that that was what she would like to do. She hadn't, she told us with some particularity, seen any clothes at all in New York. So we sent Robin off, and we three went off to Meuxynol's, arm in arm and giggling like three schoolgirls.

And at Meuxynol's she behaved in a very extraordinary way. When they saw her and Sheila they turned the shop inside out. Girl after girl walked round the room, so slim and so polished that they seemed ramrods made of beauty instead of metal, such exquisite products of luxury that they made one its partisan and created in one a longing to spend money for the sake of being money. And they showed dress after dress that were traps laid for one's personality, that would have coaxed the shyest bit of beauty that was concealed about to come out and shine its brightest for the confusion of men. Sheila bought wildly, as much as she dared. But Ruth bought nothing – not a dress.

This, in Ruth, was amazing. For she had known nothing between having no dresses at all in Syracuse and having all the dresses in the world in New York and Paris and London, and she knew no self-restraint in this matter. Especially had she known none concerning evening dresses. So infatuated with them was she that she had never been able to do as other dancers did, and sign a contract with a Paris dressmaker whereby she gets all her dresses for a nominal fee on condition that she wears them only two months and then returns them, and never wears anything from any other house. She had never been able to forgo the pleasure of buying wherever she could find them, masterpieces of lace and tulle and satin that matched the masterpiece that was herself. I had seen them in her wardrobe in her New York apartment, a confusion of preciousness a couple of yards long, which she so loved to look on that she had had glass doors put in in order that she might see them as she lay in bed.

And here she was being shown dress after dress by a girl near enough to her own physical type to show her exactly how lovely she herself could look in them, and all she did was to say in her high and faint voice, 'No – no. It's very pretty, but I'm not buying anything at all just now.'

Then it suddenly struck me what, with a supreme consummation of her passion for indirectness, she was telling us. The hour's walk, her objection to the badness of the air in the Casino, her refusal to buy any clothes although she had bought none in New York.

Since she had this temperament, I could say nothing to her of what I felt. But I slipped my arm through hers and squeezed it and wondered about a good many things. Had Issy still those delusions about that straight road that led to his arms from the good home in Syracuse? And did the jewels still worry him as they had done, I was almost certain, that day at Auteuil? I wanted it so much to be all right! And I was not sure that it was, for when I felt her arm it was braced and hard. She looked as if she were perfectly still; but touching her, I knew it was the stillness that comes of the profoundest tensity.

Her indirectness seemed very comic when we took her back to the Hôtel de Paris, for down the stairs came Issy, ebullient with a passion for directness that matched hers for the opposite. His method of descending the stairs was singular and attracted attention. He seemed disinclined in his present state of happiness to admit even in that small matter that there was any down in the world, so every time he struck a step he bounced up in the air as if to demonstrate that for every down there is an up.

Robin de Cambremer, who had arranged to meet us in the hall, is the least bit of a snob, and he died many deaths when he saw the little man enfolding us all in his arms and kissing Sheila on both cheeks, because they had known each other when she was still an actress. But even he softened to Issy when he heard his philoprogenitive crowings. He was so naïve about it that he looked a little disappointed when he heard that Robin and Sheila had three children.

You could see him calculating that it would be years before he and Ruth caught up to that, and even then he couldn't rely on Robin and Sheila not having followed up their first advantage and got ahead again. And he was so loving and concerned with Ruth; he told us so proudly of how well she had run his house in New York, how his own mother had said it couldn't have been done better. He spoke of the villa he had taken for her at Cap Ferrat and the plans he had made for the summer, not ostentatiously but eagerly and humbly so that we would suggest improvements.

And every now and then his speech went to a confused babble on his lips, just as it used to do on the stage in New York, to the delight of his audiences; and then his hand had to close and unclose and close again over her hand to show that his love had not failed with his breath.

Dear little Issy. I would have felt very happy about them both if I hadn't remembered the tensity of her arm at the dressmaker's, and in the light of that memory known that the relaxation of her pose in the armchair was acting. Also when one of the assistant hotel managers came up and whispered in Issy's ear, and Issy looked scared, apologized to us and followed him out of the lounge, she neither looked at the manager nor expressed any curiosity; and since the whole time she had been watching over Issy, as if he were her child and not the father of her child, I knew that to mean that something was happening according to plan. And it was her plan, not his. For veritably Issy had looked scared.

He came back in a minute. He flipped his hands at Robin in a sea-lion gesture that till then I had believed was practised only behind the footlights.

'Say, you're French, aren't you?' His speech went. His hands flipped and flipped and flipped. Getting his breath, he used it to comfort Ruth, who had at last raised great startled eyes. 'Say, honey, it's nothing. Not a thing, I said.' He turned to Robin again. 'Would you just help us out over this? There's a coupla fellows –'

They walked away from us up the lounge. From each side of Issy's back in turn flipped an explanatory hand. He looked up at Robin's tallness trustfully, as dachshunds do to their masters.

'Why, whatever can it all be about?' murmured Ruth.

Robin came back in a minute. 'I'm afraid you've got to come and deal with this, Ruth,' he said, and drew us in with his eyes. 'You'd better all come.'

Ruth sat up. 'It isn't – it isn't – anything horrid?' she faltered. There was a pale ghost of a shrieking quality in her voice, just the most ladylike version of a trace of hysteria, which made one remember that in her condition she oughtn't to be over-excited.

'It's nothing at all,' said Robin kindly; 'but it seems there's some bills you've forgotten to settle in Paris, and these are some *huissiers*, some debt collectors, that you've got to see about it. Don't be frightened. I dare say it's all a mistake. Come along, girls, and we'll get it over.'

We found Issy in one of the smaller salons leading out of the lounge, an Olympian apartment with marble pillars, and a ceiling on which some dozen goddesses as they were conceived by mural artists in the '80s were thrusting robust ankles through clouds – insurance refused because subjected to unreasonable strain – and offering bosoms the size of public libraries to the embraces of hundred-pound Cupids, and a vast circular table round which were arranged six enormous chairs, upholstered in purple plush, each having the air of being the wealthy widow of a prominent member of the furniture world.

Issy, who looked remarkably undersized in these surroundings, was working his way round the table, clinging to the back of one chair after another, while he attempted to express his opinion of the two gentlemen who waited for us under a colossal mantelpiece, doubtless the tomb of a specially eminent chef, which took up almost one whole wall of the room. He would have succeeded, for he seemed to have a prettier gift of language than I had supposed from seeing him in his milder moments, had it not been for this tendency of his breath and tongue to fail him and his words.

I admit I regretted it; for the gentlemen were not nice. I cannot describe them adequately. They seemed to be relevant to all the more shabby and less pleasing manifestations of French bureaucracy; or rather, to put it more justly, people who wear uniforms in France. I could imagine that their mothers were ticket collectors on the Paris, Méditerranée et Lyons Railway; that their fathers were postmen notorious for their dilatoriness. I felt that the peculiarly offensive tin trumpets which give the trains the signal to start in small French railroad stations played an important part in the courting of these pairs; gave, no doubt, the coy female warning of her lover's approach.

To the sound of that trumpet they had dedicated their children to the sacred duty of annoying the public. These gentlemen were being faithful to that dedication, to that call of the blood. They were standing drawn up to their full height; they were feeling worthy of the mantelpiece. They bowed towards the ladies repeatedly, with a juicy fervour.

'I wanted to be taught how to use my hands,' said Issy. 'God knows I wanted to be taught how to use my hands, from the time I was a small boy, but my poor mother – You know what women are.' His speech left him again.

'Do you understand French?' said Robin to Ruth.

'I do and I don't,' she answered softly.

'You had better read the writ to the lady then,' Robin said to the debt collector.

The one with the pomaded beard stepped forward. He looked round with the expression of a prize bull and, just to put us at our ease, remarked in a rich baritone, *'Moi, c'est la loi,'* and began to read a list of debts that about ten Paris tradesmen had sworn in the court of Monte Carlo that Ruth owed them.

I listened in amazement. I had been under the impression that Ruth never ran up bills. I might say, even, that I knew she did not, because once or twice I had been, on her recommendation, to tailors and milliners, and when they heard her name they gave me credit with a readiness that showed they had never lost a penny through her. But this was a formidable list. It amounted to a vast sum, and it comprised such odd items for her to have defaulted. Not only two years' dressmaking bills from two of the most expensive houses but nearly the whole of the purchase price of the villa at Auteuil.

'Oh, won't you none of you tell me what it's all about?' whimpered Issy.

We were all so thralled by the recital that we turned round and sh-sh-ed him.

He clung to one of the pillars and bubbled.

Some pictures bought from the best modern art dealers in Paris, which showed that Ruth knew a great deal more about painting than I had suspected. Who had told her it was good business to buy Derains and Utrillos? A good deal of antique furniture that had been shipped to New York last fall, and some that had gone to Auteuil. And some Persian rugs that must, from the price, have been very, very fine indeed.

The total was eighteen hundred thousand francs. We all were silent.

'How much do they want?' screamed Issy suddenly.

We turned to him, stared at him in sympathy, and having all fallen into the habit of thinking in French while the *huissier* was reading, we shouted, in unison, '*Un million huit cent mille francs.*'

'I said how much do they want.'

We were silent in amazement, then chanted in unison again: '*Un million huit cent mille francs.*'

He buried his head in his hands. Then made one more despairing effort: 'Will you tell me how much –'

It dawned on us that he did not understand French: 'Oh! Eighteen hundred thousand francs!'

Having gratified his curiosity, we turned away as if we had done him a good turn.

'Do you owe all that?' asked Sheila of Ruth, with the solemn admiration that an extravagant woman feels for a very extravagant woman.

'Well,' said Ruth, ever so faint and high, 'maybe I do.'

We all looked at her in amazement. It was a new light on the girl.

Then we all swung round at a howl from Issy. With a pencil in his hand, he was staggering back from the column on which he had been scribbling calculations.

Ruth detached herself from the group like a greyhound and was beside him in a flick of the eye. She put a loving arm round his shoulders, took the pencil from his hands and seemed to revise the calculations. I am sure I heard her say, 'Now, sweetie, you always get that wrong. You have to cross off two zeros, not one.' And I am almost certain I also heard her say, 'That makes it seventy-two hundred dollars.' Which is not true. Nothing in the world will make eighteen hundred thousand francs at the current rate of exchange anything but seventy-two thousand dollars. She drew him back into our group.

'Do you owe all that, honey?' asked Issy.

She shook her head. 'I guess I haven't kept one single receipt of the whole lot,' she said, and she began to weep very softly – tears that reminded him that she was his woman, that she was soon to be the mother of his child. 'But I want it settled. I don't like this,

Issy!' She looked with doe-like eyes at the *huissiers*. 'What do they want us to do?'

Issy stepped in front of her. 'Here you, young fellow,' he said to Robin, 'do they want her to go to prison? Because here I am.'

'Well, they don't quite want that,' answered Robin. 'They want the money.'

'Now?'

'At once. That's the point of this process. For all they know, you might get away, you know.'

'But they can't have it! I tell you, man, I haven't got it! I've just enough to pay my bill here. I sent a banker's draft over to Ruth's Paris bank account and it will only just be paid in. In fact I don't understand all this business, but Ruthie says it can't be paid till I get there next week, because there's all this foolery of identification. Poor Ruthie wouldn't have a letter of credit, because she got nervous in case somebody slugged me for it.'

Ruth shuddered at the recollection of those fears and cast herself into his arms. 'Then they'll seize your luggage.'

'My luggage! For a debt they haven't proved? For a debt Ruthie paid but didn't keep the receipt for?'

'Oh, I do owe some of it, Issy darling.'

'Honey, I won't have it!'

'Aow!' Ruth had wrested herself from his arms and given the shrillest yet the most refined scream imaginable. 'You've forgotten!'

'Forgotten what?'

'Our luggage got left behind at Ventimiglia by mistake. It's still in Italy! Don't you remember how Mary made that silly mistake so that it went into the left luggage room instead of our train? And I was sending a courier back for it today.'

'Why, sure I –'

'We haven't anything except – oh, darling, my jewels!'

She looked into his eyes and did not take them from his, though her lips trembled, when for a second his chubby little face looked grey and tired, as if he had been reminded of a family disgrace. Then she began to cry again, those heart-melting tears that reminded him of her claim on him, and his child's claim.

'Oh, let's get through with this! I always told you that my jewels were faked up old things. I guess they're not worth as much as that –'

'Not worth as much as that?' the little man echoed her, wistfully, hopefully.

'Not worth half as much as that, but they've been so mean putting these men on me, who never owed a cent in my life, that I guess they can stand the loss. Let me give them the jewels and send them away.' She broke into terrible primitive sobs. 'It isn't fair to me to have me standing talking to this kind of men. Why, they've come from the police! They're all dirty from handling criminals! I'm frightened, Issy! I feel they'll make a criminal of me! I feel they'll drag me off to prison! It isn't good for my baby! Give them my jewels and send them away!'

At this point a waiter, who must have been listening at the door, rushed in, and taking his stand in front of Ruth in an attitude of defence such as seen in Greek statuary, cried, '*Le soleil est couché!*'

The assistant manager, who had been standing behind one of the pillars, stepped forward and said, '*Ah, c'est vrai, le soleil est couché.*'

Robin de Cambremer turned to us, and with an air of warmly congratulating himself and us, exclaimed, '*Le soleil est couché!*'

The two debt collectors turned to each other and remarked gloomily: '*Piste, le soleil est couché!*'

'What are they saying?' asked Issy.

'They're saying the sun has set.'

'Is that what that waiter fellow yelled when he came dashing into the room?'

'Yes.'

'He said the sun was set?'

'Yes.'

'And that's what all the rest of them are saying?'

'Yes.'

He disengaged Ruth from his arms and made her stand by herself. 'What makes you raise Cain to have your child born in a country where the people are such darned fools that they burst into a room where people are talking important business to tell them that the sun has set? If we really got down to brass tacks, I suppose they would burst in to tell us that broccoli had just come in season.'

'Well, it is rather important,' said Robin. 'You see, in the principality of Monaco, where we are at the moment, no debt collector can do his work between sunset and sunrise.'

'Oh, I see, I see!' breathed Issy, and he took Ruth back to his arms. There immediately she began to weep again, and say, 'Tell them to come back as early as they like in the morning and take my jewels,' to which he answered, 'Sure, honey. Anything you say, honey. Only don't cry, honey.' And so we left them.

And that would have been the end of the story, so far as I would have known it, if Sheila had not had the temperament of a natural lawbreaker, and had not grown bright and rather restless after dinner.

'I hate to think of that poor little thing giving up her jewels,' she said, as we sat round the fire, safe in Cap Martin, which is over the frontier in France.

'She didn't seem to mind,' I said.

'Of course she minded. Who wouldn't? Besides, if she says she's paid some and hasn't kept the receipts, it's outrageous. And her jewels are worth far more – far more.'

'Are they?'

She nodded. 'Half as much again if I know anything about jewels at all.' For a moment she was still. Then her shoe began to tap the ground. 'Besides, it's a disgraceful law. That a firm should have the right to issue a writ by simply alleging a debt to a magistrate without having to inform the other people and giving them a chance to disprove it! It's outrageous.' And a little later: 'And I hate to think of her losing any of her lovely jewels to those *huissiers*. For they get 10 per cent, you know, of all the debts they collect.'

In the end she evolved a plan. It depended on a royal personage who lived in the very next villa. His automobile would never be stopped as it crossed the frontier of Monaco. So if he sent the automobile into Monaco and it called at the Hôtel de Paris and picked up Issy and Ruth no power could prevent them from crossing the frontier back into France and they could settle down in a hotel at Mentone for the night, proceed by motorboat to Cap Ferrat, and let the French tradesmen justify their claims according to the more formal methods of the French courts.

The idea struck us as a good joke splendidly in the Phillips Oppenheim manner. We got our evening wraps and strolled over to the royal personage's villa. He found the idea as entertaining as we did. We got a little excited over it sitting on the floor in front of his great wood fire on the deep white polar bear rugs with his Alsatians nuzzling us with their ice-cold black noses and little glasses of vodka in our hands. It was certainly fun to talk about; and rather too late Robin and I found that Sheila and the royal personage were taking it seriously. Finally we got in his automobile and went back to Monaco.

I reflected that it was because he had taken this sort of plan seriously that he was living in Cap Martin instead of the kingdom to which he was born. Issy, we were told, had gone out for a stroll. Ruth was in bed, but she telephoned down that she would be glad to see us.

Sheila and I left Robin and the royal personage in the lounge and went up to her bedroom. Ruth was lying very still with her eyes closed; and Mary, who was hovering about the room with an air of concern, looked gravely at us and whispered in passing 'She's poorly, the child.' But I did not worry too much about that, for I had a pretty good idea that what had held Ruth and Mary together all those years was a common gift for putting things over on the trustful just the way they wanted. What I did worry about was that I detected in her stillness something steely and I suspected that what was making her steely was the thought of us and our present intrusion on her.

'Darling!' said Sheila, hopping on to the bed.

'Darling!' said Ruth, higher and fainter than ever.

'Darling, we can't bear you to lose your jewels,' Sheila went on, 'and we've been planning a way you don't have to.'

'Darling, how sweet of you!' It might have been the tiniest frailest angel whispering down to earth.

Sheila briskly explained her plan, ending up with:

'So you just pop on your clothes and come down to the automobile.'

But Ruth only shook her head weakly and closed her eyes again.

'Darling, don't be silly! They can't touch you if you do as I say. It's a clean get-away! And your jewels are worth 'way more than that!'

Ruth opened her eyes and gave her a bland and innocent look. 'Oh, do you think so?' she inquired, and closed her eyes again.

'Darling, come on!' Ruth shook her head. 'But why not? The king is downstairs, and you would just love the king.'

Ruth whimpered, 'I'm too sick!'

'But, darling, you were out walking this very afternoon and you were looking fine, and it'll only mean half an hour in an automobile.'

Ruth dug her knuckles in her eyes. 'But since then I've felt terribly sick. I just feel as if it's all gone wrong – and I'm scared!'

Suddenly Mary, her eyes rolling in her chocolate face, stepped forward and joined in the whimpering. 'Yes, I'm scared too! She's real sick, I tell you!'

Ruth was apparently weeping from real fright; and, indeed, she had been so hysterical that afternoon that she might have been.

'Then where's the doctor? And where's a nurse?' demanded Sheila, utterly convinced.

'I don't need a nurse,' Ruth wailed. 'I hate strangers. Mary's my nurse. She's all the nurse I want.'

'We coloured folks are awful good at nursin',' said Mary.

'Nonsense! All the kindness in the world can't take the place of a good trained nurse!' exclaimed Sheila. 'Isn't that Issy coming into the sitting-room now? I'll go in and talk to him about it.'

Before she got to the door Ruth was out of bed and in front of it. 'You dare scare my Issy boy!' she said. Her movements were those of one in the most robust health and her voice was no longer faint and high. It was, on the contrary, probably one of the strongest and deepest voices that have ever proceeded from a female inhabitant of Syracuse. I perceived that at last she was about to adopt directness as her tactics and I had a sort of idea that we would find her as soothing as the kick of a mule. I strolled away and looked out of the window at the lights twinkling on the Casino, casting circles on the lawns and the flower beds of the gardens. After all, this was Sheila's show, and she might as well take what was coming to her for it.

'You two girls don't seem to have any sense!' said Ruth indignantly. 'I thought you'd be on to what I was doing this afternoon! You see, there's always been this trouble about the jewels.' For a minute she bent like a tired lily, and I saw that she spoke of something that had been a real oppression to her spirit. 'Issy didn't seem to like having all that jewellery. It worried him all the time. He doesn't like to see me wearing it. He doesn't like to see my jewels around. I want to get them out of the house but I don't dare send them back to the folks that gave them to me, for that would make him think I got them in ways that give him the right to feel as he does about them. And he hasn't ever been sure. I don't dare sell them, in case the money they fetch make him think things. So what could I do but what I did?'

I left the window in the subsequent stunned silence. 'But what', I inquired gently 'did you do?'

'Well, what you've seen I did!' she replied with exasperation. 'The first thing any person would think of doing! I knew darned well I had a right to those jewels, whatever anybody said. They owed me something – those blighters who gave them to me. A good boy like Issy doesn't know how much they owed me!' For a time she used harsh words that I do not think she had learned in Syracuse. I had an odd impression that though she used them of men in the plural, she was thinking of a man in the singular. Then she went on:

'And I need that money. Issy makes a whole heap, but then you got to reckon that there isn't anybody over eighty on the East Side who isn't Issy's granduncle or grandaunt, and he keeps them all. And I want my kids to be brought up right. A girl's gotta be rich. A girl can't have good time and be safe if she isn't rich. You can do anything over here if you've got money. That's why I'm keeping on the villa at Auteuil. That's a swell convent school next door for the girls to go to. If I bring them up that way' – she began to stammer – 'I mustn't hope for too much – maybe they'll have to marry Jews, but they'll be the right sort of Jews – good old families; and their children – their children –' Her ambition choked her; she made fluttering gestures with her hands.

'I understand all that,' I said, and reflected that the royal personage downstairs was waiting vainly for one that he would probably meet later in his extreme old age at the marriage of his grandson, in the person of the grandmother of the bride. 'But I still don't understand about the jewels.'

'Oh, for heaven's sake!' she cried. 'I did the thing that was as plain as the nose on your face. I had my jewels valued – all except the things like the pearls that men never can tell whether they're fake or real – and then I went round Paris buying all I could with that much money which was most likely to rise in value. And then I arranged with the people in Paris to collect payments this way. I'd heard of someone being stung this way by the *huissiers* when I was dancing here two years ago. The people in Paris didn't mind. They just had to arrange a flat rate for the *huissiers*. These boys are taking twenty thousand francs between them instead of the regular commission. And now the jewels will be out of the house. They'll be taken up to Paris tomorrow right to the jewellers who agreed to buy them. And Issy won't even know how much they were worth.

'I've taken a great deal of trouble to buy things that don't look to him like they cost two cents. He thinks I bought these pictures at five hundred francs, because a poor boy painted them; and I was sorry for him because I saw he had no talent. And he won't ever get at the inwardness of it, because if all the schoolmasters in the world had worked on Issy from the day he was born till he was eighty years of age they couldn't teach him French or give him a head for figures. He's just all balled up about it. Wasn't what I did,' she demanded, her voice going high and faint again, 'the obvious thing to do?'

When we stole downstairs and presented ourselves again before Robin and the royal personage we could neither of us find any adequate answer when they asked us why we had not brought down Ruth. Sheila only drew a deep breath.

'I feel a child!' she said in the accents of one who has just witnessed a performance of genius. 'A child!'

And I could say nothing at all. I was gazing at the royal personage, who was looking his best, with the light shining on his silver pointed beard and his waist long and slim in his evening clothes. I didn't believe he would like it when his grandson married Issy's granddaughter. But after what I'd heard upstairs, I didn't believe he had a chance in the world of not having to put up with it.

# Lucky Boy

*This, another of the stories written for an American readership, appeared in* The World's Best Short Stories of 1930, *New York, Doubleday, Doran & Co., 1929.*

F ar down the train there was the sound of a revolver shot; and then they came to fetch my husband, who is a doctor. After that there rang the scream and rave of a woman in agony; and then they came to fetch me.

They took me to a drawing-room in the very last coach of all, where my husband was bending over something on the bed, of which I could see only a face with closed eyes, a face as beautiful as one of those Greek shepherd-boy gods, not one of the powerful gods who made the world but one of those graceful gods who intensified the harmony of the world after its making by being perfectly harmonious in themselves. I was appalled by the look on that sleeping face. For it seemed to be resolved on its own unconsciousness, to be sniffing it in as one might sniff an anaesthetic

123

past what one knew to be the proper dose so that sleep might turn into death.

Bemused by the meaning of that face I moved nearer and found I was treading on a pyjama jacket. It was of silk so thick and fine that even in the presence or approach of death I felt compunction at spoiling so fine a thing and I picked it up. And the woman who was screaming in the corner stopped screaming and came forward to snatch it from my hands, because she could not bear that anybody else should touch anything belonging to him. Then as I gave it to her she drew her head back as a startled animal will do and gave me a hard, discerning look – having, as I could see, lived all her life in such unprotected situations that she had had need to look at every single person who came near her to see if he meant harm.

Seeing that I meant none, that I had nothing about me of the police matron, she flung herself on me and wept. I had beauty as marvellous as the boy's on the bed pressed close to me. Soft she was, soft and ripe and luscious. One could have picked up handfuls of her body off the bone, not because she was fat or because she was old, for she was at most two or three years older than the boy on the bed, who was in his late twenties; but because of a deliberate luxuriousness of substance which one could imagine her cultivating by odd kinds of massage and costly baths. And her sobs cut her so deep that she gave that little after-sob which is the sign of true grief, being the voice of the poor human animal's amazement that it can suffer all that much.

She was told that the boy must go on travelling through the night – for we were in the middle of the desert – that he must have quiet, that she must go with me. And after pausing for a moment to blubber and look down on the boy's sleeping face, which seemed to be growing harder and harder as he slept, so that his hardness was as noticeable as her softness, she passed along the cars with me.

In our drawing-room she slipped into the bed that was still hollowed by my body with a lack of fastidiousness that was somehow pathetic as an old soldier's. Apologetically she asked if I minded leaving the lights on and would, I suspected, not have been embittered if the permission had been refused. She found she could not lie down; she sat up propped by pillows; she snatched up a copy of a magazine and tried to read it; she stuffed her mouth with candies from a box I put beside her; she rocked herself from side to side, blubbering and crying out from time to time:

'What did he have to do that for?'

She cried it out again and again and I thought she was going to start screaming once more. So I asked her what it was all about.

And over several hours, with intervals when she butted her pillow, when the tears rolled down so that she seemed to be deliquescing into something like strawberries and cream, she told me.

She said: 'That's Martin Vesey in there. They call him Lucky Boy.'

That was good for another five minutes' weeping.

Then she went on: 'I saw him first five years ago. You don't know who I am. I'm Kay Cunningham. I guess you've seen me in the musical shows. I was the Spirit of True Enlightenment in the "Disgraces" of 1927. They spun me round and round on a spinning top made of mirrors. Well, I'd been around an awful lot in New York. I'd been going round ever since I was seventeen. I know an awful lot of people in New York. Well, there was a banker I used to run around with who's just lousy with money. Oh, gosh, I don't mind tellin' you who it was, though I never spilled a thing like that before. It was Jim Melcher of Melcher & Lockett. That's way back in 1924. I've run around with a whole lot of other men since then and a whole lot before. But it was Jim Melcher then.

'Well, we were both just crazy on Florence Mills, and that's when she used to be at the old Plantation. Were you ever at the old Plantation before it was padlocked? It was a swell place. And that second show Florence Mills used to give, round about half after two, was just grand. Jim used to take me along there after the show two or three times a week. He was one of those boys who don't need any sleep, though I guess he was all of forty-five and looked older, being bald and having a paunch on him.

'One Saturday night he took me along and we were both feeling fine. I had a new silver dress on with a cloak that matched and I guess I looked pretty good. I'm talking of 1924. I was twenty-seven then. And he'd pulled off some fierce deal that had given him just about all the money he hadn't got already. I guess we looked as if we owned the earth. And Christopher – he was the Captain there – I wonder what's happened to Christopher. Christopher had given us the best table in the room. We were just a wow, the two of us, and we knew it. And Jim put on a lot of dog when he was with me because before I took up with him I'd been going around with Jack Spencer, who'd got a pile more money than he had.

'Well, we were sitting there at the best table, feeling good, when I saw two boys at the table right next to us, only it was behind a pillar, and Christopher wouldn't give it to anybody he knew. One was a boy I kind of knew, not much of a guy, a kind of false alarm round Wall Street, a Californian called Bert Ansell I'd met at a party two or three times. But the other boy I fell for right there. He was just a kid then. Twenty-two, he must have been. Say, did you see what he looked like when you were in there? You couldn't have seen his eyes, anyway. He's got great grey eyes that lie right across his face, bigger than anybody's eyes you ever saw, and they gleam. And he's got funny yellow hair, only dark too, that goes into curls, but hard, hard, just as if they were stone curls in those statues you see in the museum if you're walking in Central Park and it comes on raining. And his skin's white, white, like hardly any of us girls at the "Disgrace" had. And he's long and thin and got a waist. He's a grand swimmer and his body looks like that, kind of as if it was shaped by the swimming and diving. But it's the look of him that is so grand. He laughs all the time. I don't mean that, because he can be awful sad, but things go big with him that other people don't notice and then he laughs.

'I said to Jim: "Who's that with Bert Ansell?" And he says: "A sucker like Bert, I guess." And I says: "Well, he looks cute anyhow." And Jim says: "Oh, is that so! Is that so!" And I knew enough to lay off. But I went on looking at them out of the corner of my eye. And I could see that they were looking at me. And I saw the kid asking Bert Ansell who I was and who Jim was and I saw Bert telling him. He went on telling him for a helluva long time and I knew he must be telling all about Jack Spencer and maybe a lot before that. So I says: "For God's sake, Jim, aren't you never going to dance with me no more? I feel blue." But as we stood up to dance the music stopped and I heard the kid say all high and excited: "Gee, it must be great to have money!" And I knew Jim was right. He was a sucker like Bert. You don't get no rich man beginning like that. Jim didn't begin to play till he had his money, and he found having money means you can play. You don't get none of them making their money because they want to play.

'But I didn't care. All the better for me if he felt that way. If he had been looking for a good girl, that wouldn't have made it my lucky day. So I just peacocked about the place, and when Jack Spencer came in, I acted up and grabbed Jim's arm like I was afraid, and I jiggled my diamond bracelets and made them sparkle, and I was just the world's expensive vamp. And the kid ate it with a spoon. I watched him whenever I dared, and I could just see him shaking his rattle and saying: "This is the life!" Gosh, he was such a kid.

'Then next day I called up Bert Ansell, and told him I was throwing a cocktail party that afternoon at six, and he could come. And I says: "Oh, and who's your kid friend you were at the Plantation with last night?"

'And he says: "That's Martin Vesey. They call him the Lucky Boy in his home town."

'"And where's that?" says I.

'"Penaranda, California," says he.

'"I never heard of it," says I.

'"Neither did any one else," he says. "It's a water-tank, and the church where Martin's minister father preaches, and a kennel where a yellow dog sleeps when it's driven out of the next town." The dirty dog – I found out afterwards it was his own home-town too!

'"Why'd they call him 'Lucky Boy'?" says I.

'"Because he looked like having more chance than the rest of the inhabitants of leaving Penaranda," says he.

'"What's he doing in New York?" says I.

'"He started some coupon-selling business to do with railroad tickets in Los Angeles, and James P. Birkett of this town thought there might be something to it, and sent for him to hear his say-so. And now James P. Birkett don't think there is much to it, and don't care a damn what happens to him, but the poor boob can't bring himself to go back to Los Angeles."

'"That's as may be," says I, "but you bring him along to my party."

'But when Bert came in, he came alone. And when I asked him about the kid, he bursts out laughing and says: "He told me to tell you he was coming in two years' time."

'"What's he mean by that?" I says.

'"I guess he means that in two years' time he's coming along with a truckload of diamond bracelets," says he.

'"I guess that means he won't ever come," I says. I was kind of peeved, but I wasn't broken-hearted. You know how it is when you're young, and something happens nearly every day. You don't break your heart over nothing.

'Then I began to drop out. You do, when you're over thirty. It can't last. It wasn't so bad, mind you, but it wasn't like it used to be. Jim Melcher had gone long ago – he was with a red-haired girl who was in a cabaret; and after him there was Bill Spennings, but he went too; and a good job too, for he was pretty mean. I still had fellas I went around with, but none of them top-notchers, nothing big. I didn't know quite what to do. You don't, you know. It wasn't that I hadn't any money; I got some bonds and a lot of jewellery. I could live comfortably, though not how I used to; but what are you going to do with yourself? That's what got me.

'It's funny just about the time I was beginning to worry about all this I met Bert Ansell and I said to him: "Well, it's three years and your kid friend hasn't been to see me yet."

'He laughs and says: "I guess he won't ever come and see you with that truckload of diamond bracelets now. He fancies himself as a big operator, but it just stays a fancy."

'And I says: "Why'd they call him Lucky Boy, then? I won't give up hope."

'And about a year later he comes to see me, after all, just like he said. I went out one afternoon for my walk in the park because I was beginning to worry about reducing and when I came in my coloured girl says: "Mr Martin Vesey called up and says he's coming to see you at six."

'Well, I just could have dropped down dead. I felt terribly excited, as if I'd been crazier about him than I'd thought I was – which was silly, as I'd only seen him once. And I was just wild to know what had happened. I had to call up Jack Spencer about some business advice. They all like you to come to them for business advice after the whole thing's over and the feeling's died down; it kind of makes them feel powerful and as if you hadn't been able to do well for yourself after they fired you, and so I did it right then. And at the end of it I said quite kind of casual:

'"Do you know anything about a boy called Martin Vesey who's been doing things on Wall Street?"

'He bursts out laughing and says: "Aw, forget it."

'I says: "But hasn't he been cleaning up a whole pile there lately?"

'"Yes," says he, "he's made a whole pile out of Grand Carfax Uniteds; but remember", says he, "that a stopped clock tells the right time one minute in the day, but that don't make it a good clock."

'"I'll remember that," says I.

'Well, at six o'clock he came. He stood and looked at me with his great grey eyes laughing and a waist on him that made you want to run your arms down his body. I says to myself: "Somehow you don't look like a rich man to me." And he says to me: "You asked me to call." And then we both burst out laughing. And I settled him down in a chair and gave him a cocktail and took a good look at him.

'He'd got a grand suit on him, the kind that Jim Melcher and Jack Spencer and Bill Spennings wear, and he'd studs and cuff-links like the kind they wear and shoes like what they wear and I guessed he's gone to live in an apartment like they have and hired an English valet like they do. I was what comes after the suits and the studs and the cuff-links and the shoes and the apartments and the English valets; and he hadn't noticed that I wasn't what a rich man would go after any longer; that I'd been out of fashion for three years. And that wasn't the kind of mistake a rich man would make. I guessed Jack Spencer was right saying what he did.

'I felt so strongly I almost cried when he said to me after we'd been to a show the next night: "You know I'm a rich man now."

'"Is that so? Is that so?" says I, trying to kid him along.

'"It's so, and it ain't no wonder," says he. "The people in my town called me Lucky Boy ever since I was a kid."

'"Is that so? Is that so?" says I.

'"Can't you say nothing but 'Is that so?'" says he, laughing at me. "Can't you talk but just like a parrot?"

'"Maybe I don't only want to talk when I'm with you," says I, for I saw he was terribly shy and I felt as if I wanted to snatch at a good time with him in case something happened and it all went wrong. And then he kissed me and it was all grand. Gee, and the diamond bracelet he gave me as his first present! It half made that joke about the truckload come true.

'We had a fine time. He used to take me around to all the places Jack Spencer and Jim Melcher and the rest used to take me. Everybody got to know me and my Lucky Boy and he made me get a silver dress and a silver cloak like what I was wearing that first time he ever saw me. I guess he was sore because the Plantation had been padlocked; he'd have given his eyeteeth to go and give Christopher a bigger tip than the biggest tip he thought Jim could ever have given him and sat at that table. And I guess I gave him a good time. I ain't so old, really. Look at me – it don't hurt the eyes. It's only that I'm out of fashion. That's the kind of thing that spoils the pleasure of a rich man so that he can't see your looks or notice how loving you are. But he wasn't like that. That was one of the ways I knew he wasn't like a rich man.

'And I got scared stiff because he didn't seem to care for anything so much as he did for being a rich man. Nights he used to tell me about how he'd made little bits of dollars and dimes out in Penaranda when the other kids never saw a cent. And he was so darned proud of that nickname of his, "Lucky Boy". I don't suppose the folks who gave it meant a thing more than that they felt heaps better for seeing his lovely-looking eyes, but he'd been reading those success magazines and he figured out they meant that he was all set to be a millionaire. And I used to kid myself maybe there was something in it and anyway he'd made this packet out of Grand Carfax Uniteds and that would carry him along. But he was spending that packet as fast as a drunken sailor and anyway he had the look of someone that's got something coming to them. I seen it before in girls. A new showgirl blows in, some girl that's just come to New York from way out in Kansas or Texas, and everybody's saying, "Oh, isn't she the cutest thing!" and you just see that she's got something coming to her. All the men she cares for will treat her like a dog and she won't get no money and she'll get sick. Well, Lucky Boy had that look to me. My heart's turned over sometimes when he's left me, turning at the door to wave goodbye to me, smiling and kind of glittering with his own good looks.

'And my heart did turn over and it darn nearly stopped when one day he was standing like that with his hand on the doorknob and he suddenly remembered something and he pulls the door to and he says:

'"Oh, I'm forgetting something! I'm sending a clerk down to you about noon with some stock you got to sign your name to. They're preference stock in Western Waybath Oilfields and that's what's going to make you and me our second pile."

'Then he comes back to me and kneels down beside me and kisses me again and says:

'"Aren't you glad you got a Lucky Boy?"

'"Have you taken advice?" I said.

'He looked at me as if he might act ugly. "Advice be damned!" says he; and I saw right there how I could lose him.

'The minute I thought Jim Melcher would be back at his office I called him up and I asked him for advice the same as I usually do. And then I asked:

'"Do you know anything about Western Waybath Oilfields?"

'He bursts out laughing. "You spend the money you want to spend on them on Scotch. It won't be any more wasted, in the long run and it'll make you a whole lot happier."

'"But a friend of mine –" says I.

'He cuts in. "I know. It's a tip for the suckers. But there isn't a thing in it."

'Then an idea came into my head. "Could I sell them short?"

'Says he: "I doubt if you could. There aren't enough suckers to set the market moving by taking the tip."

'Says I: "Don't worry about that. I'll guarantee the suckers, all right. And that's my game." So that morning I went out and sold some of my jewellery and I went down to my brokers and told them what I wanted to do. I was right back when Lucky Boy's clerk came down with the stock.

'Gee, it broke my heart to see how that kid loved this new deal of his. I used to say to him, "Baby, it ain't right to have your whole mind set on one thing like this," and he used to jolly me about it and go out and buy something. My Lord, how he could spend! I guess he had exaggerated ideas of the way rich men spend money. Some of them don't. And anyway, I've had things bought for me and I don't get any kick out of it any more. But he bought dandy things for himself. I liked him to do that. Did you feel that pyjama jacket you picked up in there? All his things are good like that. And they ought to be. There ain't silk good enough for that skin of his. And he had some jewellery, lovely studs for the evening and a watch as thin as notepaper. Well, he loved all that buying and he loved the thing itself. He used to say to me: "Listen, they don't take me seriously as a big operator, but you wait till next week! You just wait till next week!" And I would feel sick in my stomach.

'Next week came. And it was just what I expected. There were three days that were just plain unadulterated hell, when he used to call up and say in a kind of shamed, grinning way, trying to make out it was all grand: "It's me, it's your Lucky Boy. Oh, it's all fine. But it ain't going the way I want it to just yet." And then there came a time when he didn't call up at all, and if I called up he wouldn't speak to me. So I had to send a message by my maid to say that I had been taken dangerously ill; the doctor wanted him along at once. And when he'd come and he was in my arms crying like a baby, my telephone rang and I picked it up and said: "Yes, it's me, Mr Sayers. Oh, indeed, Mr Sayers; will you please ring off, Mr Sayers. I've a friend here who's ill –" which Sayers must have thought darned chilly, as he had called up to tell me I'd made twenty-five thousand dollars on the deal up to date.

'Well, he was pretty miserable for the next few weeks. We used to dine out a lot in the old way, just to show folks he'd a lot more than what he'd lost and sometimes that would cheer him up. The music would get him and then he always liked being with me. I guess he's awfully fond of me. But when we got home he'd cry most nights. There isn't anything he really cares about except being a rich man.

'After a bit he seemed to get better and I began to think I'd be able to talk to him about spending less money. Because I knew he must have a bit left – he'd made a terrible lot of money on that first Grand Carfax Uniteds deal.

'One morning he was having breakfast up in my apartment on Central Park West and he was right as rain. He opened the window so's he could feed a bird that was pecking around out there and he called back over his shoulder to me, "Gee, baby, don't these bushes look fine down there coming out all green with the trees above 'em still soot-black?" He looked grand. So I says: "Lucky Boy, I want to speak to you," I says. "Lucky Boy, you're feeling fine these days."

'And he says: "Yes, I'm fine. And would you like to know what's made me feel fine?"

'I began to feel gone at the knees and I says: "Yes, I would like to know what's made you feel fine."

'And he says: "Canadian Carnation Industrials are making me feel fine and they're going to make Wall Street learn all over again why I'm called Lucky Boy." My heart turned right over then and it did a back-flop into the first position when he kissed me goodbye and said: "You do believe in your Lucky Boy?"

'And I says: "Yes."

'And he says: "You do believe your Lucky Boy'll be rich again by the end of May?"

'And I says: "Sure."

'Soon as he was out of the house I called up Bill Spennings and I asked him for advice the same as I usually do and then I asked: "Do you know anything about Canadian Carnation Industrials?"

'He laughed like I was sick of hearing. I got mad and said: "Heard a good story?"

'"Sure," he said, "what you were telling me."

'I tried to pull myself together and keep my temper. "Honest," says I, "is it that fierce?"

133

'He says: "It's just terrible, just terrible," he says.

'"Could I sell it short?" I says.

'"I doubt it. They're dead; they can't come to life unless such a sucker as hasn't been seen in Wall Street for fifty years comes along."

'I guess I cried. He says: "What's eating you? You sound funny to me!"

'I says: "I've got a kind of notion I'm going to make some money and being a poor girl," I says, "it's too much for me."

'That time I made fifty thousand. And it was hell twenty times worse than before. I wanted to take the heart out of my body and slip it into him because his own wouldn't give him any peace. He's just a kid and he grieved like a kid – only he don't drop things like a kid. This time we didn't go out nights to the restaurants and clubs and it was partly because all the money was gone and partly because I think he'd have died if he heard anybody call him "Lucky Boy" the way he knew they would now.

'Then somebody sued him for some small bit of business he'd been doing on the side – just a small operation. He hadn't mentioned it or I could have covered it the way I had the others. It was for something like twenty-three thousand, and he hadn't got it. When he sold all his jewellery and the furniture in his apartment he got just as much as made them stop the suit and not a cent more.

'"Lucky boy," says I, "there's just one thing for you to do. You gotta get out of town."

'He says: "I could get work in California and I could stage my home comeback from there. I believe you're right, honey. But my Lord, how I shall miss you!"

'"You wouldn't miss me, Lucky Boy," I says, "if you took me along."

'He just looked at me. "You couldn't face life with a poor man," says he.

'I didn't dare tell him that when he came along I'd been nearer than I liked to facing life with no man at all; and I didn't dare tell him I'd sixty-five thousand fresh in my hands, let alone what I had before. So I says: "I won't face life without

134

you. Why, you're my Lucky Boy. If you went, where would my luck be?"

'He kinda looked and looked and looked at me. "Would you marry me?" he says.

'I could see what was in his mind over and above the plain fact that I was the woman he liked to make love to most in the world. He thought it would be just swell to have a woman that had all the rich men after her turning aside and marrying him the week after he'd gone broke. That again showed he wasn't cut out to be a rich man. Rich men don't get fancies like that. They get things dead right. But I knew darned well that it was the best thing for him, so I says: "Yes I will."

'We went down to the City Hall and there was a fuss about it in the papers. The story was news enough to give it a good deal of space. I guess that carried him through, for he was mighty blue. And we packed up and took our tickets to California, to San Francisco. This place Penaranda is right near Los Angeles and it seems that in Los Angeles too they got into the habit of calling him Lucky Boy. For me that's reason enough for keeping in the vicinity of San Francisco. And he has an uncle there who'd offered him work. I made him take a drawing-room, though it looked the way we couldn't afford it, so far as he knew, because I said we had got to leave New York in some sort of style.

'Well, it was pretty sour the first part of the trip going to Chicago. I guess he hadn't ever meant to leave New York except in his private car. He just kind of moped and I sat around and was there when he wanted me. Then he began to cheer up once we left Chicago and say: "Well, the next time I come this way they'll know I'm coming. I ain't buried yet. I ain't dead. Why, I'm not thirty yet. I'll grind them down when I make my comeback! I'll stamp on their faces!" Then yesterday he seemed to get down again and last evening over dinner he was terrible. And when we got back to our drawing-room he undressed and he lay down on his bed with his eyes on the ceiling.

'"What's the matter, Lucky Boy?" I says.

'"I'm going to be an employed man," he says. "I'm going to be an employed man in my uncle's ten-cent office with his staff of two men and a yellow dog. I, who've had my staff of twenty men and those offices looking over the Battery."

'"Baby," says I, "don't be silly. It's going to be grand."

'He wouldn't look at me. He just kept staring up at the ceiling and his eyes weren't laughing no more.'

'So I quit fussing with him and I took my clothes off and I put on this peach-coloured nightdress and this negligée that he used to carry about and I went and knelt on his bed.

'"Let me in," says I.

'"Quit that," he says, and he went on staring at the ceiling.

'"Don't be mean," says I, "because I got a secret for my baby. You ain't going to be an employed man," I says. "You're not going to work in no office; we're going to have our own farm."

'"What do you mean?" says he.

'"You forget I've got my own money," says I. "I got a hundred and ten thousand dollars in good bonds and we're going to put some of them in a farm and invest the rest," I says, "and we ain't going to think of the stock market again."

'He sat up. "What do you mean, you got a hundred and ten thousand?" He says, "You told me last March you got forty-five thousand."

'"Well, so I had, so I had," I says. "But that was March."

'"What do you mean, that was March?" says he. And he grabs my wrist. "Has some richer man than me been giving you money?"

'I could have laughed at that if it hadn't been for the way he said "a richer man than me". Oh, the poor kid, the poor kid! I said: "You know darned well I ain't touched another man since you've been with me."

'He said: "Then where'd you get the money?"

'I should have lied, but I thought it better he should have the truth. I says: "I made it on the stock market."

'He says: "But how? I never gave you a tip that wasn't such a failure that the cat would laugh it off. You always told me when you got a tip. You didn't get none in the last three months that would make all that money."

'I said, "You gave me the tips yourself."

'He says, "You're lying."

'I says, "I'm telling the truth. I always knew you weren't cut out to be a rich man. Rich men aren't like you. They haven't laughing eyes," I says, trying to kid him along. "They don't have a good time over little things the way you do; they don't hang out of the window feeding birds and hollering because the bushes are coming out green. And about stocks. They don't hope; they know. They don't love women the way you love me, nestling up the way you must have to your mammy. They go crazy about them, but they aren't sweet like you are. They're mean and ugly with them when they're through. They quit them like you couldn't. I've been out with some of the richest men that have been in New York for the last fifteen years and I ought to know. They're all different from you somehow. So when you counted on stocks making you rich, I knew they'd make you poor and I sold them short."

'He lay back. I should have known he was feeling badly. Like a fool I went on: "So I made all this money and it's yours really. We're going to buy a farm where you say, and we're going to work and we needn't work too darned hard, and we can have the grandest time, and maybe we'll make some money, but it won't be that way. Baby, take your mammy close and tell her you won't be too bored living on a farm with her!"

'He didn't seem to listen to a thing I was saying. He just stared at me. "You think there's a kind of rule that I ain't going to be rich?"

'"The men that get rich ain't like you," I says.

'"You made all that money by just going against me every time?" he says.

'"Sure I did, honey," I says. "But what's it matter?"

'"You don't believe in my luck?" says he.

'"Not on the stock market," says I.

'"Oh, is that so?" he says. "Is that so!"

'And at that he sits up in his bed and he starts looking down on the floor where our grips were, not paying any attention to me.

'"Not on the stock market you haven't got luck," says I, "but that ain't the whole of life. Don't you remember what it was like to have good times on a farm when you was a kid?"

'He'd found what he was looking for and it was in a grip I hadn't packed that he'd brought from his apartment.

'"Oh, shucks," he says, fumbling in it, "what's the good of a man being alive if he ain't got luck?"

'And I saw he was clean crazy and wouldn't hear sense. His eyes were kind of old and he didn't look like a kid any more. And I felt such a fool in my peach-coloured nightdress and this fool negligée and I turned around and chucked myself down on my own bed and howled. Until I heard – what I did. God, how I hoped for the first minute that it was me he had shot!'

And at that she wept more terribly than I had thought a human being could weep, throwing her soft beauty, whose irrelevant promise of pleasure was somehow a mockery of her own grief, from side to side of the narrow bed. I found no words to comfort her, for, though doubtless there are words to comfort the womenfolk of gamblers, I doubt if they are to be spoken on this earth. There are explanations of our sorrows which seem to be strictly reserved for the hereafter.

Then it was, as the morning stood bright to meet us over the California mountains, that my husband chose to come in, rubbing his hands and otherwise comporting himself with the air of unqualified satisfaction which doctors are apt to exhibit in the face of return from the jaws of death, with what often seems to less biased minds insufficient reason.

'Well,' he said to Mrs Martin Vesey, 'that young man of yours is going to pull through after all.'

She looked more than ever like a chorus-girl after the most debased kind of party that ever led to a patrol wagon. But she clasped her hands as if in prayer.

'Yes,' my husband went on, 'the bullet's missed his lung by a miracle and the haemorrhage is drying up nicely.'

'Can I go along to him now?'

'You can look at him. He's sleeping.'

'I'd like to look at him.'

She jumped out of bed and made for the door. But on the way a thought struck her, and looking up at my husband she muttered in an embarrassed way as if she were proposing a half-shameful compromise with a monster that she knew in the end would devour her:

'Make him feel that's good luck – about his lung. . . . He wants to think he has good luck.'

# Ruby

*This, another of Rebecca West's 'American' short stories, appeared in the* New Yorker *– to which she had been a contributor since the 1920s – of 20 April 1940.*

U sually I am repelled by those of my sex who have been often and greatly loved. My complaint against them is that they are so extremely disagreeable. So far as I can see, when a man wants a rose-wreathed companion for his hours of ease he chooses a female plainly embittered by disappointment because she was not born an alligator or one of those medieval harpies who used to haunt battlefields and rob the dead or dying, jobs in which she could have exercised her really distinctive qualities.

I know of only one exception: Ruby.

Some might wonder at my choice, for Ruby, though once beautiful, now weighs two hundred and fifty pounds. Her hair, which used to be golden and wreathed by night with diamonds, now grows thin and white from a pink scalp. During the last thirty years she has dropped through destiny like a stone. Her first marriage was celebrated in the Chapel Royal in London, with Queen Alexandra signing the register. Her last husband held a minor position in connection with the Six-Day Bicycle Race. All her life she has lost and wasted what ought to be preserved. Invariably she has turned her back on the amiable and honourable man who would have meant lifelong security and has gone off with another who was undistinguishable in his morals and manners from a gorilla. She has specialized in such negligences as letting her insurance run out and leaving all her jewels in a taxi the next day. Once she managed to get mixed up in a narcotics case, and frequently, after a certain hour, she has to speak through a bubble of alcohol. Even so, she is a remarkable woman. She has been given the power of miraculous healing, and she deserves it.

I saw her use that power not long after I first met her. I knew her through a friend of mine whom she refused to marry, since he was solvent and would not have beaten her. One night in Paris I returned to my hotel after the theatre, and when I went to claim my key I found her standing beside me. We greeted each other, but soon her eye slid past me to the night clerk, a fat and sallow Frenchman.

'You're in pain,' she said, and when he had told her that he was suffering from a gastric ulcer, she went on, 'I can always tell a hundred yards off if somebody's in pain, even if I've got my back to them. And if you let me touch you, I'll take away the pain. I can always do that. I can always stop people feeling pain.' It sounded as credible as a chorus-girl's boast that in a previous incarnation she had been an Egyptian princess.

We retired to a kind of pantry, where, with some sleepy waiters staring at us, Ruby slid her hands six times down the stripes of his old-fashioned French shirt and the pain left him. In no time his face changed from tallow to flesh and hers became lined and grey. When he put on his coat he was laughing with relief.

Sometimes I nearly detest Ruby.

She seems to me that stock figure of bad fiction, the golden-hearted courtesan. Then she reminds me of a candle softening and bending in the heat, of grease that cannot keep itself to itself. But sooner or later I see that she is uniquely good, that she performs an act of charity which others cannot achieve.

Quite a lot of people will bestow on us wise, prudent, long-term kindness. Very few have a quick, instinctive, assuaging reaction to our first cry of pain. Most people hold back; they do not know what to say, they tell us that we are exaggerating or that it is our own fault – which may be true but does nothing to salve the first, worst prick of agony. That is where Ruby showed genius. She rushed at the sufferer, not to criticize but to give pity, pity compounded to the perfect formula for each individual case. For proof of this I would bring forward the Hindu fortune-teller at Brighton. We had both gone there to convalesce after influenza, and one day we lunched and went to a cinema and afterward had tea in a department store.

We were on our way to an elevator when she stopped in front of a little booth that had been run up in a corner and said, in a voice suddenly girlish with hope, 'Oh, a fortune-teller!' A minute later I, too, had become interested in Mr Chandra Bil Bose, the Eastern mystic, who, as a notice announced, was willing to draw aside the veil of fate for all who would pay him two shillings and sixpence.

The front of his booth was plastered with letters and telegrams which the casual passer-by might have taken for testimonials to his psychic powers, but which were not. There wasn't one word pinned up on the boards which could have been interpreted as a recommendation of Mr Bose, except a letter in which a lady tersely declared that in consequence of what he had told her she had decided to return to her husband; even that might have been an incident in Mr Bose's love life. Most of the telegrams were bare requests for appointments. One was definitely irrelevant to all psychic matters, being a promise to reserve him a third-floor bedroom at the usual terms. Another was openly hostile, saying, 'PLEASE DO NOT COME DO NOT WANT YOU ON ANY ACCOUNT.'

The letters were not more satisfactory as tributes. The Aga Khan, the Duke of Kent, and several other public figures acknowledged good wishes, and some showed ill feeling under their reiteration. His Highness the Maharajah of Indore had been maddened into a final letter that thanked Mr Bose but regretted that he could not imagine any manner in which Mr Bose's services could be of the slightest use to him and begged that the correspondence might be closed. We both burst out laughing.

'You go first,' said Ruby, 'I'm laughing so.' Once I got inside the booth there was no more laughter. Mr Bose was one of the most pathetic creatures I have ever seen. He was a very ugly, small, thin Hindu, no longer young, and his teeth were stained red with betel nut. He wore a grubby white turban and a worn summer suit of a grey that made a displeasing contrast with his brown skin. He was shivering from cold, and perhaps a touch of fever, and certainly some recent personal humiliation and sorrow. He was clammy with failure. I am sure the telegrams and letters on the board outside gave an accurate account of how the world had treated him.

'Me, I am an Indian,' he said, quite unnecessarily. 'I know all the wisdom of the East. Put out your hands on the table, please.' He stared past me as if he saw a picture of his troubles painted on the wall, and then compelled himself back to his palmistry.

'Your husband – your husband – your husband is a big, fair clergyman,' he pronounced, and when I made a dissenting murmur he cried desperately, 'What, is he not a big, fair clergyman?' I saw that he believed, in the face of all experience, that he had psychic gifts, and so I agreed that it was all as he said and accepted a bogus and very dreary destiny from his hands. While he jabbered, shaking and shuddering, I wrote it all down in my notebook. 'And these are your lucky days: fourthmarchthirdapril seventhmay*donothing*junejulyaugust andseptemberseventhoctobereleventhnovemberseventeenthdecember *rest*januaryandfebruary – and please go, lady, please go at once, and I will see your friend.' As a St Bernard I was a failure. I couldn't think what to do to comfort the little man.

Ruby, however, knew what was needed. When I put my eye to the curtain to see why she was so long, it was the Hindu's hands that lay palm upward on the table, his eyes that swam in cosy, hypnotized credulity, while Ruby's forefinger hovered and indicated, and her voice spoke out of a cloud of mystical assurance. 'Now, that's a lucky line, a very lucky line, and you see it makes a turn just here. That's not just yet. Not for a day or two. You said you were leaving Brighton on Monday, didn't you? I'm glad of that. It isn't a good place for you, doesn't fit in with your stars. But once you get out of here, there's luck waiting for you, a lot of luck.'

Nobody in the world but Ruby would have thought of that.

# They That Sit in Darkness

*This story appeared in* The Fothergill Omnibus, 1931, *Eyre & Spottiswoode, London, 1931.*

George Manisty had a fine head, and so his father had had before him; pale, shining grey eyes which long vision made look at once blind and all-seeing, fine brown hair dusted with gold which seemed blown back from his high white forehead, a mouth which even when he felt most completely at repose was compressed as if under discipline by pain, a pointed chin which, because of this long vision, he carried high and thrust out so that he had an air of fastidiously disdaining the world. As he was chronically tubercular, his tall body was very thin and his skin glazed with a luminous pallor; and he was racked by temperatures which took him up to peaks where he sparkled and crackled with what was surely more than human vitality, and dropped him down into abysses where he lay spent and panting, virtue having gone out of him. So it had been with his father. They were alike even to the long blue-white fingers, so supple that they could all or each be pressed back till the nails lay against the sparse flesh of the wrist. And they were alike in trade. Each earned his living by communing with the dead.

It followed therefore that George Manisty had never known any but those who communed with the dead, or who desired to do so. His home had always been a villa in South London, the last of a road which a speculative builder had long ago led out to the open fields in an orgy of unjustified faith in the fecundity of Londoners. It was very quiet. Long grasses grew in the ruts outside its gates, and four out of the nine neighbouring houses lacked a tenant. It was also very dark. The round butt of a steep hill, blackened with clumps of gorse, stopped the afternoon sun; and as if that were not enough the builders had encumbered all the ground-floor rooms with verandahs, and had brought the slated eaves low over the upper-storey windows. Yet it was not quiet and dark enough for the Manistys. It was their habit to sit in the basement, very often with the shutters fastened to keep out the nearly imperceptible noises of this limbo between town and country.

There was a breakfast-room down there which they used during the hours the daily servant was there. When the winter mornings were dark she would ask, 'Shan't I bring in a candle?' but Francis Manisty always shook his head, and when Momma had been well enough to get up she used to exclaim in pious horror, 'Snakes and ladders, no!' There was too much of this light, so damaging to their special talents, lying about uncageable in the open streets. They had no need of it for reading the papers, for that they never did; the deeds of the living had no interest for them. But they chattered perpetually of the deeds of the dead, and a world where these were the ghostly small-talk. 'Met Jenkinson in the Underground coming home. He's going to Cardiff next week, so I told him all that I was telling you about that old woman whose father called his horse Bucephalus and goes all gooey if you fetch the old man up and get him talking about it. And when I told him I was going to York he spilt quite a lot. It seems there's a chap up there called Sprott whose wife died when he was at the war – here, George, you listen to this . . . ' and George listened, for probably there would be a sharp question when he got in from school in the late afternoon, 'Now, George, what was I telling you this morning about a chap named Sprott? And where did he live?'

For they would still be talking about the dead, though by that time they would have moved into the kitchen to do it. It was nice there. Mother would be sitting at the table, at her elbow the bottle out of which she had to drink so often because her heart was bad, and she would be looking warm and mellow and pretty. In the house she wore her hair in fat brown sausage-curls tumbling over her shoulders, just as she had been wearing it when she and her pop, Ira Wickett, the celebrated medium of Palmyra, New York, who had learnt to make raps from the Fox Sisters themselves, had found the young English conjurer sick of a fever in a Pittsburg hotel. Since the glow from the kitchen-range and the gas-jet disguised the puffiness under her eyes and made an agreeable flush of the bluish venous smears on her cheeks, and her bulky body was obscured by the shadows of a big basket-chair, she might still have been a young woman of rich beauty.

Meanwhile Father would be cooking chops or steak or fish for high tea in a frying-pan that sent up a curling incense of onions, and little George was set to make toast and founder it with a good block of beef dripping; and usually there was a glass dish of tinned fruit in syrup. After Father and George had cleared the table they would sit down to lessons: not the lessons the boy had brought from school. Since they dealt with the world of the living they were unprofitable to him. The lessons he had to learn now were in the nature of vocational training. 'That's the ticket, that's the ticket,' Father would say. 'You slip the wedge in between the slates and write – and talk, talk quick! Then if the pencil scratches they don't hear it. That's right – keep going – when you're at a loss cry out loud and happy – "I can feel them! Oh, they're so close the blessed spirits!" With a little catch in your breath. That's done already is it? Ah, whose fingers has my boy got? You won't disgrace your dad!' So the whole evening went by, all diligence and praise. Momma used to sit quietly, saying sometimes, 'I heard you move then, honey,' but sinking deeper and deeper into a drowse, until she no longer took any more doses from the bottle at her elbow. For half an hour before his bedtime the gaslight was turned out, so that he could put into practice what he had been taught. Then his father came into his own, his voice became sweet and strong and charged with ecstasy, and George glowed with a junior version of his pride. They could feel the manual and vocal tricks cohering together into a presentation that they laid before an invisible audience; they knew themselves priests and creators.

It was not so nice when Father was away. Momma had only one accomplishment, the making of raps; but that she taught him thoroughly. They would sit in the dark kitchen together while the tap-taps travelled round the kitchen along the skirting and up one side of the fireplace, like a question, and then went across the mantelpiece and down the other side of the fireplace, like an answer, or made the table quiver under the fusillade, or even the chairs beneath them. 'Make 'em ring, honey, make 'em ring out like bells!' she would exhort him, and cry out, 'That's Momma's boy!' when he got the right hopeful resonance. But after a certain hour she would forget to teach him, and would pass into a delirium of tapping, rocking to and fro in her basket-chair, and making the kitchen echo till it seemed the house must fall in on them, while in her rich yet flat voice she sang hymn after hymn, freshening the tone every now and then with a dose from the bottle. In the end, as always, she fell into a drowse; and it was difficult work shaking her awake so that she would go to bed. Sometimes, indeed, she would not let herself be roused and would only settle herself deeper in the basket-chair, chuckling, 'Run away to bed, honey, and let Momma rest till she feels better.'

It was not so nice, and it happened more and more frequently. For it was not often now that the Manistys could work at him. Occasionally, especially on Sundays, they mounted to the rooms above, and were very busy dusting the aspidistras and the glass aeolians that dangled at the doors, taking the pleated papers out of the grates and lighting fires, until Father looked at his watch and said 'They'll be here in five minutes if they found old Parkyns's fly at the station. Better begin.' Then Momma and George would stand by the harmonium and sing 'Let Us Gather by the River', while Father swayed over the keyboard, milking the melody out of the keys with his long supple fingers, until

150

the crepey widow or the palsied old gentleman had infirmly descended at the gate. Time was when the searchers after the dead had been younger: had been comparatively young as the fathers and mothers of young men are apt to be, as pitifully young as their widows must be. But that time had not lasted long – 'You'd think they'd be ashamed to forget so soon,' Father used to say – and George had then been too small to be trusted in the company of believers, though he had crawled about on the floor and received instruction in the art of wire-laying. Since then the rush had dwindled year by year; and now Father had to travel about, seeking after the seekers for the dead, and would be at home for at best three days out of the week.

It was mainly the seekers for the dead he sought; though about his pursuit there was a certain delicacy. Mr Sprott of York might have been a gold-mine, particularly as dead Phyllis Sprott's maid had come into the fold of the faithful in Birmingham, and 'there's nothing', as Father used to say, 'they won't tell you, without having the faintest idea they've told you anything.' But he always preferred to rely on the mere séance fees alone. 'After all,' he used to say, exchanging a nod with Momma, 'we're luckier than most.' Momma sighed. 'Yes, poor blessèd Pop,' turning up her eyes to the shadowed ceiling. 'So we'll leave 'em be, we'll leave 'em be,' he used to say, jerking his head over his shoulder, as if there stood behind him hosts of the credulous bereaved; and through the half-light one could see his fingers darting and interweaving in some new technical trick.

For lately his technique, from being his joy and pride, had changed into an agonized preoccupation. It accounted for the lesser but far more harrowing part of his trips about the country. First of all he would read, either in the daily papers or in some journal of his craft, an account of some new medium, and sit swaying his cooling cup of tea in the air and groaning aloud, 'They can't do that. No one could do that! Yet I wonder. I wonder – I wish I could see this fellow working.' Then he would get up and walk about the room saying, 'I couldn't do that, you know, I couldn't do what the papers say that chap does. But they're all such liars.' Nevertheless he would know no rest till he had made arrangements to attend one of the new medium's séances, and usually not even then. He was himself again only when he was able to push open the door into the flame-driven darkness that was his home and cry out, 'Momma! George! Are you there? Why of course you're there! Well it was nothing, nothing at all! He did that old trick that Herb Waterbury taught me way back in nineteen hundred. Say, have you got sausages the way I asked you to? Now watch me do a swell piece of cooking.' And he would have a happy time with the frying-pan, explaining to them just how long he had been baffled and what had given the show away. 'It's all right!' he used to end up by saying; and then, after a pause, he would add, 'It's all right, up till now.'

His return was always as triumphant, though the advent of ectoplasm sorely grieved him. A real or fancied identification with inflated calves' lights touched his professional dignity. '"I'm a spiritualist medium," I said to him, "and a spiritualist medium I remain, without setting up for a tripe-shop,"' he once reported, 'and me that never has any insides in the house except liver, and that I wouldn't if it weren't good for the blood.' But in spite of this invariable triumph Father seemed to be suffering from these researches. Perhaps the suspense was too much for him. At any rate he lost weight, he began to cough, when he put up his hand to the gas-jet one seemed to be able to see the light through it. 'For crying out loud,' said Momma at breakfast one morning, 'why do you want to run around the country snooping after fellows like these fellows that don't matter two hoots anyhow?' 'Oh, one wants to know,' said Father, stirring his tea. 'Oh, for the Lord's sake what is there to know?' asked Momma. But he answered her only with the resolute, weak, and apprehensive stare of a very ill man; which indeed he was now to such an extent that he could no longer conduct a séance by himself. For some time past he had fallen into the habit of taking George with him, although the boy was only sixteen, and handing the séance over to him. Shy as the boy was, this was heaven to him. He loved the feeling of sitting in the blackness facing his father, with their four perfect hands weaving unseen a web of emotion that fell on their companions and made those their subjects. He loved hearing his father's voice throb and soar in the ecstasy of the seer, and letting his own voice come jagged out of his throat, and recognizing them as the same voice. He loved leaving the hot room and the tearful thanks, and the moist handshakes, and travelling home in the tube beside his wonderful father, who was insubstantial as flame, as delicate as a pointed church window.

Every day his father was looking more and more wonderful. But he had been looking very old, and the night he came back from Liverpool, where he had gone for the double reason of holding a séance and seeing a medium who claimed to get spirit writing without the slate, he looked very young. That was what struck George when he raised his eyes from his hands and saw his father standing at the open door. 'I don't believe Dad's looked as young as this all the time I can remember him,' he thought, and shot a glance at Momma, wondering if she would notice it too; but for some time she had been drowsing, her chin was down among her sausage-curls on her bust. Looking back at his father, he saw that the gaslight was showing crystal beads of rain on his coat, and that his draggled hat hung from his lax hand. He had not, as he always had done before, left his wet clothes in the hall above. 'Why, Father, let me take your things!' he said. His father allowed it but did not help, standing quite still, and murmuring 'My dear boy.' When he was free of his things he went over and sat down on the floor in front of Momma, leaning back against her knees. 'I'm sick, Cora,' he said, 'the way I was when you found me in that hotel in Pittsburg.' She stirred in her drowse and, putting out her hand to the new weight on her knee, stroked his hair. 'It's grand to be back,' he said, stretching back his throat, seeking her with his blazing eyes, his bright cheeks. 'I know you'll look after me.' Then his head slipped forward, and he sat nodding into the shadows, trouble growing in his eyes. 'Maybe it was because I was sick, but I couldn't see how that chap worked his tricks. Not one of them. But maybe it was because I was sick. Cora! Cora!' he called quite loudly. 'Do you think there's something in it after all?'

Momma was nearly fetched out of her drowse. She made her automatic response at that hour, her raps began to travel round the skirting, up the side of the fireplace; but sleep took her before they crossed the mantelpiece. It sounded as if a question had been asked, but the answer was not given. Father's chin dropped, his lips twitched in a desperate grimace, his hands began to practise with an

153

invisible slate. George ran forward and knelt beside him. 'Father, let me help you to bed,' he begged. 'I don't want to go to bed,' said Father, 'you'd think bed was a medicine the way some people talk. It's just something you lie down on.' 'Well let me get the doctor.' 'I don't want a doctor,' said Father, 'he couldn't tell me what's worrying me. That's all that's the matter with me. A bit of worry. And anyway no doctor knows as much about sickness as your momma here. She's a grand nurse. I never would have got out of Pittsburg alive if it hadn't been for her. Would I, dear?' 'But, Father –' 'George, let me alone. Leave us alone. You mustn't come between Momma and me. We're all right together. See?' He looked up into the boy's face and his eyes changed as if a cloud of colder thought had blown across his mind. In a remote whisper he said, 'Kiss me, boy.' Then he went on, 'We'll be all right, we'll go to bed when Momma's ready. And in the meantime I want to practise something. So goodnight, son.'

When George and the daily maid tiptoed into the room in the morning they found him still sitting with his head against Momma's knees; and Momma's grief at the moment of waking, and for ever afterwards, was frenzied and despairing. She offered George no help – but then for years it had been taken for granted that her relationship with the practical was tenuous in the extreme – in working out the problem of how he must live. Their position was not desperate. Ira Wickett had left some provision for his daughter. The house was theirs, and there was a little money. But it was not quite enough. There was needed exactly that sum that Father had made out of his séances. It was plain, therefore, that the problem was virtually solved: George must give the séances his father had given. It was an easy solution, and indeed there was no other. The lessons in mediumship his father had given him every evening had gravely interfered with his general education; he had no friends outside the spiritualist world whose influence he could evoke to give him employment; and, indeed, if he had been able to do so it would have been useless, for his mother's state of health would have prevented his going out to work every morning. For she was not getting over her loss, on the contrary she was every day more subject to it. She was in a perpetual state of hysteria that seemed at times to be verging on a more delusionary condition. Almost every day she would sit in her basket-chair making raps, and would suddenly forget what she was doing and shriek with fear at the raps, and wonder if they were Father coming back to her, and then cry because she had been so cowardly as to be afraid of dear Father. In the evening it was better, for she fell into her drowse earlier and earlier; but it was quite impossible to think of leaving her every day.

So, though without vanity, he expected to be civilly received, as one who is properly shouldering his responsibilities, when he told his schoolmaster that he was leaving school at the end of the term and was going to be a medium. He was surprised, he was hurt, when he saw a look in the man's eye that plainly meant something very different. He had always known that all his teachers pitied him for something to do with his parentage, but he had thought this due to the preference for insipidity which is almost part of education. So far as he had seen anything of the homes of other children, their mothers were far inferior to his own in richness, their fathers far inferior to his in every conceivable quality that could be admired. But now he perceived that his parents had been blamed for a specific reason, and that now he too was going to be blamed instead of being pitied.

George did not like it, because the little man had always been very kind to him. He had an impulse to defend himself, to explain how his father's lessons in legerdemain had kept him back in his studies. But he had to bite his lip and break off the sentence. People did not understand about that. It would seem to the schoolmaster as if he was confessing that his father had been a cheat and that he was going to be one; and he could not find the words to explain that really it was not like that at all. He felt helpless and unhappy, and more than ever conscious of the coldness of the little man's eyes. He wanted to rouse his sympathies by telling him about his mother, how ill she was, how she thought that the rappings she herself had made were spirit messages, but it struck him immediately that that also would not do. He had to stand stupidly looking down at the floor till the schoolmaster, speaking to him more icily than he had ever done before, told him he could go.

That was the first time that George felt conscious of a difference

155

between himself and other people, which consisted in his inability to be candid about many of the things concerning which they had nothing to hide. It depressed him every time he thought of it during the following winter, although his happiest moments came when he was giving his séances. He would leave the dark house, made desolate by Momma weeping and moaning, or laughing loudly over some small inexplicable joke, he would travel across London, or across England, it might be, to a room where something so delightful was to happen that at any point in his journey he could dismiss its tedium by resting his forehead on his hand and thinking how presently he would be sitting in the blackness, using his hands as his father taught him, palming the slate without a sound so quickly that it never showed a trace of the hand's heat, and letting his voice bell in his throat so that it sounded like his father's and whipped up the passions of the hidden people all about him, so that though the eye saw nothing the mind saw a circle of blazing light. There was always a point in the séance when this light grew so strong that he knew that he himself could not be responsible for it and he felt his father's spirit sitting close to him. Whatever he said then meant something to all of the sitters. The light would blaze higher, it would recede, when the poor real light flooded the room it was obvious that virtue had gone out of him. As they pressed in on him he would forget how he had spent weeks piecing together the convincing messages from the dead for which they thanked him, it would seem that the unknown dead had spoken through his lips, that the known dead had kissed him on the lips, and he would go out into the night dazzled and smiling and drunken. But in the third-class carriage he would remember that he had lied, and his chin would fall lower and lower inside his turned-up collar. When he got back to the silent house Momma would be lying in her bed, breathing stertorously, but as unlike herself as she had been a year or two ago as if she were dead; as unresponsive to the hand he laid on her, the mouth he pressed on her forehead, as if she were dead; dumbfoundingly just a body. He would stand beside her, looking up at the ceiling, asking what that which is not the body is, and where it goes, as if he expected to find it a small moth folded somewhere on the cornice of the discoloured plaster.

George slept late after such nights; but after one such he woke early, one morning in the March following his father's death. For his mother stood by his bedside, calmer than she had been for months, and more brisk and purposeful than he had seen her since his childhood, though she was so bodily destroyed that for a second or two he looked at her in horror without listening to what she had to say. Her sausage-curls, which she now neither dyed nor brushed, were greasy, grey, soiled springs, her cheeks were purple, her stoutness was so increased that her dressing-gown did not meet. He cried out in pain, 'Oh, Momma, Momma!' But she hushed him with a finger and said, 'Quiet now, your dad's right nervous.' The hair standing up on his head, he lay still. She went on, 'You know well's I do he hasn't been home for months. And here was I thinking he was just like the ones I had before him. But he's back sitting in the kitchen, and he's looking peaked. He's got a story of having been on a long journey.' She passed the lapel of her dressing-gown across her lips and stared in front of her under knit brows, as if weighing evidence. 'It's a queer story, but I believe it. So we'll treat him right. Come down and talk to him while I cook him some breakfast. He's looking real peaked I tell you.'

George followed her down the creaking stairs into the kitchen where there was nothing but the raw morning light. She nodded to an empty chair and said, in the ironical tone of one who forgives but dreads to be laughed at for forgiving so tries to put a complexion of mockery on it all, 'Well, here's the boy,' and sharply bade George in an undertone, 'Give your dad a kiss.' Then she turned to the kitchen-range and busied herself with a frying-pan of bacon. 'Momma,' said George. 'Momma.' Over her shoulder she said, 'It's your dad you should talk to. Make him feel at home. We've both wanted him at home, I'm sure.'

He knelt down beside the empty space she kept on looking at, and whispered, 'Father, father.' It might be so. But he had hardly time to drop his lids, so that in darkness he might see better, before a whimper from his mother brought him up again. She was leaning against the mantelpiece, shaking with a fever and crying out in a delirium which did not leave her until three days after, when she died. George's grief was greater than he had expected, for he had never felt much emotion

157

about her other than a joy in the lusciousness she had had before she got so ill. He admired the doctor very much, and was puzzled and worried because he had an air of impatience and even disgust when he came into the house, and always spoke curtly to him. He was relieved when the doctor said that he would come in the day after the funeral to have a look at him. It showed there was no actual ill-feeling.

But the doctor was still curt when he said, 'I thought so. Your lungs are pretty bad. Be careful of yourself, or there'll be TB and a sanatorium. No hard work, no indoor work.' He gave brief directions for a regime, and was out in the garden on his way to his car as he gave the last. 'And, above all, no drink.'

'I never drink,' said George.

'Not yet, perhaps, but you'd better guard against it.'

'Why?' asked George. Then, as his eyes met the doctor's, he cried out indignantly, 'My mother didn't drink. She took it sometimes as medicine because her heart was so bad. But she didn't drink.'

The doctor was silenced. He made a step back towards the boy, and stopped; and his hands described a gesture of apology.

George bowed his head in acknowledgement and stood staring at something light on the ground that had caught his eye. Up till that moment he had always taken his mother's behaviour as just a mother's behaviour. He did not know that all mothers did not become comatose in the evening after a gradual mellowing; the very smell that hung about her he had accepted as the usual attribute of a mother. But he was suddenly and immediately convinced.

'She must have been a very remarkable woman in her youth,' said the doctor uncomfortably.

'Who told you that?' asked George; and with a rush of hope he added, 'Did you know my father?'

'No,' said the doctor, 'but I have read about her.'

'Where, where?' asked George.

'Goodbye, I will look in again,' flustered the doctor.

George's eye went back to the light object on the ground. He had been convinced of something else. If the doctor had read of his mother it could only be because she had at some time been exposed as a fraudulent medium. He remembered now that it had always been

158

kept a secret that she had been Cora, that he had been told from his childhood that he must never mention Grandpop Ira in front of any of the believers.

He was conscious that the light object he was looking at was a cluster of snowdrops. Their whiteness and the innocence of their slenderness and drooping bells were to him a symbol of everything that his circumstances were not. For a minute he had a wild impulse to run through the gate and throw himself on the mercy of the doctor, who was sitting in his car, having some difficulty with his clutch. But he reflected that the doctor, though plainly possessed of full affinity with success and respectability, would not help him. Did not the advice the doctor had just before given him sentence him to being a medium and nothing else?

The next six years passed slowly, miserably, successfully. George was at first known as the boy medium, and as he grew into manhood ladies often likened him to the poet Shelley. He would look like a young, dying god when they bound his hands and tied him up in the cabinet, a lock of his fine goldish-brown hair falling over his forehead, his mouth pressed as if in pain, his thin frame heaving with the deep sighs breathed in expectation of his ordeal. While they sat in darkness it was as if a living god moved among them, showering prodigies, writing messages, giving flowers, creating out of space the hands of beloveds that caressed as they had done when living, filling the air so full of spirits that some, unable to insert themselves in the sequence of materializations, rapped the walls and furniture till it was like a bombardment. When they untied the knots at the end of the séance he was very nearly a dead god. His white skin, glazed with the most delicate conceivable form of sweat, looked like fine porcelain; he hardly breathed, but joy lingered on his lips. He would refuse all company to the station, and would sit with bent spine, with hanging head, to his journey's end. He was hungry not only for the immortality of his dear ones, but for honour, so that when he re-entered the dark house he could comfort himself with no fantasy about them. If it had been Father's step he had heard on the stairs, if suddenly Momma's raps had started in the basement below, he would have remained sitting on his bed, with his head on his hands. There were too many accusations to be made if he had opened the door; there were too few conceivable defences.

Loneliness was George's tragedy. He could make no friends, among the believers, not so much because he felt he could not be friendly with people whom he cheated, as because he knew that those with whom he would much rather be friends would feel like that; and soon, too, he found himself calculating that this remoteness was of commercial value to him, in enhancing the effect of his personality. Since he was so successful he was able to afford good holidays, to stay at moderately expensive hotels in England and in Switzerland where he could come in contact with the friends he desired; but though he had the presentability that is cultivated by those who are doubtful of themselves it was cancelled by the sense of guilt that tied his tongue. It was during one such holiday that, shut in his room in the evenings, he wrote an article on the sorrows of a man who was brought up to be a fraudulent medium and could do no other work, and sent it to a London newspaper which published it over a pseudonym and sent him a few guineas for it. It relieved his feelings for a time, and he got a bitter and contemptuous kind of pleasure from seeing the article attacked as untrue in the correspondence columns by believers whom he had often cheated. It brought him a letter from a female medium, who was careful to give only a box number at a stationer's shop, confessing that she too was in a like position, having been reared to deceive and having no other means of livelihood nor relations who could help her to them. George was sorry for her, though for some reason he visualized her as being like Momma in her last stages, purplish and stout and bedressing-gowned, and he answered her kindly. But the correspondence naturally languished after a few exchanges; it could hardly consist of anything but reiterated complaints and commiserations. Perhaps the best thing his article did for him was to mitigate his sense of unimportance and isolation; for the newspaper liked to keep in touch with him, since he could supply them with possible explanations of the miracles imputed to any sensational new medium.

But often George thought that he should not have written that article, particularly while he was conducting a séance or had just given a very successful one. Was it right to make people think that there was nothing in spiritualism when night after night he felt his father close to him in the darkness? There might be tricks, and tricks again, but there was also a magical transfusion of matter, a sieve-like quality of this world that let in siftings from eternity. It was little enough when he wanted the whole of his father back again just as he used to be, but was it not something that that very night he had been certain, as the knots round his ankles fell unloosed in a second, that his hands had superhuman agility because they were not his but his father's? He was thinking that very thought as he stood putting on his overcoat after a séance at Barnet when a man he knew, one of the believers, came in and told him he would be welcome at a demonstration by a voice medium that was taking place at a private house not far distant. He said he would go, because of a hope that there his father might be also, which turned, as soon as the open air fanned his face, into a weariness that he should leave one circle of fools sitting in darkness round a cheat to go to another.

But this other séance was not in darkness. Round a large drawing-room furnished in the Victorian style with brass chandeliers, a prodigious mantelpiece crowned by a large marble presentation clock, and many gold-framed pictures representing Highland cattle, undaunted by the bright lights, undaunted by all the respectability, the medium was running about with a long trumpet in her hand. She was the most fairylike person he had ever seen. She wore a dress of accordion-pleated blue muslin, falling from a band of silk that girded a bust as flat and narrow as a child of ten's though she was perhaps eighteen; and because of her floating skirts and the way her light brown gold-dusted hair blew back from her forehead, she seemed to flutter and poise like a winged sprite as she ran about the room, holding out her trumpet to each of the dozen persons that were sitting there in turn. Her lips perpetually curved in a gentle smile; she waited till each had alternately put his ear to the trumpet and spoken into it, for perhaps three minutes, then, breaking into a freshet of nervous, high-pitched yet soft laughter, she pulled the trumpet away and sped on with it to someone else. She came to George very soon after he had entered the room, but at first he did not take the end

161

of the trumpet from her, he was marvelling so much at her extreme
pallor, which suggested not that she had no blood but that her blood
was more ethereal than other people's. But she remained in front of
him, rising and falling slightly on her toes, and perpetually smiling,
till he put his ear to the trumpet. A far whisper said, 'It's . . . ther.'
It must be Father; for nobody had ever called his mother anything
but Momma. He said, 'Is that you, Father?' The whisper answered,
'Yes.' He stared along the trumpet into the medium's pale shining grey
eyes, which looked at once blind and farseeing, which brightly turned
about and seemed to bless by not recognizing the essential quality of
anything on which they lay. In full faith he cried down the trumpet,
'Did you help me with my hands tonight?' and the whisper answered,
'Yes, my son, and in many other ways.' He dropped his end of the
trumpet, and stood with his jaw dropping, wishing that he had not
been one of the fools he himself habitually cheated, asking questions
that suggested their correct answers. But on the medium's face was
a smile so sweet that it might well have been the centre and source
of a halo. He shuddered, knowing that he was in the presence of a
true medium; and then shuddered again, for as she stepped away
from him she had laughed, and he had desired her as he had never
desired any woman.

After the séance George was introduced to her; her name was Ivy
Bentham. She talked to him pleasantly with that wonderful laugh
coming up to the surface, sometimes merely shimmering behind her
words. When somebody told her that he too was a medium he thought
she looked distressed, and his heart stood still lest it had got abroad
that he was a false medium, and she had heard. But she let him travel
with her back to London, and leave her at the boarding-house where
she lived with her mother, who at the moment was, she explained,
absent in the North nursing a sister through a dangerous illness; and
she told him too that he might telephone the next day. There was no
question but that she liked him, and though of course he was not good
enough for her he might have been her husband and her servant had
he not been cursed with this heritage of fraud and trickery. When he
got home to the dark and empty house that night he shouted oaths at
the creaking on the stairs, the stirrings down in the basement. If they

were what he had sometimes thought they were, so much the better. He told them three weeks later that it was because they had made him what they had that he was going to do this dirty trick and marry Ivy while her mother was away, and not tell her the truth till he had had one month of perfect happiness. But he did not abuse them. He felt a kinship with all evil, a need for alliance against the good, for he was haunted by a fear that one of the angels who spoke through Ivy's trumpet, who, she had shyly and even uncomfortably told him, had watched over her since she was ten years old, might tell her what he was. He even planned that he would bring her back there to make his confession. For he felt that Father with his twisting white fingers would bring a touch of legerdemain to the situation which would turn it all to the family's account; and he felt that Momma, sitting in the basement making her raps, would wear it all down, would make the angels sink into such a thick drowse as her own. He knew himself doubly a Judas for these plans because it was not until he had heard his father whispering down her trumpet, and had asked her solemnly if there was no trickery in her voices, and she had as solemnly denied it, that he had known for certain that the dead are alive and can be called on for aid according to their quality.

'You look so white!' Ivy had said to George as they left the Registry Office. They had had no difficulty in getting married, although her mother was still at Whitley Bay, and seemed from her letters frigidly displeased at the mere notion of her daughter's engagement, because, to his surprise, she was as old as he was: she was twenty-three. But that whiteness, which was indeed excessive, vanished almost as soon as they started their honeymoon at Swanage. He was delighted simply to be there, a married man, which was such an ordinary, unexceptional sort of thing to be, and had great delight in getting into conversation with people and telling them that in London he was a bank clerk; and he was amazed to find that Ivy was enjoying the same sort of pleasure. She had, it appeared, told the landlady that before her marriage she had been a private secretary. But their chief delight was their possession of each other. Ivy was magic, she was marvellous, she was worthy of these gifts which, when he thought of them, cooled him with reverence. She had everything, even a beautiful melancholy, which he thought not unnatural in one who was in touch with the secrets of eternity. Sometimes she would look wildly into his face and then dissolve into weeping that was the sad and enchanting sister of her laughter. He would comfort her until she slept, and then he would go out and walk by the sea thinking how wicked he was: the false that had seduced into union the true. He had deceived her utterly. She would look into his face sometimes and say, 'You know I can't imagine your doing anything wrong.'

But for the most part it was ecstasy, if they embraced, or if they did not. Perhaps George's highest ecstasy was when for three days he had spared her his passion, and he felt in tune with her purity, so that like her he was unassailable. He felt a great pity for all other human beings. He even thought of the poor fat and mottled old fraudulent medium who had written to him about his article, and routed her address out of his notebook, and sent a letter telling her not to despair, because there was some truth in spiritualism, there were mediums so holy that they could pierce the veil between the worlds and could let loose the radiance of eternity on mortal man. It was unfortunate that just after that his passion broke loose and he was her lover more urgently for a night than, he thought, any man had any right to be to his wife. He was afraid he had offended her, for she was very remote all that morning, and would not go out with him, saying she wanted to write a letter. But she had really written a letter, she had nearly finished the box of pale blue fancy stationery they had bought.

As the time for his return drew nearer his distress grew more unconcealable. He would bury his face in the pillow, groaning, 'I don't want to go back!' And she, poor thing, thinking she understood, thinking merely that he meant that he had been happy here and did not want to go back to his work, was kind to him. Sometimes he even played with the idea of not telling her. But he would not let the dead that are damned master him quite to that extent; even if he invoked their aid after he did it, he must align himself with the beloved saved by that one act of confession. He must, to raise one practical point, give her the chance of leaving him, of deciding, even though she would forgive his prostitution of what was to her a holy cult, whether she could face being his wife if he was exposed as a fraud. Remembering the sickening hours he had spent in a Public Library reading up the exposure of Momma in the nineties, he felt he had to put that to her; although he meant to put it to her in the dark house, where Momma's raps under their feet might somehow turn the balance.

So she said again, 'You look so white!' when the cab stopped among the grassy ruts in the road that was already shadowed by the butt of the hill in front of the afternoon sun. George smiled at her, and told her to take her time in collecting the smaller packages, and lifted out the suitcases. Very slowly he carried them up the path and rang the bell at the front door. The patterns of clear glass on the panes of frosted glass seemed to let out darkness into the day, instead of letting the day into the darkness, as it was meant. When the old daily maid came he said, 'How are you, Mary?' and carried the suitcase into the hall. For a minute he stood feeling the full weight of the shadow on his shoulders. Then his eye was caught by something on the hall table, and he bent forward. Then he straightened himself again and looked down the black staircase that led down to the basement. 'Poor old Father!' he said. 'Poor old Momma.'

He turned and went back into the garden, and called out to the cabman who was unstrapping the bigger suitcase, 'No, wait a minute.' He was not sure whether he would ever take Ivy into this house. He thought not. There was a nice big villa opposite the station which called itself a Private Hotel, and they could stay there till he had settled up everything. There was a nice big garden where Ivy could sit. He suspected her of needing sun and fresh air as much as he did. He went to meet her as she came through the gate, took some of her packages, and began to lead her about the garden. 'Here's where a big clump of snowdrops comes up every spring,' he said, and was touched to see that though nothing could be less interesting, she was interested for his sake. Abruptly he asked her if she would mind very much if they gave up being mediums, if they sold this house and went to somewhere like Swanage and kept a shop; and because he saw in her eyes the look of a trapped creature that feels at last kind fingers loosening the spring on its leg, he looked away and squeezed her arm and said, 'That's what we'll do, then.' Then his eyes went back to the patch of earth where the snowdrops came, and he said irrelevantly, 'Poor Momma, poor Momma.' He hardly knew why he said it, he was only filling in time while he wondered whether he would or would not tell her about the two pale blue envelopes, both readdressed, that he had found lying side by side on the hall table. But it did not matter, it would be all right anyway.

# Madame Sara's Magic Crystal

*This savagely satirical short story lampoons the Allies' attitude towards Yugoslavia and its factions during the Second World War, as Rebecca West perceived it. It was found in manuscript and typescript form in a file marked 'Unpublished'. The reason for this is to be found, Diana Stainforth writes, 'in Rebecca West's diary/memorandum of 1942/44, where she says, concerning a visit to Buckingham Palace, "There I met Sir Orme Sargent, Assistant Under-Secretary of State for the Foreign Office, whom I had last seen when I lunched with him at the Ritz. He had persuaded me that the recognition of Marshall Tito was made by reason of our military necessities, and for no other reason. I had sent him 'Marshal Pierrot' (the alternative title), a parody of our press comments on Tito, which imagined the emergence of such a Communist puppet in France, and had informed him I was not publishing it, thus giving guarantee of my willingness to sacrifice myself to the needs of the country".'*

## Marshal Pierrot

In the North of London a wedge-shaped block of flats balances on the top of an Express dairy which is situated between a cemetery and a reservoir much used by sea-gulls in time of storm. In the topmost of the flats Madame Sara, clad in a long robe of clairvoyants' purple, is to be found sitting among that rickety kind of bamboo furniture which is so often found on the frontier between the worlds. She is much the least authentic crystal-reader I have ever discovered in a lifelong search for the psychically gifted, but I frequent her society less for the sake of her revelations of the future than for the beautiful example she affords of fidelity in love. At the turn of the century she had a love affair with a journalist, which she now dismisses lightly by remarking how bad and mad and sad it was, but oh! how it was sweet. All the same she never sees anything in her

167

crystal except newspaper-cuttings. An occasional private letter may creep in, but very rarely. I consider that after forty-three years that is a feather to stick in Fleet Street's cap.

Usually I get little entertainment from her crystal-reading. I can wait till next Sunday to read the cookery column from *The Sunday Pictorial*, which is the kind of thing her unconscious digs up from the future. But the other day I got something from her which interested me. I don't, mind you, believe a word of it. It is plainly impossible that we should ever betray a number of French generals, and that we should ever impose on France first an unauthorized Commander-in-Chief and then a puppet Government. Yet, somehow, the whole thing seems to remind me of something. But I will let my readers judge for themselves.

(From the *Daily News-Lamentations*, 15 May 1944)
The present struggle will probably be known to historians as the Half-hearted War. It is unfortunate that the inertia which has always characterized the Prime Minister seems from the very outset to have left its mark on the enterprise, which is supremely important because it practically marks our first entrance into the fighting arena – of the Second Front. We start this enterprise with a black mark against us, in view of our inexplicable tardiness in embarking on it. Readers will remember that it is more than a year since a Gallup Poll of children under eight showed that seventy-five per cent of little boys of that age and seventy-two per cent of little girls could understand that to reach the Continent, it was only necessary to cross the Channel.

It must now be admitted that, though the invasion has now started, we are doing little to lift that black mark from our name. No detached observer can doubt that the Second Front is being grossly mishandled. For what reason it is hard to understand, there have been heavy casualties; and the failure to establish complete social order in the invaded areas, even after as long a period as three weeks has elapsed since the first landings, can only be ascribed to widespread Fascist sympathies in our military and administrative units. Progressive opinion must keep a vigilant eye on the course of events, and must remember that if we want an early victory against Fascism we must always be ready to blame without reserve every person who is holding any position of responsibility whatsoever, and outside that field of certainty must be ready to suspect everything, of whatever nature. The one source of satisfaction in an otherwise gloomy landscape is the emergence in France of what seems to be likely to be a real popular leader, in the person of Marshal Pierrot. His partisan troops have apparently done valiant work all over France, which it may be hoped will act as an inspiration to the British and French regular armies. His firm and manly proclamations, which declare that he and his men, who number about a hundred thousand alone, can claim to represent France, strike a sound democratic note.

(From any newspaper, Madame Sara couldn't say which. 17 May 1944)
As well as the communiqués issued from the British and French military headquarters, there has been a bulletin issued by Marshal Pierrot. He states that his men have had brushes with the enemy at Tours, Orléans, Bourges, Clermont-Ferrand, and many other points in Central France. A bridge near St Etienne has been destroyed, and the Paris–Lyons railway has been blown up at several points.

(From the report of a correspondent attached to French Military Headquarters, published in any newspaper, 19 May 1944)
. . . Towards dusk a painful incident occurred. Some of the troops returning from the engagement I have just described made contact with certain French guerillas, believed to be followers of the so-called Marshal Pierrot. The regular troops hailed them as friends, but the guerillas opened fire and killed and wounded many of them.

(Again from any newspaper, 15 June 1944)
Marshal Pierrot's Radio Station today broadcast yet another

attack on the French Regular Armies now fighting on the Second Front. He declares that his partisans frequently find themselves attacked by German and French regulars acting in concert, and that they have found many documents proving that certain French Generals have signed pacts with various German commanders, promising them immunity from aggressive action, provided that they themselves are left free to hunt down Marshal Pierrot and his men.

(From the *Daily Toiler*, 17 June 1944)

We are able to give the text of an agreement between General de Chose, commander of the French armies in the Loire district, and General von Ding, commander of the German armies in the same area. This shameful document was apparently signed the day after General de Chose and his gang of traitors had landed on the shores of France in barges made by the blood and sweat of British working-men. It provides that General de Chose should hand over to the Germans twenty tanks, thirty Bren guns, a number of Wellington boots, and four thousand hand grenades, on condition that they permitted him to pass freely about the countryside to harass Marshal Pierrot and his men.

(From 'Simon's Diary' in *The New Simpleton*, 30 June 1944)

I must own that I was very favourably impressed by the three French soldiers who arrived here last week in order to acquaint British public opinion with the treachery of the French generals. Unfortunately I speak no French, and they speak no English, but what they said was translated by interpreters whose impartiality was guaranteed by their membership of the Union of Democratic Control. But in any case the quiet, unassuming manner of the three soldiers spoke for itself. I do not know why some people have been doubtful of these men because they happen to have arrived in London via Sweden. They are obviously of peasant stock, and peasants very easily lose their way when travelling. It also seems to me quite unimportant that when they first arrived in London they went to Free French headquarters, expressed themselves as anxious to rejoin the French army in France, and accepted the usual allowances, returning only after a lapse of some days to say they had made a mistake and that all the French generals were traitors. This again seems to me a very natural error for peasants to make.

Certainly, I found their story of what they had seen going on in France quite plain-sailing and convincing, though sad enough in all conscience. According to them, the French Generals always greeted each other with 'Heil, Hitler!' 'A bas les ouvriers!' 'Merde les pauvres!' 'Passez muscade!' and other recognized Fascist salutes. They made no effort to fight the Germans, and constantly entertained the German higher command to extravagant lunches and dinners. They frequently shot large numbers of their own soldiers who were reported to have democratic sympathies, and regularly went out every evening to ambush Marshal Pierrot's men, whom they brought home and tortured with utmost barbarity. All this seems very credible.

(From the *Sunday Tory*, 30 July 1944)

Reports from the British Military Mission attached to the headquarters of Marshal Pierrot which, under the leadership of Brigadier Prendergast Macwhirter, MP, and Major Thomas J. Smith, DCM, are very encouraging. They suggest that in Marshal Pierrot we at last have a French leader in whom we can feel full confidence as a representative of his people, and with whom we will at last find Anglo–French collaboration a happy and easy task. He is a typical Frenchman. Born in Alsace in 1892, he fled to another country in 1914, and remained abroad until 1928 when he entered France. There he has since led an active life as a strike-leader, often acting in opposition to the orthodox Trade Unionists. He freely opposed the present war in its earlier stages, speaking eloquently at many meetings held to discourage the workers from participating in an imperialistic struggle, but after June 1941 he revised his opinion of how to serve the real interest of France, and ever since has been the life and soul of all that was significant in French resistance.

171

This interesting career has made a truly magnetic personality. He is strongly built, with penetrating eyes and a firm chin, and his manner is at once simple and commanding. He is adored by his men, being stern but just. He rides on a white horse and is said sometimes to walk on the water.

(From any newspaper, 4 August 1944)

Toronto: The mystery of Thomas J. Smith, the Canadian Major fighting with Pierrot's patriots, is today dispelled. A distinguished veteran of World War No.I, he has spent the time between the wars operating in the insurance business in Toronto.

In February of last year he was transferred suddenly to the Army with rank of Major.

Back here in his home town Mrs Thomas J. Smith insists that her husband, DCM, underground fighter, infuriator of the Germans, is fundamentally a little boy and all this is part of a game of cowboys-and-Indians.

(Telegram sent to the Rt Hon. Anthony Eden by Denis Saurat, Professor of French Language and Literature in the University of London, Directeur de l'Institut Français du Royaume Uni. 15 October 1944)

ON BEHALF OF VAST MAJORITY OF FRENCHMEN IN ENGLAND WISH TO RECORD HORROR AND DISTRESS FELT BY YOUR ANNOUNCEMENT MADE THIS AFTERNOON IN THE HOUSE OF COMMONS THAT THE BRITISH GOVERNMENT HAS RECOGNIZED MARSHAL PIERROT AS LEADER OF FRENCH MILITARY RESISTANCE AGAINST THE GERMANS STOP WE ARE UNABLE TO UNDERSTAND WHY THE FUTURE OF OUR GREAT COUNTRY SHOULD BE DECIDED BY REPORTS DRAWN UP BY YOUNG ENGLISHMAN WHO SPEAKS RUSSIAN FLUENTLY AND WEARS KILT AND BY CANADIAN INSURANCE AGENT HOWEVER COURAGEOUS THEY MAY BE AND FIND IT DIFFICULT TO BELIEVE THAT THE CABINET CAN BE SERIOUS IN CLAIMING THAT SO MOMENTOUS A CHANGE OF POLICY HAS BEEN DETERMINED SOLELY ON THE ADVICE OF THESE TWO AGENTS STOP WE BEG YOU TO REMEMBER THE FREE FRENCHMEN WHO IN THE

DARKEST DAYS OF 1940 DID NOT ABANDON THE STRUGGLE AGAINST
THE NAZIS AND WERE PROUD TO STAND SHOULDER BY SHOULDER WITH
THE BRITISH.

DENIS SAURAT.

(From the *Daily Barometer*, 24 October 1944)
. . . and those of us who respect Professor Saurat for his
well-known *History of Religion* and his scholarly studies of the
works of Milton will hope that in future he will realize that a
cobbler should stick to his last. Meanwhile Marshal Pierrot is
showing himself a figure well fitted to promote friendship abroad
and unity at home. Scenes of enthusiasm are reported in all those
parts of France where he has appeared on his white horse. I hear
that he is introducing many reforms into his country which have
been long overdue. There were till recently a surprising number
of illiterates in France. All those in the area controlled by Marshal Pierrot have been taught to read and write during the fourteen months during which Marshal Pierrot has been in power.
Indeed, he has visited many of the schools where these illiterates
have been taught, and has personally given them their lessons.
On these occasions, of course, he leaves his horse outside.

(From a newsletter called *Seven Days*, 27 October 1944)
Those who know smiled when they read of the basinful of
scurrilous abuse of Marshal Pierrot which Professor Saurat
emptied over Mr Eden last week. The explanation lies in the
private interests of the Professor. He is a director of the French
Institut, an organization which made itself notorious a few years
ago by a function it held to inaugurate its new premises. The
Princess Royal, the President of the French Republic, several
peers, and many other notabilities of the same kidney sat on
the platform, many of the women in the audience wore furs,
and a large proportion of the audience arrived or left in motor
cars and taxis; and there was a general feeling that there
was something behind the party which left none too good a
taste in the mouth. But the really amusing thing about the

173

Professor is that when he took the trouble to write *A History of Religion* it was not for nothing. It was to get a reputation for superiority to worldly interests, which he badly needs. For as all his friends say, 'he has given his whole life to Milton'. In other words he owns a controlling interest in Milton, the well-known disinfectant, and thinks of it first, last, and all the time. Hence, the famous telegram of last week. For nobody knows better than the Professor how urgently 'Milton' needs new continental markets, and he knows well enough that Marshal Pierrot will put an end to that kind of filthy exploitation.

(From a letter written by a Frenchman early in November 1944) At last we have fuller details of the incident about which you had heard.

There is a pitiable mistake into which responsible people here are being pushed by someone unknown whose interest seems to be to rob the British of the immense moral prestige with which, after *such* a war, they could have renovated Europe. No nation, however great, can live on broken pledges. And the present mistake in the British policy is transcribed down there with the blood of the elite that has been and is and was bound to be the natural ally of Great Britain's civilizing mission. These letters are so difficult to efface in history.

May I tell you that, in consequence of this mistake, we, the French, oppressed and starved by the Germans through so many years, have seen six thousand four hundred of our elite still left alive savagely massacred by so-called partisans in the second week of September, 1944. It was in the district of Lyons. There were eight thousand of them, amongst them twenty-eight seminarists, scores of students, the best boys of our peasant stock, who left their homes and went into the woods to wait for the Allies. The Free French representative with a War-Council of regular officers was with them. The Allies did not come. But Marshal Pierrot's partisans came, accompanied by Italian soldiers from the North of Italy, and armed with Italian guns, and massacred them down to 1500, who escaped into the Cévennes. That happened when there was not a single shot fired at the Germans, at a time when the BBC was saying that 'Marshal Pierrot is mopping up the last pockets of enemy resistance'. It was with the applause of the BBC that men made mad by fanaticism killed the flower of the youth of our dying people. Such tragedies cannot be forgotten. Imagine the confusion of our people. They did not think that Great Britain and America would make it a condition of helping them that they would submit to a form of government to which Great Britain and America themselves do not submit.

I thought up to the present that this mistake was only a special form of tactics. I thought that Pierrot was only a tactical stroke in circumstances which impose a consideration of Pierrot's political friends. But we have collected sufficient proof now that Pierrot is not tactics but a well-determined *policy* of the Conservatives over here. And now my mind is blank when I look at the future.

(A drift of these passed across the crystal)

M. et Mme Louis Delaye, Mlles Yvonne et Thérèse Delaye, M. et Mme Delaugerre née Delaye, M. et Mme Stephane Négre née Delaye et leurs enfants, et M. et Mme Eustachy et leurs enfants, font part du décès de M. Robert Delaye, leur fils, frère, neveu, et cousin, survenu accidentellement à l'age de 17 ans. On ne reçoit pas.

(Extract from 'Simon's Diary' in *The New Simpleton*, 30 December 1944)

The long and sorry tale of the French Generals has not yet come to an end. I hear these encumberers of the earth are still skulking with a remnant of their troops in the valleys of Auvergne, obstinately refusing to surrender to Marshal Pierrot and pay the just penalty for their collaboration with the Nazis. It shows how half-hearted our Government is in its democratic sympathies that no punitive expedition has been sent to wind up this intolerable situation. I think, by the way, there is a great deal of veiled Fascist propaganda in the criticism of Marshal Pierrot's Government. I do not see that it is any matter for regret that it contains no well-known names. Such a vigorous leader as Marshal Pierrot can easily find new blood. I think too much has been made of the circumstance that an important Ministerial post is filled by the former crossword puzzle editor of the newspaper *Mensonges de Paris*. We English progressives are far too apt to have a soberside contempt for the recreational side of life. And it is certainly most unfair to reproach Marshal Pierrot for his inclusion of certain Ministers who collaborated with the Nazis during the period of occupation. Surely we fought the war in order that we might have the opportunity to make such gestures. The restoration of France by this great man is a great encouragement; and we can turn with lighter hearts to the international task of which I think all right-minded people have become more and more conscious as our special moral obligation. I mean the creation of some sort of Borstal system for the treatment of all our allies except, of course, Russia and America. They must be purged, and purged soundly, for their reluctance to accept social revolution; and our own humiliating failure to produce social revolution, which is entirely due to the refusal of the governing classes to allow the most able of the population to take control of the community, at least leaves us free to administer this purgation. I think we may look forward to 1945 as a happy and busy year.

(There is some doubt as to what the following excerpt can be. Madame Sara declares she saw it in newspaper print, but says that 'the letters looked a bit funny', and I imagine it is a leading article which would be published somewhere on 31 December 1944, if various people should tell the truth, an eventuality which, however, will not happen.)

In reviewing the events of 1944 . . . in reviewing the events of 1944 . . . in reviewing the events of 1944 . . . what fun it would be if one could say what one really thought. Then we could admit that there was one event of 1944 on which we of the Right Wing could look back with satisfaction, and that was the recognition of Marshal Pierrot. Quite apart from the reasons which made us take that step, the way it was taken made us feel fine. We are always a little afraid of the Left-Wing intellectuals. But that's all over now. We feel quite safe in the saddle, thank you.

For the recognition of Marshal Pierrot was a Right-Wing stunt from first to last. We might have told the truth about him. We might have owned up that there was civil war in France, and that the revolutionaries were led by a man called Marshal Pierrot, and that the others who wanted to live in the same sort of society as ours were fighting against him, and that there were good people on both sides, and that probably the best man would win, and anyway it was France's business. Instead we played him up as if all conceivable kinds of right were on his side and all conceivable kinds of wrong on the other side. It was some of our Right-Wing boys who got that idea and worked it out to the last detail. But not only did the Left-Wing intellectuals not offer any opposition to the policy, though it was dead against half their principles, they swallowed it hook, line, and sinker, and even took on the job of selling it to the public. There wasn't any question of leading them up the garden path. They ran up it of their own accord, and fetched up just at that dark spot in the shrubbery we wanted them to be. Honest, it was a shame to take their money. There wasn't a silly story they wouldn't believe, on evidence that wouldn't justify hanging a cat; and I don't think it ever struck them that most of those stories were told them by Government officials. No, we don't worry about Left-Wing intellectuals any more.

Why did we recognize Marshal Pierrot? For several reasons. There are some of us who carry the people in their minds as a good man carries his wife and children. A man works for his wife and children. If he is out of luck he may have to work for them in torturing conditions. Many a man has woken up in the night and said to himself, 'I cannot go on working in that sweat-shop for one more day, it would be better to starve.' Then he has heard his wife and children breathing quietly, and he has known that he was lying, and he has gone on working the next day, and the next, and the next. There are some of us who when they wake up in the night hear the people breathing quietly and know that they would pay any price to keep safe those poor dear afflicted millions. So they go back to their sort of sweat-shops, and do what is demanded of them. And if it is demanded of them in that sweat-shop that they should sacrifice a scruple, they make that sacrifice.

There are others who are not of this kind, who do not read their files and have no notion that the matter is not simple, or who have a fancy that when the mob bursts open the library door they will flash a wide grin, lay a hand on the decanter of second-best port (the best being buried in the gladiolus bed) and roar genially, 'Come right in, boys, and drink a toast with me to Marshal Pierrot.' But most can claim to care for the people, and if the special form of our care is to be called appeasement, in this hour we will not be ashamed of that name. Surely it is not a disgrace to seek the salvation of the people, and often, as many of us have found in our lives, appeasement answers. But if it fails, it is not easy to see what we can do. For then we will have to defend ourselves in the real situation; and then, since the people are now utterly confused by lies, it is not possible to know how we can acquaint the people with the truth in the amount of time which will be left to us. And that is where those others were to blame, for we are men of action whose profession is the deed, but they were intellectuals, clerks, whose profession was the truth. So may the Lord have mercy on all our souls.

As I said at the beginning, I do not really believe that anything in this monstrous sequence of revelations from Madame Sara's magic crystal will take place in the future. Yet all the same, it disquiets me. For, somehow, it reminds me of something, but I can't think what . . .

*30 January 1944*

# The Second Commandment:
## Thou Shalt Not Make Any
## Graven Image

*This appeared in an anthology,* The Ten Commandments, Ten Short Novels of Hitler's War Against the Moral Code, *Cassell and Company Ltd, London, 1945. Avowedly propaganda – of a very high order – it was edited by Armin L. Robinson, who commissioned internationally renowned writers. As well as Rebecca West's story, there are contributions from Thomas Mann (a magnificent tale of the life of the prophet Moses and the formulation of all ten commandments; the commandment in question here is the first, 'Thou Shalt Have No Other Gods But Me'), Franz Werfel, John Erskine, Bruno Frank, Jules Romains, André Maurois, Sigrid Undset, Hendrik Willem Van Loon and Louis Bromfield. Even allowing for unusual despatch in commissioning and publishing, it is unlikely that this project dated much later than 1944, when the tide of war was starting to turn in favour of the Allies and, significantly, considering the theme of Rebecca West's story – and others in the collection – the full monstrosity of what Hitler was doing to the Jewish population in his territories was just beginning to emerge.*

When Elisaveta woke she rang the bell for her coffee, but Marta did not come. When she had rung again and nothing happened, she thought, 'This is the third time Marta has not come this month. She is getting old, probably she will not stay with me much longer. But I will not know what to do without her, she has been with me ever since I was a little girl.' Her eyes brimmed. 'I am still young, but I am being left alone as if I were very old. Everybody is going away from me.'

She reached out for the bottle of rose water and the pad of cotton wool she kept by her bedside to repair the damage done by the tears she shed so much more frequently than was wise in an actress. Then she picked up the script of her new part, which had fallen to the floor when she had at last dropped off to sleep, and began reading the lines

179

to try to drive out of her mind the thought of her husband, David, who might be alive, who might not. With the Nazis there was no knowing, and no hoping.

Dropping it, she pouted the smiling defiances of an imaginary happy woman while she pulled on her dressing-gown, which had to go unmended now that she lived alone, then went along the corridor, drawing back the curtains and wincing as the strong morning light fell on her tired eyes. She went to the kitchen to make the strong coffee her nerves needed before she could face the day.

'No,' she murmured, 'I don't want to go on a trip to Paris – not unless you can move Paris out of France, to some new, exciting country. I've been to France so often. And I don't want any diamonds. I don't want any jewels – unless you can get me some stone that's a cross between a diamond and a pearl. That I might like – though I can't be sure.'

The problem was to say the lines, not as if the woman were a complete fool and meant it, or meant to be funny, but as if she were a sensible woman who was talking nonsense because the cause of her dissatisfaction was so wounding to her pride that she could not name it, yet at the same time to keep on the plane of comedy, even light comedy.

Soon, however, she ceased to say the lines. She was seduced into gentle contentment by the clean white and green paint of the kitchen and the glittering stove and pots and pans, all very bright in the spring sunshine, by the bowl of hyacinths on the dresser, by the good coffee and rye bread and butter, and, above all, by the view she saw between the checked curtains of her window.

People thought it strange of her to live so far away from the centre of the town, in the most distant apartment house, right up on the heights beyond the navy dockyard. Indeed, it cost her a fortune in taxis after the theatre. But it was halfway to being in paradise, looking down on the town from these windows. It might be one of the smallest capitals in Europe, beautiful Copenhagen, but it was like the seat of a king in a fairy-tale. Even when she had dreamed of it as a girl in her father's parsonage at the other end of the country, pouring into the dream all she could imagine of beauty, and knowing nothing of ugliness, she had not seen it as lovely as it was.

Beneath her windows the little white houses stood on the sloping hillside among the budding lilacs with the touching, hopeful quality of a new suburb; there young people were beginning life, or old people ending lives that had been successful enough, since they were still together and had the means for comfort. All turned their faces toward the wide, high floor of the dark-blue sea, crisped now to white horses by spring winds, strewn with the hundred islands, dark with pine trees, bright with the wakening maples and birches, stretching to the white bar of the southern horizon.

At the foot of the hillside the red-roofed cottages of the old fishing village and the long, low, butter-coloured buildings of the naval establishment hid all of the docks save the funnels and masts. From that the raised causeway, blue water and gentle surf on the one side, emerald salt marshes on the other, ran to the tortoise-shaped rock on which the city lay. With its gables and towers it made a shape as clear, as easy for the eye to grasp, as an intaglio on a ring. Its colour was red, a soft drowsy red with nothing harsh in it, the colour that some rose petals turn in potpourri. Behind it rose the pointed hills, dark with firewoods, and above them the pyramids of the snow peaks, all angular, all shapely and austerely cut yet not ungentle, like the houses and churches in the city below.

'Spring is here,' thought Elisaveta. 'Someday soon I will get old Sven to take me to the fisherman's pavilion on the other side of the city, where they give one those lovely prawns, just out of the water and cooked.' Sven was the oldest actor in the State Theatre and he had been very kind to her since David had gone, taking her about to pretty places that were not too noisy and yet were a distraction, and being patient with her when the distraction failed and she wept. She poured out another cup of coffee.

'No,' she murmured, 'I don't want to go on a trip to Paris – not unless you can move Paris out of France . . .'

Then it was that she saw what was happening. She set down her cup and saucer on the table so that the coffee spilt. She ran to the window and grasped the ledge and stared, her mouth falling open as if she were dead, as she might well soon be. The causeway was no longer dust-coloured, empty save for an occasional lorry or tradesman's cart, as it always was at this hour. It was dark with a moving column of men and vehicles more brutal than lorries, monstrous even when seen from a great distance. Crying out, she ran from the kitchen into the living-room and turned on the radio. A voice, smug with successful treachery, was shouting that the city need feel no further fear, for Hitler had taken it under his protection.

Elisaveta threw herself down on the divan, sobbing and cursing and drumming with her fists on the Chinese silk coverlet. A part of her which remained calm thought wistfully 'I am not a great beauty, I am not a great actress, I am only so-so. It is not fair that I should be asked to take part in great events of history. I could have borne with misfortunes that are like myself, within a moderate compass. I could have nursed David through a long illness. I could have kept my dignity if the Director had taken a dislike to me as he did to Inga and pretended that I was old long before I really was, and made me play character parts.

'I could have gone on all my life long being patient if David and I had had a child and it had been delicate or stupid or wayward, but all this abduction and killing and tyranny, I cannot stand up to it.

'When Truda married and left the theatre and it was a question who should play the leading parts, the Director said to me, "Now, Elisaveta, this you can play and that, but not Hebbel's Judith and not Ann Whitefield. You have not the big bones, you have not the broad veins." I wish somebody would come and say to me: "You cannot be expected to live under Hitler. You have not the big bones, you have not the broad veins."'

She sobbed for a little while, and then thought: 'And it is all wrong. It is like having suddenly to start acting without any make-up on in the middle of the lounge at the Excelsior Hotel, or in the silk department in Lacherman's store, to have to face these tremendous events in the familiar places where one has lived all one's everyday life.

It would have been better if these horrible things were happening to one in some fantastic country which one had reached only after many days' travel.'

It had been at the holiday resort which everybody in the city went to in summer, which she had visited two or three times a year ever since she had become an actress, that they had taken David away. It was on the road going through the pinewoods to the lake with the overhung cliff called the Trolls' Castle, to which every family in the kingdom had at some time or other made an excursion, that the grey automobile had stopped and the four men had got out and thrown the raincoat over David's head. It was there that David had fallen to the ground and been kicked by the heaviest man in the crutch of the loins. As she heard again his scream, she prayed at one and the same time that he would come back to her again; that he had long been dead.

Then the automobile had driven off in the direction of the frontier, and she was left alone, looking about her in horror at the pinewoods she had known so long, as if they had lied to her.

There had been nobody on the road, for it was lunchtime. She had run into the woods and had found a picnic party and had stood in front of them with her hands stretched out, as if it were of them she was asking mercy, and had said: 'My husband is a Jewish refugee, he is David Adler, the writer. The Nazis have come in an automobile and kidnapped him. What shall I do?'

The men and women and children had sat quite still on the grass, holding bitten slices of bread and sausage in their hands, staring at her in hostility because, though they were kind, she looked so strange, what she said was so strange. When they understood, they had gathered round her in a circle, helpless as if the sun had turned black. They looked about them at the forest as she had done, as if they were victims of a betrayal, as if they had been asked to a bridal and had found themselves at a funeral, their dress improper and an unexpected grief taking advantage of them. Their country which had always promised small delights, small comforts, small, swiftly terminated sorrows, and had kept its promise, would henceforth, now that the Nazis had come, practise such bizarre deceptions against which the mind could not forearm itself, being committed to health.

'Whom shall I turn to now?' she wondered. 'Who will be strong enough, who will be a refuge in whom I can find shelter, and remember the time when everything was healthy, so that I do not go mad? I will be poor, of course. Even if I could bear to act now, they would not let David's widow play in the State Theatre. Probably they will steal my savings. But that does not matter. It is seeing horrible things I will mind. My head will go. Even if it had not been David whom they took away in the automobile, even if it had been a total stranger I had never set my eyes on before, the mere sight of what happened would have shattered me. I am afraid of going mad, all alone. Who will come to save me now?'

Old Sven was too old. He had wept sometimes at the thought of the Nazis coming; now he would be utterly overcome, no shelter for her but a charge on her kindness. Besides, it was not an actor to whom one would wish to turn at this time. If there had been a great actor in the State Theatre, then that would have been all right; he would have been co-creator with the greatest men whose works they had performed. He would have been wise, as they were. But there was nobody at the State Theatre now who was more than an interpreter; one might as well look to a violin apart from its player for comfort in a crisis.

If one knew a great author, though he might be helpless as a child in material matters and in human relationships, and perhaps even naughty as a very naughty child, he would have wisdom. He would know what to put in the other pan to counterbalance the evil that was dragging down the scales. Because writers, if they were good, really knew something. She did not care for books and rarely read one from year's end to year's end, but she knew from the plays in which she had acted that writers were not just trying to amuse people or to make money. They were making clear a pattern in life that was there but had not been noticed by ordinary people. Often in her own life, something would happen to her that would strike her as important and strange, and yet not altogether unfamiliar; as if she had been told long ago that that was how it would be in such circumstances. Then she would remember, 'But, of course, that is what the play *A Pack of Cards* was about! That was what Feierabend was trying to say . . .'

Well, there was Egon, and there was Nils. They were certainly the greatest dramatists in the country; and some said they were among the greatest dramatists in Europe or in the world. Their plays were performed in Germany and France and England and the United States. They were wise; she had learnt that over and over again. And she was so sure of their friendship that as soon as she had thought of them she stopped weeping and got up from the divan and set about dressing. As she filled her bath she wondered which of the two she liked better. She knew them equally well; she had acted in all the plays they had written during the last ten years, and each had been her lover. As she lay in the warm water she wondered which she would find the kinder friend. She had always thought of them as being, as nearly as is possible for two human beings, of exactly the same value. They were, indeed, so much alike physically that people often took them for relatives; of middle height and slim though not unsturdy, with strong blue eyes and light-brown hair and high cheekbones, they might have been fishermen from the islands constrained to an elegance unusual even in dwellers in the city. For they had beautiful clothes and shoes and gloves, all from London, much more beautiful than those worn by the shipping millionaires who could have bought them up ten times, successful though they were. They practised their dandyism as a joke, because of its incongruity with the other characteristics they had in common; for they were alike in being grimly industrious, quietly indifferent to the opinion of the community, and able to pass at a moment's notice from life as it is lived by intellectuals to life as it is lived by sailors and farmers and timbermen. They seemed to have nothing in common with the bourgeoisie into which they had been born. They were a mixture of peasant and aristocrat. Of course the resemblance was not necessarily innate. They had probably developed it in the course of their lifelong friendship; for as neighbours' children they had gone to school together, they had left home together to go to Berlin University, they had worked side by side in a shipping office and had been sent to work for the firm's correspondents in London and New York at the same time.

185

They had both had plays produced when they were twenty-five. Fame had come to them soon and simultaneously and shortly afterwards they had married two very beautiful girls belonging to the best families in the city, girls of very much the same type, Magda and Hildegarde.

Tears came into Elisaveta's eyes as she thought how terrible the coming of the Nazis would be to Magda and Hildegarde, to whom life was entirely a matter of happiness, running up the scale from fur coats and pearls to loving husbands and perfect children. There was no consolation for the moralist in their reverse, for like Egon and Nils they had taken their good fortune with laughing modesty, as undeserved good luck and an occasion for generosity. It was just like seeing a bowl of lovely fruit overturned in the mud. 'Perhaps I can do something for them,' thought Elisaveta, 'help them pack up if they are going to their farms up in the country.'

Drying herself, she thought: 'But which will be best able to help me, to make me bear it, to keep me from going mad? Egon or Nils? Which is the wiser?' She tried to remember their plays, though her mind was shocked; she did not find it so easy to grope her way back to the parts she had acted in the happier times. Egon's plays were more complete, of course. It was as if a home were shrunken to the size of a doll's house, and the front taken away. The rooms were as if flooded with soft bright light; that was the effect of the dialogue, which was always tactfully balanced, never too brilliant to divert the audience's attention from the development of the story, but never dull. One could see everything the family was doing, and with exquisite art their visible life was made to reveal their invisible life. She had often found it necessary to follow dramatists round the theatre till there was an opportunity of saying: 'Please, I know I am very stupid, but I would like to understand why I have to say this line in the third act?'

But Egon's characters were written in the script as plain as lifelong acquaintances; doubt was not possible. Looking back on the roles she had played for him, she saw herself in a party dress with a bodice glittering with sequins and a full skirt of white net, dancing about an attic, twitching away dark cloths that were draped over a dozen or so of these doll's houses, which had been stripped of their façades and were emitting bright light, against which the silhouettes of tiny people told the truth about themselves.

To act in Nils's plays was quite different, and perhaps not so agreeable, though one received great praise, and the audience was given over to one in a disarmed state, almost in a trance, out of which their weeping and their laughter proceeded in a natural, uncensored form. It was as if one had become a totally strange woman and walked in and out of darkness on to the lighted stage, with one's face veiled; and as if the attention of the audience became a person and crossed the footlights and tore off the veil and was at first disconcerted and then either enormously amused or enormously horrified by what it saw.

'They are both great men,' Elisaveta said to herself, 'but in different ways. You can't compare things that don't set out to be the same. Anyway, I am not clever, I can't judge their work.'

But she had other material that she could consider. Both Egon and Nils, she remembered, had been sweet lovers, giving her much, going from her without unkindness. Though she would now have preferred that there had been nobody in her life but David, it nevertheless made her happy to remember how they had first made love to her.

Egon had come on her as she was sitting waiting for the Director in his office, which was built right on the roof of the theatre and opened many windows to the sky. She had come to show the costume she was to wear in a nineteenth-century comedy: a little bonnet with a feather, a close jacket edged with dark fur, a tiny muff, a crinoline, all of which made her feel fragile and remote, the sort of woman who is cherished. Egon burst in without expecting to see her and came to a halt, crying: 'But how lovely you look! How lovely you are, Elisaveta!'

That was eight years before; but she still smiled with pride at the memory. She had not been a great beauty, but she had been lovely enough, she had no reason to feel sorry for herself. And she was not merely a pretty woman, she had something that would go on when she was old and ugly.

Nils taught her that. He had first noticed her one day when he had passed her in the corridor and had seen that she had been crying. He had paused, stared, looked away, and gone on, and then turned back and gripped her by the shoulders.

'Why are you crying? Little one, you must tell me why you are crying.'

She had not wanted to tell him, for it was a childish matter of hurt pride, of professional vanity, and he had ceased to press her for the explanation, crying:

'Elisaveta, do you know I have never thought of you before as a human being! I've thought of you just as an actress, just as somebody who acts in my plays, but of course you're a human being, you laugh and cry, and I believe you're a wonderful human being! Elisaveta, put on your hat and come out with me, I want to talk to you, I want to learn what you are like.'

He had really liked her. Ever since he had treated her with respect and interest. He evidently felt that she was one of his kind of person. To think that had often given her back her self-confidence when she had lost it.

With both of them she had been very happy; but all three of them belonged to the breed of artist to whom no love affair can mean anything unless it leads to domesticity. Love that is not a solid background for artistic achievement, that did not build a home to write in, or to come back to after the theatre, might be very beautiful, but it was not worthwhile going to any trouble to keep it alive. Egon and she had ceased to be lovers when he went on a trip to the South Seas; Nils and she had mislaid each other when he went to the United States to produce a play and she went as guest artist to the state theatres of three neighbouring countries. But ever since they had been close friends, not that they saw each other so very often, since they were all very busy, but when they met, whether at a party or café or in each other's homes, they found it difficult to separate, the two men talked so well when she was listening.

'To which of them shall I go first?' she asked herself and could not give an answer. It was pure chance that took her to Egon's house. The two men lived only a few doors from each other, at the foot of the hill in her part of the city, in a row of seventeenth-century brick houses looking on to the quay which was no longer used. It was always as quiet as a convent garden, and it was horrible to turn around the corner and find the German troops there among a crowd of townsmen, screaming and jerking at their weapons. But they were screaming dismissal. Evidently some high German dignitary had been addressing the people, for they were streaming back into their houses, their heads down, their faces blank with shame. They knew what she knew, that many of them would soon know pain and death, and that goodness would, from now on, be mocked. These people in the turd-green uniforms were those who had taken David away. Her knees gave way under her and she went to Egon's house because it was nearest.

The old servant, Johanna, was bent and weeping. Her famous lace-encrusted cap, which she made after a fashion that used to be followed by the women of the outer islands, flapped over her shaking, bluish face. With the obstinate formality of a proud servant she greeted Elisaveta as if this were an ordinary visit and there was nothing terrible about the day, and when Elisaveta spoke to her sympathetically, she asked coldly if she wanted to see Mr Egon and announced her in proper fashion. Elisaveta clapped her hands with joy as the door opened, for they were both there. Egon and Nils.

They made a very pleasant picture, the two handsome men sitting in a room which was famous for its beauty. It ran from the front to the back of the house, and the great windows let in the lovely Scandinavian sunlight, the clean spray-washed sunlight. On the windowsills there stood a line of model ships, the lovely nervous systems of their masts and riggings in silhouette, and on the walls there were pictures of the sea and portraits of old sailors and their wives. The furniture was such as the sailors and merchants of the city in the times gone past had bought for their own comfort and that of their descendants. Some had been fetched from England, because the workmanship of Chippendale and Sheraton was so well reputed. There were Persian carpets also bought in those times by the townspeople; and the floorboards had been polished with such frenzy as sailors bring to the keeping of a beloved ship. Sometimes Elisaveta had thought it a shame that the descendants of the men who had made this room had not followed the sea like their fathers, but were merely writers. But when she saw Egon and Nils sitting there, as quiet as if an end to all happiness and safety had not come, she knew that they had done better than following the sea, they had followed danger wherever it might be found.

They stood up, exclaiming with pleasure at the sight of her.

'I came here', Elisaveta said, 'because – oh, first of all, because I feel frightened and I wanted some comfort and you have always been my dear friends, and secondly, because I thought you might be going away and I wondered if I could be of some help to Magda and Hildegarde, in packing or looking after the children –'

'But, Elisaveta!' they said to her, 'have you forgotten?'

'Forgotten what?' she asked happily. It was lovely when they laughed at her; it was as if they were picnicking up in the mountains, or dancing in a sailors' inn at a little port.

'Have you forgotten that Magda and Hildegarde and the children all went off for a holiday in England just a month ago?' asked Nils. 'Why, you came and gave all the children presents to amuse them on the journey and you waved them goodbye!'

'But of course I did!' cried Elisaveta. 'Oh, but how wonderful! Oh, Egon! Oh, Nils! To think that Magda and Hildegarde and all the children are safe! What a blessing!' She flung her arms around the neck of each man in turn and kissed him. Their eyes became wet; they looked down on her tenderly, as if in gratitude for speaking of what they could hardly trust themselves to speak.

Egon muttered, 'Yes, as you know, now it is, comparatively speaking, all right for us.'

'But how mad of me to forget that Magda and Hildegarde had gone to England!' exclaimed Elisaveta. 'I actually saw them off on the boat. We stood on the quay and waved to them!' She looked at them with troubled eyes. 'But you know my memory is not what it was before they took David. Oh, it's all right for parts, but about real things it is very wrong, it is as if my mind were running away from them. Hitler has begun to kill me. You will see, he will kill us all.'

'No,' said Egon.

'No,' said Nils.

'Do you really think anything will survive him?' she asked.

'Yes,' said Egon.

'Everything,' said Nils.

'And in the meantime,' said Egon, 'he will not prevent us from drinking a toast to Magda and Hildegarde.'

'No,' said Nils, 'not just to Magda and Hildegarde. To all our beloveds. To David as well.'

Egon hesitated for a moment and Elisaveta could see what was in his methodical mind.

'No, Nils,' she said. 'Perhaps it is not in good order to drink to people who are alive and to people who may be dead all in the same toast. We will drink to David later. But now the toast to Magda and Hildegarde, may they be happy and well, may you all be together again before long.' They drank, and she set down her glass so that she could dry her eyes. 'I am not weeping because I am sad,' she explained, 'or frightened – though of course I am frightened. But it is only now one realizes what people mean to one, and I have had such glorious times with Magda and Hildegarde and the children – up in the mountains in summer, and here on birthdays and on Christmas Eve. You have been lucky, getting those two – not that you don't deserve it, my dears.' Her words died into her handkerchief.

They watched her tenderly, nodding. 'You must come and live with one of us,' said Egon.

'Yes, indeed,' said Nils.

She shook her head. 'No, no, hadn't you thought? I am not a nice person to be associated with. David was a Jew and I am polluted. Besides, I must stay in my home. Don't you feel that? You wouldn't either of you want to leave your houses and go somewhere else just to be safe. One has to stand by what one is. I lived in my apartment with David. I won't stop living there just because they have come.'

'Yes,' said Egon, 'that is how it must be. One must go on living, just as one used to do, not modifying one's conduct in the least.'

'Oh, my dear!' she cried. 'Do nothing rash!' As the two men gently laughed, she spoke more wildly, seeing again the tallest of the four Germans kick her husband so that he fell in the dust of the road. 'No, do not laugh, you are too good to be destroyed by the devils. You must stay quiet.'

191

'No, Elisaveta,' said Egon, 'we cannot stay quiet. We are going on exactly as we went on before our country was invaded at three o'clock this morning.'

'So that was when it happened?' sighed Elisaveta. 'I have heard nothing. Did anybody resist?'

'On the frontier about three hundred of our soldiers died,' he answered. 'They told us that when they gathered us together on the quay. They told us that without shame, almost as if they thought it would make us respect them and like them better.'

'That is why we must go on behaving just as if they were not here,' said Nils, 'to avenge those three hundred men.'

'We must maintain the right,' said Egon.

'That's not the reason that I see for standing out against them,' said Nils. 'The right can maintain itself. If it can't do that it isn't the right. If we all behaved like rascals and licked the swines' boots, sooner or later something would prove to the people who came after us that that had not been the way to happiness. Something would recommend honour and decency to them. I think we have got to stand out against the Germans because it is a necessary scene in this drama we are enacting.

'You see, Elisaveta, you are a distinguished actress and a distinguished woman. Egon and I are certainly good playwrights and we have tried to be good men. None of us three has lived falsely to what we believe. What we have thought to be true we have said, what we have thought to be right we have done. This has given us power, wherever we are known, partly because people respect courage, partly because they know we have thought a little further past the point where they themselves stopped thinking. Now, because of some earlier scene in the play, at which we were not present, the Germans want that sort of power, and believe that they can take it from us as they could, and probably will, take these lovely glasses out of Egon's cupboard, the pictures off these walls, those model ships away from the windows. They think that burglars can really rob. If we go on showing that we have power, that we have an inexhaustible fount of it within ourselves, which is there because of what we are and what we do, and cannot be ceded to any other person or seized by him, then we will make the burglar doubt the efficacy of burglary, then the world will become safe for good people. Now, Egon, fill up our glasses again and let us drink to David.'

He broke the stillness that fell after they had drunk the toast by saying, 'Are we not fortunate, we three? For we have glory thrust upon us. Not one of us could, however weak our flesh might be, collaborate with the Germans. For you, Elisaveta, are married to David Adler, who was a Jew, and, thanks be to God, Egon and I have never written a play that was not good for a Nazi noose around our necks.'

Out on the quay there were scuffling, and some cries, and the pitter-patter of machine guns, but none of the three turned to look through the windows.

'But it is not going to be easy,' said Egon.

'It is not going to be easy or difficult,' said Nils. 'It is going to be not so much the thing one does as the thing that life does to one.'


But Elisaveta found the winter after the coming of the Nazis easier to endure than the one before. She no longer felt so empty for lack of David. It was more as if she were working her way to him. Materially, of course, life in Copenhagen was hard enough. As one who had polluted her race by marriage to a Jew, she could not see many of her friends. Old Sven, she knew, was actually frightened lest she come to see him, though he sent her loving messages. By the invention of new taxes and by levies for special purposes the Nazis took possession of the better part of every citizen's income; and this looting was carried out more thoroughly when the citizen was Jewish. She had not been extravagant, and had taken her manager's advice about investments, and consequently had fancied she would never be in want, but she would have gone hungry now if she had not been able to eat with Egon and Nils whenever she needed.

She was able to help herself by going around to the few Jewish households in the city and giving the children, who were now debarred from all but a single unsanitary school, lessons in foreign languages and elocution. That pleased her. The Jewish parents felt an inordinate concern because their children's education had been interrupted, and when she listened to their complaints she was reminded of David's intellectual greed. What with these lessons she had not much time on her hands.

Egon and Nils were still allowed to live in their houses, though their defiance of the invaders was uncompromising, but most of their servants, except the very old ones, who were now in a state of collapse, had been taken away to wait on German officers in their billets; so Elisaveta could be of real service to her two friends by sometimes helping the old women with the cooking and mending.

The great physical discomfort was cold, of course, because the Germans had taken all the fuel, but everybody was suffering that alike, and one did not feel that one was being cold because people did not like one enough to share their warmth with one.

Elisaveta might almost have described herself as happy with this new, narrow, and impoverished, but glorious way of living, had she been sure that it was going either to continue until the English won, which she thought unlikely, or to end in the simultaneous annihilation of herself and her friends. But Egon and Nils denounced the invaders and their doings not to their fellow townsmen, whom they refused to involve in their activities, but to the Nazi officials and German officers.

They constantly visited the law courts where townsmen were being tried for offences against the invaders and afterwards they made protests to the authorities and plagued the tax collectors with complaints against irregularities. Indeed, whatever was left of legality in the country they fearlessly exploited. On days that had been kept as national festivals they went through the streets carrying flowers which they laid before the statues of great men which the city had taken pride in placing in its most beautiful squares and esplanades.

It was said that the Germans had not imprisoned Egon and Nils because of their great reputation in the United States; but it seemed certain that that slight strand of consideration would presently break under the strain they both put on it. Elisaveta did not know how she would be able to go on if the Nazis took Egon and Nils as they had taken David. Nor did she know how she would be able to go on if she saw any more horrible things. Once she started to cross the

Clocktower Square on her way to a Jewish pupil and, noticing the upward stare of horror on the faces of the people about her, followed it with her own eyes to its sources, and saw six young men hanging from electric standards.

Thereafter she went about the city carefully, watching the people in front of her as she came to any public place, in case they came to a sudden halt. But one Sunday morning she forgot her carefulness. She was hurrying down to Egon's house to help Johanna cook a goose which some peasant had smuggled down to the city under his coat as a gift to the man who, as was known all over the country, was keeping the habit of its freedom alive. Egon had asked some of his friends to share it, and Nils was going to send along some of the last of his French wine. Wrapped in a big cloak she had once worn in a historical play and bought afterwards because it was so becoming, she turned the corner of the quay where Egon and Nils lived, with her head down, butting the February winds. She was thinking what good things they would be able to cook for days to come with the goose fat, when she heard a yelled word of command, raised her eyes, and had just time to cover her ears against the sound of the shots. Ten young men, some of them blindfolded, were standing at the end of the quay, where the little light tower was. At the other was a party of soldiers with raised rifles. The ten young men all fell forward on their faces. Near her was another crowd of young men, surrounded by soldiers, who prodded them with bayonets to make them look at the ten figures lying face downwards on the cobbles. She ran to Egon's house and brought the knocker down rattling on the door until Johanna opened it.

They sat together, the two women, talking about how they should cook the goose, in the great airy kitchen, which looked out on a little garden where in summertime tall roses bloomed between the dark savory kitchen herbs. Now the roses were sticks tied up in sacking, and the herbs were stumps level with the ground, and a light miserable snow was falling.

Suddenly old Johanna burst into tears. 'Yes, I know,' said Elisaveta, 'it was terrible, it was terrible; however, one must go on.'

When the goose was in the oven Elisaveta went up into Egon's study. It was right at the top of the tall house, just below the

attics. He was sitting at the window, looking out at the angry sea
and the distant pine-black islands. His desk was littered with sheets
of manuscript covered with unfinished paragraphs, thrown down in
a disorder usually alien to him, and when he greeted her he was
careful not to turn his face towards her. She went and stood beside
him, looking out at the dark skies and the darker waters.

'Did you see it?' he asked.

'Yes,' she said, 'I walked straight into it. Why was it done? Who
were they?'

'Just ten young men of all sorts who had not seemed amenable,'
he answered. 'The beasts read out their offences, but it was all very
vague. I didn't recognize them all. There was the son of an orchestra
conductor, and the son of the Greek professor up at the University, and
Dr Brand's son, and the boy who used to serve ice-cream sodas in the
pastry cook's by the Cathedral. And there was old Sven's nephew.'

'Oh, poor old Sven!' she wept. 'But, Egon, such children!'

'Such children,' he agreed. It came back to her, what she had seen:
the ten bodies lying lumpishly like amateur actors practising a fall, on
the familiar, pretty cobbles, the crowd of boys looking at their dead
comrades with eyes that did not dare grow bright with rage and pride,
that were like the eyes of defeated old men.

'Do you mind if I cry?' she asked Egon.

'I am crying,' he said.

They sat silent for a time.

'I am trying to think out something that Nils and I are going to
write together,' he told her. 'Something in quite a new style for us.
Much more concentrated, much more impressive. It will have to tell
stupid and wicked people what their stupidity and wickedness are, in
quite a few words.'

'It is to be about this?' she asked.

'Yes,' he said.

'Oh, be careful,' she mourned, 'be careful!'

'We are being careful to do what we must do at the right time for
the sake of our city,' he said.

It was in her mind to cry out, 'But then what will become of me?'
That would have been, however, wholly disgraceful.

'I hope', he said, 'you have not brought trouble on yourself by associating with us. You must certainly not come near us tomorrow or the day after.'

They were silent for a moment, and then he muttered a phrase, repeated it, repeated it again, and then broke off with an exclamation of annoyance. 'It won't do,' he said. 'It's not the sort of thing I'm used to doing, and, anyway, it's very difficult in our language. It would be easier in English or in French.'

'I do so admire you for knowing what you want to say,' she said. 'To be so certain of what should be said you must see quite clearly the meaning of this event, how it fits into the scheme of the universe. That's what I don't know, and I feel lost for want of knowledge.'

'I don't quite understand you,' he said. 'Whatever Nils and I know, you know it better. There's nobody with greater moral sensitiveness than yourself. I can't imagine you doing a dishonourable or cruel action.'

'You speak too well of me,' she said, 'and, anyway, I am not the keeper of my own conscience. My father and my mother taught me that certain things were wrong, and I have always feared to do them and feared the people who did them. Also the other way of behaving is more happy and cheerful. There is really no choice between them for a sensible person. But, indeed, there I often fail. You would be surprised if you knew how horrid I am. But this is not what I mean. You have some knowledge about the universe which I have not got. That is shown by the fact that you are going to write something about what they did to the boys on the quay this morning which is going to explain it to people, which is going to move them to do something. I wish you would tell me what it is.' Her tears broke out, but she spoke through them. 'Because it would make me able to bear what happened to those ten boys, it would make me able to bear what happened to David. You must tell me, Egon, because I cannot go on like this, seeing evil lording it everywhere, seeing good and wise and pleasant people done to death. What does it mean? Why is God doing this to us?'

Egon said slowly, his eyes looking far out to sea, 'The problem isn't easy to formulate, but one knows where one is, I think. There are certain things in life which are beautiful. If there is a God they would please Him. If there is no God they would still represent ultimate values. That is proved by our assumption that they would please Him, for if He does not exist He is the embodiment of our dreams of what is highest. So one must give one's life to preserving these values, to letting love, and justice, and truth have their way with men.'

She twisted her fingers in and out, acting her perplexity. 'But the boys on the quay were innocent.'

'Certainly.'

'But they are dead. Nothing will make them live again. What is there in existence that makes that right?'

'We must pit ourselves against those who killed them.'

'But that will not give them back their lives. It won't bring David home to me.'

'If there is a God,' said Egon, 'then we shall all of us live again, and you shall be reunited with David. If there is not a God, then it will still be well with us. It is well with the boys on the quay because they died on the side of virtue. It will be well with you and me and Nils because we too kept our integrity. You must try to remember, Elisaveta, that defeat such as Europe has suffered at the hands of the Nazis is not of real importance. You cannot reverse the meaning of an abstract noun by an event on the material plane. Love and justice and truth remain what they were before Hitler came to power, and we are participants in their unchangeable glory. Forgive me', he added shyly, 'if I sound priggish, but I am a writer of comedies and it is not my trade to write expressions of faith. But that, my dear, is what I believe.'

'It is a very beautiful belief,' said Elisaveta. She crossed her knees and swung her foot backwards and forwards, staring at it. It came into her head how much she had disliked Rome. She had liked the country outside it, she had enjoyed eating at wayside inns under vine pergolas and going to see the waterfall at Tivoli; but she had hated those great columns which were everywhere, either lying about on the ground or standing up in quite insufficient numbers to make a comfortable building. She saw love and justice and truth as just such columns.

'You have comforted me greatly, Egon,' she said. But the feeling of bleakness in her bosom was so absolute that she got to her feet, anxious to go somewhere where she need not think of this desolate faith and see the dreary winter sea. 'I must go down and baste the goose now.'

She would have been glad if Johanna had wanted her help; but the old woman was querulous and asked it to be remembered by all parties concerned that she had been cooking geese long before anybody else in the house was born. So Elisaveta wandered into the great sitting-room on the ground floor, where the ships were, and the pictures of great sailors and their wives. There the table had been laid for the lunch-party, and at the sight of the gleaming table silver, it occurred to her that the rest of the silver in the room, the candlesticks and the French winetasters which were used as ashtrays, was less bright. So she went to Johanna and asked if she should polish it, and Johanna said that she might, so she sat down by the fire, which was larger than usual, for Egon and Nils had been saving up their fuel for the party, with a candlestick on her lap and a soft cloth in her hand and a saucer full of polish. She was busy rubbing away and crying her eyes out when Nils came in with a basketful of decanters in each hand.

He set them carefully down on the floor and went over to her and knelt before her. When she covered her wet face with her hands he took them in his own and made her look at him.

'Were you thinking of David?' he asked. 'Or of what happened today?'

'Of neither,' she sobbed, 'of the world. Of life. Oh, Nils, it is all so dreary.'

'So dreary?' he repeated. 'Do you mean what we are going through, the lack of food, the darkness, the cold, those brutes? Dear heart, it will not last for ever.'

'That is not the point,' she cried, 'for even if it goes, even if it does not come back in our lifetime, it will come back some time. History is full of suffering. And I have asked Egon what it all means, and he tells me it has no meaning except that love and justice and truth are beautiful things, and that we must serve them always, and that if there is a God, He will let us into heaven as a reward for our service, and if there is not we will have the satisfaction of having done the right thing. And it is so dreary. It is like going to school for ever. Nils, it is so dreary!' She put down the candlestick on the floor and wept into the crook of his arm.

'Hush,' said Nils, 'hush. That is what Egon thinks; and it has taken him a long way. There is obviously much in his creed, because the way it has taken him is all in the opposite direction from barbarism. But I do not think like Egon.'

She drew back from him and looked into his face. 'What is your belief?'

He was disconcerted. 'My belief,' he said, 'my belief . . . why, Elisaveta, it is written behind all my plays, as yours was written behind all your performances. I do not know how to put it into words directly. But I must try . . .' Abruptly he lifted her out of the chair and held her by the shoulders, facing him. 'Run away and put on your cloak. There's no use merely talking about these things. They must be made visible. We of the theatre know that. I'll take you somewhere where you'll see what I mean. I intended to go there anyhow, and finding you has made me forget it. Hurry, or we will be late.'

'Where are we going?' she asked in the hall, as he wrapped the cloak around her.

'If I told you,' he said, 'it would not be true, the words would give you a false picture of what we are about to do.'

The day was so harsh that when they got outside the door they ducked as if they had been shot at, and Elisaveta moaned. But he said, 'It is not far,' and he took her up one of the steep alleys leading off the quayside.

'But this only leads to the St Sebastian Place,' she said, 'and there is nothing there but the church.'

'Trust me, trust me,' he said, 'and hurry, hurry, we must hurry.' When they came to the square he guided her straight across it to the church, but she hung back.

'But surely we are not going to church. I cannot go to church, I am an unbeliever, I have not been to a service for many years.'

But he said, 'Hurry, hurry, this is such a service as there has never been before, and as for unbelief, there is more to be said on that subject than we used to think.'

And indeed the old red church, which was not large but very noble, having been built at the time when the fishermen were simple yet rich, held such a gathering as she could not have conceived coming together in real life. All the people in the village were listening to the service, all the people she had known for many years, and they all looked changed as by a long illness. She could not have imagined such a uniformity of appearance save as the result of make-up under common instructions. Yet they did not look weak. On the contrary, a strong pulse seemed beating through them, and in the eyes they turned to the altar there was a fervour as if there was great acting about, and they were all exalted by it, as often happens in a theatre when a genius is playing. But it was not the pastor who was that genius, for he was in the same state as his flock, and had he been among them he would have been undistinguishable from them. He, like they, seemed astonished by the words of the service as they left his mouth. They seemed to linger in the air before him that spoke them and those that listened to them, like the spray that rises from a great waterfall and hovers as if considering the greatness of the leap and slowly rejoins the stream below.

Elisaveta did not wonder why this talk of God and man and giving His only son should have moved her deeply, for it had nothing to do with her troubles; it was impossible to work out from it any way of regarding what had happened to David as anything but an undeserved suffering. But sometimes a play whose total effect was true was made up of lines that, taken by themselves, carried no great significance. Certainly the total effect of the service was true. As she stood among the pale and anguished but not passive people she felt her courage like an eagle in her breast, she felt herself capable of going on tunnelling until the earth crumbled and she was with David.

'Go forward now,' whispered Nils, as the worshippers went forward to the communion table.

'I have not fasted,' she murmured.

'What happened this morning is like a fast for all of us,' he said. 'Let us go forward.'

They had to stand a long time, for almost everybody in the village had come to take communion. When at last Elisaveta came to the pastor and brought down her lips to the chalice, the meaning of her act escaped her. She wondered, as the wine passed her lips, why Nils had made her do this thing, but when she stood erect again, and passed on, the action achieved, she would have liked to utter a high clear cry of relief. But she was doubtful lest she had done an unreasonable thing, lest she had been, as men say, hysterical.

Out in the street, she turned to Nils and looked at him in question. He drew her to him and kissed her on the lips. There were many people standing about, but even those who were gazing at them with interest, remembering that in other times this man and this woman had been the embodiment of romance and art, did not look offended or even startled. The kiss was grave, it was a part of that terrible day.

'But why did you make me go there?' she asked. 'Why did you make me take communion? I tell you, I have long been an unbeliever. And God did nothing to save David.'

'Why did we all go there today?' he said. 'All but Egon, who does not think as we think. We went to keep faith with someone who is hidden from us because he is at the end of time. Someone to whom we have promised that though man is born in ignorance of the meaning of life, in ignorance of his own nature and the nature of the universe, and though his environment perpetually tempts him to remain in this ignorance, he shall come to understanding. That someone may be man himself, or it may be God. I do not know. My ignorance on that point is part of the ignorance we have promised to dispel.'

'But how do you know?' she asked. 'How do you know we made that promise?'

'Idiot, idiot!' he cried, laughing and pressing her arm against his body as they hurried down the alley. 'I know we made it because I find myself keeping it. What have I done all my life but write and write and worry out a little more of the truth than was known before? And if I had stopped doing that, if I had retired on what I made, and had lived here in my fine house on the quay and sailed my boat among the islands and gone up to the mountains when it was time for the snow or the flowers, I would have felt and you would have felt, and all the world would have felt, that I was guilty of a breach of faith. And you, too, if you had left the stage, then too we would have felt that a vow had been broken.'

'Oh,' she said, smiling faintly, 'how could anything I do matter?'

'In each of your performances you told us something of what a woman is, and that is something we do not yet know. We do not fully know what a woman is, we do not fully know what a man is, we are working in the dark even when we try to train and discipline ourselves, which we must do before we start out to explore the universe. You did a great thing for the people who saw you, and you must not forget it, for without that you cannot understand what you are or what you meant to David. You are a wonderful and important person, Elisaveta.'

'But I cannot play the great parts,' she murmured.

'Idiot, idiot!' he cried again, 'you filled out the parts which the author had not known how to write completely. But we are talking too much about ourselves, we artists cannot get off the subject. That is right in a way. I would never have written if I had not been the kind of child that runs about all day saying, "See what I've done," you would never have acted if you hadn't been the kind of child that runs about all day saying, "Look at me." But what I tell you about, this vow, is not special to us because we are artists. All the world takes it and keeps it or breaks it. There are fishermen, there are shipwrights, there are industrialists, there are politicians, about whom we feel, "So! That man is showing the world what it is to go out to sea for fish, to build a boat, to handle machinery, to govern the state," and there are housewives about whom we feel, "There is a woman showing the world how to be a man's mate and bear children," all showing how a human being can bear himself under such a destiny. Then there is a feeling amongst all that it is well, that the harvest has been brought in. But there are other men and women who never master a craft, whose lives never take on recognizable form before the eyes of the world. They die without learning anything or teaching anything, and we have the feeling not only of loss but of resentment, as if they had not played their part in a common enterprise. All this must mean something, it must relate to something in the future. So I go to church, though I am not certain that Jesus was in fact the Son of God, and I take communion with Him, because I know what I promise has relation to what he demanded of men, and I do not think He can find my action offensive, for I am willing to give my life, which is all I have, to keep my promise. And I am sure I was right, for I felt happy doing it. Didn't you, Elisaveta?'

'Yes, I did,' she said. 'But I wish I could see what was happening more plainly.'

'But this is not a plain matter,' he said. 'We have been put in a ridiculous position by Providence, let us admit it. We find ourselves acting in the second act of a play, and trying to do justice to our parts, without any recollection of the first act, and no knowledge of what the third act is to be. There is nothing to do but to guess, and use the guesses of other men whom we recognize as likely to have guessed well. And one can do it, one can get through. Why are you not dead, seeing what happened to David?'

'That surprises me too,' she said, nodding.

'I tell you, there is something afoot, it is not merely a question of maintaining standards which already exist; of preserving love and justice and truth. It is a question of finding out something, of discovering what we ourselves are, what God is, and what the two, mankind and God, are to make together.

'Why, that is the reason the Nazis are wrong. It is not just that they come into this country, which is ours and not theirs, and that they kill us and put us in prison and take away our food. That would be justified, if they could achieve any respectable end by doing it. But they cannot. It interferes with the keeping of the promise.

'It is the duty of mankind to understand the universe. We need, as people say when there is a lot of work to be done, every pair of hands. And no man can say for another what is his best way of increasing his understanding.

'We must all follow our own path to reality. And that is what Nazism will not let us do. It puts this man here and that man there, and it takes no heed if each says: "But from this place my eyes can see nothing." And it will not listen when men who are in places where they can see tell us what they have seen. If what they have seen is of any moment, the Nazis will choke their voices in their throats, lest the new things they have discovered should weaken the Nazis' claim to govern. They wish to repudiate the promise, they want to disappoint the person who is waiting for us at the end of time. They wish to make the world a dead planet. We who rebel against the Nazis are keeping it bright. Elisaveta, did your mother and my mother ever think we should do anything as wonderful as this? As keeping a star alight?'

'I think that is what they hoped,' said Elisaveta, 'but we did not think their hopes would come true.'

They had turned the corner and were on the quay, which was still commanded by the death of the young men. There were many of the townspeople standing about looking towards the place where they had died. It was still guarded by German soldiers, looking gross and trivial in their health.

They ran into the house and she picked up the candlestick off the floor where she had left it, and sat down and went on with her polishing. Nils went over to the basketful of decanters he had set down and clicked his tongue with annoyance.

'This room is not warm enough for wine,' he said. 'See, we will have to put it close to the fire. Chambertin it is, to drink with the goose. A man's food, a man's drink.' As he bent over the hearth he looked up at Elisaveta, 'All the same, it will be difficult, you know, before the end. For me certainly, for you probably, if you are not careful.'

'I have always taken the coffee as it comes out of the pot,' she said, 'strong or weak. I am not boasting of the strength of my character, it is probably a sign of weakness.'

'That is not what I mean,' said Nils. 'Now what I believe comforts us, but it may fail us when we are in very great pain.'

'Oh, perhaps,' she said.

Presently she went out to help Johanna with serving the goose. When she returned, Egon had come down from his study and the room was full of guests. They were all old friends of hers. There was the Director of the State Theatre, and two other dramatists, and the leading actor, and the editor of the newspaper, with their wives. All were haggard as if after prolonged weeping, but they were gay.

'What a lovely colour you have, Elisaveta,' said the Director, handing her a glass of spirits.

'Yes,' said the editor's wife, 'and we know it's all natural. We have no cosmetics now. Tell us, Elisaveta, how is it done?'

'Bending over an oven!' laughed Elisaveta.

'But none of us have anything to put in our ovens,' said the Director, 'so that raises another question.'

They were poor jokes, these people would have been ashamed to make them in the old days. But they served. Everybody moved through warmth, they spoke and held their heads as if the Director still had the theatre he had spent his life in making, as if the actor and the dramatists could still fill the loving and attentive air of the theatre with what in their breasts longed to be out there; as if the editor's office were not given over to his enemies; as if the wives were sure that none would come to their houses by night in lorries.

There was a great ohing and ahing when the goose was brought in, and much laughter when Nils told them they could eat up Egon's bird with an easy conscience, and not think guiltily of those they had left at home, for he also was a dramatist and a peasant had brought him a goose too, and he had had it cooked, so that each guest could take away a slice or two for his family. And there was a great deal of joking about the affinity between geese and dramatists.

Then when the wine was poured out, the men had much amusement in guessing the vintage, which was easy, and then the year, which was more difficult, while the women mocked them for their solemnity over what, after all, was meant to be swallowed.

It was at that point in the meal when the door was flung open and the Nazi major came in. He stood on the threshold and stared at them. Egon and Nils rose to their feet, but with quick movements of their hands bade the others remain seated.

'*Heil Hitler!*' said the major.

There was a silence. They all thought of the dead boys and felt ashamed as they murmured '*Heil Hitler!*' but it was not worth suffering for such a little thing.

'Who are these people,' the major asked Egon, 'and why are they here?'

'They are my friends,' said Egon. 'They are here to have their Sunday dinner with me, as they often did before you and your people invaded our country.' He indicated the spread table, his guests, with their fine heads, the delicate glasses holding wine, the polished silver candlesticks. 'This is how we lived before you came.'

The major did not answer for a moment. He looked about him with a steady, absorbed gaze as if he were trying to take away what he saw with his eyes. Then he shouted: 'I have come to warn you that if you have gathered together in protest against today's disciplinary action, you do so at your peril. In the past we have been too gentle with your people, you intellectuals who refuse to collaborate with the New Order. But after today there will be no more forbearance.'

His voice stopped suddenly. His hungry eyes, his pale, angry, resolute, and perplexed eyes stared ahead of him. The guests stirred on their chairs. The Director licked his dry lips and put out his hand for his glass, but stopped when it was halfway to his lips, fearing to offend the intruder. He looked as if he were about to propose a toast, and the editor picked up his glass and held it likewise, and murmured so softly that only those who sat about the table could hear it: 'To the ten young men.' Then all the other guests raised their glasses and Egon and Nils too bent down and found theirs.

The gentle movement, which seemed concerted and yet surely could not have been, startled the major. 'Stand up!' he cried, as if in fear. 'Stand up!' They all stood up. More than ever they looked simply like people drinking a toast, not like threatened people, nor yet like defiant people.

It was the actor's wife, her whispered words merely a faint pulse of sound not to be heard save by stretched senses, who said again, 'To our ten young men.' They all raised their glasses to their lips, halting them before their breasts according to the custom of their country.

'What are you doing? What are you doing?' shouted the major, striding into the room.

Egon explained wearily, 'My friends were about to drink a toast. When you told them to stand up, they naturally continued.'

'To whom is the toast?' shouted the major.

'To some other friends,' said Egon. 'You must excuse us, Major. This was a great city for friendship before you came.'

Rage flamed in the major's face. 'Why do such people as you

continually reproach us? We came here to protect you from the British, we came here to bring you prosperity by giving you full rights in the New Order. And we are your brothers, our people and your people are Nordic Aryans.'

Around the table all stood with their heads down, looking at the heeltaps of their toast.

'We have discovered the way of living which is right for mankind,' cried the major, 'and we are trying to share our discovery with you, and you will not accept the gift.'

Around the table all shifted from foot to foot, still looking down at their glasses.

'But tomorrow,' cried the major, his voice rising, 'it shall be different.'

The door crashed behind him. At the table all sat down again. They laughed, as people do who see somebody behaving in a way which betokens him their inferior, but who are not naturally unkind. Nevertheless, there was a chill wonder in the centre of their laughter, for they knew that tomorrow it would indeed be different, perhaps by the considerable difference that lies between life and death.

'Thanks be to God,' said the editor's wife, who had two chins and was as plump as a pigeon, 'he did not stay so long that the gravy grew cold,' and she polished her plate with a crust. The others broke into affectionate jeers and teasing, then Elisaveta told them there was something else to come, and there were many exclamations of surprise, the party forming again into what it had been, but harder, more impregnable.

When she and Johanna brought in the sweet they had made the day before of bottled fruit and sago flour, the sweet which was the unvalued standby in the town before the Germans came and took everything away, they clapped and cheered so that it was heard outside on the quay; and they were not sure that there were not some soldiers among those who came and peered through the windows. But they did not turn their heads to look.

'That German', said Nils, taking his seat after he had been around the table pouring out some sweet French wine to drink with the fruit-pudding, 'said that he and his kind had discovered the way of living that is right for mankind. That means they believe they could draw a picture of God's mind, and another picture of man's mind. What blasphemy! For we know almost nothing.'

Egon put down his spoon and fork. 'I am not with you there. I think we can draw a picture of God's mind, and it is not like the picture that he drew, and the Major is wrong and we are right.'

'No,' said Nils, 'that is why it was written in the Tables of the Law, "Thou shalt not make unto thee any graven image or any likeness of anything that is in heaven above, or that is in the water under the earth."'

'But I have read the reason for that commandment somewhere,' said one of the guests, 'and it was an attempt of the Jewish priesthood in the time of Moses to shepherd the faithful away from the competitive religions of the day, which practised an attractive form of idolatry.'

'Yes, yes, that was the reason in the first place,' said Nils, 'but it has survived, like the rest of the commandments, because Moses had an eternal mind, and his thoughts have meaning upon meaning on which the centuries have hardly time enough to ponder. For me that commandment means that man must never pretend to have accomplished that task which will be unfinished so long as he himself exists. He was set upon earth in order that he may acquaint himself with reality, which is an impossible task, since reality creates itself anew as fast as the learner learns. It cannot be achieved until the end of the earth, the death of the stars; and until then a man lies if he says that he has learnt his lesson and can make a graven image of anything that is in Heaven above, or that is in the earth beneath, or that is in the water under the earth. Little sketches we can make, but that is all, and they are worthless unless we know that they are worthless, that we as yet lack the knowledge to make them true images. It seems to me that a man's work is dead and a man's soul is ideas, if he does not make this admission that all sacred truth is still veiled, for this relationship between us and a mystery is what constitutes life. Why need we go on living if all is known? Why do we love life so if it is not that it enchants us with its magnificence of undisclosed secrets?'

Egon said, 'I would not agree with you. One wants to live because life is agreeable!'

'Today,' said Nils, 'I have a good opportunity of pointing out to you that quite often it is not.'

Egon smiled and shrugged his shoulders. 'And as for man's mind, we know enough to say we know all.'

'Yes,' said someone, 'since Freud has shown us the way we are justified in saying we know all.'

'I feel', said Nils, 'that our experience during the last few months has transcended all the experience of our previous lives.'

'What you mean', said Egon, 'is that we have adhered to our principles, and that we have been happy in doing so.'

'No,' said Nils, 'I have thought thoughts and felt passions which were unknown to me before. I have learnt many things about my own nature which had before been hidden from me.'

Some of the guests said, 'Yes, I know what you mean,' and one said: 'No, one is what one always has been,' and the others were silent.

'Yes,' said Nils, 'one is always what one has always been, and what one always will be. But what is that? And how extraordinary it is that we should be here at all on this earth, which spins about in space, incommunicado, knowing nothing of other stars or of the limits of space! And how extraordinary it is that being alive makes other things, trees and flowers and fish! And how extraordinary it is that anything should exist at all! I thought these things when I was a little boy, and then I was distracted by immediate problems. Now they come back to me, and I remember the words of the Bible "– for I speak of a mystery".'

'But Saint Paul used them when he was speaking of marriage,' said one of the dramatists, smiling, 'and there is nothing more ordinary than marriage.'

'There you prove my case,' said Nils, 'for there is nothing more ordinary than marriage, yet it is a mystery.'

A stir ran about the table, and they all smiled, a troubled and reflective smile. Some of the husbands and wives were happy, some were not.

'No,' said Egon firmly, 'it is something very reasonable. Reasonable and beautiful.'

One or two of the guests laughed aloud, the rest were silent. The editor's wife wiped her mouth and said, 'Are not all marriages happy since the Germans came? A stick is something to lean on, whether it is straight or crooked.'

'Yes, yes,' said the guests, nodding their heads.

'Then there is something mysterious about marriage,' said Nils, 'as mysterious as the action of the molecules that make a stick solid and not liquid.'

'Oh, you mean mysterious in that sense,' said Egon.

Nils's hands made an exasperated flutter and Elisaveta rose and pushed back her chair, saying, 'And now I must go out to the kitchen, for our hosts are giving us coffee, real coffee and some real milk!' At which the company clapped their hands, and the editor said, 'Ah, they have sold themselves to the Nazis. You can see. There's everything here.'

When all the guests had gone home they called in Johanna and thanked her for preparing the feast. Elisaveta stood up, stretched herself and yawned, looking at herself in a mirror. She was still slender, it would be years before she looked old. 'Oh, dear, I would have liked that party to go on for ever,' she said. 'It was fun. But now I must go and help Johanna wash the dishes.'

'And we must go upstairs and get on with our piece of work,' said Egon. 'Have you thought of anything, Nils?'

'Yes, I have it all in my head,' said Nils.

'Then we had better go upstairs at once,' said Egon. 'The printers will be here early this evening.'

'I will say goodbye now,' said Elisaveta, 'so that I won't disturb you when I have finished. Goodbye, dear Egon and dear Nils. And thank you for all the good food and all the good wine, and the lovely gay party. It . . .'

She had been about to say that it had made them forget what was happening outside, but that was not true. The gaiety of the party had existed inside the terror of the day, enfolded by it.

'Elisaveta,' said Egon, 'we must say goodbye. A real goodbye. You must not come back here. It will not be safe.'

'Please do as we say, Elisaveta,' said Nils. 'It would be a heavy

211

burden on us if we were to bring suffering on you. And you must be here when David comes back.'

She thought, 'But I am going to David. Why should he come back here, where there will be nothing?' But in order not to burden them, she opened her arms to them and raised her face for their kisses.

'Goodbye, Elisaveta,' they said.

'Goodbye, my dear, dear friends,' she answered. She stood in the hall and watched the two men go up the wide, wooden stairs and bending over the banisters of the landing to kiss their hands to her before they passed out of sight, and then went to wash the dishes.

That evening she burned everything in her apartment which she did not want to fall into the hands of strangers. She made up her best silver spoon and china into brown-paper parcels and marked them with the names of her closest friends, and left them with her neighbours. She burned all of David's letters quite without regret, for she felt she would not need them much longer. Then she went to bed and slept well, and woke up early the next morning. She emptied all her little stock of sugar into her cup of coffee and had it sticky-sweet, as she liked it but had never dared have it for fear of growing fat.

She dressed with care, choosing her warmest clothes. Then she went out into the lifting darkness and took the way down to the fishing village. As she was hurrying through the square which marked where the village and the new suburb met, her eye was caught by a patch of white on the wall of a house, which had not been there the night before. Shuddering in the morning cold, she stood in front of it and waited till the light should be clear enough for her to read it. Some passers-by joined her. When the patch could be seen for what it was, some moved away, others raised a defiant cheer. She read it with excitement that brought her heels off the ground, that set her bobbing up and down like a dancer waiting for her solo to begin.

It was a manifesto, signed by Egon and Nils, telling how the people in the city looked upon the killing of the ten young men the day before. It said that they considered the Germans common burglars for invading their country; it said they knew the German story that they had come only to forestall the English was a stupid lie; it said that they regarded the murder of the ten young men on the previous day not as an impressive display of power, but as the kind of idiot brutality that burglars might show to householders whom they had bound and gagged.

It said that the people of the city did not respect the Germans because they had conquered them; a feat that an organized band of gorillas could have achieved. They despised the Germans as undermen who had interrupted the normal course of life towards greater goodwill and understanding because they were unable to take part in it. The people in the city, the manifesto said, had many faults; they were often shamefully petty and mean. But they had tried to make their city a glory to the earth.

Generation by generation they had had more and more recourse to the kindnesses of science, they had listened more attentively to art, they had felt greater charity towards children and the unfortunate, they had been juster masters of themselves and more willing servants of their fellows and had asked more urgently what purpose their lives should fulfil. And they had availed themselves gratefully of such happiness as had existed since the beginning of the world.

Now the Germans were trying to cancel this achievement, they were trying to blot out the city and make it as if people had never come out of the forest centuries ago and built huts on the sea-shore and carved boats out of tree trunks. They had blotted out freedom, they had blotted out virtue, they had made time meaningless. But those who wanted to be meaningless were likely to be successful; what was nonsense was soon forgotten. An idiot's babble was not remembered. The Germans would perish.

Elisaveta wished David were standing beside her reading it. He would have appreciated it. It was written in a style that was peculiar to this city. A man born there who read this while far away, without signatures, would have said to himself, 'This was written by one of the townsfolk.' But it would have been understood anywhere in the world. It reminded those who might have forgotten what life was like before the Germans came, and what it had been like afterwards.

It reminded those who might have forgotten what the difference is between good and evil. It set down in black and white what the city had been, and what the Germans were.

'How I would have liked to speak that from the stage!' thought Elisaveta, and she turned away and hurried off, as to a rehearsal. She went to Egon's house; not from the quay but by the back door, for fear that Egon would try to turn her away, and be distressed by her resistance. It was the day when the family washing was done, so she helped Johanna collect the linens. A great deal had been used the day before.

Then there came a thunder on the door, and Johanna went to open it. She came back, saying, 'They have come!'

Elisaveta kissed her and thanked her for all she had done for her in the years she had come to the house, and then went out of the kitchen.

In the living-room Egon and Nils were standing face to face with a group of soldiers, one of whom was reading something aloud to them. When she came in, a soldier said, 'Yes, this is the woman who is always with them. We have orders to arrest her also.' Nothing could have been more convenient. She had feared she would have to strike one of them before they would take her.

She and Egon and Nils looked at each other and laughed, full of the joy that had visited them every now and then during the last few days. But at the same time they swayed on their feet, sick and dizzy with fear. For now began the pain and torture.


They were in prison for some weeks, and were frequently taken before a kind of judge and questioned about a conspiracy which did not exist. As their answers were necessarily unsatisfactory, they were always beaten after these inquiries. During this time they did not see each other, but one night at the end of three weeks they were all brought into the hall of the prison and were then taken to the railway station and put on a train that went through the darkness in an easterly direction. It was pleasant to be together again, but the guards would not let them talk much.

Elisaveta was at first ashamed of letting Egon and Nils see her as she was. Her hair had become lank and greasy, her face powder had been taken from her, and of course she was not properly clean. But they did not seem to mind, and they were dirty and unshaven.

In the morning they got out at a railway junction on a plain and they were made to sit all day and to lie all night in a small room with stone floors where the railwaymen filled their lamps. The air stank with oil and it was very cold. They had to sleep on pallets laid on the stone floor. But now they were over the frontier and the railwaymen spoke a foreign language, so that they felt as if they were a stage nearer the end of their journey, which would be the extremity of foreignness.

In the night Egon said to Elisaveta, 'Did you think our manifesto was all right? People who read it would remember how things were, wouldn't they?'

'You did not think it was too long, did you?' asked Nils.

It was just like a first night in the old days. Before the guard could tell her to shut up, she said, 'No, not a word too long. I said to myself as I read it, "I would do anything to speak that from a stage."'

The next day, towards noon, they heard a train puff in and shortly afterwards they were taken out on to the platform. The train was made up of cattle trucks. They had been looted from France, for they had *8 chevaux, 40 hommes* painted on them. But when the guards led them up to a truck and slid back the doors, they saw more than forty human beings inside. There were men, women, and children, all strange in appearance. Their skins were yellow and greasy, their black hair was screwed up into tight verminous curls, in their eyes black irises swam in oily yellow whites, and they stank.

As the door opened they cried out in terrible squawking voices, 'Let us empty the bucket, let us empty the bucket!' and they pointed to a bucket in the corner, standing in an overflow of excrement. One of them by a clumsy touch upset the bucket and it streamed to the open door where Egon and Nils and Elisaveta were standing. They shrank back, but the guards pressed them in, jeering at them, 'You chose to be with the Jews, you shall go with them to Poland and you shall see what fine friends they have.'

They had to pass over the spilt excrement to enter the truck.

The door slammed behind them and they looked about at the filthy

215

and lousy people, smiling insincerely and thinking 'Perhaps Hitler was right about the Jews after all.' But an elderly man, his face red with insect bites where his beard met the smooth skin, put out a hot and slimy hand and pulled at Elisaveta's skirt and said, 'I cannot see you, lady and gentlemen, because the brutes have broken my glasses, but this I know, you do not smell. And it makes me remember that once I did not smell, that in those days I despised people who smelled. Do not despise us, lady and gentlemen, for till we got on this train, we did not smell. I was a lawyer, most of the people here were superior workmen, and we used to be clean and have clean homes. But we have been three weeks coming across Germany in this train. So do not despise us. It will not be just, if you despise us.'

'No,' said Elisaveta, 'we are artistic people and so not much in the way of despising people. And in any case, I am the wife of a Jew.'

'For God's sake,' said Nils, 'do not think we despise you. We respect you and we need your help. For the joy that sustains me against the Germans comes and goes. And now it has gone from me.'

'Let us tell each other who we were,' said Egon, 'and who we shall be again.'

For a time the Jews found relief in recalling their names, and where they had lived, and in what comfort, and which of their kin had been unusual in talent. But soon they fell silent, for they were cold and hungry and tired and sick, very sick. There was one man who seemed to be near death; he sat with his eyes closed and never spoke.

When night came, they found there was no room to lie down straight, but Egon and Nils and Elisaveta were able to huddle into a heap. Their bodies ached, and presently the tears began to stream down Elisaveta's face.

'What is it, little one?' asked Egon.

'What is it, darling?' asked Nils.

She blubbered like a child, 'Things are crawling over me.'

The two men burst out laughing and hugged her, saying, 'Poor little Elisaveta,' and it seemed no shame to her.

In the middle of the night she awoke and smelled the stench of the degraded animals around her who had been people, and shuddered with horror because that was what the Nazis would make of her also.

But Nils felt her shudders and drew her close to him, and she saw that his face was shining.

'That joy,' he whispered, 'it goes away, but it comes back.'

'Yes,' whispered Egon, 'one cannot be anything but proud of being here.' They listened to the roll of the carriage wheels and the snoring of the people around them, and ecstasy flowered in them. 'We will not always be happy like this,' Nils warned her. 'One must keep on remembering that. It goes away, though it comes back.'

During the morning, towards noon, there were a grinding noise and an upheaval. Everybody shrieked. When there was stillness again they found they were piled up on the wall of the truck which was opposite the door. The truck had been tilted on its side. Some of the metal stanchions had freed themselves and were sticking out dangerously. Some of the people at the bottom of the pile were quite still. Egon had injured his left arm and shoulder. There was blood trickling down Nils's brow. Elisaveta's body had been bruised. After a little, guards came and opened the door, which was now above them, and helped them to get out. They found themselves on a vast, unbroken plain, covered with light snow. Many people were screaming. The guards told them to go over and sit on an embankment that marked an irrigation ditch, about two hundred yards from the railway track.

'Come on,' cried Elisaveta to Egon and Nils, when she found herself on the ground, happy as she had been all her life when she found herself starting to do a new thing. But they answered only faintly, and she perceived that their injuries were not like hers. She found herself crying, as she still did when she woke from a bad dream: 'David, David!'

She turned to the guards and told them that her friends were ill, but remembered, before their faces told her so, that they were pitiless. There was nothing to do but guide Egon and Nils to the embankment. But long before they got there she saw that Egon could not go any farther.

'Can we carry him together?' she said to Nils. But Nils did not hear her. He looked at her with the blue, blue eyes of a fisherman from the isles, and she saw that he too had nearly gone from her. 'Go on to the embankment,' she said to him. 'Sit down with the others and I will come to you.'

217

Egon had sunk on his knees. She laid him flat on his back, hoping that he was only faint. 'What is wrong with you, my little child?' she asked. As she spoke, she noticed that his eyes were immense and pellucid as a child's.

He said, 'Under my arm.'

She could not look for a second, for a spurt of light had caught her eye and she had to see what was happening to the train. It had been derailed and flame was passing from the engine, where it had already died, and there was a ghost of smoke haunting a pile of twisted metal along the whole long line of trucks. The telegraph pole had been brought down and the broken wires were like twisted fingers pointing to the sky. Then her mind returned to Egon. She put her hand under his armpit and found that blood was pouring down inside his waistcoat. One of the metal stanchions had struck him and cut a vein.

A guard was passing, clubbing some Jews before him. She cried out: 'Among these Jews, there may be a doctor. Find him. This man is dying. He is a great man.' The guard looked at her with empty eyes, that made nonsense of the fact that there are Jews who are clever and not animals to the extent of being doctors, that Egon was a great man. Again she cried, not from habit, but out of a desire that a miracle would happen, 'David, David!' But in this place there was no one to bear Elisaveta's part but Elisaveta. She put her hand under her dress and tore her chemise away from its shoulder straps, rolled it into a pad and put it against his wound, set her knee to it and pressed.

'Elisaveta,' said Egon, 'I regret nothing. I have served the ideals of love and justice and truth.'

'My little one,' said Elisaveta, 'my sweet one.' The pad against her knee was wet. Egon's face was becoming white, blue white.

'I have done what is right,' he said faintly.

'And more than that,' said Elisaveta. But she knew as she spoke that he was about to die.

'What is right,' he repeated more faintly still.

'My baby, my little baby,' said Elisaveta; and before she had ended, he was dead.

She stood up and looked about her. The train was now wholly

consumed by fire; the guards were beating towards the embankment such of the Jews as were old or so infirm as not to have already accomplished the passage. On the white snow all human beings were like small, black flies. She scanned the horizon and saw no farmstead save one that might be six or seven miles away. The Jews would not be able to walk so far; she herself doubted if, after her less exhausting imprisonment, she still had the strength to do it. She remembered that this was a country of vast estates. It might well be, now that the electric wires had gone, that it would be many hours before help reached them. The cold was so extreme that it ran in a network of fire through her body. Most probably she, and everybody she saw before her, would before very long be dead of exposure.

She looked down on the calm and noble face of Egon, from which life had in this little time completely departed. Then she looked up at the grey sky, across which an army of violet-blue clouds was riding.

'So this is where doing what is right leads me,' she said to herself. 'This is the reward of serving love and justice and truth. One dies on a snowy plain under an empty sky.'

She knelt down beside Egon and tried to say a prayer, but her friend was gone; she might as well have been praying beside a cod laid out on a fishmonger's slab. She said, 'And it is just Egon's word against the Germans. Love against hatred, justice against tyranny, truth against lies.' Under this sky it seemed uncertain that a wise man would take one side rather than the other. She stood up and walked away. Even if there had not been Nils to look after, she would not have stayed with him. He was dead, he had gone away; and it seemed as if David was gone away too, farther than she could go to find him.

There were many people lying on the embankment, moaning and crying out against the pain of injuries and the searching cold. The lawyer whose face was red with insect bites was walking up and down at the foot of the embankment, calling out in mockery: 'Hail, Jesus Christ, King of the Jews.'

She found Nils stretched out between two children who were nuzzling against him for the sake of the warmth of his body. The blood was still running down his brows, and she bound it with what was left of her chemise. He smiled, but his eyes were set on the sky

219

above him, and he said, 'Thank you, Anna.' Now she was entirely alone. Nobody in the world was thinking of her.

'I am thirsty,' he said later.

She melted a little snow in her hand and propped his head up while she poured the water into his mouth. But his eyes sought the sky again and his head tilted back, and the water dribbled down his chin.

'Nils, Nils,' she said, 'keep your chin down or you cannot drink.' But she spoke half-heartedly, because she liked to watch him looking up so eagerly. It made her heart live again.

'I have had enough water,' he said, 'and I want to look at the sky. I am watching a great battle.'

She sat back on her heels and watched the clouds ride above her. The cold was torturing her, but the sustaining joy had returned.

'No,' said Nils, and shut his eyes. 'It is no use. One cannot see the battle. The sky is too small a frame.'

But every now and then he opened his eyes and looked up at the sky, until the dusk came, and the snow began to fall.

# Parthenope

*This short story, previously collected in* Rebecca West: A Celebration, *The Viking Press, New York 1977, first appeared in the* New Yorker, *November 1959.*

My Uncle Arthur had red hair that lay close to his head in flat, circular curls, and a pointed red beard, and his blue-green eyes were at once penetrating and bemused. He was the object of mingled derision and respect in our family. He was a civil servant who had early attracted attention by his brilliance; but the chief of his department, like so many English civil servants, was an author in his spare time, and when he published a history of European literature, my uncle reviewed it in the leading weekly of the day, pointing out that large as was the number of works in the less familiar languages that his chief supposed to be written in prose, though in fact they were written in verse, it was not so large as the number of such works that he supposed to be written in verse, though in fact they were written in prose. He wrote without malice, simply

221

thinking his chief would be glad to know. My uncle never connected this review with his subsequent failure to gain a promotion that had seemed certain, or to have the day as snug as civil servants usually had it in the nineteenth century. But in the course of time his chief died, and my uncle rose to be an important official. However, he did a Cabinet Minister much the same service he had rendered his chief, and he never received the title that normally went with his post.

So he seesawed through life, and I liked his company very much when he was an old man and I was a young girl, for it was full of surprises. When I asked him a question, I never knew if his answer would show that he knew far less than I did or far more; and though he was really quite old, for he was my father's elder by many years, he often made discoveries such as a schoolchild might make, and shared them with an enthusiasm as little adult. One day he gave me no peace till I had come with him to see the brightest field of buttercups he had ever found near London; it lay, solid gold, beside the great Jacobean mansion Ham House, by the river Thames. After we had admired it he took me to nearby Petersham Church, to see another treasure, the tomb of Captain Vancouver, who gave his name to the island; my uncle liked this tomb because he had spent some years of his boyhood in Canada and had been to Vancouver Island when it was hardly inhabited. Then we had tea in an inn garden and it happened that the girl who waited on us was called away by the landlord as she set the china on the table. His voice came from the kitchen: 'Parthenope! Parthenope!' My uncle started, for no very good reason that I could see. There had been a time when many ships in the British Navy were called after characters in Greek history and mythology, male and female, and therefore many sailors' daughters had been given the names of nymphs and goddesses and Homeric princesses and heroines of Greek tragedy. The only strange thing was that it was a long time since British ships had been christened so poetically, and most of the women who had acquired these classical names by this secondary interest were by now old or middle-aged, while our little waitress was very young. She had, as she told us when she came back, been called after a grandmother. But my uncle was plainly shaken by hearing those four syllables suddenly borne on the afternoon air. His thin hand plucked at the edge of the tablecloth, he cast down his eyes, his head began to nod and shake. He asked me if he had ever told me the story of the Admiral and his seven daughters, in a tone that suggested that he knew he had not and was still trying to make up his mind whether he wanted to tell it now. Indeed, he told me very little that day, though I was to hear the whole of it before he died.

The story began at the house of my grandmother's sister, Alice Darrell, and it could hardly have happened anywhere else. When her husband, an officer in the Indian Army, died of fever, her father-in-law had given her a house that he had recently and reluctantly inherited and could not sell because it was part of an entailed estate. He apologized for the gift, pleading justly that he could not afford to buy her another, and she accepted it bravely. But the house lay in a district that would strain anybody's bravery. To reach it, one travelled about eight miles out of London along the main Hammersmith Road, the dullest of highways, and then turned left and found something worse. For some forgotten reason, there had sprung up at this point a Hogarthian slum, as bad as anything in the East End, which turned into a brawling hell every Saturday night. Beyond this web of filthy hovels lay flatlands covered by orchards and farmlands and market gardens, among which there had been set down three or four large houses. There was nothing to recommend the site. The Thames was not far distant, and it was comprehensible enough that along its bank there had been built a line of fine houses. But at Alice Darrell's there was no view of the river, though it lay near enough to shroud the region in mist during the winter months. It was true that the gardens had an alluvial fertility, but even they did not give the pleasure they should have done, for the slum dwellers carried out periodical raids on the strawberry beds and raspberry canes and orchards.

These stranded houses had been built in Regency times and were beautiful, though disconcerting, because there was no reason why they should be there, and they were so oddly placed in relation to each other. They all opened off the same narrow road, and Aunt Alice's house, Currivel Lodge, which was the smallest of them, lay at the end of a drive, and there faced sideways, so that its upper windows looked straight down on the garden of the much bigger house beside it, as that had been built nearer the road. This meant that my grandaunt could not sit on the pretty balcony outside her bedroom window without seeming to spy on her neighbours, so she never used it. But when my Uncle Arthur went to stay with her as a little boy, which was about a hundred years ago, nothing delighted him more than to shut himself in his bedroom and kneel on his window and do what his Aunt Alice could not bear to be suspected of doing.

Currivel Lodge should have been a dreary place for the child. There was nowhere to walk and nowhere to ride. There was no village where one could watch the blacksmith at his forge and the carpenter at his bench. In those days, nobody rowed on the Thames anywhere but at Oxford, unless they were watermen earning their living. There was little visiting, for it took a good hour to an hour and a half to drive to London, and my needy grandaunt's horses were old crocks. Her children were all older than little Arthur. But he enjoyed his visit simply because of the hours he spent on that windowseat. I know the setting of the scene on which he looked, since I often stayed in that house many years later; for of course my grandaunt's family never left it. When the entail came to an end and the property could have been sold, there were the Zulu Wars, the South African War, the First World War, and all meant that the occupants were too busy or too troubled to move; and they were still living there when the house was swept away in a town-planning scheme during the twenties. What Arthur in his day and I in mine looked down on was a croquet lawn framed by trees, very tall trees – so tall and strong, my uncle said with approval, that though one could not see the river, one knew that there must be one not far away. Born and reared in one of the wettest parts of Ireland, he regarded dry weather and a dry soil as the rest of us regard dry bread.

To the left of this lawn, seen through foliage, was a stone terrace overgrown with crimson and white roses. Behind the terrace rose the mellow red rectangle of a handsome Regency house with a green copper cupola rising from its roof. What my uncle saw there that was not there for me to see was a spectacle that gave him the same sort of enjoyment I was to get from the ballet 'Les Sylphides'. When the weather was fine, it often happened that there would come down the broad stone steps of the terrace a number of princesses out of a fairy-tale, each dressed in a different pale but bright colour. Sometimes there were as few as four of these princesses; occasionally there were as many as seven. Among the colours that my uncle thought he remembered them wearing were hyacinth blue, the green of the leaves of lilies of the valley, a silvery lilac that was almost grey, a transparent red that was like one's hand when one holds it up to a strong light, primrose yellow, a watery jade green, and a gentle orange. The dresses were made of muslin, and billowed in loops and swinging circles as their wearers' little feet carried them about in what was neither a dance nor the everyday motion of ordinary people. It was as if these lovely creatures were all parts of a brave and sensitive and melancholy being, and were at once confiding in each other about their griefs, which were their common grief, and giving each other reassurance.

Some carried croquet mallets and went on to the lawn and started to play, while the others sat down on benches to watch them. But sooner or later the players would pause and forget to make the next stroke, move towards each other and stand in a group, resting their mallets on the ground, and presently forget them and let them fall, as the spectators rose from their seats to join them in their exchange of confidences. Though they appeared in the garden as often as three times a week, they always seemed to have as much to say to one another as if they met but once a year; and they were always grave as they talked. There was a wildness about them, it was impossible to tell what they would do next, one might suddenly break away from the others and waltz round the lawn in the almost visible arms of an invisible partner; but when they talked, they showed restraint, they did not weep, though what they said was so plainly sad, and they rarely laughed. What was true of one of them was true of all, for there seemed very little difference between them. All were golden-headed. The only one who could be told apart was the wearer of the lilac-grey dress. She was taller than the rest, and often stood aloof while they clustered together and swayed and spoke. Sometimes a woman in a black gown came down from the terrace and talked to this separate one.

The girls in the coloured dresses were the seven daughters of the Admiral who owned the house. My uncle saw him once, when he called on Alice Darrell to discuss with her arrangements for repairing the wall between their properties: a tall and handsome man with iron-grey hair, a probing, defensive gaze, and a mouth so sternly compressed that it was a straight line across his face. The call would never have been made had there not been business to discuss. The Admiral would have no social relations with his neighbours; nobody had ever been invited to his house. Nor, had such an invitation been sent, would Aunt Alice have accepted it, for she thought he treated his daughters abominably. She could not help smiling when she told her nephew their names, for they came straight off the Navy List: Andromeda, Cassandra, Clytie, Hera, Parthenope, Arethusa, and Persephone. But that was the only time she smiled when she spoke of them, for she thought they had been treated with actual cruelty, though not in the way that might have been supposed. They were not immured in this lonely house by a father who wanted to keep them to himself; their case was the very opposite.

The Admiral's daughters were, in effect, motherless. By Aunt Alice my Uncle Arthur was told that the Admiral's wife was an invalid and had to live in a mild climate in the West of England, but from the servants he learnt that she was mad. Without a wife to soften him, the Admiral dealt with his daughters summarily by sending each of them, as she passed her seventeenth birthday, to be guided through the London season by his only sister, a wealthy woman with a house in Berkeley Square, and by giving each to the first man of reasonably respectable character who made her an offer of marriage. He would permit no delay, though his daughters, who had inheritances from a wealthy grandfather, as well as their beauty, would obviously have many suitors. These precipitate marriages were always against the brides' inclinations, for they had, strangely enough, no desire but to go on living in their lonely home.

'They are', Aunt Alice told her nephew, hesitating and looking troubled, 'oddly young for their ages. I know they are not old, and that they have lived a great deal alone, since their mother cannot be with them. But they are really very young for what they are.' They had yielded, it was said, only to the most brutal pressure exercised by their father. It astonished my uncle that all this was spoken of as something that had happened in the past. They did not look like grown-up ladies as they wandered in the garden, yet all but two were wives, and those two were betrothed, and some of them were already mothers. Parthenope, the one with most character, the one who had charge of the house in her father's absence, had married a North Country landowner who was reputed to be a millionaire. It was a pity that he was twice her age and had, by a dead wife, a son almost as old as she was, but such a fortune is a great comfort; and none of her sisters was without some measure of that same kind of consolation. Nevertheless, their discontent could be measured by the frequency with which they returned to the home of their childhood.

The first time my uncle visited Currivel Lodge, the Admiral's seven daughters were only a spectacle for his distant enjoyment. But one day during his second visit, a year later, his aunt asked him to deliver a note for Miss Parthenope at the house next door. Another section of the wall between the properties was in need of buttresses, and the builder had to have his orders. My uncle went up to his bedroom and smoothed his hair and washed his face, a thing he had never done before between morning and night of his own accord, and when he got to the Admiral's house, he told the butler, falsely but without a tremor, that he had been told to give the note into Miss Parthenope's own hands. It did not matter to him that the butler looked annoyed at hearing this: too much was at stake. He followed the butler's offended back through several rooms full of fine furniture, which were very much like the rooms to which he was accustomed, but had a sleepy air, as if the windows were closed, though they were not. In one there were some dolls thrown down on the floor, though he had never heard that there were any children living in the house. In the last room, which opened on the stone terrace and its white and crimson roses, a woman in a black dress with a suggestion of a uniform about it was sitting at an embroidery frame. She stared at him as if he presented a greater problem than schoolboys usually do, and he recognized her as the dark figure he had seen talking with the tallest of the daughters in the garden.

She took the letter from him, and he saw that the opportunity he had seized was slipping out of his grasp, so he pretended to be younger and simpler than he was, and put on the Irish brogue, which he never used at home except when he was talking to the servants or the people on the farms, but which he had found charmed the English. 'May I not go out into the garden and see the young ladies?' he asked. 'I have watched them from my window, and they look so pretty.'

It worked. The woman smiled and said, 'You're from Ireland, aren't you?' and before he could answer she exclaimed, as if defying prohibitions of which she had long been weary, 'What is the harm? Yes, go out and give the note to Miss Parthenope yourself. You will know her – she is wearing grey and is the tallest.' When he got out on the terrace, he saw that all seven of the Admiral's daughters were on the lawn, and his heart was like a turning windmill as he went down the stone steps. Then one of the croquet players caught sight of him – the one who was wearing a red dress, just nearer flame colour than flesh. She dropped her mallet and cried, 'Oh, look, a little boy! A little red-haired boy!' and danced towards him, sometimes pausing and twirling right round, so that her skirts billowed out round her. Other voices took up the cry, and, cooing like pigeons, the croquet players closed in on him in a circle of unbelievable beauty. It was their complexions that he remembered in later life as the marvel that made them, among all the women he was ever to see, the nonpareils. Light lay on their skin as it lies on the petals of flowers, but it promised that it would never fade, that it would last for ever, like the pearl. Yet even while he remarked their loveliness and was awed by it, he was disconcerted. They came so close, and it seemed as if they might do more than look at him and speak to him. It was as if a flock of birds had come down on him, and were fluttering and pecking about him; and they asked so many questions, in voices that chirped indefatigably and were sharper than the human note. 'Who are you?' 'You are Mrs Darrell's nephew?' 'Her brother's child or her sister's?' 'How old are

you?' 'What is your name?' 'Why is your middle name Greatorex?'
'Oh, what lovely hair he has – true Titian! And those round curls
like coins!' 'Have you sisters?' 'Have they hair like yours?' Their little
hands darted out and touched his hands, his cheeks, his shoulders,
briefly but not pleasantly. His flesh rose in goose pimples, as it did
when a moth's wing brushed his face as he lay in bed in the dark.
And while their feathery restlessness poked and cheeped at him, they
looked at him with eyes almost as fixed as if they were blind and
could not see him at all. Their eyes were immense and very bright
and shaded by lashes longer than he had ever seen; but they were so
light a grey that they were as colourless as clear water running over a
bed of pebbles. He was glad when the woman in the black dress called
from the terrace, 'Leave the boy alone!' He did not like anything about
the Admiral's daughters, now he saw them at close range. Even their
dresses, which had looked beautiful from a distance, repelled him. If
a lady had been sitting to a portrait painter in the character of a wood
nymph, she might have worn such draperies, but it was foolish to wear
them in a garden, when there was nobody to see them. 'Leave the boy
alone!' the woman in black called again. 'He has come with a letter
for Parthenope.'

She had not been one of the circle. Now that the others fell back,
my uncle saw her standing a little way off, biting her lip and knitting
her brows, as if the scene disturbed her. There were other differences,
beyond her height, that distinguished her from her sisters. While they
were all that was most feminine, with tiny waists and hands and
feet, she might have been a handsome and athletic boy dressed in
woman's clothes for a school play. Only, of course, one knew quite
well that she was not a boy. She stood erect, her arms hanging by
her sides, smoothing back the muslin billows of her skirt, as if they
were foolishness she would be glad to put behind her; and indeed,
she would have looked better in Greek dress. Like her sisters, she had
golden hair, but hers was a whiter gold. As my uncle and she went
towards each other, she smiled, and he was glad to see that her eyes
were a darker grey than her sisters', and were quick and glancing. He
told her who he was, speaking honestly, not putting on a brogue to
win her, and she smiled and held out her hand. It took her a little

time to read the letter, and she frowned over it and held her forefinger to her lips, and bade him tell his aunt that she would send over an answer later in the day, after she had consulted her gardeners, and then she asked him if he would care to come into the house and drink some raspberry vinegar. As she led him across the lawn to the terrace, walking with long strides, he saw that her sisters were clustered in a group, staring up at a gutter high on the house, where a rook had perched, as if the bird were a great marvel. 'Should I say goodbye to the ladies?' he asked nervously, and Parthenope answered, 'No, they have forgotten you already.' However, one had not. The sister who wore the light-red dress ran after him, crying, 'Come back soon, little boy. Nobody ever comes into this garden except to steal our strawberries.'

Parthenope took him through the silent house, pausing in the room where the dolls lay on the floor to lift them up and shut them in a drawer, and they came to a dining-room, lined with pictures of great ships at war with stormy seas. There was no raspberry vinegar on the top of the sideboard – only decanters wearing labels marked with the names of adult drinks he was allowed only at Christmas and on his birthday, and then but one glass, and he always chose claret. So they opened the cupboard below, and sat down together on the carpet and peered into the darkness while he told her that he did not really want any but if it had gone astray he would be pleased to help her find it. But when the decanter turned up at the very back of the shelf (and they agreed that that was what always happened when one lost anything, and that there was no doubt that objects can move), they both had a glass, talking meanwhile of what they liked to eat and drink. Like him, she hated boiled mutton, and she, too, liked goose better than turkey. When he had finished and the talk had slowed down, he rose and put his glass on the sideboard, and offered her a hand to help her up from the floor, but she did not need it; and he gave a last look round the room, so that he would not forget it. He asked her, 'Why is your chandelier tied up in a canvas bag? At home that only happens when the family is away.' She answered, 'Our family is away,' speaking so grimly that he said, 'I did not mean to ask a rude question.' She told him, 'You have not asked a rude question. What I meant was that all but two of us have our own homes, and those two will be leaving here soon.' It would not have been right to say that she spoke sadly. But her tone was empty of all it had held when they had talked about how much better chicken tastes when you eat it with your fingers when you are out shooting. He remembered all the sad things he had heard his aunt say about her family, the sadder things he had heard from the servants. He said, 'Why don't you come back with me and have tea with my aunt?' She said, smiling, 'She has not asked me.' And he said, 'Never think of that. We are not proper English, you know; we are from Ireland, and friends come in any time.' But she thanked him, sighing, so that he knew she would really have liked to come, and said that she must go back to her sisters. As the butler held the front door open for my uncle, she gave him a friendly slap across the shoulders, as an older boy might have done.

After that, my uncle never watched the Admiral's daughters again. If a glance told him that they were in the garden, he turned his back on the window. He had not liked those staring eyes that were colourless as water, and it troubled him that though some of them had children, none had said, 'I have a boy, too, but he is much younger than you,' for mothers always said that. He remembered Parthenope so well that he could summon her to his mind when he wished, and he could not bear to see her with these women who made him feel uneasy, because he was sure that he and she felt alike, and therefore she must be in a perpetual state of unease. So when, the very day before he was to go back to Ireland, he looked out of his bedroom window and saw her alone on the lawn, he threw up the sash and called to her; but she did not hear him.

She was absorbed in playing a game by herself, a game that he knew well. She was throwing a ball high into the air, then letting her arms drop by her sides, and waiting to the last, the very last moment, before stretching out a hand to catch it. It was a strange thing for a grown-up lady to be doing, but it did not distress him like the playground gambolling and chattering of her sisters. They had been like children as grown-ups like to think of them, silly and meaningless and mischievous. But she was being a child as children really are, sobered by all they have to put up with and glad to forget it in play. There was currently some danger that his own father was going to get a post in some foreign place and that the whole family would have to leave County Kerry for years and years; and when he and his brothers and sisters thought of this, they would go and, each one apart, would play this very same game that Parthenope was playing.

He did not want to raise his voice in a shout, in case he was overheard by his aunt or his mother. They would not understand that although Parthenope and he had met only once, they knew each other quite well. He got up from the windowseat and went out of his room and down through the house and out into the garden. There was a ladder in the coach house, and he dragged it to the right part of the wall and propped it up and stopped it with stones, and climbed to the top and called 'Miss Parthenope!' When she saw him, she smiled and waved at him as if she really were glad to see him again.

'Where are your sisters?' he asked cautiously.

'They have all gone away. I am going home tomorrow.'

'So am I.'

'Are you glad?'

'Papa will be there,' he said, 'and my brothers and sisters, and Garrity the groom, and my pony.'

She asked him the names of his brothers and sisters, and how old they were, and where his home was; and he told her all these things and told her, too, that his father was always being sent all over the world, and that of late he and his brothers and sisters had heard talk that someday, and it might be soon, he would be sent to some foreign place for so long that they would have to go with him, and they didn't want this to happen; for though they loved him and wanted to be near him, they loved County Kerry, too. At that, she stopped smiling and nodded her head, as if to say she knew how he must feel. 'But perhaps it won't happen,' he said, 'and then you must come and stay with us for the hunting.'

He thought of her in a riding habit, and at that he noticed that she was wearing a dress such as his own mother might have worn – a dress of grey cloth, with a tight bodice and a stiffened skirt, ornamented with braid. He said, 'How funny to see you dressed like other ladies. Don't you usually wear that lilac-grey muslin dress?'

She shook her head. 'No. My sisters and I only wear those muslin dresses when we are together here. My sisters like them.'

'Don't you?' he said, for her tone had gone blank again.

'No,' she answered, 'not at all.'

He was glad to hear it, but it seemed horribly unfair that she should have to wear clothes she did not like, just because her sisters did; nothing of the sort happened in his own family. 'Then don't wear them!' he said passionately. 'You mustn't wear them! Not if you don't like them!'

'You're making your ladder wobble,' she said, laughing at him, 'and if you fall down, I can't climb over the wall and pick you up.' She started across the lawn towards the house.

'Garrity says that you're lost if you let yourself be put upon,' he cried after her, his brogue coming back to him, but honestly, because he spoke to Garrity as Garrity spoke to him. He would have liked to have the power to make her do what she ought to do, and save her from all this foolishness.

'Goodbye, goodbye,' she called across the growing distance. 'Be a good boy, and come back to see us next year.'

'You will be here for sure?' he asked eagerly.

'Oh, yes,' she promised. 'We will always be back here for some time in the summer. My sisters would rather be here than anywhere in the world.'

'But do you like it yourself?' he asked angrily.

It was no use. She had run up the steps to the terrace.


My uncle did not come back the next year, because his fears were realized and his father was appointed to a post in Canada. But from his aunt's letters to his mother he learnt that even if he had returned to Currivel Lodge, he would not have seen Parthenope, for the Admiral sold the house later that year, as soon as his two remaining daughters went to the altar, which they did with even greater reluctance than their elder sisters. Alice Darrell's maid happened to be at the window one winter day and saw the two of them walking up and down the lawn, dressed in those strange, bright muslin gowns and wearing no mantles, though the river mist was thick, while they wept and wrung their hands. Aunt Alice felt that even if the Admiral had felt obliged to bundle all his daughters into matrimony, he should at least not have sold the house, which was the one place where they could meet and have a little nursery happiness again.

In the course of time, Uncle Arthur came back to Ireland, and went to Trinity College, Dublin, and passed into the English Civil Service, and was sent to London. The first time he went back to Currivel Lodge, he stood at his bedroom window and stared out at the croquet lawn of the house next door, and it looked very much like other croquet lawns. Under the trees two men and two women were sitting round a tea table, all of them presenting the kind of appearance, more common then than now, that suggests that nothing untoward happens to the human race. It occurred to him that perhaps his boyish imagination had made a story out of nothing, but Aunt Alice gave him back his version intact. The Admiral had really hectored his daughters into early and undesired marriages, with the most brutal disregard for their feelings, and the daughters had really been very strange girls, given to runing about the garden in a sort of fancy dress and behaving like children – all except Parthenope, who was quite remarkable. She had made her mark in society since then. Well, so they all had, in a way. Their photographs were always in the papers, at one time, and no wonder, they were so very pretty. But that seemed over now, and, indeed, they must all be out of their twenties by now, even the youngest. Parthenope's triumphs, however, had been more durable. It was said that Queen Victoria greatly approved of her, and she was often at Court.

My uncle always thought of Parthenope when he was dressing for any of the grander parties to which he was invited, and he soon found his way to the opera and ascertained which was her box, but she was never at the parties, and, unless she had changed out of all recognition, never in her box at Covent Garden, either. My uncle did not wish to approach her, for he was a poor young man, far below her grandeur, and they belonged to different generations; at the least, she was twelve years older than he was. But he would have liked to see her again. Soon, however, he received an intimation that that would not be possible. One morning at breakfast he unfolded his newspaper and folded it again almost immediately, having read a single paragraph, which told him that Parthenope had met a violent death.

He had failed to meet her at parties and to see her in her opera box because she had been spending the winter abroad, taking care of two of her sisters who had both been the victims of prolonged illness. Originally, they had settled at Nice, but had found it too urban, and had moved to a hotel at Grasse, where they spent some weeks. Then a friend had found them a pleasant villa at Hyères, and the party had started off from Grasse in two carriages. Parthenope and her sisters and a lady's maid had travelled in the first, and another maid and a courier had followed in the second. The second carriage had dropped far behind. Afterwards, the coachman remembered that he had been oddly delayed in leaving the inn where they had stopped for a midday meal; he had been told that a man was looking for him with a letter for his employers, and failing to find him had gone to a house some way down the village street. The coachman sought him but there was nobody there; and on his return to his horses he discovered that a harness strap was broken, and he had to mend it before they could resume their journey. After a sharp turn in the road, he had found himself driving into a felled tree trunk, and when the courier and the maid and the coachman got out, they could see no sign of the first carriage. It was found some hours later, abandoned on a cart track running through a wood to a river. There was no trace of any of its occupants. Later that same day the maid crawled up to a farmhouse door. Before she collapsed she was able to tell the story of an attack by masked men, who had, she thought, killed the three sisters outright because they refused to tell in which trunk their jewel cases were packed. She had escaped during the struggle, and while she was running away through the woods, she had heard terrible prolonged screaming from the riverbank. As the river was in flood, there was no hope of recovering the bodies.

After my uncle had read all the accounts of the crime that appeared in the newspapers, and had listened to all he could hear from gossiping friends, there hung, framed on the wall of his mind, a romantic picture of a highway robbery, in the style of Salvator Rosa, with coal-black shadows and highlights white on hands lifted in imploration, and he felt no emotion whatsoever. When he had opened *The Times* at breakfast, his heart had stopped. But now he felt as if he had been stopped before an outmoded and conventional picture in a private gallery by a host who valued it too highly.

A year or so later, Alice Darrell mentioned to him an odd story she had heard. It appeared that Parthenope had been carrying a great deal more jewellery than would seem necessary for a woman travelling quietly with two invalid sisters. To be sure, she had not taken all the jewellery she possessed, but she had taken enough for the value to be estimated at fifty thousand pounds; and of this not a penny could be recovered, for it was uninsured. Her husband had left the matter for her to handle, because she had sold some old jewellery and had bought some to replace it just about the time that the policy should have been renewed, but she had failed to write the necessary letter to her lawyers till the very night before the journey to Hyères, and it was found, unposted, at the hotel in Grasse.

'Parthenope!' my uncle said. 'Let an insurance policy lapse! Parthenope! I'll not believe it.'

'That's just what I said,' Alice Darrell exclaimed. 'Any of the others, but not Parthenope. She had her hand on everything. Yet, of course, she may have changed. They are a queer family. There was the other one, you know – the one who disappeared. That was after the accident.'

It seemed that another sister – Hera, Aunt Alice thought it was – had also suffered ill health, and had gone to France with a nurse, and one day her cloak and bonnet were found on the bank of a river.

'I wish that things turned out better,' Aunt Alice remarked sadly. 'They do sometimes, but not often enough.'

This was the only criticism of life he had ever heard her utter, though she had had a sad life, constantly losing the people she loved, to tropical diseases or to wars against obscure tribes that lacked even the interest of enmity. What she uttered now made him realize that she had indeed thought Parthenope remarkable, and he said, smiling, 'Why, we are making ourselves quite miserable about her, though all we know for sure is that she let an insurance policy lapse.'

He did not hear of the Admiral's daughters again until after a long space of time, during which he had many other things to think about: his career, which was alternately advanced by his brilliance and retarded by his abstracted candour; a long affair with a married woman older than himself, some others that were briefer; and his marriage, which, like his career, and for much the same reason, was neither a success nor a failure. One day when he was reading the papers at his club, he heard two men speaking of a friend who was distressed about his mother, whose behaviour had been strange since she had been left a widow. She had rejected the dower house and gone off to the Continent to travel by herself, and now refused to come back to see her family or to meet them abroad. The mother had an old Greek name, and so had a sister, who had got herself murdered for her jewels in the South of France. My uncle went on staring at his newspaper, but it was as if a door in his mind were swinging backward and forward on a broken hinge.


Many years later, when Aunt Alice was dead and my uncle was a middle-aged man, with children who were no longer children, he broke his journey home from a conference in Spain at a certain town in the southwest of France, for no other reason than that its name had always charmed him. But it proved to be a dull place, and as he sat down to breakfast at a café in the large and featureless station square, it occurred to him to ask the waiter if there were not some smaller and pleasanter place in the neighbourhood where he could spend the rest of the day and night. The waiter said that if Monsieur would take the horse-bus that started from the other side of the square in half an hour, it would take him to the village where he, the waiter, was born, and there he would find a good inn and a church that people came all the way from Paris to see. My uncle took his advice; and because his night had been wakeful, he fell asleep almost as soon as the bus started. He woke suddenly to find that the journey had ended and he was in a village which was all that he had hoped it would be.

A broad, deliberate river, winding among low wooded hills, spread its blessings at this point through a circular patch of plain, a couple of miles or so across, which was studded with farmhouses, each standing beside its deep green orchard. In the centre of this circle was a village that was no more than one long street, which looked very clean. The houses were built of stone that had been washed by the hill rains, and beside the road a brook flowed over a paved bed. There were bursts of red valerian growing from the cracks in the walls and in the yard-long bridges that crossed the brook. The street ended in a little square, where the church and the inn looked across cobblestones, shaded by pollarded limes, at the *mairie* and the post office. At the inn, my uncle took a room and slept for an hour or two in a bed smelling of the herbs with which the sheets had been washed. Then, as it was past noon, he went down to lunch, and ate some potato soup, a trout, some wood strawberries, and a slice of cheese. Afterwards, he asked the landlord how soon the church would be open, and was told that he could open it himself when he chose. The priest and his housekeeper were away until vespers, and had left the church keys at the inn.

When he went to the church, it was a long time before he unlocked the door, for there was a beautiful tympanum in the porch, representing the Last Judgement. It was clear-cut in more than one sense. There was no doubt who was saved and who was damned: there was a beatific smile on the faces of those walking in Paradise, which made it seem as if just there a shaft of sunlight had struck the dark stone. Also the edges of the carving, though the centuries had rubbed them down, showed a definition more positive than mere sharpness. Often my uncle played games when he was alone, and now he climbed on a wooden stool which was in the porch, and shut his eyes and felt the faces of the blessed, and pretended that he had been blind for a long time, and that the smiles of the blessed were striking into his darkness through his fingertips.

When he went into the church, he found, behind an oaken door, the steps that led to the top of the tower. He climbed up through darkness that was transfixed every few steps by thin shafts of light, dancing with dust, coming through the eyelet windows, and he found that though the tower was not very high, it gave a fine view of an amphitheatre of hills, green on their lower slopes with chestnut groves, banded higher with fir woods and bare turf, and crowned with shining rock. He marked some likely paths on the nearest hills, and then dropped his eyes to the village below, and looked down into the oblong garden of a house that seemed larger than the rest. At the farther end was the usual, pedantically neat French vegetable garden; then there was a screen of espaliered fruit trees; then there was a lawn framed in trees so tall and strong that it could have been guessed from them alone that not far away there was a river. The lawn was set with croquet hoops, and about them were wandering four figures in bright dresses – one hyacinth blue, one primrose yellow, one jade green, one clear light red. They all had croquet mallets in their hands, but they had turned from the game, and as my uncle watched them they drew together, resting their mallets on the ground. Some distance away, a woman in black, taller than the others, stood watching them.

When one of the croquet players let her mallet fall on the grass, and used her free hands in a fluttering gesture, my uncle left the top of the tower and went down through the darkness and shafts of light and locked the church door behind him. In the corner of the square he found what might have been the château of the village – one of those square and solid dwellings, noble out of proportion to their size, which many provincial French architects achieved in the seventeenth century. My uncle went through an iron gateway into a paved garden and found that the broad door of the house was open. He walked into the vestibule and paused, looking up the curved staircase. The pictures were as old as the house, and two had been framed to fit the recessed panels in which they hung. The place must have been bought as it stood. On the threshold of the corridor beyond, he paused again, for it smelled of damp stone, as all the back parts of his father's house in County Kerry did, at any time of the year but high summer. It struck him as a piece of good fortune for which he had never before been sufficiently grateful that he could go back to that house any time he pleased; he would be there again in a few weeks' time. He passed the open door of a kitchen, where two women were rattling dishes and pans and singing softly, and came to a closed door, which he stared at for a second before he turned the handle.

He found himself in a salon that ran across the whole breadth of the house, with three French windows opening on a stone terrace overlooking the garden. As he crossed it to the steps that led down to the lawn, he came close to a bird cage on a pole, and the scarlet parrot inside broke into screams. All the women on the lawn turned and saw him, and the tall woman in black called, '*Que voulez-vous, Monsieur?*' She had put her hand to her heart, and he was eager to reassure her, but could not think how, across that distance, to explain why he had come. So he continued to walk towards her, but could not reach her because the four others suddenly scampered toward him, crying 'Go away! Go away!' Their arms flapped like bats' wings, and their voices were cracked, but, under their white hair, their faces were unlined and their eyes were colourless as water. 'Go away!' shrilled the one in light red. 'We know you have come to steal our strawberries. Why may we not keep our own strawberries?' But the figure in black had come forward with long strides, and told them to go on with their game, and asked again, '*Que voulez-vous, Monsieur?*'

Her hair was grey now, and her mouth so sternly compressed that it was a straight line across her face. She reminded my uncle of a particular man – her father, the Admiral – but she was not like a man, she was still a handsome and athletic boy, though a frost had fallen on him; and still it was strange that she should look like a boy, since she was also not male at all. My uncle found that now he was face to face with her, it was just as difficult to explain to her why he had come. He said, 'I came to this village by chance this morning, and after I had luncheon at the inn I went to the top of the church tower, and looked down on this garden, and recognized you all. I came to tell you that if there is anything I can do for you I will do it. I am a civil servant who has quite a respectable career, and so I can hope that I might be efficient enough to help you, if you need it.'

'That is very kind,' she said, and paused, and it was as if she were holding a shell to her ear and listening to the voice of a distant sea. 'Very kind,' she repeated. 'But who are you?'

'I am the nephew of your neighbour, Mrs Darrell,' said my uncle.

'I brought you a letter from her, many years ago, when you were all in your garden.'

Her smile broke slowly. 'I remember you,' she said. 'You were a fatherly little boy. You gave me good advice from the top of a ladder. Why should you have found me here, I wonder? It can't be that, after all, there is some meaning in the things that happen. You had better come into the house and drink some of the cherry brandy we make here. I will get the cook to come out and watch them. I never leave them alone now.'

While she went to the kitchen, my uncle sat in the salon and noted that, for all its fine furniture and all its space and light, there was a feeling that the place was dusty, the same feeling that he had noticed in the Admiral's house long ago. It is the dust of another world, he thought with horror, and the housemaids of this world are helpless against it. It settles wherever these women live, and Parthenope must live with them.

When she came back, she was carrying a tray with a slender decanter and very tiny glasses. They sat sipping the cherry brandy in silence until she said, 'I did nothing wrong.' He looked at her in astonishment. Of course she had done nothing wrong. Wrong was what she did not do. But she continued gravely, 'When we all die, it will be found that the sum I got for the jewellery is intact. My stepson will not be a penny the worse off. Indeed, he is better off, for my husband has had my small inheritance long before it would have come to him if I had not done this.'

'I knew you would have done it honestly,' said my uncle. He hesitated. 'This is very strange. You see, I knew things about you which I had no reason to know. I knew you had not been murdered.'

Then my uncle had to think carefully. They were united by eternal bonds, but hardly knew each other, which was the reverse of what usually happened to men and women. But they might lapse into being strangers and nothing else if he showed disrespect to the faith by which she lived. He said only, 'Also I knew that what you were doing in looking after your family was terrible.'

She answered, 'Yes. How good it is to hear somebody say that it

241

is terrible, and to be able to answer that it is. But I had to do it. I had to get my sisters away from their husbands. They were ashamed of them. They locked them up in the care of strangers. I saw their bruises.' My uncle caught his breath. 'Oh,' she said, desperately just, 'the people who looked after them did not mean to be cruel. But they were strangers; they did not know the way to handle my sisters. And their husbands were not bad men, either. And even if they had been, I could not say a word against them, for they were cheated; my father cheated them. They were never told the truth about my mother. About my mother and half her family.' She raised her little glass of cherry brandy to her lips and nodded, to intimate that that was all she had to say, but words rushed out and she brought her glass down to her lap. 'I am not telling the truth. Their husbands cheated, too. . . . No, I am wrong. They did not cheat. But they failed to keep their bond. Still, there is no use talking about that.'

'What bond did your sisters' husbands not keep?' my uncle asked.

'They married my sisters because they were beautiful, and laughed easily, and could not understand figures. They might have considered that women who laugh easily might scream easily, and that if figures meant nothing to them, words might mean nothing, either, and that if figures and words meant nothing to them, thoughts and feelings might mean nothing, too. But these men had the impudence to feel a horror of my sisters.'

She rose, trembling, and told him that he must have a sweet biscuit with his cherry brandy, and that she would get him some; they were in a cupboard in the corner of the room. Over her shoulder, she cried, 'I cannot imagine you marrying a woman who was horrible because she was horrible, and then turning against her because she was horrible.' She went on setting some wafers out on a plate, and he stared at the back of her head, unable to imagine what was inside it, saying to himself, 'She realizes that they are horrible; there is no mitigation of her state.'

When she sat down again, she said, 'But it was my father's fault.'

'What was your father's fault?' he asked gently, when she did not go on.

'Why, he should not have made us marry; he should not have sold our house. My sisters were happy there, and all they asked was to be allowed to go on living there, like children.'

'Your father wanted his daughters to marry so that they would have someone to look after them when he was dead,' my uncle told her.

'I could have looked after them.'

'Come now,' said my uncle, 'you are not being fair. You are the same sort of person as your father. And you know quite well that if you were a man you would regard all women as incapable. You see, men of the better kind want to protect the women they love, and there is so much stupidity in the male nature and the circumstances of life are generally so confused that they end up thinking they must look after women because women cannot look after themselves. It is only very seldom that a man meets a woman so strong and wise that he cannot doubt her strength and wisdom, and realizes that his desire to protect her is really the same as his desire to gather her into his arms and partake of her glory.'

Moving slowly and precisely, he took out his cardcase and was about to give her one of his cards when a thought struck him. She must have the name of his family's house in County Kerry as well as his London address, and know that he went there at Christmas and at Easter, and in the summer, too. She would be able to find him whenever she wanted him, since such bootblack service was all he could render her.

She read the card and said in an astonished whisper, 'Oh, how kind, how kind.' Then she rose and put it in a drawer in a *secrétaire*, which she locked with a key she took from a bag swinging from the belt of her hateful black gown. 'I have to lock up everything,' she said, wearily. 'They mean no harm, but sometimes they get at papers and tear them up.'

'What I have written on that card is for an emergency,' said my uncle. 'But what is there I can do now? I do not like the thought of you sitting here in exile, among things that mean nothing to you. Can I not send you out something English – a piece of furniture, a picture, some china or glass? If I were in your place, I would long for something that reminded me of the houses where I had spent my childhood.'

'If you were in my place, you would not,' she said. 'You are very kind, but the thing that has happened to my family makes me not at all anxious to remember my childhood. We were all such pretty children. Everybody always spoke as if we were bound to be happy. And in those days nobody was frightened of Mamma – they only laughed at her, because she was such a goose. Then one thing followed another, and it became quite certain about Mamma, and then it became quite certain about the others; and now I cannot bear to think of the good times that went before. It is as if someone had known and was mocking us. But you may believe that it is wonderful for me to know that there is someone I can call on at any time. You see, I had supports, which are being taken away from me. You really have no idea how I got my sisters out here?'

My uncle shook his head. 'I only read what was in the newspapers and knew it was not true.'

'But you must have guessed I had helpers,' she said. 'There was the highway robbery to be arranged. All that was done by somebody who was English but had many connections in France, a man who was very fond of Arethusa. Arethusa is the one who spoke to you in the garden; she always wears red. This man was not like her husband; when she got worse and worse, he felt no horror for her, only pity. He has always been behind me, but he was far older than we were, and he died three years ago; and since then his lawyer in Paris has been a good friend, but now he is old, too, and I must expect him to go soon. I have made all arrangements for what is to happen to my sisters after my death. They will go to a convent near here, where the nuns are really kind, and we are preparing them for it. One or other of the nuns comes here every day to see my sisters, so that they will never have to be frightened by strange faces; and I think that if my sisters go on getting worse at the same rate as at present, they will by then believe the nuns when they say that I have been obliged to go away and will come back presently. But till that time comes, I will be very glad to have someone I can ask for advice. I can see that you are to be trusted. You are like the man who loved Arethusa. My poor Arethusa! Sometimes I think', she said absently, 'that she might have been all right if it had been that man whom she had married. But no,' she cried, shaking herself awake, 'none of us should have married, not even me.'

'Why should you not have married?' asked my uncle. 'That the others should not I understand. But why not you? There is nothing wrong with you.'

'Is there not?' she asked. 'To leave my family and my home, to stage a sham highway robbery, and later to plot and lie, and lie and plot, in order to get my mad sisters to a garden I had once noted, in my travels, as something like the garden taken from them when they were young. There is an extravagance in the means my sanity took to rescue their madness that makes the one uncommonly like the other.'

'You must not think that,' my uncle told her. 'Your strange life forced strangeness on your actions, but you are not strange. You were moved by love, you had seen their bruises.'

'Yes, I had seen their bruises,' she agreed. 'But,' she added, hesitantly, 'you are so kind that I must be honest with you. It was not only for the love of my sisters that I arranged this flight. It is also true that I could not bear my life. I was not wholly unselfish. You do not know what it is like to be a character in a tragedy. Something has happened which can only be explained by supposing that God hates you with merciless hatred, and nobody will admit it. The people nearest you stand round you saying that you must ignore this extraordinary event, you must – what were the words I was always hearing? – "keep your sense of proportion", "not brood on things". They do not understand that they are asking you to deny your experiences, which is to pretend that you do not exist and never have existed. And as for the people who do not love you, they laugh. Our tragedy was so ridiculous that the laughter was quite loud. There were all sorts of really funny stories about the things my mother and sisters did before they were shut up. That is another terrible thing about being a character in a tragedy; at the same time you become a character in a farce. Do not deceive yourself,' she said, looking at him kindly and sadly. 'I am not a classical heroine, I am not Iphigenia or Electra or Alcestis, I am the absurd Parthenope. There is no dignity in my life. For one thing, too much has happened to me. One calamity evokes sympathy; when two calamities call for it, some still comes, but less. Three calamities are felt to be too many, and when four are reported, or five, the thing is ludicrous. God has only to strike one again and again for one to become a clown. There is nothing about me which is not comical. Even my flight with my sisters has become a joke.' She sipped at her glass. 'My sisters' husbands and their families must by now have found out where we are. I do not think my husband ever did, or he would have come to see me. But there are many little indications that the others know, and keep their knowledge secret, rather than let loose so monstrous a scandal.'

'You say your husband would have come to see you?' asked my uncle, wanting to make sure. 'But that must mean he loved you.'

At last the tears stood in her eyes. She said, her voice breaking, 'Oh, things might have gone very well with my husband and myself, if love had been possible for me. But of course it never was.'

'How wrong you are,' said my uncle. 'There could be nothing better for any man than to have you as his wife. If you did not know that, your husband should have made you understand it.'

'No, no,' she said. 'The fault was not in my husband or myself. It was in love, which cannot do all that is claimed for it. Oh, I can see that it can work miracles, some miracles, but not all the miracles that are required before life can be tolerable. Listen: I love my sisters, but I dare not love them thoroughly. To love them as much as one can love would be to go to the edge of an abyss and lean over the edge, farther and farther, till one was bound to lose one's balance and fall into the blackness of that other world where they live. That is why I never dared let my husband love me fully. I was so much afraid that I might be an abyss, and if he understood me, if we lived in each other, he would be drawn down into my darkness.'

'But there is no darkness in you,' said my uncle, 'you are not an abyss, you are the solid rock.'

'Why do you think so well of me?' she wondered. 'Of course, you are right to some extent – I am not the deep abyss I might be. But how could I be sure of that when I was young? Every night when I lay down in bed I examined my day for signs of folly. If I had lost my temper, if I had felt more joy than was reasonable, I was like one of a tuberculous family who has just heard herself cough. Only the years that had not then passed made me sure that I was unlike my sisters, and until I knew, I had to hold myself back. I could not let the fine man who was my husband be tempted into my father's fault.'

'What was your father's fault?' asked my uncle, for the second time since he had entered that room.

Again her disapproval was absolute, her eyes were like steel. But this time she answered at once, without a moment's hesitation: 'Why, he should not have loved my mother.'

'But you are talking like a child!' he exclaimed. 'You cannot blame anyone for loving anyone.'

'Did you ever see him?' she asked, her eyes blank because they were filled with a distant sight. 'Yes? You must have been only a boy, but surely you saw that he was remarkable. And he had a mind, he was a mathematician, he wrote a book on navigation that was thought brilliant; they asked him to lecture to the Royal Society. And one would have thought from his face that he was a giant of goodness and strength. How could such a man love such a woman as my mother? It was quite mad, the way he made us marry. How could he lean over the abyss of her mind and let himself be drawn down into that darkness?'

'Do not let your voice sink to a whisper like that,' my uncle begged her. 'It – it –'

'It frightens you,' she supplied.

'But have you', he pressed her, 'no feeling for your mother?'

'Oh, yes,' she said, her voice breaking. 'I loved my mother very much. But when she went down into the darkness, I had to say goodbye to her or I could not have looked after my sisters.' It seemed as if she was going to weep, but she clung to her harshness and asked again, 'How could my father love such a woman?'

My uncle got up and knelt in front of her chair and took her trembling hands in his. 'There is no answer, so do not ask the question.'

'I must ask it,' she said. 'Surely it is blasphemy to admit that one can ask questions to which there are no answers. I must ask why my father leant over the abyss of my mother's mind and threw himself into it, and dragged down victim after victim with him – not only

247

dragging them down but manufacturing them for that sole purpose, calling them out of nothingness simply so that they could fall and fall. How could he do it? If there is not an answer –'

He put his hand over her lips. 'He cannot have known that she was mad when he begot his children.'

Her passion had spent itself in her question. She faintly smiled as she said, 'No, but I never liked the excuse that he and my sisters' husbands made for themselves. They all said that at first they had simply thought their wives were rather silly. I could not have loved someone whom I thought rather silly. Could you?'

'It is not what I have done,' said my uncle. 'May I have some more cherry brandy?'

'I am so glad that you like it,' she said, suddenly happy. 'But you have given me the wrong glass to fill. This is mine.'

'I knew that,' he told her. 'I wanted to drink from your glass.'

'I would like to drink from yours,' she said, and for a little time they were silent. 'Tell me,' she asked meekly, as if now she had put herself in his hands, 'do you think it has been wrong for me to talk about what has happened to me? When I was at home they always said it was bad to brood over it.'

'What nonsense,' said my uncle. 'I am sure that it was one of the major misfortunes of Phèdre and Bérénice that they were unable to read Racine's clear-headed discussions of their miseries.'

'You are right,' said Parthenope. 'Oh, how kind Racine was to tragic people! He would not allow for a moment that they were comic. People at those courts must have giggled behind their hands at poor Bérénice, at poor Phèdre. But he ignored them. You are kind like Racine.' There was a tapping on the glass of the French window, and her face went grey. 'What has happened now? Oh, what has happened now?' she murmured to herself. It was the cook who had tapped, and she was looking grave.

Parthenope went out and spoke with her for a minute, and then came back, and again the tears were standing in her eyes. 'I thought I might ask you to stay all day with me,' she said. 'I thought we might dine together. But my sisters cannot bear it that there is a stranger here. They are hiding in the raspberry canes, and you must have heard them screaming. Part of that noise comes from the parrot, but part from them. It sometimes takes hours to get them quiet. I cannot help it; you must go.'

He took both her hands and pressed them against his throat, and felt it swell as she muttered, 'Goodbye.'

But as he was going through the paved garden to the gateway he heard her call 'Stop!' Stop!' and she was just behind him, her skirts lifted over her ankles so that she could take her long strides. 'The strangest thing,' she said, laughing. 'I have not told you the name by which I am known here.' She spelled it out to him as he wrote it down in his diary, and turned back towards the house, exclaiming, 'What a thing to forget!' But then she swung back again, suddenly pale, and said, 'But do not write to me. I am only giving you the name so that if I send you a message you will be able to answer it. But do not write to me.'

'Why not?' he asked indignantly. 'Why not?'

'You must not be involved in my life,' she said. 'There is a force outside the world that hates me and all my family. If you wrote to me too often it might hate you, too.'

'I would risk that,' he said, but she cried, covering her eyes, 'No, no, by being courageous you are threatening my last crumb of happiness. If you stay a stranger, I may be allowed to keep what I have of you. So do as I say.'

He made a resigned gesture, and they parted once more. But as she got to her door, he called to her to stop and hurried back. 'I will not send you anything that will remind you of your home,' he said, 'but may I not send you a present from time to time – some stupid little thing that will not mean much but might amuse you for a minute or two?'

She hesitated but in the end nodded. 'A little present, a very little present,' she conceded. 'And not too often.' She smiled like the saved in the sculpture in the church, and slowly closed the door on him.

But when he was out in the square and walking towards the inn, he heard her voice crying again, 'Stop! Stop!' This time she came quite close to him and said, as if she were a child ashamed to admit to a fault, 'There is another thing that I would like to ask of you. You said that I might write to you if I wanted anything, and I know that you meant business things – the sort of advice men give women. But I wonder if your kindness goes beyond that; you are so very kind. I know all about most dreadful things in life, but I know nothing about death. Usually I think I will not mind leaving this world, but just now and then, if I wake up in the night, particularly in winter, when it is very cold, I am afraid that I may be frightened when I die.'

'I fear that, too, sometimes,' he said.

'It seems a pity, too, to leave this world, in spite of the dreadful things that happen in it,' she went on. 'There are things that nothing can spoil – the spring and the summer and the autumn.'

'And, indeed, the winter, too,' he said.

'Yes, the winter, too,' she said, and looked up at the amphitheatre of hills round the village. 'You cannot think how beautiful it is here when the snow has fallen. But, of course, death may be just what one has been waiting for; it may explain everything. But still, I may be frightened when it comes. So if I do not die suddenly, if I have warning of my death, would it be a great trouble for you to come and be with me for a little?'

'As I would like to be with you always, I would certainly want to be with you then,' he said. 'And if I have notice of my death and you are free to travel, I will ask you to come to me.'

My uncle found that he did not want to go back to the inn just then, and he followed a road leading up to the foothills. There he climbed one of the paths he had remarked from the top of the church tower, and when he got to the bare rock, he sat down and looked at the village beneath him till the twilight fell. On his return to London, he painted a water-colour of the view of the valley as he recollected it, and pasted it in a book, which he kept by his bedside. From time to time, some object in the window of an antique shop or a jeweller's would bring Parthenope to his mind, and he would send it to her. The one that pleased him as most fitting was a gold ring in the form of two leaves, which was perhaps Saxon. She acknowledged these presents in brief letters; and it delighted him that often her solemn purpose of brevity broke down and she added an unnecessary sentence or two, telling him of something that had brightened her day – of a strayed fawn she had found in her garden, or a prodigious crop of cherries, which had made her trees quite red. But after some years these letters stopped. When he took into account how old she was, and by how many years she had been the elder, he realized that probably she had died. He told himself that at least she had enjoyed the mercy of sudden death, and presently ceased to think of her. It was as if the memory of her were too large to fit inside his head; he felt actual physical pain when he tried to recollect her. This was the time when such things as the finest buttercup field near London and the tomb of Captain Vancouver seemed to be all that mattered to him. But from the day when he heard the girl at the inn called by the name of his Parthenope, he again found it easy to think of her; and he told me about her very often during the five years that passed before his death.

# Short Life of a Saint

*This was discovered in typescript form among Rebecca West's unpublished works. There is no date for it, but readers familiar with Rebecca West's life and works will recognize its autobiographical content and its relation to the family saga of* The Fountain Overflows, This Real Night *and* Cousin Rosamund.

G erda was an immensely admired baby, because she was very fair and had bright blue eyes. 'What a little angel!' her mother's friends used to say, and so did strangers that saw her in shops and trains. Her mother said that and more, for Gerda was as good as she was pretty. She never cried as other babies do, although she used to scream sometimes in a curiously dictatorial way if nobody was paying attention to her; and even for that they never wanted to scold her, because she smiled so adorably when they went to her. She was endlessly affectionate, rubbing her soft little cheeks against her father's face, always a little harsh with the quickly growing beard, and the roughness of his coat, rubbing them against her mother's prettiness and slenderness, rubbing them against her Boer nurse's warm solidity. She wanted nothing out of life but to be good, to earn praise. In the garden she never did any damage, she would touch nothing but the daisies on the lawn, which she made into little posies to give people. No grown-up could have been more careful of possessions than she was of her toys and her little dresses. So praise she earned indeed; and because she was so very good, and one did not ascribe vanity to her any more than one would to the angels, this praise was usually spoken in her earshot.

It was a disputable matter which loved her best, her father or her mother. It was natural enough that Mrs Heming should love her. She was a nervous, excitable woman, dark of hair and eye, who belonged to what is called the maternal type. She liked neither love nor men, but brooded with the most intense passion over the fruit of her dealing with these. Mr Heming was not the kind of man one would expect to become absorbed in a child. Mrs Heming's sole motive for marrying him could have been that of all men he was most likely to confirm her opinion of men and to render her experience of love brief and transitory. He was a rake and a rogue. Yet here, for once, those characteristics led him to a virtuous emotion. His sensuousness made him alive to the beauty of his little daughter and to her endless petitioning complaisance; and his roguery made him contemplate her goodness with a peculiar agonized rapture. So little Gerda was the joy of them both, and became their idol when she began to show what a remarkable intelligence she had. She spoke some months earlier than most children, she never tired of learning, she asked extraordinarily intelligent questions. Her parents loved to sit with her by the hour, marvelling at the wonder-child they had accomplished.

The closeness of their companionship, of course, had to come to an end when their second child was born. There was not only the distraction of the running to and fro that a new baby means, there was the competition of its rival beauty. For it was almost as lovely as Gerda, but dark, as dark as she was fair. At first Gerda did not welcome her little sister. When she was taken to see her mother and the new baby in bed, she pushed at the little red bundle and said, 'Take your hands off my mamma!' That story was told in front of her, to shame her out of jealousy, and soon she took to laughing at it louder than anybody with her jolly, sunny gurgle. In no time she had taken on her little sister as a charge that she must train up in the way she should go. Everybody loved to come on her teaching her little sister not to do some babyish trick. 'Naughty baby!' she used to say. 'Mustn't do that!' When they were taken to be photographed neither the nurse nor the photographer had any trouble in keeping the younger in order, so thoroughly had Gerda got her in hand.

It was unfortunate that the younger child, who was called Ellida, turned out as she grew older to be of a very different temperament. She was moody, she seemed to feel lonely and yet to be under a compulsion to flee from the companionship that Gerda so sunnily offered her. She was given to fits of stormy weeping, during which she was given to screaming out that she was an intruder whom nobody loved. Her teachers and nurses had no hesitation in calling this wicked temper, for no child could have less reason to feel an outcast, considering how good Gerda was to her. She did not tempt them to form kinder judgements, for she was unresponsive and suspicious. It used to make Mrs Heming's heart sink to see her returning from a walk with her head lowered and sullen tears flowing down her checks, with an angry governess on one hand and on the other little Gerda, looking up into her face and then up into her governess's, crying, 'Oh, Elly, why can't you be good? Miss Smith, why can't Elly be good?'

As time went on she became more troublesome. The family left South Africa and went back to London and, while Gerda kept healthy and rosy, Ellida responded to the change in climate by ailing perpetually; and it was impossible to help blaming her for this, because she so obviously liked being ill. She liked having her mother's full attention, and pestered her to spend whole days by her bedside, and as Mrs Heming was beginning to feel the full force of her husband's roguery, and was distracted by her efforts to keep a middle-class house on an income that had by now dwindled to a working-class level, she found this an intolerable tax on her time and strength. When Gerda, her cheeks glowing with a long walk, ran into the sickroom where Ellida was obstinately keeping her bed on the plea of a mysterious pain, Mrs Heming could not restrain herself from crying, 'Oh, Ellida, if only you were more like Gerda!'

There was also constant trouble with the second child at school. She had actually a better brain than Gerda, but she could not profit by it because of the antagonism she aroused. Her teachers and her schoolfellows were prepared to find her odd, for as Gerda came into the schoolhouse every morning with her sister, her eyes were set gravely before her and her very short upper lip was raised right off her teeth, as if she were carrying a load so heavy that she did not know if she could get it to its destination; and everyone who heard her cry out to her sister, 'Ellida! you'll be late for prayers!' 'Ellida! what have you lost now? Your pencil? Oh, I told you –' knew very well that that load had consisted of crushing responsibilities. And Ellida amply justified the expectations of both the teachers and the girls. She did not seem to have any instinct of self-preservation, for she made no attempt to cover up her unlikeable qualities. When another little girl was born to the Hemings she showed open and malignant jealousy. She proclaimed glumly that after this she would get no attention at home at all. But Gerda bubbled over with pleasure, and went about telling everybody, 'I've got the loveliest little baby sister!'

She was as sweet and good-tempered with the baby as could be wished, though just at the time she had a severe shock. One day she went out to tea with a little girl, about her own age, who was a doctor's daughter. The family was well-to-do, but the child was neglected. There was nobody in the house when Gerda got there except the servants, so the little girl was able to take her visitor into the surgery. She said to Gerda as they stood in the room, which was full of the cloying smell of ether, 'There's a new baby in your house. Do you know how it came?' Gerda answered, 'Of course I do. Mother told me. Our doctor brought it in his bag.' The little girl laughed and said, 'Oh, you silly! That isn't how babies come! They just tell you that. I'll show you how babies really come,' and she took down from her father's shelves books on anatomy and obstetrics, with drawings in them, which she explained with a grin. Gerda refused to look after she understood what it was all about, and ran down the steps of the house into the street with her fair hair flying out behind her. That afternoon worried Gerda dreadfully. She could not dismiss what the girl had said as nonsense, because her shrewd little brain told her that the story hung too well together to be anything but true. The undesired knowledge made her suffer terribly, for she was instinctively very pure, so pure that she could not bear to tell even her mother what had happened. It was then, at the age of about nine, that she first turned to religion and found in it the help that life itself denied her. She had always liked saying her prayers, learning hymns, and going to church. Now she found that praying and reading the little devotional books her mother had given her, and looking at the pictures in them of angels in shining raiment, made her feel clean again; and by cleansing her made her feel she was an active participant in holy things.

That helped her, perhaps, to be so good to her baby sister Ursula. It is true that she started with a most passionate fondness for her. When she was away from her she continually talked, with an absent look in her eyes, of her wonderful little sister, of her beauty and her cleverness and her warm sweetness; and when she was with her she watched over her, without cease, correcting all her baby faults. But this feeling might soon have worn off, for Ursula was an unusually trying child. She was darker than Ellida, and far more troublesome. She was not puny or malingering; but she was insanely rebellious. She was a creature of immense vitality, which she expended in insane destructiveness and rebellion. Toys that Gerda and Ellida had kept all through their childhood survived her strong little fingers not a morning. She was disobedient to an extent that made her scandalously untidy both as regards her person and her possessions. The mere fact that she was told to button up her dress made her look on any such proceeding as a silly waste of time; and she did not seem to see any reason why she should clear up her toys from the nursery floor. Praise evidently meant nothing to her. The schoolteachers were sorrier than ever for poor little Gerda, who had a more worried look than ever when she drove before her two recalcitrant charges instead of one. They had the greater sympathy with her because the family fortunes were plainly going downhill. Mr Heming had departed in search of a very mysterious job in America, and there was nearly no money at all. The children had no new clothes, their boots and shoes were a disgrace. Gerda felt the situation very bitterly, and suffered deeply from her loneliness. For of course Ellida was far too deeply sunk in morbid fancies about her unpopularity to notice what was going on, and Ursula was obviously far too young. Poor little Gerda used sometimes to come to school red-eyed with the tears she shed over her responsibility. Her teachers noted it and talked among themselves, admiring her.

Then she was deprived of one of her few consolations: that Ursula, though troublesome, was robust and not bad-tempered. Gerda was never able to cheer herself with that after a curious scene which happened during the holidays when Ursula was about six. The Hemings were staying in a Somerset village in a cottage that stood in the High Street. One day, just after Ursula had been given her week's pocket money, she had looked through the window and seen an old man playing a hand-organ on the opposite side of the road. She cried out, 'Oh, I'll give him a penny!' and before Gerda could stop her she had run to the front door, and ran across the street, right under the hoofs of a horse that was being ridden home from the hunt. The rider checked his horse in time, she was unhurt; and she smiled up at him for forgiveness. Then an arm fell on her shoulder and she looked up into Gerda's face. Gerda had followed her sister to the front door and had got there just in time to see her run under the horse's hoofs. A red mist had covered her eyes, something had seemed to cleave her body down to the heart. Then the mist had cleared and she had seen that Ursula was safe. At once she had run forward to take her back and punish her, because of course she must be punished severely for doing anything so silly and wicked. She was shaking all over at seeing her darling little sister so near to danger.

But it oddly happened that Ursula, who had not been frightened of the horse, seemed very frightened indeed of what she saw in her big sister's face. She stared for a minute at Gerda, and then began to scream. Afterwards Gerda used to say that of all the troublesome moments she had had with Ursula, that was the worst. The child seemed driven mad by terror, and fought like a wild cat when her sister tried to get her back into the house. It was such a pandemonium as the High Street had never seen, and when they got her back into the house she continued for half an hour to give out these high, piercing screams that could be heard half across the village. Moreover, this was not the end of it. Thereafter she was given to attacks of hysteria that were to Ellida's crying fits as a thunderstorm. They made her a hopeless nuisance at school, which the teachers greatly resented. They were always having to send for poor little Gerda to take her home. What added to Ursula's unpopularity just about this time was that she developed a disfiguring facial twitch. She had always had a tendency to exaggerate all her expressions, to raise her eyebrows and pout her lips more than other people when she smiled. Of this Gerda had vainly tried to cure her, saying, 'Don't make those horrible faces!' Now she had only to utter this admonition for Ursula's face to be convulsed. Gerda kept at it, but the condition did not seem to improve. Her task of caring for her little sister became more and more thankless. Ursula seemed incapable of gratitude, and was ready to form the most passionate resentment against her for trifles.

There was, for example, the affair of Miss Fenwick's tea-party. Miss Fenwick was the only teacher for whom Ursula felt any liking; and to her she gave an outpouring of devotion that worried Gerda by its abandonment. She was a kind, absent-minded woman, who never listened to gossip, and she liked Ursula's brains. She seemed to like her very much. One summer term she gave out invitations to a tea-party for all the children in her class; and Ursula was the only child who did not get one. She went home in tears and sobbed out what had happened on her mother's breast. Her mother told her that the most likely explanation was that she had been naughty in Miss Fenwick's class. At this she had the usual fit of hysterics. But Gerda said that she did not think Ursula had been in any particular trouble lately. Then her mother told her to wait, that the invitation might be coming nearer the day. But the days passed, and every day Ursula, who was an honest child, had to admit to her playfellows that she had not been invited; and her behaviour in Miss Fenwick's class became so overwrought that she earned rebukes more than once. Every evening she cast herself into agonies of mourning at her rejection by her idol; and Gerda was as kind as could be. The day of the tea-party she tried to distract Ursula by taking her out to a tea-shop and giving her ices.

The next day Miss Fenwick said to Ursula, as she came into the cloakroom, 'What was the matter with you, dear, that you didn't come to my tea-party?'

Ursula choked and answered, 'But, Miss Fenwick, you never asked me!'

Miss Fenwick said, 'But of course I did, dear. I gave the invitation to your sister, Gerda, and she put it in her satchel to keep for you.'

Gerda was standing close to them, ready to intervene as she always did when she could save Ursula from the consequences of her oddness. When she heard these words she gasped, and slipped her hand into her satchel, and took out the letter, and cried, with tears standing in her clear blue eyes, 'Oh, Miss Fenwick, I shall never forgive myself!'

At that Ursula leapt on Gerda in a biting and scratching mass. Miss Fenwick was extremely shocked, and never could bring herself to like the child again.

Shortly after Gerda left school and went to a distant University, and Ellida got a scholarship at a boarding school. Ursula was left alone with her mother, who was in an irrational state of melancholy on account of the death of Mr Heming in America, and had formed a delusion that she had angina pectoris. Ursula did not know it was a delusion. For two years, from that time till she was twelve, she lived alone with the sad woman, in daily expectation of her death, in the dreariest poverty, with her sisters' company only in the holidays. Then Ellida came home, but that was not such a relief as it might have been. She had just completed her first year at a training college, where she had done brilliant work, when she was sent back in a state of profound neurasthenia. The only thing she wanted to do was to lie in bed and weep, lamenting that no one really cared for her, that there was no place for her in the world. She lived with her mother and Ursula for a year, by which time she was well enough to go out and take a job as an uncertified teacher. At the end of this time Ursula had a curious collapse of conduct and health. The first term she was free of Ellida, she got in with a rough crowd of girls and got into trouble by playing a practical joke on a teacher and by editing a magazine that satirized school life. There was a great fuss over that, and she proceeded to have a nervous breakdown, which was followed by a prolonged threat of weakness about the lungs.

Gerda almost broke down when she got the news. She was doing very well in her post-graduate post; and she had thought that surely her family would see that the least they could do was to relieve her of care for them. It was true that she did not actually have to go home, but the responsibility was there all the same. What broke her heart was her realization that her beloved little sister, Ursula, was evidently not going to grow out of her queerness after all. It was then for the first time that she realized that all her struggle had been in vain, that all her unremitting efforts to drag her sisters into line with normal people had been wasted, and that her family was going to be her cross. She prayed humbly for strength to bear it.

The actual material responsibility for Ursula was, as it happened, not so insoluble a problem as it might have been, because just about that time an aunt of Mrs Heming's died and left them a moderate income. Ursula, who was now seventeen, wanted to go on the stage. As a famous actress had seen her in amateur theatricals, and had declared she had great talent, she was allowed to go to a dramatic school. There, however, she failed miserably. She had the kind of self-mistrust that leads people to make the worst of themselves once they are observed. Once she was being watched she turned from something interesting and vital to something clumsy and stolid. At the end of two terms the authorities could give no hope that it was worthwhile continuing her studies. Gerda had from the first warned Ursula that she must expect some such disappointment, and fortunately, as she had just taken a post near her home, she was there to comfort her when the blow fell.

'Don't you think, dear', she asked her, 'that you would do better to choose some occupation in which your appearance would not be so important?'

This seemed to irritate Ursula, yet Gerda felt that she should have understood. When Gerda had gone to see Ursula act she had wanted to cover her eyes every time her sister had come on the stage, there had seemed something so odd and disturbing about her. Surely she must know how terribly different from other people she was? If she did not, it must be because she was so far from the normal that she had no standards. There was certainly something unpleasant about the doggedness with which she went on hunting for an engagement after she should have seen that a dramatic career was hopeless. She did eventually get one, but it was in a painfully second-rate company, and Gerda very sensibly pointed this out to her. Ursula seemed to lose pride in it, after that, and resigned during rehearsals, greatly to Gerda's relief. She then tried to make Ursula do what she had always wanted her to do, which was to become a clerk in the Post Office. It was not much of a career, but then Ursula had lost the chance of going to a University by her naughtiness at school, and she must take the consequences. It happened, however, that just at this time Ursula was given the opportunity to write an article for an evening paper, and she wrote it so brilliantly that she was given a post on the paper. Everybody was pleased except Gerda. She was enormously proud of her sister's work, but she also knew that too early and too easily won success would be the worst thing in the world for Ursula's undisciplined temperament. As it turned out afterwards, she had good ground for her fears.

The evidence for that accumulated very quickly. Ursula began to make her work an excuse for being tiresome at home. She began to pretend that she could not do her work unless her mother exercised some self-control and ceased to give way to hysteria and melancholy. That was obviously not the right thing for a daughter to say, and Gerda stopped that briskly enough. But her work itself was a worry. She expressed her views in such a downright way, and they were of a revolutionary sort that made Gerda wince. She had hated with the most passionate loathing her poverty-stricken home, with her disreputable father, her melancholic mother, poor, moping Ellida, and queer, rebellious Ursula. She would have given anything to be born again into a respectable family, such as the other girls at school had had, with a stout father who went to the City every day, a mother who was handsome and well-dressed, and brothers and sisters who were tidy and popular. But Ursula seemed at odds with the world of people who were like that, to be destroying all chance of the family getting into that world through social contacts. Gerda did her best for her sister's literary work. She read all her articles, telling her at once when they dropped below standard, and trying to prevent her from getting conceited. But she could not help feeling that it would all end badly.

But she was even more worried about Ursula's social life. The two sisters were asked out a great deal. Ellida was not; she was too strained and nervous to be readily liked. But the other two were always being invited to parties, and at these Ursula always behaved so unsatisfactorily that Gerda suffered agonies on her account. To begin with, it always seemed to Gerda that Ursula looked all wrong. One could not quite say what it was, but she was odd, she was not like other people. Gerda used to hover round her before they started, trying to make her look right, and she used to be tiresomely ungrateful. Once somebody lent her a Vionnet model to copy, and she had it made up in white crepe. Gerda almost cried when she saw it. It had loose wings on each side that parted and showed the arms up to the shoulder. It is true that women in evening dress usually have bare arms, but somehow she could not endure Ursula to do it, so she went straight away and got a needle and thread, and began sewing the wings together. At this Ursula gave way to an attack of temper that Gerda, for all her love for her sister, felt a little bit disgusting. Ursula would not let the sewing be finished, and just as if she were a naughty little girl again, she slapped her. Poor Gerda had hardly been able to get through the evening. Ursula had started out flushed and over-excited, and her arms had looked dreadful. They must have done so, for people kept on staring at her; and they would keep on making her talk, and she had not the sense to see they only wanted to make her show off and then laugh at her. She hated the way they made a laughing stock of Ursula at parties, and of course she could not do anything about it in other people's houses. When Ursula brought guests home, Gerda could more or less keep control of things. She always sat close by Ursula and when it was needed said something quiet and sensible that put matters on a proper footing. But when they were the guests of others she could do nothing, until they got into a taxi to go home, when she would try to make the girl realize what a fool she had made of herself. But that was uphill work. However kindly and tactfully she tried to do the disagreeable business, Ursula showed a childish resentment that made one feel it was useless.

That was a trial to Gerda's nerves; but not so much as the evenings when Ursula went out alone. No one was happier than Gerda that her little sister should have a gay time, but these occasions filled her with sick apprehension. She used to sit up reading by the fire, wondering whether the hosts were people that it was really wise for Ursula to know, and, as the hours went by and it drew near eleven o'clock, whether she was not staying monstrously late. Before her there appeared a humiliating picture of a drawing-room with everybody gone home except Ursula, who sat there talking and laughing in her over-excited way, while the host and hostess looked stonily at the clock. When Ursula came in she used to tax her with these things. 'Did everybody else go first? Are they really nice people?' she would ask. At first Ursula used to answer sunnily and reassuringly, but then she began to be impatient, and soon she was taking it worse and worse. With horror Gerda slowly realized that there must be something very wrong in Ursula's life, for she began to behave in the strangest way. As soon as Gerda started to ask harmless and necessary questions she used to throw herself down in her chair, covering her face and sobbing as if she were utterly tired out and utterly desperate.

Very soon Gerda knew that her suspicions were fully justified. One day Ursula ran away with a married man, Gordon Ayliss, the artist. It was an act of madness. There she was with a brilliant career opening in front of her, and a perfectly happy home life, and she had made this suicidal dive into an illicit love affair, which had even less promise of happiness than most, since Ayliss had run away with other young women and made them very unhappy. Mrs Heming went almost mad with grief, and Ellida, who had a peculiar horror of sex, turned from her sister in a pallid stupor of disgust. But suddenly Gerda knew that though they were feeling what was right and natural she could not feel it with them. She discovered that she loved Ursula far more, even, than she supposed. She remembered – and at the memory the blood seemed to leave her heart for a minute and rush down into her hands and her feet and back again – how warm and sweet her little sister used to be when she was tiny. She could not have what survived of that darling companion, however much it had let itself be soiled by the world, cast out into the darkness. Moreover, she felt that Ursula's going had left a hole in the air of the house, that stood before her in her sister's shape, forever calling her to mind, but empty of her sister's beloved substance. In spite of all her mother's shrieks and Ellida's peevish shudders, she went to see Ursula, who ran to her arms with a lack of shame that she found maddeningly characteristic in its oddity, its inability to appreciate the normal and proper view of things. And a month or two afterwards, Ursula, just as characteristically, tarnished Gerda's sacrifice by starting to have a child.

At this Gerda suffered the last bitterness of agony. The birth of this child fixed on her family for ever the stigma of undesirability that she had struggled from her infancy to remove. It took from her all hope of ever breaking into that world of conventional homes for which she longed far more than she had yet longed for Heaven. In her bed at night she sometimes envisaged the sort of home which she had seen when her schoolfellows asked her to tea, when they had thick red wallpaper in the dining-room and a massive sideboard glittering with silver-boxes and decanters, and in the drawing-room a grand piano; and she wept like an exiled angel. She remembered how she had always felt humiliated because her mother had no 'At Home' day, and though she laughed at herself for that she knew that it still humiliated her. Nevertheless she still wanted to cherish her little sister, to be a shield between that dark and merry thing and the destruction the others wished for it. She felt, too, as if some higher power compelled her to stand by Ursula's side just then, as if an essential part of her destiny would escape her did she not take her place there. The approaching birth of the child could not, she thought, have meant more to her had it been she who was to be the mother. It was not only that she felt full of the tenderest love for the little creature; she was also in a state of rapt anticipation regarding the actual hour of its birth. Of course she shrank from thinking of it, because she could not bear to think of her little sister undergoing such terrible pain. Yet she was sure that at that moment something wonderful was going to happen. The universe would be struck by a blow, and shattered, and then remade in a new and beautiful and purified form. Thinking of it, her heart used to beat quicker and quicker till she had to let her head droop back and draw in her breath through her parted lips.

She could no more have kept away from Ursula during this time than she could have done without food or water or air. In spite of Mrs Heming's protests, which were by this time almost maniacal, she went to see Ursula before the baby was born, at the watering-place where she was hiding. It was something of an anticlimax when she got there because Ursula had not yet abandoned her repellently odd point of view regarding her situation. With amazing egotism she seemed to consider that the welfare of herself and her child ought to count exclusively at this time. When Gerda told her how Mrs Heming was going about the streets of the suburb where they lived with tears running down her cheeks, Ursula said grimly, 'That's going to do a lot to keep down scandal,' and began complaining about her mother's lack of self-control. She did not seem to see that she was the person who was the proper object of blame in the family, and that of course everybody else was in the right. Gerda spent the weekend trying quietly to make her see things in the normal way, and she seemed more subdued by Sunday night. But then they walked down to the station and the sea air gave her better spirits. The train was late in starting, and they had some moments to pass with Gerda leaning out of the window and Ursula standing on the platform below. 'Look at the evening star,' said Ursula, and turned away to regard it. As she stood there the serene absorption of her profile and the straightness of her back filled Gerda with despair. She must do something to make her understand. Leaning further out of the window, she began gravely, 'I don't think you realize what you've done, dear,' when Ursula, not hearing, and still looking at the star, said, 'I wonder if I will die.'

Gerda dropped back into her seat. It had never occurred to her that Ursula might die. Thereafter the thought haunted her, making her more liable than ever to violent palpitations of the heart. When Mrs Heming railed at her because of her intention to be with Ursula when the child was born, she kept her eyes down on the floor and did not answer, nursing within her the reason why in this matter she must go against her mother as she had never done before. At last, very shortly before the date that had been foreseen for the birth, she felt that she must not hold it back any longer, and, with a curious feeling of pride as if she were lifting a curtain on some great drama, she said, 'But Ursula may die!' When Mrs Heming replied, petulantly as a tragedy queen who sees the centre of the stage usurped by a rival, 'Nonsense, Ursula won't die, she's so strong!' Gerda's heart turned over in her, and she felt herself pierced by two griefs. The one was horror that Ursula should be so uncherished by her mother. She did not know what the other was. It felt like disappointment. She supposed it was because she had raised the whole matter on to a certain plane and her mother had dragged it down to a lower one. The house became distasteful to her. She was not at ease until she found herself in the train on her way to Ursula. It was a long and uncomfortable journey; Ursula had always annoyed her by talking and writing as if her willingness to face it were the remarkable feature of her sacrifice, instead of her disregard of the conventional aspect of the situation. But she felt relaxed and content once she could sit face to face with her fear of Ursula's death, contemplating and arguing with her, not having to think of anything else.

When she got to Ursula's lodgings and had her supper with her and the nurse under the gaslight it all seemed like a dream. She looked at her sister's face, which had an expression of fatigue and power, as if she were performing a task that called for an immense expenditure of energy but she knew she had enough to last her till its completion, and she thought, 'Mother was right, Ursula is very strong, there is no danger of her dying.' All at once she became very tired. She felt that the vast amount of emotion she had expended on Ursula during the last few months had been got from her on false pretences. As soon as supper was over she got up and said she could not keep awake any longer. Ursula looked up at her apprehensively, as if she were a little girl again and were frightened of a scolding from her elders. That made Gerda laugh and bend down and kiss her.

She fell asleep very quickly, turning sullenly away from the thoughts that had occupied her nightly for many weeks as if she had been deceived by them. But she was to stay awake in that bedroom till dawn, three nights later. For Ursula's strength after all did not settle everything when the child was born. She began to suffer late in the evening, just before supper, but not severely. The doctor came and looked at her, and said that all was going well, and he would come back in a few hours. But about ten o'clock she suddenly lost all self-control. She began to moan very loudly, and even to cry out. Gerda ran at once to shut the windows, which were very wide open, as it was a hot night. The house backed on to the garden of a very nice villa, and she did not want the people living there to hear. Ursula sat up in bed to watch her doing this, shaking with hysterical laughter which changed, as she dropped back on the pillows, to shrieks. Gerda had done everything she could to make her pull herself together. She felt sure that other women did not behave like this when they were having children. But soon the nurse told her that she must go and tell the doctor to come at once. She ran down the road to his house, her eyes set gravely before her and her very short upper lip raised right off her teeth. She did not like asking him to come, when he had said he would come later. Probably he was resting after a hard day's work. It was so like Ursula to have her baby in the night. She was so apologetic that indeed he did not hurry himself, but when he got to the house and saw Ursula he seemed greatly perturbed. He sent Gerda back to tell his wife to telephone another doctor in the town. She did it very quickly, and then ran back to the house. Nobody said how quick she had been. The doctor held the door of Ursula's room while he spoke to her. It was hard to hear what he was saying because of the dreadful noises Ursula was making, but she gathered that he was telling her to go to her room, but hold herself in readiness to be called at any moment. To try and make excuses for Ursula, she said, 'She has been very brave till now, Doctor.' He looked at her strangely and said, 'She isn't quite conscious now, you know.'

Gerda went and knelt by her bed. In his face she had seen quite clearly that he thought Ursula was going to die, that he was being faced with some technical problem which he did not think he could master. The hour she had anticipated was striking now. The hair stood up on her scalp, her skin was goose-fleshed. She whimpered, 'Ursula, my baby Ursula!' and rolled her head about. She heard the steps of the second doctor coming up the stairs. He moved heavily; it did not sound as if he would be much help in an emergency. In her misery she groaned aloud, and stretched herself on the rack of intense prayer. It mysteriously seemed to her during the hours that followed as if the battle between life and death that was being waged in Ursula's body was being waged within herself also. It was true that she was praying, that her soul was going up in a steady flow to God, but she felt other forces raging within her. Sometimes she felt as if she were slipping off a ledge into a black abyss where there would be eternal agony. Sometimes she knew an inrush of pleasure that made her sway from side to side till she remembered with a start that no good news had come as yet. Then it was as if these two feelings were trying to enter into her at once; she wanted to laugh and cry at the same time and felt as if she were tickled to the degree of the most exquisite torture. There was also the feeling she had always anticipated that this was the supreme hour of her life, that everything which passed was of the highest importance. Then her mind seemed to split, like a canvas too tightly stretched. It no longer held up to her a picture of what was happening. She still was conscious of the physical signs of her alternating states, the sweat and driving heartbeats of her pain, the easier breathing of its relief, but it was no longer apparent to her what mental events were causing them and she had to search for these, naming them slowly and repeatedly, to make herself understand. Then everything went save expectation of the moment when they would knock on the door and tell her. Hour after hour passed and her brain was blank of everything but that. Presently she completely forgot what it would mean; but she still lay stark with attention.

At last the windows let in white daylight; and then it came. Gerda was on her feet in an instant, and her fingers found the handle of the door. She had to steady herself for a minute before she opened it, because a red mist covered her eyes and something seemed to cleave her body down to the heart. She did not know which of the doctors it was that said, 'The patient is doing very well now, and there is a fine little girl.' While she leant against the door-post and sobbed there ran through her mind a desire, which she knew to be childish and unkind, to hurry along the corridor and scold Ursula for having given everybody so much trouble, but that was immediately eclipsed by another feeling even more strange than anything that had happened during the night. It was not merely the relief that was bound to come when she heard that her dear little sister was out of danger. It was an

269

unmistakable feeling of redemption from guilt. Happy tears gushed up in her as if their source had been sealed and was now opened. She felt as if at the last moment she had been saved from committing a terrible crime. Yet she had been in no danger whatsoever of committing any crime. She perceived that no explanation for her emotion could be found on the rational plane; and that it must therefore be sought in the sphere of mystical experience to which, as she had been increasingly conscious for some years, she seemed to have some special right of entry. In a flash she realized that what she had been doing the whole night long was to take upon her own soul the burden of Ursula's sin, for which no doubt God had meant to punish her by death; and God had rewarded her sacrifice by sheathing His sword and letting there be not death but life. She clasped her hands and, raising her eyes in thankfulness, looked up a shaft of light.

It was something of an anticlimax to go into Ursula's bedroom, and find her sleepily self-satisfied and aware of nothing but the merely material events of the night; and of course one could not tell her, she was not on that plane. But anticlimax was to be the note of Gerda's life for many years to come. If she had not known that it was God's way to test those whom He had honoured with special spiritual blessing by subsequent tedium, she would have despaired at the flatness and savourlessness of the days that followed that miraculous night. She returned alone, since Ursula would not leave Ayliss, and resumed her life at home. Again she tried to take her family in hand, and make them lead a life more like other people's. But she was frustrated there by the development of a new phase in Ellida's eccentricity. From being exceptionally shy and retiring, and reluctant to be in the society of men, she became frank and frenzied in her efforts to marry. She began to dress with desperate and inexpert frivolity, attaching untimely frills to the soberest garments, and to make up her face with a determination that hardly compensated for lack of practice. Formerly she had spoken with disgust of a certain schoolfellow of hers, who was understood to have been leading rather a fast life since her marriage; but now she sought her out. The woman was amused at the adoration of this odd fish and took her about with her. Ellida came back laughing knowingly and repeating silly libidinous jokes and stories. Gerda suffered agonies of shame till, as it happened, Ellida met a simple scholar who was too inexpert in social ways to realize that she was behaving oddly, and only realized that here was someone who was offering him freely the affection which he had always wanted and had been too shy to ask from the more reserved. They married; and at once Ellida abandoned her extravagant demeanour. It was as if it had been a brightly coloured flag that she had waved out of a window to tell the passer-by that she was a prisoner and wanted to escape. Thereafter she took no interest in her family. She had two children, but she did not welcome any of the help that Gerda tried to give her with them. She muddled away at their upbringing as if they were her toys and she were a poor child who had never had any of her own before.

She had gone. Ursula had gone. Gerda felt very lonely. She was now well over thirty, and it seemed certain that she would never marry. It was difficult to understand the reason for this. Of course her circumstances had worked against it. When she was young she had had many admirers, some of whom had seemed to have serious intentions regarding her; and that these had never matured into definite proposals she had put down to the handicap of her family. When the time came when it was natural for her to ask them to her home, she used to be overcome by the hopelessness of it all when she had to bring them in and introduce them to her mother and sisters, so odd, so different from other people's mothers and sisters. Her embarrassment used to make her unable to speak, she would sit with her head down, looking at the floor. It was never a success. Of course the men never wanted to come back. She could not blame them: though she could not help feeling that they should have seen her value and realized that it was worth their while to overlook the awfulness of her family. But oddly enough, things did not get any better now that she was free of all her family except old Mrs Heming, who had now exchanged most of her individual characteristics except the generalized ones of age. Gerda supposed it was because she was no longer young, and because most men would not want to marry a woman whose sister had behaved like Ursula. But she had to admit that two men had seemed mysteriously chilled. It was as if they had found in her character either not as much as they had expected or something definitely repellent. Yet what could she have done to be better than she was? She felt amazed and hurt, until it became plain to her that it had been laid on her as a special cross that nobody should appreciate her.

Even her mother seemed resolved not to give her due credit. Presently nothing would please Mrs Heming save that she should be reconciled to Ursula. Nothing could have been nearer Gerda's heart than that her little sister should be taken back again, but she could not help feeling that Mrs Heming's joy over it all was a little ungrateful to her, when she had always been such a good daughter to her. She felt, too, that Mrs Heming and Ursula combined together in an attitude towards her that was not quite loyal. One afternoon at tea she gave Ursula a slice of cake and said, 'Now, mind you don't make crumbs on the carpet!' and both her mother and her sister burst out laughing. She asked them what they were laughing at, but they would not tell her, and went on looking at her as if they were sharing a secret. But altogether she was worried about Ursula. By this time she was desperately unhappy with Gordon Ayliss. He would not give her enough money to keep their joint home going, and she had to work hard to pay the bills; and at the same time he insisted on her being a devoted wife to him, and nursing him through his frequent attacks of hypochondria. She continually complained of over-work and lack of money. Of course Gerda would have been delighted if she had left Ayliss on moral grounds, but she was sure she was wrong on these particular issues. Ursula had always been neurotic, and work was good for her. After all, as she was always pointing out to Ursula, she was not doing so very much work; most of her contemporaries were turning out far more stories and novels. And it was no use her saying she had exceptional handicaps. Everybody knows that the best work is done under difficulties. As for money, Gerda felt sure Ursula was extravagant. So she did not encourage her at all in these complaints. Obviously what she needed was not sympathy, but bracing, for she was letting herself go to pieces, looking years older than she ought to have done, and dressing like a drudge. But it was no good, for she let herself go more and more, and finally sent the little girl away to boarding school when she was only five years old. This made Gerda really angry. Ursula's excuse was that she could not look after her as well as Ayliss and make money, with only one servant to help her. But surely she could have made an effort.

Gerda was not living so unhappily, when her mother died. She took a flat in town after that, but could not settle down. She missed her mother, and the life she had led after the two others had gone. It had been nice living in the suburb where everybody knew her, and used to stop her in the street to ask her how her mother was, and to say, 'It must be a heavy responsibility now you're the only one at home.' She turned for consolation to Ursula, but could get none there. For one thing, the little girl, Miriam, for whom Gerda had always felt a mystical love, had a curious dislike for her aunt. When Gerda spoke to Ursula, Miriam used to dash over to her mother as if to protect her. For another, Ursula's career worried Gerda terribly. Although she had not yet succeeded in ridding herself of Ayliss she had got on with her work, and was becoming well known as a journalist and playwright. Nobody could have been happier at Ursula's success than Gerda was, but obviously it was all on a wrong footing. Gerda winced at her articles, they were so outspoken, and frequently she contradicted what quite important people said; and her photographs were all over the place. Why did they have to have so many more photographs of her than of other people? And many of them made her look much younger than she really was. And the plays worried Gerda still more. They always seemed to her to contain a character that might have been taken from somebody in real life. Sometimes Ursula would deny this with such exasperation that it showed she was guilty. Other times she would admit it and try to pass it off by saying that the portrait was quite flattering, and that she had asked the original permission, and that they quite liked it. But that was nonsense, nobody could like being put into a play, and lots of people could not like it to be published abroad that they were friends of anybody with a reputation like Ursula's. However, there was no way of making Ursula see reason. She got quite hysterical when Gerda taxed her with putting into a play a dressmaker Mrs Heming had employed in their childhood, and had said that the woman would

almost certainly be dead. But she admitted she had taken no steps
to find out, which would have been the scrupulous thing to do. She
was so showy and rash in everything she did. She was always with
people who were well known; she must be pushing herself forward
all the time instead of making sensible friendships with people of her
own kind. Gerda suffered agonies when, as often happened, she went
to Ursula's house and found her talking familiarly with some quite
celebrated visitor. They could not resent it, of course, as they were in
Ursula's house, but of course they must be hating it. What made it
all so much worse was that it was impossible to tell her anything. One
night when Ursula was on the eve of sailing to America to superintend
the production of one of her plays, Gerda made a point of visiting her
in order to warn her not to give indiscreet interviews. Her sister took
it so badly and ungratefully. At first she kept on demanding when she
had ever given an indiscreet interview, which was surely not the point;
and then, sitting on the top of a trunk, she burst into a storm of tired
and angry weeping.

It got worse as Gerda drew into her forties. Ursula had induced
Ayliss to leave her, and was doing more work than ever. Her name
and photograph seemed to be everywhere. A comedy had a prodigious
success in America and was brought over to England with a great deal
of preliminary trumpeting. Gerda, as its production drew nearer, grew
more and more apprehensive, for she felt that such a success probably
meant that there was something unwise and conspicuous in it, and
when she had asked Ursula if she might read it her sister had merely
uttered a loud and meaningless groan. When the actual day came she
was so disturbed that she could not eat, and wandered out into the
streets during her lunch-hour. Presently she saw a church, and she
went in to pray for help in bearing her cross. When she got inside
she found that it was a Roman Catholic place of worship, but she
did not mind that. She had always been attracted by the superbly
consequential appearance of nuns as they floated by with their black
draperies and the spread white sails of their linen headgear. But she
felt that as a Protestant she had no right to join the main group
of worshippers, so she tiptoed across the church to a side altar.
Raising her eyes she saw that she was in the Lady Chapel, and

that she was looking up at a statue of the Virgin Mary, which meant more to her than any religious emblem had ever done before. There was no obvious reason for this. It was a very commonplace statue, representing the Virgin as fair and blue-eyed, like herself, and it had an unusually unaesthetic feature in the rays of light proceeding from her head, which were painted the same colour as the metal of great guns. Yet Gerda felt a wave of longing to unite herself in the spirit with this figure, that had such power and was so perpetually and unquestionably in the right. At the same moment a priest walked briskly and confidently between her and the altar, and passed a door in the wall which the casual visitor would never have suspected to be there. His air of being about some business that was kept private from the mob but was sanctified by the very highest authority aroused the most passionate envy in Gerda. She would have given anything in the world to feel herself lifted up above the general ruck of people who did not know where they were going or why on to this plane of divine certitude. Then suddenly it occurred to her there was no reason why she should not know this elevation. Like a flash of light there broke on her the realization that it had not been mere chance which had led her to this chapel. God in His infinite lovingkindness had guided her steps to this happiness, which had always been waiting for her but which she had hitherto blindly overlooked. She dissolved in joyful tears.

Six months later she was received into the Roman Catholic Church, and was not disappointed. She flung herself into the good works of the faith, and served on innumerable committees. Her flat was always full of priests and nuns and devotees, chattering together with happy immersion in technicalities, and a good-tempered merriment at the expense of the unbelievers, that never ceased to delight her. Never was she without plenty to occupy her, never did she feel depressed and abandoned. Even she could bear up under the cross laid on her by Ursula, though there things had got no better. One day Gerda went to see her and was worried by her pallor and her lack of animation, and asked her if there was any reason for it. Ursula had hesitated, and with an assumption of frankness had told her that the death of a certain politician six weeks before had meant the frustration of all her dearest hopes, since she had expected to marry him. Poor Gerda had not known what to do. It was impossible this man could have proposed to Ursula; he could have had anybody. Either she had misinterpreted some casual flirtation, or she was making up the whole story. It was the kind of fantasy a neurotic woman would invent after the death of a well-known man. Gerda looked Ursula straight in the eye and said, very gravely and gently, 'Are you quite sure he wanted to marry you, dear?' At that Ursula went quite white. She lay back on the sofa and closed her eyes, and seemed to want Gerda to go. It had evidently all been untrue, like the stories she spread about her being tired and ill. It was hard on Gerda to have a sister who did these odd things, and who was so ungrateful too; for there was reliable evidence that she had once said at a dinner-party that what she would have liked more than anything in the whole world was a family who really cared for her. All Gerda's kindness and tenderness had melted like snowflakes thrown on the hard, hot metal of Ursula's egotism. It was disheartening. Nevertheless, such was the fortifying effect of the Roman Catholic Church on Gerda that she felt an increasing love for Ursula. She went to her house quite often, and usually enjoyed the visit very much. If any other guest took her home she would tell them how sweet Ursula had been when she was a baby; and if she were alone she would pass into a daydream in which it seemed as if they were all in the nursery together again, and her little sister was just a lovely warm bundle, whom she could pick up and carry about at will. The next morning she would always remember to ring up Ursula, and say how pleasant the evening had been and point out anything that had been wrong; such as, for example, that she had made a tactless remark or that the dress she had worn was cut too low.

One day, when Gerda was about fifty-five, she heard a rumour about Ursula which was more specific than these hypochondriacal legends she spread about herself usually were. It reported that she was suffering from a mortal disease. Gerda had gone at once to Ursula to talk about it, because it was really absurdly undignified for a woman of her age to go spinning these fairy-tales, and very inconsiderate. The first minute Gerda had heard the story she had felt sick with fright. She went that evening to see Ursula about it, and found her lying on a sofa, looking very tired: she had probably been out to too many parties. At first they talked about family things – about Miriam, who was finding it difficult to accommodate herself to school life. Gerda suggested that perhaps it had done the child's character permanent harm to be sent away from home so early. Ursula said in a worried, excited way that she thought it might have done, but that she did not see what else she could have done. She said, 'It was all so difficult then! And I was only twenty-two.' Gerda corrected her, because she did not like to see her giving way to self-pity on false grounds, 'But you were twenty-three.' At that Ursula broke into that silly hysterical laughter that Gerda found so annoying. Ursula ought to be embarrassed, not amused, at the correction. Gerda went on rather severely to ask her if it was true that she had this disease. Ursula sat up on the sofa and stared at her, evidently in great confusion. She looked for a minute as if she was going to utter a long cry and fling herself on her sister's breast; but then she pulled herself together. After a pause she said rudely and impatiently that of course she was suffering from nothing like that, that what was the matter with her was that she was tired to death. Gerda told her as tactfully as possible that she thought it a pity she should let such alarmist rumours be spread about her, and described how it had upset her when she had heard it. Ursula's eyes slid past her to the window, and with that evasiveness Gerda had always hated in her, she turned the conversation to the beauty of the night-scented stocks that were growing in tubs on the balcony. They were indeed beautiful, but there were more of them than were necessary, and they must have been very expensive. Gerda felt she ought to point this out, but all the thanks she got from Ursula was a kind of groan. Gerda was very worried to see that her sister's face was twitching as it used to do when she was a child. Evidently she was caught in one of those nerve-racking complications that her untidy way of living brought on her. Since Gerda knew by long experience that there was no means of helping her, she left her and went home, heavy of heart.

For three weeks after that Gerda heard nothing of Ursula. She rang up the flat several times, but there was no reply at any hour, so she knew it was shut up. Ursula must be travelling. The journey could not be necessary. Ursula was not having a new play produced anywhere, she had been passing through one of her neurotic spells when she did not work. She must have been moved to travel by sheer restlessness. Gerda sighed and wondered if Ursula would ever accept the way of peace. Then one evening she got a telegram telling her that Ursula had died that day at a nursing home in a town about an hour from London. It asked her to come to the funeral two days later, but she went down that evening. She sat in the railway train with the tears running down her cheeks. Though the people in the carriage looked quite nice, she did not care what they thought about her. When she got to the nursing home she found Miriam there, overcome with grief. She looked terribly like her mother, very odd in the wildness of her grief. Gerda tried to say a few consoling words to her but was repelled because there came into the girl's eyes the same look that had so often come into Ursula's eyes when she had been the object of Gerda's kindness; insanely lacking in the appropriate gratitude, insanely seeming to reverse the real state of affairs and claim that patience and forbearance were being not accepted but given. A cold sense of how trying Ursula had been stood up in her mind like a post that the tempest of her grief could not blow down. But Gerda forgot all that when she went into a room and saw lying on a bed the tired woman, tired to death just as she had said, who was what life had made of her darling baby sister.

She spent much of the next two days in the Roman Catholic chapel of the little town, praying for the soul of her sister, and trying to subdue the confusion, the storm of emotion, which was distressing her. She could not help but feel that it was characteristically odd and cruel of Ursula to have kept her state a secret. Why had she denied the rumour that Gerda had taken to her? It had been true; Ursula had been killed by the malady it had named. Why, too, should she who had hated loneliness, who had always liked to fill her house with people she had not known well, have chosen to die alone save for Miriam? It was almost as if she had felt that Gerda had failed her. But looking back on their lives, right to childhood, Gerda could not see that for one moment she had failed in her duty to her darling baby sister. There could be no reason for Ursula's unkind rejection of her save her insane suicidal tendency to rebel against everything that was good for her. That inexplicable madness which had wrecked her life had dominated her to her last breath. All that Gerda could hope was that now, in the hereafter, Ursula was beginning to understand.

Thanks to these religious exercises she was able to go to the funeral in a state of composure. But it was shaken when they lowered the coffin into the earth, for then a part of her that had existed in her long before she heard of religion, and that did not seem to have heard of it yet, stood up and cried that they were taking from her all that she had truly loved. She was wrung with anguish, she seemed to be spinning like a top further and further away into desolation, when she was brought back by people shaking her hands. It heartened her immensely to realize how kind men and women were. For these people must obviously have a kindly motive in talking as they did of Ursula as if her life had not been a tragic failure. They might have been sorry for her, they might have discerned what potentialities were wasted in that desperate career, they might have seen what real sweetness was hidden behind the oddness; but they could not really have admired her as they were pretending. Gerda wept with gratitude, for she felt they were doing it because they recognized what it must all have meant to her.

That evening she went back to London; and thereafter day followed day. When she came back to her flat every night she used to sit down and cry, she was so utterly alone. Ursula was dead; Ellida was submerged; unaccountably she was nothing to Miriam. There was no liking there, and no material bond, for though she had imagined the girl might need financial help there had turned out to be plenty of money for her; since Ursula was such a bad manager she must have been very lucky. Gerda was in the deepest anguish; and it seemed to her as if her loneliness had more than the ordinary degree of horror. It had a shuddering quality as if she were expecting a veil to be thrown back and something to stare her in the face. Sadness even worse than anything she had known in her martyred life seemed about to swallow her; but it was then that she was rewarded for the dedication of her life to holiness. There came a letter from a Catholic committee called to organize the opposition to birth control, saying that their secretary had resigned and asking her to take on the post. She sat with the letter in her hand, and for the first time she had a mystic revelation of the sin that is involved in birth control. She saw Ursula's face, as it was

279

when she was a baby, pressed against the night sky as if the stars were points of a grille; and she was appalled to think that any human beings could find it in their hearts to shut out of life that which could be as sweet and dear as this.

So began Gerda's mission: which was to lift her to the ranks of the saints, which she was to carry on till her dying day with a courage that never flinched under an attack and an unfailing energy that, as she truly said, was not hers alone. It did indeed appear to proceed from the Lord. For whenever she relaxed in her labours, whenever she tried to take a holiday of body or spirit, she was not permitted. Always there came to scourge her back to her divinely appointed work a sense that the universe was being polluted by some vast crime against children, by an offence against these little ones on a huge scale, and that she, even she, was responsible. If she did not at once start again to buy expiation through her toil and her prayers it appeared to her that the blackness of guilt was about to engulf her. But she was not dismayed, knowing that thus mysteriously does the Lord deal with even His most innocent saints.

# Deliverance

*This story, never before collected, appeared in* Ladies' Home Journal, *August 1952.*

One autumn evening a woman in her early forties walked along the platform of the Terminal Station in Rome and boarded a *wagon-lit* in the Paris Express. She sat down on the made-up bed in her compartment, took off her small, perfect, inconspicuous hat, and looked about her with an air of annoyance. It was a long time since she had travelled by rail, and she had been pushed to it against her will, because there had not been a seat free on any of the planes leaving Rome that day or the next. But this was the least of her worries, and she wasted no time on it, but set about arranging her passport and her tickets in order to have them ready when the *wagon-lit* attendant arrived. This required close scrutiny, for although she was a Frenchwoman named Madame Rémy, another impression was conveyed by her passport, her tickets and the labels

281

on her luggage, and she had to remind herself what that impression was, for only a few hours before she had been yet a third person.

Such inconsistencies, however, never made her nervous. They were unlikely to be noticed because she herself was so unnoticeable. She was neither tall nor short, dark nor fair, handsome nor ugly. She left a pleasant impression on those she met in her quiet passage through the world, and then these people forgot her. She had no remarkable attributes except some which were without outward sign, such as a command of six languages and an unusually good memory.

When the door opened, Madame Rémy had not quite finished getting her papers out of a handbag which had more than the usual number of pockets and flaps in it, and some very intricate fastenings. Without raising her head, she asked the attendant to wait a moment, in her excellent Italian, which, just for verisimilitude, had a slight Florentine accent. Then, as he did not answer, she looked up sharply. She had only time to remark that he was wearing not the uniform of a *wagon-lit* attendant but a dark grey suit with a checked blue muffler, and that his pale face was shining with sweat. Then the door banged between them. She did not follow him, because she was as highly disciplined as any soldier, and she knew that her first concern must be with the tiny ball of paper which he had dropped in her lap.

When she had unrolled it she read a typewritten message: 'A man is travelling on this train under orders to kill you.' She rolled it up again and went into the corridor and stood there, looking out at the crowds on the ill-lit platform. It would have been unwise to leave the train. A clever man with a knife, she calculated, could do his work among the shadows and get away quite easily. Several times she had to step back into her compartment, to get out of the way of passengers who were coming aboard, and at these, if they were male, she looked with some interest. She was standing thus, looking up with a noncommittal glance, neither too blank nor too keenly interested, at a tall man in a tweed overcoat and wondering if he were so tall as to be specially memorable, and therefore ineligible as an assassin, when she heard shouts from the platform.

The tall man came to a halt, and she crushed past him and stood beside him, looking out through the wide corridor window at a scene still as a painted picture. Everybody was motionless, even the porters with their luggage barrows, while four men made their way back to the platform gates, at a quiet and steady pace, two in front, and two behind who were walking backwards. Their faces were darkened by masks, and all held revolvers which they pointed at the crowd. The man beside Madame Rémy made a scandalized and bluff noise which told her that he was not an assassin, and at that moment the train began to move. He went on his way to his compartment and left Madame Rémy standing alone at the window, waiting to see what had happened at the end of the platform. But she saw nothing unusual till the train was leaving the station behind it and sliding out into the open evening. Then her eye was caught by the last iron pillar that held up the platform roof. A man was embracing it as if it were a beloved woman to whom he was bidding farewell. His suit was dark grey; and as he slid to the ground and toppled over and fell face upward, it could be seen that he was wearing a checked blue muffler.

Madame Rémy went back to her compartment and said a prayer for his soul. She looked at her hands with some distaste, because they were shaking, and took the little ball of paper out of her bag and read the message again. This was not because she feared she had forgotten it, or thought she had overlooked any of its implications, but because it interested her as a technician to see if there were any distinguishing marks in the typefaces which recalled any typed letters that she had received before. Then she thought of all the things it would be sensible to do, such as ringing for the attendant and showing him the message, out in the corridor, in front of some open door, in the hearing of some other passenger, preferably a woman, and she decided to do none of them.

She said aloud, 'I am a lucky woman.' Leaning back her head against the cushions, she repeated, 'How very lucky I am.'

There had seemed no way out of the wretchedness that was all around her. She was under no illusion as to the reason why the doctor she had consulted in Rome concerning a slight but persistent symptom had begged her to go into hospital for an X-ray examination the next day, and had urged her, when he found she was resolved to go back to Paris, not to let one day pass after she got there without seeking a surgeon. The thing was in her father's family, and she was familiar with its method of approach.

She was, moreover, in financial difficulties to which there could be no end. She had loved her dead husband very much, so much that she felt that she could deny nothing to the child of his first marriage. But Madeleine was sullen and unaffectionate, had early insisted on marrying a worthless young man and had three children already and might have more; and her only remarkable characteristic was a capacity for getting into debt without having anything to show for it in purchased goods. Madame Rémy really did not see how she could meet this last crop of bills without selling either the few jewels remaining to her, which were those she wore so constantly, except when she was on duty, that they seemed part of her body, or her little house in Passy, where she had spent all her married life. In either case it would be a joyless sacrifice, for Madeleine had nothing of her father in her.

Also, it was evident to Madame Rémy that her long-standing friendship with Claude was over. Just before she left Paris she had heard again the rumour that he was going to marry the Armenian heiress, and his denial had left her in no doubt that they were going to part before very long, perhaps even without tenderness. That would take from the last five years of her life the value which she had believed made them remarkable. She had always thought that she had taken up her peculiar work because she and a distinguished member of the French Foreign Office had fallen in love with each other, and that had made it a romantic adventure. But now she suspected that a member of the French Foreign Office had had a love affair with her because she had an aptitude for a certain peculiar kind of work; and though she recognized that even if this were so, Claude had formed some real affection for her, and that she owed him gratitude for much charming companionship, she knew that she would never be able to look back on their relations without a sense of humiliation. Even her work, in which she had hoped to find her main interest as her life went on, would now be darkened in her mind by association with a long pretence, and her own gullibility. There was nothing at the end of her journey except several sorts of pain, so if the journey had no end there was no reason for grief.

When she had worked it out to her final satisfaction she found that the *wagon-lit* attendant was standing in front of her, asking for her tickets and passport. She gave them to him slowly, feeling a certain sense of luxury, because his presence meant her last hope of life, and she was not taking it. They wished each other good night, and then she called him back, because it had occurred to her that it would be hardly fair if he had to go without his tip in the morning just because she was dead. Agents were trained never to make themselves memorable by giving more or less than the standard tip, and she acted according to habit, but regretted it, for surely the occasion called for a little lavishness. As she explained to him that she was giving him the tip in case they were rushed at the other end she noted his casual air. He was evidently to be the second-last man she was to see, not the last.

Once she was alone, she burned the message in her washbasin, and pulled up the window blind so that she could look at the bright villages and the dark countryside that raced by. She thought of the smell of anaesthetics that hangs about the vestibules of clinics, and she thought of the last time she had met Madame Couthier in the Champs Elysées and how Madame Couthier had looked through her as if they had never been at school together, and how it had turned out that Madeleine had run up a huge bill with young Couthier, who was finding it hard to make his way as an interior decorator. She thought of an evening, just before she had heard the rumour about the Armenian heiress, when Claude had driven her back from dinner at Ville-d'Avray, and she had rested her head against his shoulder for a minute when the road was dark, and had kissed his sleeve. Claude and she were the same age, yet she felt hot with shame when she remembered this, as if she had been an old woman doting on a boy.

She pulled down the blind, and began to make very careful preparations for the night. Her large case was on the rack, and she did not care to ring for the attendant and ask him to move it for her, lest somebody else should come in his stead and the attack be precipitated before she was ready for it. But she was obliged to get it down, because she had packed in it her best nightgown, which was made of pleated white chiffon. For a reason she had never understood she had always liked to carry it with her when she went on a specially dangerous enterprise; and now she saw that it had been a sensible thing to do. It was very pleasant to put it on after she had undressed and washed very carefully, rubbing herself down with toilet water, as she could not have a bath. After she had made up her face again and recoiffed her hair, she lay down between the sheets. Then it occurred to her that she had not unpacked her bedroom slippers, and she made a move to get out of bed before she realized that she need not take the trouble.

She turned out the big light in the compartment ceiling, and left on only the little reading lamp at the head of her bed. She had not locked the door. Her careful toilette had made her tired: and indeed she had been working very hard for some days, preparing all the papers that were now safe in her embassy. She thought of Madeleine and Claude, and bleakly realized that she had no desire to see either of them ever again. She tried to remember something pleasant, and found that for that she had to go back to the days when her husband was alive. It had been delightful when he came back in the evenings from his office, particularly at this very time of year, in the autumn, when he brought her sweet-smelling bouquets of bronze and gold chrysanthemums, and after tea they did not light the lamps, and sat with the firelight playing on the Japanese gilt wallpaper. It had been delightful, too, when they went for holidays in Switzerland and skied in winter and climbed in summer, and he always was astounded and pleased by her courage. But dear Louis was not at the end of her journey. There was nothing waiting for her there but Madeleine and Claude, and the smell that hangs about the vestibules of clinics.

The train slowed down at a station. There were cries, lurchings and trampings in the corridors, long periods of silence and immobility, a thin blast on a trumpet; and the train jerked forward again. That happened a second time, and a third. But still the man who was travelling under orders did not come to carry them out.

Madame Rémy turned out the reading lamp and prayed to the darkness that he might hurry; and then for a little, retreating again from the thought of Madeleine and Claude to the memory of her husband, she passed into something nearly a dream. But she was fully awake as soon as someone tried the lock of the door with a wire. It was as if a bucket had been emptied over her, a bucket filled, not with water, but with fear. There was not a part of her which was not drenched with terror. She disliked this emotion, which she had never felt before except in a slight degree, just as much as added to the zest of an enterprise. To escape from this shuddering abasement she reminded herself that she wanted to die, she had chosen to die, and she sat up and cried, '*Entrez! Entrate!*'

The door swung open, and softly closed again. There followed a silence, and, feeling fear coming on her again, she switched on the light. It was a relief to her that the man who was standing with his back to the door did not wear the uniform of a *wagon-lit* attendant, and that he was the sort of person who would be selected for such a mission. He was young and lean and spectacled, and wore a soft hat crushed down over his brows and a loose greatcoat with the collar turned up, in a way that she tenderly noted as amateurish. It would be very hard for him to get away from the scene of a crime without arousing suspicion. There was also a sign that he was the man for whom she was waiting, in the woodenness of his features and his posture. He knew quite well that what he was doing was wrong, and to persuade himself that it was right, he had had to stop the natural flow of not only his thoughts and feelings but his muscles.

Yet he made no move to commit the violent act for which this rigidity had been a preparation. Simply he stood there, staring at her. She thought 'Poor child, he is very young' and remained quite still, fearing to do anything which might turn him from his resolution. But he went on staring at her. 'Is he never going to do it?' she asked herself, wondering at the same time whether it was a cord or a knife that he was fingering in the pocket of his greatcoat. It occurred to her that with such a slow-moving assailant she had still a very good chance of making a fight for her life and saving it. But then there came to her the look of surgical instruments on a tray, the whine that came into Madeleine's voice when she spoke of the inevitability of debt, and the fluency, which now recalled to her a conjurer's patter, of Claude's love-making; and she was conscious of the immense distance that divided her from the only real happiness she had ever known. She flung open her arms in invitation to the assassin, smiling at him to assure him that she felt no ill will against him, that all she asked of him was to do his work quickly.

Suddenly he stepped backwards, and she found herself looking at the door with a stare as fixed as his own. She had made an absurd mistake. This was simply a fellow passenger who had mistaken the number of his compartment, and all the signs she had read in his appearance were fictions of her own mind, excited by the typewritten message. It was a disappointment, but she did not allow it to depress her. When she thought of the man in the dark grey suit with the checked blue muffler, sliding down the pillar and turning over as he reached the ground, it was as a child might think of an adult who had made it a promise. She contemplated in sorrow and wonder the fact that a stranger had given up his life because he wished her well, and switched out the light and again said a prayer for him into the darkness. Then, although she had no reason to suppose that the man who was travelling under orders would come sooner or later to carry them out, she grew drowsy.

'What, not stay awake even to be assassinated?' she muttered to her pillow, and laughed, and was swallowed up by sleep, deep sleep, such as had often come on her at the end of a long day on the mountains.

The next morning a spectacled young man, wearing a soft hat and a loose greatcoat, who had made his way back to Rome while the sun came up, stood in a hotel room and gave a disappointing report to his superior.

He said, 'Madame Rémy was not on the train. It was all a mistake. There was one woman who answered to the description, and I went into her compartment, but I found she was quite a different sort of person. She was not at all haggard and worn; indeed, she looked much younger than the age you gave me, and she was very animated. And though we know that if Ferrero found Madame Rémy on the train he must have warned her, this woman was not at all frightened. She had left her door unlocked, and when she saw me she showed no fear at all. Indeed,' he said gloomily, 'she was evidently a loose woman. Though she was in bed her face was painted, and her hair was done up as if she were going to a ball, and it was really quite extraordinary – she even stretched out her arms and smiled at me. I think', he asserted, blushing faintly, 'that if I had cared to stay in her compartment I would have received quite a warm welcome.'

His superior expressed an unfavourable opinion regarding the morals of all bourgeois women, but had his doubts, and made certain inquiries. As a result the spectacled young man was doomed not to realize what was at that time his dearest ambition, for he was never given another chance to commit a political assassination. He regretted this much less than he would have owned. Even then, standing in the golden sunshine of a Roman morning, he was not really disturbed because the night had been so innocent.

At that moment Madame Rémy was sitting in the restaurant car of the Paris Express, eating breakfast. She could have had it brought to her in her compartment, but she had felt a desire to have it where the windows were wider and she could see more of the countryside. Her first pot of coffee had been so good that she had ordered a second, and she was spreading the butter on a roll, smiling a little, because it seemed so absurd that after such a night she should have awakened to find herself suddenly freed from the wretchedness that had hung about her for so long. Certainly she had lost none of her troubles; but they no longer appalled her. There came to mind the names of several among her friends who had survived serious operations. As for Madeleine's debts, if nobody paid them it might help the poor silly child to grow up; and the wisest thing, even the loyalest thing, for her stepmother to do was to keep the jewels and the house that Louis Rémy had given her and leave them intact to Madeleine's children. It might well be true that she could no longer support the desperate nature of her present work, but there was no need for her days to be idle, for the great dressmaker, Mariol, had always had a liking for her and had more than once offered her a post in his business. And there was no need for her to think of Claude. If she wanted to think of someone who was not there any more, she could remember Louis.

Some other names occurred to her: the names of people who had not survived operations. But they cast no darkness on her mind; she was conscious only of a certain grandeur, and they went from her.

For all her interest was given to looking out of the window at what she was seeing again only because of some inexplicable carelessness on the part of those who were usually careful.

Now the train was running toward the mountains, and was passing through a valley in the foothills. There were cliffs, steel-grey where the sun caught them, dark blue in the shadow, rising to heights patterned with the first snows, glistening sugar-white under the sharp blue sky. At the foot of the cliffs a line of poplars, golden with autumn, marked the course of a broad and shallow river racing over grey shingle; and between the river and the railway track was a field where a few corn shocks, like dried, gesticulating men, were still standing among some trailing morning mists. Across this field, through the mists, an old man in a dark blue shirt and light blue trousers was leading a red cart, drawn by two oxen the colour of the coffee and milk in her cup. Deliberately the two beasts trod, so slowly that they seemed to sleep between paces, so dutifully that if they were dreaming it must be of industry. There was nothing very beautiful in the scene, yet it was wonderful, and it existed, it would go on being there when she was far away.

As the train met the mountains and passed into a tunnel, she closed her eyes so that she could go on seeing the cliffs and the snow and the poplars, the man and his cart and his oxen. Amazed by what the world looked like when one had thought it lost and had found it again, she sat quite still, in a trance of contentment, while the train carried her on to the end of her journey.

# The Only Poet

Among Rebecca West's unpublished works there were fragments of what was evidently to be a full-length novel, together with an outline of the plot. It opens with Leonora Morton, a widow of over eighty, going to a party where, in the cloakroom, she meets a woman who seems to be effusively grateful for something Leonora has done in the past. In plotting terms this incident has no importance, though we learn something of Leonora's character and past. She had been married first to Philip Le Measurer, by whom she had two daughters before he died. The incident prompting the flashback which, it seems, was to form the heart of the novel, is Leonora's seeing an old accredited beauty, Avril Waters, the woman whom Leonora perceives as having ruined her life. Leonora's first husband had died 'confident that she will marry a millionaire, Gerard March, who has long professed a passion for her. But once her husband is dead Gerard March loses all interest in her. She feels hurt and humiliated, and goes to Paris to get over it'. There she meets the rich Greek, Nicholas, with whom she is to have a long and passionate affair which is ended by a brutal incident involving Avril Waters. She returns to London and marries Lionel Morton, with whom she lives in East Africa for some years before returning to London. On a visit to Vienna she encounters Nicholas, ten years after their affair. They spend the night together, and have a long conversation before parting again. And so we return to the party and the novel's conclusion.

Diana Stainforth sorted and typed the mass of existing material, and chose a logical order for it all, while providing the many alternatives. I am more indebted than I can say for the lovingly scrupulous work she has done, and for the notes she has provided. The material was, she writes, 'in manuscript (handwritten) books or part manuscript books, frequently muddled up with other works, many loose manuscript pages, one short, incomplete typescript version and a number of loose manuscript pages. The typescripts have no [corresponding] manuscript, although there are similar versions. There are many rough drafts of some sections.

'Most of the material is very rough and heavily corrected, and very difficult to read. Most is in the form of notes. The manuscript book "Notes for Nicholas", which covers much of the affair and forms the core of the story, is entirely in note form with no regard for chronological order. Amongst the rest there are several

*"Chapter 1"s and from this it is deduced that Rebecca West was trying out alternative beginnings.*

*'The manuscripts are written in ballpoint pen, with the odd page in fibretip. The probable dating is therefore between the late 1950s to the late 1970s. Mention of the New Berkeley hotel, which opened in 1972, shows that some of the . . . material was written then or later.*

*'It is also likely that this book was worked on at varying times between the dates given. The evidence for this is not only in the type of ballpoint pen used, the paper and the handwriting, but also in the inconsistencies, i.e. the number of husbands Leonora had (two or three), their names, her age at the time of the party (seventy or eighty).*

*'Although the notes and drafts span most of the outline there are gaps. One point not clear in the material is the moment when Leonora recalls her affair. It appears that Rebecca West had not quite decided if the long recall should come immediately after Leonora sees the woman who ruined it, and then she feels ill and dies, or if she feels ill and then recalls the affair.'*

*With some conflations and recensions, Diana Stainforth's is the order used here, with Leonora seeing the woman she blamed for ruining her love affair, recalling the love affair and then falling ill. It should be emphasized that this makes no pretence at being a scholarly version: it has been ordered to give as much of the original material as is consonant with providing a coherent narrative. Thus the different names which Rebecca West tried out for many of the characters have been reduced to one name each, usually following the 'Notes for Nicholas' manuscript, and Leonora has two husbands rather than the three of some drafts. Dating has been left vague, since more than one decade seems to have been tried out. The story seems to work better if Leonora is eighty or more at the time of the party. Her first husband fought in the 1914–18 war, and she foresees her second husband rejoining the army for the threatened Second World War. Her affair with Nicholas, therefore, would have occurred in the middle to late twenties, when she was thirty-one, and their meeting in Vienna when she was forty-one.*

*The arrival at a coherent reading version has meant that a few passages of attractive material have had to be omitted. For instance, there are two versions of the house in which the party is held, the alternative one with some beguiling details of rooms plundered from a demolished Mayfair house. These, however, were too incomplete, hinted at too many subplots, to do more than confuse the narrative. A very few passages have been omitted even when there was no alternative version, because their inclusion would have muddled the narrative or characterization. However, the passages in note form which were often all we have of the central love affair have been left as they are: they are charged with life and narrative suggestiveness. The selection and conflation of various versions have left some minor inconsistencies, but these have been left on the principle of including as much of the original material as possible.*

*Wherever feasible, Rebecca West's characteristic light punctuation has been left as it is. Material in square brackets and Roman type comes from her notes. Italic type indicates my editorial interpolations.*

# The Only Poet

*The only poet is the nervous system – (Paul Valéry)*

**B**eing over eighty, Leonora Morton often fell asleep quite
suddenly in what are usually counted as working hours.
That was how it looked to her juniors, but actually she
was passing judgement on the moment and sentencing it to oblivion
if it lacked interest, and she was doing that as she drove through the
spring night to Patricia Stone's birthday party. In a fusion of dream
and memory she had gone from London, which was now simply
a stage where she had once given a performance of no particular
interest to her, and was back in the country house where she had
lived for thirty years: lying in bed in the room which ran right across
the house behind the pediment of the colonnade, a window in each of
the four walls to show the raspberry-stained night sky over the towns
that lay beyond the hills to the north and south and east and west. Half

a dozen books lay scattered over the counterpane so that her mind could nibble itself into a doze, and outside the hoots of the owlets in the spinney across the road fell through the night softly as feathers, making wakefulness restful as sleep. She should never have left the country. There was always something to do, from morning till night; and in her remembrance, in her dream, it was morning, and she was dawdling down the garden with the old labradors – but that showed the folly of wishing she had died a year before she sold the house – and she was kneeling by the rubble-poor bed on the south side of the walled garden. She was thrusting her fingers deeply and delicately down into the coarse rampage of flags to find the minute tight-fisted pencils of iris slytosa that would unfurl in the warmth of the house and be a high, singing blue. They were odd flowers, uncertain like stocks and shares; perhaps forty in all in a bad season, and one hundred and twenty a day if the year was good, and no reason for it.

As the car slowed down and went into the gates she awoke, and looked out across the lawn at Patricia's house, frosted in the light of the moon that was caught like a kite on the topmost branches of an elm tree over towards Lord's Cricket Ground. How time changed that which seemed unchangeable, and in fact had not changed. Fifty years ago people had been so rude about the house, so sorry for poor Patricia, who was so elegant, so like Gertrude Lawrence, and who simply had to live in the horrible thing, since it was a wedding-present from her father-in-law, who had been brought up in it and thought it the most beautiful house in London, and anyway revered his own father, who had built it in the eighties. It had been ironical, he was suffering as much from leaving it as poor Patricia was from moving into what one of her friends had likened to a deserted wife of the old National Liberal Club, dumped down on the edge of mediocre Maida Vale, to sulk over an inadequate alimony. But now nobody would have denied it was simply splendid, the moonbeams glistening on the turrets and balconies and *oeils-de-boeuf* and creatures on the upper storeys, and underlining them with sooty shadows and the golden glow of the party shining through the huge windows on the ground floor and making patterns through the trefoils and quatrefoils of the tracery, so silly anywhere but in a cathedral, so nice. Somebody with no self-consciousness had managed to think of Winenberg and Venice at the same time, in a thoroughly English way, and it was as succulent a morsel of Betjeman-meat as could be found in all London. Patricia would die if she had to leave it.

As Leonora Morton came up the steps, which were covered with the confetti of blown-about cherry blossom, she called to the butler, 'Am I late, Mr Macnab? Has everybody come except me? Had I better go home?' and he answered, coming out into the spring night chill to give her an arm up the last step, 'Oh, there's a few to come yet, Mrs Morton.' When they got inside, under the chandeliers, he did not let her go, but said soothingly, 'Anyway, if we had to stay up all night for you, you'd still be welcome,' and helped her up the inner staircase to the octagonal hall, though the steps were shallow and she could manage them perfectly well. 'I must be looking ghastly,' she thought, but that was not unnatural at her time of life, and Mr Macnab could easily fall back on the brighter memories of her he must have accumulated in the forty years of their acquaintance.

Leonora Morton crossed the octagonal hall slowly, she did not want to hurry through it, Gordon and Patricia had made it so pretty when they had had the house redone. Though Lord's Cricket Ground was only a hundred yards away, the room had a country air to it, which in her eyes was a great recommendation. Who would not be in the country if they could? The country was the place to live, there alone could one see the change every day brought to the look of the land, the only justification of time. Had she still lived at Buttermilk Hall she would have walked out early that morning, through the lemon-sharp sunshine to the shaw nearest the house, and peered about among last year's rust-red beech leaves for the first white violets, not for picking, just for looking, while the two old labradors (but this was simply dreaming, she was dreaming as they used to as they lay before the library fire after dinner, for they had died a year before she sold the place. Both dogs were like the ideal family solicitor, chasing the woodland smells as if they were getting concessions out of the Inland Revenue). But it was no use going on about that. When one was old, one had to creep back to London, it was the only place where one could get what one needed, good dailies and indoor swimming-pools, which were oddly enough not what she had expected. Nobody had told her that when one is over seventy what one wants more than anything else is access to a good indoor swimming-pool. One got something of what one had got from love-making, from that first thrust into the water, the surrender of the whole body to an unusual element.

She hurried across the hall to the powder-room, though it was so pretty, unfastening her coat as she went, for she really was too late, it was sheer impudence to come to a party when everybody would be thinking of going home. She briskly handed the coat to the woman in black among the hangers, who, she noted, was not the nice fat blonde Italian whom Patricia usually got for her parties from Willowes-Aumbrie, the caterers in Sloane Street, but an older woman with a rather odd stare. 'I am so late,' she chattered, because she saw that the woman in black was still staring at her, but seemed to be in the grip of an emotion, even to be about to burst into tears. 'She is unhappy,' thought Leonora. 'Perhaps somebody she loves has died. Perhaps she's just poor.' It struck her and amused her that though her coat was quite a good mink – wild, and very well cut – once the woman had got it safely among the powder-room hangers any other guests who caught sight of it would not say, 'That's a nice mink,' they would deduce, 'That must belong to someone old.' For some years now Patricia and her friends had held the belief, strong though they might lose it overnight, that all furs short of sable were dowdy, and by night and by day they wore cloth coats, of such remarkable simplicity that, allowing for the difference in wear between cloth and fur, they could have saved little or no money that way.

She herself was unlikely to join in that movement. The people who had been about her in her youth were as sensible as she had ever known, and she had let what they taught her stay in her mind, even if she did not act on it. One of their precepts related to the buying of clothes. Her home had not been actually poverty-stricken but every halfpenny had been bespoken for warmth and repairs to the roof and books and good plain food and drinkable wine, and it had been impressed on her that before buying any article of clothing one must divide the price by the number of years the thing was likely to be wearable, and if the figure was high, well, obviously one abandoned the project. There was some sense in it, of course, though the sum had to be altered just a little to work out the right answer. Nowadays it was only prudent to divide the price of any dress or coat she bought by the number of years she might live. 'But, God,' she said to herself, 'how ridiculous I would have looked in the intervening years, had I not thrown that precept out of the window.' All sorts of things would not have happened, she vaguely thought, not specifying what things. 'No, I did not look ridiculous,' she thought with dreamy unspecifying pride, but she supposed she looked ridiculous now, people did when they were old, but when she peered into the glass it did not seem to her that she did, though such vanity as she had been born with had long since evaporated, as scent does if one leaves it long enough in the bottle. It was many years since her appearance had raised any important issue. But, scanning her image with such matter in mind (and that was how it seemed to her now, just 'such matters', no faces and no names floated up to the surface), she felt a stirring memory, and it seemed to her that her hair had something special about it, it had been unusually soft and fine, and had some other and rarer quality as well. To pass a comb through it had been to give it a life of its own. It had risen in a cloud round her head, and had drifted about her shoulders, floating far out from her body, and if she brushed it in the darkness that followed, it gave off sparks, she was her own night-sky and shooting-stars.

Her lips were dry. This happened all the time now, whenever she had been out in the open air, however briefly. She pressed the lipstick against the tedious surface, and continued to consider her mink. Dear Philip, her first husband, would have been pleased at her refusal to jettison her mink. He had always encouraged her to buy good clothes, he had often embarrassed her by taking it for granted that she must have what she wanted before his wants were even clearly conceived, which had the tiresome result that when she tried to describe the sacrifices this husband had made for her she found herself able to specify them less clearly than she would have liked. The pattern had been pleasant enough. But it had to be faced whenever they went to Paris, which they did every three months because of his work, and then it was all so pleasant, it flowered into such a pretty occasion. He would urge her to go and buy herself a suit from Chanel or an evening dress from Vionnet, and she would at first put him off by saying every evening that she had preferred to visit an art gallery where they were showing some panels by Bonnard or see a new Guitry film or meet a friend, and then on the last morning, when his work would be done and he would offer to take her to see the collections himself, she would flatly refuse to go; and he always rewarded her with an astonished admiration, that was fresh and candid as if he were a boy in love for the first time, a boy much younger than he had been when he first fell in love with her.

The only thing was that his emotion was founded on a double error. He believed that she did not fit herself out at Chanel's and Vionnet's because she was true to her parents' deliberate avoidance of vulgar expenditure. In fact what prevented her from shopping in Paris was her knowledge that Philip had not got that sort of money, and that anyway there were few people in Dorset who would not, had they seen her in a Chanel suit, think her under-dressed, or think her over-dressed had they seen her in a Vionnet dress; and as for her parents, the reasons that they lived in a house lent by a relative and travelled and entertained very little was that a heart ailment had forced her father to retire early. It was not tragic, they were happy enough reading and gardening and listening to music, and it was quite unemotionally that they said to each other every now and then: 'We'll be all right if we don't run into debt'. They had meant just that, and nothing more. But how like dear Philip it was to make so much of what was simple hard-headedness and hail it as the restraint which was the attribute he valued most.

Why, she wondered, did he overprice by so much that necessary but negative quality – that dangerous quality, which might only be disguise for a deficiency? There must be some deep reason, for he had pledged himself to his belief in it, he had laboured to cultivate it. Yet why was that? She could not imagine what he feared he might do if he let his nature have its head. There came into her mind a photograph she had once seen in a newspaper, showing a crowd moved by rumour to gather on a foothill near Los Angeles and wait for the Day of Judgement. She told herself it was all part of his humble resolution to make his goodness, which was already remarkable, still better. There were many facets of his personality which she could not understand because she was so far beneath his level. Yet there sounded in her ears, as clearly as if she had said the words to a deaf companion, 'Philip would have liked me to wear a mink coat till it was bald'.

That was the worst of being old. One had time to think over things which really required no further mental attention, only a sort of physical fostering made one familiar with them over a long time so that one could look at them from every angle, every useful angle, and judge them by their consequences over the decades, and one surely might have left it all at that. But suddenly one found that one held opinions which were nothing like what one had worked out through one's lifetime, and these were sometimes subversive and ungrateful, and always, that was the treason, superfluous. It was no use starting chewing over things all over again. But she was so unsettled by what she had been thinking about Philip that she had to remind herself that her second husband's attitude to money had been the exact opposite and had been just as irritating. Lionel had liked her to spend money – no, it was worse, he loved her to waste it. But his attitude was not so simple as that. It sprang from deep roots, being involved, she sometimes imagined, in a far-fetched fantasy about the abundance of womanhood, overturning her conscience. He enjoyed her having large bills and running up an overdraft in much the same spirit that he insisted on her keeping her hair long at a time when all her friends were bobbed and shingled.

A distant pleasure warmed her, she was on the point of return to a long unvisited satisfaction, but she was too tired to make the long journey. She looked away from the cheval glass, closed her eyes and put her right forefinger between her lips and bit it, as she had done when she was a child and wanted to be somewhere other than where she was. Then suddenly she opened her eyes and turned about. The woman in the black dress had left her place beside the hangers and was standing close behind her and had just called her by the name of her first husband, who had died fifty years before.

'You are Mrs Philip Le Measurer, aren't you?'

She supposed the woman was the child of someone who had worked for her father-in-law in the house in Dorset or who had possibly herself worked there when she was very young. But Leonora felt no curiosity about that. She was conscious of nothing except that the three words 'Philip Le Measurer' had pierced her with horror. Not that Philip's name could raise any horrible image. Sometimes, even now, when she had passed in the street or seen in a group of young people at a friend's house some boy not yet spoiled in skin or smile or look of candour, she had said to herself, 'Philip was like that when he was forty'. What was so terrible about hearing his name was simply that it was so many years since it had been spoken. By now all his friends were dead; he had been twenty years her elder. Her two daughters had been eight and six when he died, and had married in their teens; 'Le Measurer' must be to them what they had burnt on to their pencil boxes with a magnifying glass when they were at school. She herself had remarried only four years after she became a widow, and had then passed into a world he had never known. The last time she had heard him mentioned was in a lawyer's office five years or so before, when a young solicitor (grandson of the one she had started with) had read out the list of parties affected by the breaking of a family trust, paused to ask who Philip Le Measurer might be, and on hearing, crossed off his name without comment.

She stood quite still, in her ears the humming which is the abstract sound of the night, and she ached because she had given Philip no son to keep his name alive. 'But this is nonsense,' she told herself, 'we had our children as they came, and if I didn't have a son it was because there wasn't a son about for me to have.' There was no occasion for self-reproach; but one must shudder in the pervading chill.

But now the woman in black was surely speaking to her in the warm and soaring voice of affection. 'Forgive me. I knew I should call you Mrs Morton. I've known for years you're Mrs Morton, I cut the notice from the *Continental Daily Mail*. You'll understand,' she added huskily, 'there's nobody in the world whose life I'd be more likely to follow than yours.'

Leonora smiled insincerely and raised her eyebrows as if in eagerness to arrive at some recognition which she could trust to be delicious when it came. 'No relation to that odious housekeeper I do hope,' she thought, 'but thank goodness, by now she must be dead and in hell.' But then she felt a sharper twinge of curiosity. When one came to look at the woman in black she was not at all the kind of woman whom caterers sent out to take charge of the cloakroom at parties. For one thing, she was too old, in her middle or even late sixties, and for another her elderly good looks were being expensively maintained. Her black dress was no uniform, Leonora would not have minded wearing it herself for a lunch at, say, the New Berkeley, and her thick silver hair was arranged in the casual order which meant costly hours and carefulness from hairdressers who were respecters of persons. The jewellery, too, didn't fit. The string of pearls would be worth little enough now, they had that look of being bought long ago, a reward for a first child, perhaps, but when this woman was young they would have stood for a large packet of stocks and shares; and she had combed forward two cushioning curls of hair in an effort to hide earrings which were really prodigious, the sort of thing one saw if one still crossed the Atlantic by liner, worn by the women at the next table in the restaurant, who were always much richer than oneself. She plainly had all she wanted in a material sense, though she was not, as people used to say, a lady. But that was only because she did not want to be taken for a lady. She was being industriously deferential as she explained how she happened to be in Patricia's cloakroom. Leonora did not believe a word of it. Whoever she was, she was supported by a group, a family, an association, which had stopped at a lower step on the social staircase than Leonora's own people simply because they were not going to risk their dignity by a dispute about their right to mount any higher, and anyway they were all right where they were. And they did not mind being deferential because they were used to exacting deference themselves.

But her explanation, which was going on and on without actually explaining anything which Leonora wanted to know about this encounter, threatened an outburst of emotion which would crack the opaque varnish of her manner; and at this Leonora felt the sweat form on her forehead, for that emotion must be purely illusory, product of a mistake which would have to be laughed off although it was probably not in the least amusing. Not a single word was enlightening. It seemed that this woman had come from her home in Brussels to London a day or so earlier, to visit her grandson, Jean-Pierre, who was going through the mill at Willowes-Aumbrie, and was, in fact, at this very moment carving at the buffet in the next room. He had, of course, had his full training already, in the original establishment in Brussels. But his father (who was, the woman in black explained, with what would have been a sob had she not been solid like an Ingres portrait of a Louis Philippe matron, their eldest child, yes, her first-born) was starting a catering business in Antwerp.

'Our third,' she said, and paused. Then started again, in a pure gush of pride and joy. 'Our third. Not counting, *not counting*, the original establishment. Oh, Mrs Morton, I do want you to understand. It's all been as successful as that.'

Leonora picked up the cue. 'I'm so glad,' she breathed. If this went on she would have to sit down but goodness knew how long that would protract this huge and springing jet of misunderstanding.

'My son's reason for sending Jean-Pierre to London and to Willowes-Aumbrie', continued the woman in black, 'was that he wants this new branch to have the same classic air as the mother establishments his grandfather and his father founded and we feel that London is the last capital where there remains some vestige of style. So when we open at Antwerp we hope to create an atmosphere which suggests that the clients will find, just round the corner, Buckingham Palace and its sentries.' Her eyes, which were the colour of certain topazes, suddenly cancelled their own hardness by tears, and she ceased to talk as if she were translating from a brochure. 'So Jean-Pierre settled down in London for six months, and I took the opportunity to come over and visit him, and that wasn't simply an excuse, I'm very fond of Jean-Pierre and I miss him. I'm a great one for keeping my own about me. After all, as you know, I nearly had none. But I haven't been back here, not once since I left, and I really wanted to see it all just once again before I go. It's only the look of things I wanted to see,' she said, suddenly icy. 'God is my witness that I had nobody over here to thank, for I had heard that

you had gone to live in Africa for good. To tell the truth if you won't
be offended, I thought you were dead, and don't laugh at me, I had
planned to make sure whether you were for if you were I'd have had
a Mass said for you, and so I will, if you go before me. But how glad
I was when I got Jean-Pierre's bit of news.'

'Why, what was that?' asked Leonora. She felt half-asleep. The
woman's passion was reversing the world, she was now wondering
not so much who the woman was as who she herself might be.

'I must tell it my way, if you'll forgive me, I do realize I'm keeping
you. But being you you'll like to know. Jean-Pierre met me at the
Airport, so funny when you think that when I left there was no flying
except for soldiers. Then he took me to my hotel –'

Leonora could not resist asking where she was staying. She always
had a feeling that it was nice to know as much about people as if they
were not real but were characters in a book one was writing.

Of course it was Brown's. 'Then he took me out for some supper
at the Savoy Grill, and when we'd ordered he said, "I've got a lovely
present for you Granny." It seems that he came to this house, this
very house where we are this minute, and what a fine house it is,
I can see nothing grudged in the past when that was right, and he
was waiting at a dinner-party. From the very first he noted that
there was one lady who came by herself and wasn't young, but
very distinguished-looking. At one point it had interested him to
note that the conversation had become general, which was the rule
at dinner-parties in France and Belgium, but was not usual, he had
observed, in England. Though it was difficult for a waiter to follow
a conversation at table, he had gathered that this unusual unity of
interest was caused by the pleasure everybody felt at a pleasant event
in the family of the distinguished lady of a certain age. One of her
sons-in-law had received from a learned society a medal which was
the highest honour attainable in his profession, whatever that might
be; and they were congratulating the distinguished old lady on this
honour and the charming appearance her daughter had presented at
the ceremony. Then someone asked her how it happened that this
daughter had been given the unusual and tragic name of Cassandra,
and she explained that this was the child of her first husband, in

whose family it had been the habit for generations to call their eldest daughters Cassandra. She owned she could not imagine why, and had hoped, since Jane Austen's sister was named Cassandra, that they had some ancestress in common, and she added, in case someone present knew enough to give a clue, that her first husband's name had been Philip Le Measurer.

'At that,' said the woman in black, trembling, 'Jean-Pierre pricked up his ears. For I can assure you that I've brought up all my children, and my grandchildren too, to revere you.' She laughed nervously. 'I didn't, of course, tell them exactly what you did for me. For us. My poor husband would have been glad to tell you as much, if he had had the privilege of meeting you. For certainly you saved him as well as you saved me. I don't know what Leon's uncle might not have done to him had it not been for you. He was a terrible man, with a cash-box where his heart should have been. So, though Jean-Pierre doesn't exactly know what you did for us, he realizes that it was something extraordinary and saintly, and he knew when he said, "I've found your Mrs Le Measurer" he was doing something like bringing down to earth my guardian angel to reassure me before I die.'

'Why this is real. This is too frightful,' thought Leonora. 'I mean something tremendous to her. What seems unchangeable in her is changed when she thinks of what she imagines I did for her. It's evidently the big thing in her life. And what a fool she'll feel when she finds she has mixed me up with someone else –' But it suddenly occurred to her that this was impossible. The Le Measurer family had long been thin on the ground, and the only other Mrs Le Measurer in living memory was her own mother-in-law, and the woman in black, who had an air of being even too good at sums, would certainly have realized that if old Maisie were alive today she must be well up in her second century. But then Leonora remembered poor Geraldine, the wife of Philip's younger brother, and at that she mildly blazed. Surely old age had not altered her so much that this woman, who had a head on her shoulders, could not see that she was far, far better-looking than Geraldine always had been and always would. Why, poor Geraldine was guilty of the supreme immodesty of having white eyelashes and not darkening them and her skin, however desperately powdered, had the high glaze of bathroom fittings. 'Geraldine was quite nice, really awfully nice sometimes,' thought Leonora, 'but it would be absurd of this woman to think I could be her,' and then, but without pleasure, she faced the fact that the woman had done nothing of the sort. She had to accept the only other alternative. She had indeed rendered this woman some service, which was vital to her happiness, but which had attached her own interest so little that she had clean forgotten it. 'What an insult,' she whispered, almost aloud. She could not offhand think of a worse thing for one human being to do to another.

She was perhaps not well. The room seemed very hot, though a minute before she had wondered how it could be so cold in late spring. Perhaps this forgetfulness of hers was not so disgraceful, so important, so cruel, as she supposed, but she could not be sure. Her mind was as slow as if she were ill, and she longed to do what of all things she must not do, break down and end the matter by confession. But she decided: 'I will get out of this somehow. There must be a loophole, there is always a loophole.' For that belief she had real reason. In various parts of the world she had faced attack from tiresome people, usually proclaiming themselves inspired by principle, but rendered unsympathetic by their taste for the handling of disgustingly unsubtle weapons. Her mind wandered off in meditation on the barbarism of the panga, simply a strip of sharp-edged steel. She was back again sitting between her two daughters on one of the twin beds in the bedroom she shared with Lionel Morton, who did not happen to be there, who should return from Nairobi any moment now. She and her girls each held a revolver. The floor was striped with the arrows of sunlight that struck down through the shutters; the stripes had altered their angle quite extensively since the three of them had first come into the room and locked the door. It must have been hours before they heard the sound of furniture falling over in the room below. 'What did you do then?' people asked her afterwards. She had never given the truthful answer: 'I pretended to be someone else.' Instead she said, 'I hadn't to do much, the girls were so good.' That was true, then and afterwards. She never had to reproach herself for exposing them to an experience which had shattered them. Cassandra had languidly announced the day after, 'I'd much rather spend the afternoon doing

307

that than playing hockey at school,' and Harriet, perpetually ready to
trump her elder's ace, had positively drawled, 'Hockey, yes. Tennis,
no.' They were imitating her they imagined, but in fact they were
imitating her imitation of someone else. She must have imitated him
very often; for even now, on any occasion when the extraordinary had
to be treated as the ordinary, her daughters surprised her by speaking
with Nicholas's voice, which they had never heard.

From that she averted her mind, and listened to the story the
woman in black was telling with a passion which failed to make it
interesting. It seemed that Jean-Pierre had made inquiries from his
fellow-waiters as to the distinguished lady of a certain age, and had
been told that she was often at parties, particularly those given at this
house, and was herself in a small way a client of Willowes-Aumbrie.
Jean-Pierre had greeted his grandmother on her arrival in London
not only with the news that he had seen her beloved Madame
Le Measurer, Mrs Morton, and thought her distinguished and
sympathetic and all he had been taught from his cradle to expect
her to be; but he was going to see her again the very next evening
– which was now: this puzzling now. For he had heard her say to her
hostess that she would be back in a month's time for her birthday
party; and he was booked to wait at that very party.

'At first I looked you up in the telephone book,' said the stranger.
'I thought I'd leave some flowers and a note asking if I could call.
But –' she paused, and continued with an air of flinching delicacy,
'I've forgotten London, and I don't know any more where you would
be likely to live.' It struck Leonora that she did not like to say that
she had found too many Mortons in the telephone book, and that
the unrevealed incident which linked them owed an essential part
of its power to infatuate her for between forty and fifty years to the
rarity and vague picturesqueness of the name Le Measurer. 'A good
thing she doesn't know the Le Measurers were nobodies, Huguenots
who settled down as linen-drapers in the City during the nineteenth
century and put their savings into railways at the right time and took
them out at another right time. Oh, it's all an illusion, somewhere she's
got it all wrong, it's all going to be such an anticlimax for the poor
dear,' she mourned, but forgot to grieve when the poor dear said, 'So

all I could do was to ask Mr Aumbrie if I could take the place of the girl at the cloakroom, and though he didn't like it he's not, of course, in a position to refuse.'

There was nothing to do but wait. How wonderfully, Leonora thought, Coleridge had distilled the essence of boredom into the two lines, 'The wedding-guest then beat his breast, for he heard the loud bassoon.'

*From the manuscript book 'Notes for Nicholas'*: The woman in the powder-room had been a girl working in the house of Leonora's (first) father-in-law and mother-in-law and she was dismissed because she was pregnant, at the time when Leonora and Nicholas were having a love affair.

Leonora felt unhappy because the girl was being dismissed for what she herself was doing. Nicholas felt even more unhappy. He said the Mother of God would forgive. (But I suppose she wouldn't approve, she might want to punish the girl.) Nicholas said in astonishment, 'She, of all people!'

Leonora never identifies the woman in the powder-room with this girl. But she recalls the girl when, during the night when she was dying, she recalls her love affair with Nicholas.

She did not hurry to the drawing-room, though she was so late, finding herself alone in the octagonal hall, which always enchanted her. Really, she must get herself to the drawing-room. But she had disarranged the hair at the back of her neck when staring up at the painted ceiling. With the nervousness of the old, who are always on a slide under the microscope of the middle-aged, using their last critical advantage, she used her mirror and her little comb, rehearsing the white lie she had to tell Patricia. In fact she had been sitting in front of her TV, watching the World's Pair Skating Championship at Bratislava, and the Russians were the last in the programme. These ones were good, but not like the wonderful champions of five or six years ago. She could think of no event that could take precedence over this concourse of mythic creatures, but one could not say so, she would have to tell Patricia that she had had to dine in Richmond, and remember not to change it to Dulwich when she spoke to George. Several times she repeated, 'Richmond, Richmond, Richmond,' and braced her spine and raised her head to make her entrance.

As soon as Leonora Morton entered the great new white room, a woman said to her, 'This is a far grander party than I expected, look at me, a short dress and no jewellery, and absolutely everybody's here. Avril Waters is over there by the fireplace.' Leonora, thinking peripherally while she took the shock, asked herself, not at all seriously, why it was that even now, when she and Avril were quite old, it should be natural for a woman to tell her at a party, 'Avril Waters is here,' and most improbable that anyone would say to Avril Waters, 'Leonora Morton is here.' While the temperature of her inner mind slowly rose as she remembered what Avril Waters had done to her, forty-eight years ago, her outer mind wondered coolly enough why this woman had been given precedence over all the women of her generation, by a judgement almost unanimous though nonsensical. She was beautiful, but not very. Her bones were flimsy and her mouth was constantly falling open with the gape of a fish. She was not nice. Strangers she met with the worst manners; it was then that her mouth was most apt to fall open, as if she really could not believe what she saw, what she heard. With her familiars she bounced like an Edwardian schoolgirl, she was full of larks and calendarish sentiments; she infected her friends with her silliness, quite distinguished men looked, when they were with her, nimble and jolly like morris dancers. She was also notoriously avaricious.

It was at this point that the knowledge of Avril Waters which she shared with all the world fused with her particular experience of the woman, and the memory, substantiated, proved not a mere fantasy, burned her memory like an ember held in the hand. The curious conspiracy to associate Avril Waters with brilliance was building up a dazzlement in front of her. She had, of course, found the brightest spot in the room, where light poured down from the sconces set close together and, with her still golden head duplicated in a mirror, she was acting out her legend before a group round-eyed as if they were

310

watching fireworks. She looked well enough and was shining with diamonds, and Leonora thought to herself, her memory seeming the blacker in contrast with this gaudiness, 'She should not have diamonds, she should have nothing.' She took a glass of champagne from a tray and raised her eyes to the face of a friend whom she found standing in front of her. While she talked to him she said to herself, 'Why should you hate her so? She did not mean to hurt you. She did not know that it was you in that room. She does not know it now.' But that argument failed as it always did. Her mind insisted, 'But after that everything went wrong.'

That, of course, was nonsense. On the contrary, after that everything had gone right. She had skipped out of an affair which could lead to nothing, and had pursued the direct path to the very pleasant situation in which she found herself in her old age, widow of a well-loved second husband, with two affectionate and handsome daughters who had married nice men and given her agreeable grandchildren, as well as a world of friends and a pleasant house. But these were the terms used by people when they talked of strangers. The truth was that though Avril Waters could not have ruined her life, since her life was not in ruins, her life had been ruined ever since that day in Paris. That became certain just at this very hour in the day. When the night looked in at any uncurtained window she looked back at it, and saw that when she came to die she would have had nothing out of life. The French windows of this grand house gave on a garden fresh from the nurseryman's spade and hoe, its lawn as opaquely green as if it were painted, each annual in its bed and each rose and clematis on the walls in its exact prune. It was without the gravity which comes soon to any garden, the elegiac touch given by spreading creepers and the thickened shade under mature trees. Yet if no one drew the curtain soon enough, the garden would become unbearable in its melancholy. Pressed against the panes would be a message to her. She would know that when she came to the turnstile of the next world, there would be no money in her purse. If things had turned out differently, her life would have had an absolute value which would have made it last for ever. As it was, she would perish. Indeed, she had perished.

Yet her friend was saying, his eyes bright because he was a kind

311

man and liked things to go agreeably, 'You're looking well.' And so she probably was. When Nicholas came back into her mind as the sight of Avril Waters had brought him now, she was always pricked with grief as sharp as if it had happened yesterday, but she also glowed, imagining herself once more the object of desire. That had been his great gift to her, and she had needed it. She was then thinking of herself as valueless and unprized, and was the more unhappy about it because people thought that what she was mourning was the death of her husband, and she felt a hypocrite because she could not tell them the truth. But she could not have grieved over the end of her marriage, for it had been too long in ending, and had changed as it ended. When she was nineteen, she had married Philip Le Measurer, a friend of her father's, an officer in the same regiment, a widower in his middle forties. Bright images flooded her mind as she thought of that man, who was then so much older than she was, and now was so much younger, since he had died in his fifties, and she was over eighty; and they were all images of childhood. She had been in love with Philip Le Measurer ever since she was a little girl. He was a silent, handsome, slow-moving man, who lost his silence and became alert only when he was playing with children, and because his first marriage had been childless he had constantly visited Leonora in her nursery. Her Nanny had once said in her presence that 'Major Le Measurer keeps his tongue in our toy cupboard', and it gave her a happy sense of power over a grown-up. The immediate cause for their marriage was her father's announcement that he was going to marry a woman whom both she and Philip saw with horror as the stepmother of the fairy-tales: a view in which there was a solid foundation of sense, for she would certainly have been disagreeable to Leonora, but which showed an infantile bias, for the woman was not whiskery and pointed in hat and chin but the sort of stupid bully, round in hat and head, whom men unaccountably trust, whom male hospital committees choose as matron.

She made a necessary escape from a real danger which was nevertheless quite imaginary as she saw it, into a world as sharp and brightly coloured in her memory as the hand-coloured picture postcards of the time. She had spent her honeymoon at the old monastery high above the Reckitt's Blue Mediterranean, when the oranges were orange-coloured and the lemons lemon-coloured in the terraced gardens, and went home to a little white box in a small flowery Kensington square, purple with lilacs at the time of her return. They were just well enough off to look at the future confidently. After Philip had left the Army he had held a not very important post in a mining corporation; and though his family were far from rich they had possessions which were as good as money in the bank. Their estate was on the outskirts of a Dorset market-town, with a William and Mary house built of stone pale yellow as farm butter, and famous fishing, some of it let and some of it kept for relatives who came to stay. His father and mother were delighted that their son should have taken another wife and a young one; and they showed their delight by treating her as if she were the first of the children they might now expect to find in their house, and as good and pretty and well-behaved as they could have hoped. She spent all summer with them. The weather was perfect. Each limpid day was followed by another, and life was limpid too, with a purity unknown in the nursery, because there was no wild real childhood to break into despair and sin.

In August the First World War broke out. But not in its full force for her. Though Philip went back to the Army, she felt no intense fear for him. He told her that he would not get killed, and she believed him, and even after sixty years did not think herself a fool for her credulity, since about that sort of thing he had a way of being right. So she spent the four years of the war almost unperturbed in having her two daughters. It had been glorious when peace came. The little house in Kensington, the great house in Dorset, were real nurseries now, and the two children, she and Philip, and the grandparents chattered together in happiness from morning to night. What had they said to each other? She could not now recall one single sentence. But when she was thinking of Nicholas, her mind was his mirror, it reflected no other images. She only remembered that when they had all been together it had sounded like the hymns of praise which the birds sing to the dawn. There are no words to that either. Five years passed and they were still with their innocent and exultant chorus. Then Philip was taken ill, and he announced, just as certainly as he had told her he was not going to be killed in the war, that he was going to die.

He became silent again, and not even the little girls could give him back his speech. After he had been operated on the doctors told him that he was well, but he grew quieter and more indifferent every day. Presently he had to have another operation which left the doctors as pleased as they had been by the first. But he counted their assurances as nothing compared to the disposition he felt, when he went home to Dorset, to move out of his own room which had always been his into one far away from the other bedrooms, though he had not slept in it since he had had measles there when he was a boy. 'This is too damn like the way a cat chooses a corner to die in,' he told Leonora, speaking as if he were at one and the same time a vet kindly breaking bad news to the owner of a pet, and the doomed pet itself. It was the last characteristic thing he ever said to her. She thought of him as having really died only a few days after that: one of his daughters was thrown and rolled on by her pony, and though he tried he could not care. Looking back, it seemed to her as if after that there had been no fine weather, a drizzling rain set in. But he lived for nearly another two years, never seeming very well though once so nearly recovered that they went on holiday to France. But he behaved there like a man in a theatre-party sitting out a boring play out of politeness to his host, and shortly after their return he had to have another operation and then all of him was gone.

She had loved Philip, he had loved her, they had the good fortune to do nothing in all their married life to displease each other and a great deal which they both found pleasing; and she mourned him deeply. But her grief could not have abased her spirit, for happiness and loss happened in a world where her value was set high. What had made her such a broken-winged, shameful creature when she met Nicholas in Paris was an incomprehensible humiliation. The squat, magnetic little man named Gerard March. She had believed, Philip had believed, Philip's parents had believed, all her world had believed, that Gerard March was in love with her. It was true that he had often been talked about in connection with other women, some of them very beautiful. But he was the first to mention them to her, in his deep, soft, virile growl, sadly as if they were concessions to his lower nature, while her power was over his higher nature. He talked perpetually about her to their circle of friends, always with adoration. He had asked Philip and her to his London house far more often than any other of his executives, he regularly had them to stay at his villa in Monte Carlo and on his yacht, and if he found himself alone with her during these visits he behaved with the choked tenderness of a lover who for creditable reasons cannot speak what he feels, but will not cease to feel it. Back in England he often sent her scribbled notes which told her he had been seized by a desire to communicate with her, it did not matter what, and sheaves of flowers came to the door with no anniversary to account for them. At Christmas the presents, particularly for the children, were sumptuous, even though they often came from a Bond Street shop not liked by the Le Measurers, who, when passing its windows, grossly splendid with gold fitted dressing-cases and crocodile handbags and what Philip called cad's cuff-links, used to ring an imaginary handbell and say, 'Unclean, unclean,' which was part of an old family joke.

Philip Le Measurer had not liked March's attentions at first. The homage sometimes took forms that invited comment; in defiance of the rules of precedence he always placed her on his right at his birthday dinner-parties, even if there was a Duchess there. 'He never says anything?' Philip had anxiously inquired. 'When he talks of you to me I just think how queer it is that people think he's ruthless and materialist, he seems to care so much for what you and I have got. It's odd that he's never married. But really the things he does are a bit much. He doesn't ever get tiresome when you're alone?' 'No, indeed,' she had said. 'I would have told you if he had. There's just this long drawn out impersonation of a Landseer dog.' But as his last illness settled on him he began to speak of March's devotion to her in another tone, and one night in their bed he said suddenly through the darkness, 'When I am dead March will ask you to marry him, that's quite certain, and if you like him at all you must accept him, for my father and mother are very old, and there'll be nobody who can really take care of you and the children.' The ghost of the warm and living love he had had for her walked dimly through the long, dim, weary sentence. She gave her promise with a laugh, telling him that he was not going to die, kissed him through the blackness and got a tired kiss in return. She supposed that he was being sensible enough. Philip always knew best; and Gerard March had been so kind during this long illness that she could not doubt his devotion. She should not want a second husband, but on the other hand, she could not conceive of life without one, since she had been married throughout the whole of her adult life.

But there had been some huge mistake. It happened that only half an hour or so after Philip had been found dead by his nurse Leonora had been standing beside the telephone when Gerard March rang up to make his usual daily soft, concerned inquiry. When she told him the news through her tears, he suddenly cried out in a high-pitched voice, 'But the doctors said he'd live another ten years!' Her tears stopped, she stared into the black throat of the telephone. But in a second it was bringing her his usual gruff compassion, couched now in biblical terms out of respect for the occasion; his father had been a Low Church parson. In half an hour he was there himself, casting his charm and strength and sympathy like a fur cloak, warm yet so fine as to be weightless. It had always been his great attraction that he seemed to promise security without making the slightest demand in return. The wreath he sent to the funeral was enormous, and he came all the way down to Dorset to sit in the front pew with the family, his smallness sunk down in a large overcoat, his bowed head nodding sadly in its depths. She was slightly disconcerted when he was the writer of one of those letters about Philip which old Mr and Mrs Le Measurer considered beautiful but which Philip would not have liked at all. Reading it, she remembered though she could not say why, Gerard's sudden shrill explosion down the telephone, and was repelled. In spite of all that had surely been his real sweetness and kindness, in spite of the promise she had made Philip, she found herself not at all eager to hear from Gerard again. But she was astonished and disappointed when she did not. For one thing, she found it embarrassing that so many friends should ask, 'And have you seen anything of Gerard March lately?' and could hardly hide their wonder when she answered that she had not, and presently, with alarming unanimity, stopped putting that question.

More than six months later he asked her to dinner; and she was very glad indeed to hear from him. Her life had become disagreeable in a way she had never anticipated. She had never been rich, before her marriage or after; but she had always had enough, and everybody round her had had rather more than enough, so that her life was full of presents. It now appeared that a carelessly drafted family trust had left her in her widowhood only half as well-off as Philip had thought she would be. The funds were equally divided between her and her daughters, and the income from their share had to accumulate till they were twenty-one. She could not touch it for their school fees or their keep. This meant that she had, at once, to sell her little white house in Kensington. For eighteen months she went about thinking of herself as valueless and unprized. So, at the time she met Nicholas she had had great need of reassurance.

*Eighteen months after Philip's death Leonora is visiting Paris with a friend.*

She went out to buy some books and some scent, and was walking round the corner of the Place de la Concorde into the rue de la Paix, when a man came out of a jeweller's shop and stopped dead in front of her. He looked at her in a searching way. He might have been a detective waiting to make himself quite sure that the person he intended to arrest was in fact the person pursued by justice. Then he smiled and said, 'You have forgotten me, but you and your husband came to lunch a year ago at our house in Deauville.'

She had already recognized him by his eyes. They were blue-grey with very long black lashes; a curiously feminine inset in a face otherwise bleakly masculine. He was indeed very male in a way she did not particularly like. He was tall and in ten years' time, when he got into his fifties, he might be too heavy, there was already a thickening about his neck. His shoulders were very broad and seemed more so because his waist was slender, he had

317

something of the top heavy look of a boxer. She found the effect of all
this massiveness unpleasing, disconcerting, because she had a feeling
he would use it to force things to go his way when it was hardly fair
that they should. His mouth was sulky. But the brute was tamed. He
was very carefully dressed. But though his taste was sober she was
sure that he and her dead husband would have detected all sorts of
things wrong with each other's clothes. They would have been quite
subtle points, almost imperceptible to a woman. It was odd that she
could not remember his name. He did not look entirely French, he
might have been Italian or Spanish, yet she thought his name was
more exotic than that.

'Your house was full of flowers,' was all she could find to say.

'Yes, we overdo it,' he answered, as if they had already been talking
for some time. 'The place always looks like a flower-show. We overdo
everything. We're half French, half Phanariot Greek. Both of us. I
married my cousin. We're an exuberant group, the Phanariots. When
was it you were with us? Last June, I think. There were probably more
roses in our drawing-room than actually exist.'

'It can't have been last June,' she said, 'my husband has been dead
for eighteen months.'

They had begun to walk round the square together, in the opposite
direction to which she had intended to go. He came to a halt, and she
stood by him, slightly bewildered, but not much. Then he began to
stroll on again. He said, 'I am sorry. But he was quite old, wasn't
he? Much older than –' she expected him to say, 'Much older than
you,' but instead he said, 'Much older than I am.' In either case it
was a strange remark. He couldn't expect her to say, 'Yes, so it really
didn't matter.' It would not even have been true. Yet surely there was
no other answer.

She found he was guiding her across the road, and he said, 'We'll
have tea at the Ritz.' She protested that the friend with whom she had
come to Paris was ill, that she was taking her back some books and
some medicine, but he said amiably that that could wait for half an
hour. When they got into the Ritz she had the impression that she
was going into a theatre with one of the principal actors rather than
into a hotel which she modestly yet impudently thought simply of as

318

a place where one stayed. The concierge came forward to greet him and give him a letter, one of the chasseurs ran up to assure him of a message performed, he moved with the assurance of someone more wanted than wanting, but pleased that he was wanted. He said, 'I am a son of the house, one of my uncles and his wife have lived here for thirty-five years.' As they sat down at the tea-table she liked the air and the light, the beautifully dressed women. She noticed they brought him tea without him having to order it.

He said, 'How long are you staying in Paris?'

'Two or three weeks,' she answered.

He thought for an instant then held out a cigarette case to her. It was of an odd gold that looked too much like gold and too heavy, and she did not quite approve. He said, 'Your husband was Philip Le Measurer. My family are in hydroelectrics, and have done a lot with Gerard March. That was why you came to luncheon with us. I see you are slightly embarrassed, it can only be because you have forgotten my name. You will not remember it even when I repeat it. I am Nicholas –' and indeed she could not take in his long Greek surname. 'I will write it down.' He took out a little diary and tore out the leaf and held it out to her, but took it back, and folded it up, and gave it to her again. 'Don't bother about it now,' he said, 'take it home and learn it by heart.' She was, again, a little disconcerted. Faintly he smiled. 'Then you'll know what's happening when my wife rings up and asks you to dinner.'

*He pursues the acquaintance and Leonora evidently meets his wife, Yolande. She feels the growing attraction between them, but '[b]ecause of Gerard March she thought she was imagining it – and the proof was when at [a] gala she saw Nicholas put his arm tenderly round his wife's shoulder'.*

Her left hand was lying on the table. His right hand went to it, covered it for a moment, while she stared at him, her lips parted, and then closed on it. Gently he crushed her bones, then his grip slowly tightened. She could not divine from his face whether he knew he was hurting her, whether he was not gone from her into a trance and was unconscious of what he was doing. She could not think ill of him for crushing her hand, because in fact she had found the pain delightful. She felt a tense delight, as if she were herself the sound of a trumpet, and great fainting pain, and a disinclination for disobedience. Suddenly his grip relaxed, but he kept his hand over hers and said, 'I want to take you somewhere outside Paris. On Tuesday, starting in the morning. Is there any place you would like to go?'

She said, 'Chartres, I haven't been there since I was a schoolgirl.'

He repeated, 'Chartres. No, not Chartres.'

'Why not?'

'A cold place. On a hill in bare country. Two large crowded hotels. How unsuitable. We can do better than that. Somewhere more genial.'

'Where?' she asked.

'You needn't know. Just pack your bag.'

'What?'

'I said, pack your bag. We're going to stay the night. It's time we were lovers.'

She hated him because he had not said he loved her, because he had never made an opportunity to kiss her, and hated him still more when he said, 'I am not waiting for a conventional period and saying the conventional things. You see, I hate the idea of getting a woman by pursuing her as if she were an unusually inefficient species of big game, clumsy on her feet, who got caught. I'd think nothing of any animal who didn't succeed in running away if that was what it wanted to do. We could make love beautifully. Inevitably you'll give me greater pleasure than I can give you. I'm a middle-aged man, beginning to get a little thick round the neck and the waist, and I think I'm rather a bore. I'm not really interested in anything but molecular chemistry and engineering. I'm completely unromantic. You're a beautiful though rather strange-looking young woman and a much more amusing human being than I am. I can't give you what I'll get out of you, but it would be foolish to pretend I can't give you something.'

She said nothing, and he went on, 'You needn't decide now. It's Monday. Ring me up if you don't want to go. I shall feel quite ill if you do. Since I met you outside Van Cupels I have had a continuous singing in my ears, I feel as if I had mountain sickness. I see from your expression you have the same symptom. Is there any reason why we shouldn't?'

*He takes her to a cathedral town, unnamed.*

'Why does it mean so much to you to be here with me?'

She could only look at him and ask with her eyes how he could imagine that it would not mean much to her; but his hard handsomeness showed no sign of understanding.

He went on: 'You're thirty-one? You were married for nine years? You've had two children?' She nodded her head to each of the questions. But then he asked, 'You must have had lovers?' and when she shook her head he said, 'How strange,' and was silent for a minute.

'This isn't at all what I expected,' he said. 'How strange.'

'Why are you surprised?' she asked. 'Lots of women don't have lovers.'

'I'm prepared to believe that but it's beside the point. I thought you would have had lovers.'

'Why?'

'Simply because of your eyes. I apologized to you a moment ago, it was because I should have liked to make my addresses to you at a proper pace. With pomp and ceremony. But to be the second man in your life, the first one that you have not walked down an aisle with in your white dress. My apology would have been a little different.' He stroked her shoulders. 'But even so why are you trembling as if we were doing something extraordinary? This is something so normal.'

'If this is a matter of routine,' she said, 'why have you brought me a hundred and fifty miles?'

He was taken aback. 'There's some sense in that.' He took out a cigarette and lit it.

321

'Your hand is trembling too,' she said. He looked at it and smiled and nodded.

'Yes, my hand's trembling and my ears are ringing and you are right, we are doing something quite extraordinary.' He extinguished his cigarette and said, 'Let's go to bed now.'

'Aren't we going to the Cathedral?'

'Certainly not. It would be very rash. The heavenly powers might work a miracle on me, or on you, or on both of us, which might upset all my careful plans. So we'll go to bed now.'

'No,' she said, 'no. You said I wouldn't have to do anything I didn't want to.'

'But you want me to make love to you,' he said. 'I am aching for you, and by the happiest of coincidences you are aching for me.'

'No,' she said, 'no. I don't feel in the least amorous, I feel ill.'

'I never make love to young girls. I am exemplary about that,' he said. 'I'm not making love to a young girl, how mean and unjust of you to contrive that I should feel as if I were. My dear, you are a woman, a grown woman, and I am a man, and it's time we threw away shame. We've something to do.'

He was so harsh, he was so bleak. 'There could be nothing we could do that would be any good to either of us,' she said. 'I want to go back to Paris.'

'You don't want anything of the kind,' he said, and bent forward and took her in his arms and for the first time kissed her on the mouth. It was very nearly a blow and nothing else. When he let her go she shrank back, covering her lips with her hands in case he did it again, and he said, 'Too late. You know quite well that now we've done that we've in effect done everything. Stop worrying about it. We're lovers, we must make love, it's an ingrained habit of our species.' He took her jacket off, then her blouse. She became hallucinated. There seemed to be a sun beating down on her, a sea before her in which she wished to swim. She wrenched herself out of his arms, stood up, and took off her skirt, keeping her eyes shut, as though the light of that sun were too much for her. 'You are horrible. I'm doing this', she said, 'because I want to, not because you do.'

'I hope that's true,' he said. She did not think she would ever forgive him. 'Why does he make me go through this without one word of tenderness?' she cried out to herself, as he laid her down on the bed. 'I would like to love and be loved, why will he not say one word about love?' She was enraged because he stripped off the rest of her clothes. It did not seem like rape – it would have been absurd to complain of rape – but theft. When he released her she drew the sheet over her face and thought that she would not be able to endure it. When he came back to her he too was naked. She thought how safe she had been with her husband, she wished she had married Gerard March, she did not want to be here in this strange place with this strange man. She thought with fear and hostility of the dark vein on his forehead.

He stopped and said, 'Can it be possible that I can desire you so that I'm ill? I'm stupid. I'm like a concussion case, and that you don't feel any desire for me at all?' He buried his face against her hair. 'Then let me make love to you out of pity.'

'It won't be pity if I do. Or cruelty if I don't. I can't do this. It's too awful.' But then his skin was on her skin as a widespread caress, his mouth travelled about her breasts, his arms cradled her, she knew an extremity of pleasure, which was wild, then became peace itself. She became a bird that soared, but as pierced and brought down through space by an arrow that was also herself, fused with him. It was as if she slowly discovered that her body was interpenetrated with another body, that was at once more physical and more ethereal, that existed just to receive and transmit pleasure; and it was being revealed to her because he too had such a body.

She had no idea what had happened to her. She did not know whether she was the slave of the intense pleasure he had given her, or whether she felt that pleasure only because she loved him. It struck her that he knew which it was, but would not tell her; and she would not ask him. She would not dare to admit to him that she might love him, in case by some covetous and unspoken brutality, a mere failure of his eyes to lighten, a preoccupied movement of his fingers across his lips, he showed that he did not welcome such a possibility.

*Later that evening, Nicholas speaks:*

'My plans weren't carefully laid. I forgot when I made love to you this afternoon that this meant that I wouldn't see you through the night with my love-making. I thought of myself walking with you beside the river in the afternoon and then having dinner and taking you up to our room in a celestial haze. Instead I've got to take you up to that bedroom stone cold. What have I done? You'll hate sleeping in the same room with me. That's familiarity. You know me well enough to let me make love to you but not for that. The thing is, I can't have blundered. I made this idiotic gaffe because I wanted to move in on you. I wanted to behave as if we had known each other for a long time.'

[He sleeps in the sitting-room. She wakes up and goes into him and sees him on his knees on the balcony, and goes and caresses him. He puts his head against her breast. They watch cats playing in the garden.]

She shuddered strangely. 'You want to go back to bed, you're cold,' he said, and took her there. She drew him down to her and he put his arms round her and she whispered, 'Oh, I wasn't asking you to make love to me, I only wanted to show I didn't mind you sleeping beside me.' And he said, 'But if I'm here I shall make love to you. Not much. Not a symphony or several movements like this afternoon, just a little more than the cat gets when it is stroked by a little girl when she kisses it good night.' But it was this embrace which delivered her over to him for ever. She was not curious or frightened by either his intensity or by her own, or by their delirium. This was an extension of the quiet night above their roof and it passed beyond pleasure to serenity and then to sleep.

When she awoke after their first night together he said, 'I am sitting here staring at you as if I were afraid I might forget you. But I will remember. My dear, I am so sorry that I must hurry you.'

He stood at the end of her bed and said, 'You're looking very pretty. Much prettier than before. And no wonder. "*Le seul poète, c'est le système nerveux.*"'

'Who wrote that?'

'One of our ambassadors,' he said, turning and straightening his tie in the mirror. 'They're always scribbling that sort of thing in the margin.'


## As they return

Nicholas said, 'I can't see you for two days now. It's hateful, but I've got some work I must do. I'm not even going out at night. I'm working on something I must get finished by the weekend. You won't think it's disrespectful of me to leave you alone till then? But you must know I'd like to be with you all the time. For several reasons. To go on making love, of course. I should like to spend eternity in your arms, as people so politely put it. How soberly I mean that. To go on and on feeling what you make me feel, that fierce refinement of sensation. Also to hear the ridiculous things you say, and look at the inappropriate way you look as you say them. Mysteriously you manage to be much wilder than your mind. But I have to work. So hard that while I'm working I shan't even think of you. I won't be telephoning. I'm stupid. I can only think of one thing at a time. Then when I'm finished I'll ask you when we can be together again. I want you to come and have luncheon at my apartment.'

But that evening he came with more flowers (he had sent her some) and stayed with her only a quarter of an hour. And all that time told her that she must come to him in Paris.

He said to her, 'Where do you live?'

'In Dorset. With Philip's father and mother. And my two children.'

He thought over that. 'Two children. Are they boys or girls, or, neatly, one of each?'

'Two girls. Cassandra and Harriet.' He did not comment. 'Ten and eight,' she added. He still said nothing. 'The names are family names.

325

It's awkward, nobody calls their little girls Cassandra, everybody calls their little girls Caroline. But', she repeated, 'they're family names.'

He said, 'I never thought of you as having any children.' He sounded rather cross.

She gave a foolish little laugh, and just stopped herself from repeating, 'They are ten and eight.'

'Why do you live with your husband's father and mother? Did you always live with them?'

'No. We had a house in London. We went down to Dorset for weekends and holidays. But after Philip died I sold the house.'


[And so on . . . and so on. . . . He badgered her with question after question. When does she get up for breakfast? She takes the children to school? What clothes she wore? He seems irritated, his reason for asking these questions seems to spring from his irritation.]


'It's so exasperating. I can't imagine you at any moment of the day, as you are over there. I want to get a clear picture of you in my mind. I would like to see you as you are –' he paused, and even more resentfully repeated – 'at any moment of the day.'

She was angry. He had no right to speak as if she had laid him under some obligation to acquaint himself with the whole fact of her being, and to talk as if this imagined obligation was an inconvenience to him. 'It isn't necessary that you should,' she said.

'Should what?'

'Be able to imagine me at any moment of the day.'

He looked at her. 'You don't admit anything, do you?'


*Leonora is telling Nicholas about her humiliation by Gerard March*

'Stop,' he said. 'I've heard this story before. He said he wanted you and then when you were free he didn't come through and there was a queer humiliating scene. He asked you to dinner and there were two of you, and a rather ambiguous relative who might have been a mistress, and he behaved as if it were all rather a bore, and never raised a finger. I'll tell you the name of your friend. It's Gerard March. African mines. I know him. I don't sympathize with your taste. He's a little man. What do women see in little men? But then I don't really understand any woman surrendering herself to anybody except me or some men who look rather like me, though no man ever does, darling, say no man ever does. But don't give March another thought. He used you as a cover for something. Either he's a pederast or impotent. In any case he isn't a man. I think from what I've heard he's impotent. You'd be an irresistible companion for an impotent man, he could imagine all sorts of things about you. What hell it must be to be impotent. Like having your hearing and your sight and being dumb, not being able to say anything about it. What's happened to you is like being hit by a cripple with his crutch. But what extraordinary people the English are. Don't other men want to do something about a man who goes about hurting and insulting their women? Not perhaps if he does it by being impotent, which gives the rest of us an advantage. Oh, you poor darling. How vulnerable all you English women are. You all grow up believing in romantic love, among a lot of men who've never heard of the thing. I wouldn't let Yolande send Gilberte to school in England, though it's the fashion. Do you want your daughter to have lovers and take money from them? I would never think of my daughter in that way. I turn my imagination away from my family. I don't try to know what love affairs my sons are having. But all the same I wouldn't give them an education that would incline them to take a wrong direction when they make that journey into a territory I must never think about.'

'Who can have told you about Gerard March?'

'Oddly enough, I can't remember.'

It came to her mind that there had been other women whose names had for a time been linked with March's. 'Would it have been Nini Corder? Harriet O'Shea? Jean Murdoch?'

'No,' he said, 'none of them,' and yawned.

'Don't you know any of them?' she said.

'As it happens I know all of them,' he said. 'Nini Corder I've met at Suvretta. Harriet O'Shea was dancing at Cannes when we spent Easter there. Jean Murdoch's often at Cap d'Ail. But none of them do I know well enough to ask them if they've ever had a wasted evening. And let's not waste any part of this evening.'

When they were making love he sometimes looked at her with the downcast lids and sideways smile of a proselytizing priest, urging a convert over another hurdle of the faith. It was indeed like being absorbed into a religion. She lived a dedicated life. She did not want to see people, she did not want to go to picture galleries or theatres, she went for walks only because the open air was good for her skin. But this was not idleness. She contemplated his image perpetually. She said, 'What can I do for him?' She bought clothes very carefully, going to several of the great dressmakers before she chose a dress, entirely with reference to his taste. In the hotel room, she hardly read, she sat by her window varnishing her fingernails and her toenails, looking down on the tops of the chestnut trees; and thinking of him, with love, with lust, with wonder. She would grow fascinated by memories. Once when she went to his country house she had seen him riding, and it filled her with ecstasy to remember how his ugly hands had looked among the reins on his horse's withers.

Sometimes as he sat beside her in an automobile, he would draw the fingertips of the hand nearest her along his mouth and then press them for a second against the bare flesh of her forearm. It was the remotest form of caress imaginable. It was as tenuous as a whisper on the telephone. It bewildered her that sometimes when he had made extravagant love to her and they were lying side by side, he would brush his lips with his fingertips and then put them to her forearm, just as if they were in public and their bodies dead again with clothes. What did that mean? That he wanted to warn her that making love was making love, but they were still separate people? That he wanted to own that when they were not joined by desire they were still joined in some way that had almost nothing to do with the body?

When she entered his flat he used to put his hands on each side of her face, kiss her on both cheeks, then draw his hands down her throat and over her shoulders, and down her arms till he took her wrists and brought her hands up to his mouth. Sometimes in the midst of her joy at seeing him, she would feel bewildered because of the sadness of his face.

'Do you think when we die there's anything?'

'I'm sure there is. I believe in the existence of God and the Son of God and the Mother of God. They're there. I knew it in the war. But they're two-dimensional, no deeper than a picture or a mosaic, though they work miracles and save us. It'll all be absurd, winged giraffes in the Place de la Concorde, but otherwise just like the world as we know it.'

He liked to pour out wine into a goblet, for both of them to drink from.

He liked to call her 'you wicked little thing'.

In bed when he wanted to read he used her back as a book-rest.

'We always make love all the time as if God were looking at us.'

When he was naked he was more like a Roman statue than a Greek one.

He was untidy. He was always taking his possessions out of his pockets and putting them down. But they always fell into groups like a seventeenth-century still-life. They made the room look beautiful. He bought antique scientific intruments and once left one in her hotel sitting-room – a fifteenth-century astrolabe.

'You hate walking along this passage, you wish there was some way by which you could be transported from the windowseat of my living-room straight into my bed, without having to give away that you go to my bed by your own free will. You nearly die of embarrassment every time, I can feel it. But why? You aren't a humbug. You never try to suggest that you're doing something for my sake which you don't want to do. It puzzles me. But it's your folly. You may have one little folly.'

'You are a little mad. I'm complimenting you. You know, you get a horse, and then you try it out, and you find there's something a little mad about it, and you know then it is going to be a good horse.'

His feeling that to kiss a woman on the mouth was something as intimate as the sexual act, that it would be as shameful to be seen by a third person doing the one as the other. Old fashioned.

'Whores don't attract me, but I've nothing against them. They are realists who face reality for the sake of practising an art or making easy money or doing both at the same time. And I respect them for escaping one humiliation. A whore's the only woman who goes to bed with a man without running the risk of the man thinking that she's in love with him though he's not in love with her. If I were a woman I couldn't bear that.' But isn't that, she thought, just our case? Or isn't it?

He hated pederasts but thought it pardonable for women to be lesbians. But he found this difficult to explain.

'Wouldn't you think it odd for me to go to bed with, let us say, Yvonne Achille?'

'No, she's pretty, you're pretty, it would be quite charming.'

'But what would we get out of it? When I make love it's for the sake of being as close as I can to someone' – she dared not say it – she dared not ever speak of love – 'who is strong as men are, who gives a sense of protection.'

'You take it all too seriously. Can't you see that it might be pleasant for two women to use each other's prettiness to give each other sensations?'

'It's odd, you're so professional about sex,' she said, 'and then I suddenly realize you don't know a thing about it. Sensations.'

Nicholas thought Frenchmen brutal to and about women. 'It's their livers. We Greeks have killed off all our own people with weak digestions by the badness of our food, and left a digestively strong people that isn't interested in food.'

Nicholas did not care much for food and drank wine with an impatient liking; he complained he could not taste it after the first glass. But he had a passion for sweets, not chocolates, which he would not let himself indulge. She bought all the local sweets she could, and left them about her hotel sitting-room so that he would see them and she could watch him eat half a dozen wolfishly, and then check himself with difficulty. It seemed so odd that this was evidently the only thing he thought it wrong to do. He developed this habit of coming in to see her in the evenings if they were not to make love that day. He used to come in before he went out to dinner, very correct in his evening clothes, his public self, a hard, rich man, arrogant and unsympathetic and impassive. It was as odd that he should be the lover she knew, half out of his body with subtlety and desire and revelation, as it would have been if he were a poet or a musician. She would be dressed for her dance or her dinner-party or her theatre, and he would tell her how she looked. He would tell her what he had been doing that day, either not troubling to make it comprehensible, or perhaps hallucinated into thinking that everything he said was comprehensible to her simply because he said it. He would ask her what she had been doing, and always found her answers surprising and comic, as if the idea of her being able to do anything independently of him was amusing, as if she showed great hardihood continuing to exist and moving about when she was not in bed with him. He had usually arranged for his car (a huge Rochfort Schneider) to take his wife alone to the house where they were to dine and send it back for him, so that he should have stayed with Leonora only ten minutes, but sometimes he stayed longer. Once, on such an occasion, he looked at her and sighed 'I must go, they'll think I'm making love to someone, and how I wish I were.' At the last moment as he turned away he took a crystallized walnut as a compensatory sweetness from a box. It turned out to be full of syrup in a thin shell of sugar which broke between his fingers and the syrup ran down his dress-shirt. He sat on the edge of the bath while she sponged the syrup off his shirt front, and they laughed together.

'An improbable reason for being late!' he said. 'Even Yolande won't believe it! A walnut!' Laughter lightened his face, it lost its heaviness, she was surprised by its beauty, she bent over him and dropped a kiss on his lips, then retreated back into laughter, and as he had ceased to laugh went further back into silence. He looked up at her wickedly and said, 'I win point by point. You never kissed me before without being asked. Now I go without regret. To make love after that would be an anticlimax.'

Once when she went to stay at his country house there was an afternoon when it was raining, and she could not make love. When the others sat down to play bridge they went out and had a walk in the woods, amused by the sound made by the artillery of summer rain. Sometimes they stood still and listened to it, face to face, smiling with happiness, while he held her clasped hands to his breast. The arcades between the trees. . . . He said under the rain, 'Oh, my girl, my sweet girl,' and drew her to him, and kissed her as he rarely did except when they were making love. Both their faces were wet with rain. 'We might both have been crying,' she said. 'It's not our thing to do.'

His two sons were tall and dark and hard like him, but more graceful. She wondered if he had ever been as beautiful as they were, and if it were simply time that made him so unpliable, so like a rock. They had that sad look too. 'We all, my sons and I, look subtly awful. Just a hairbreadth's difference and we might all be the sort of man Josephine Baker might employ as a chauffeur.'

His wife was his cousin. 'I'd as soon be in love with my sister. Indeed sooner. Chateaubriand gives one that idea in one's romantic youth. I think someone has been very unkind to her. But naturally I don't discuss that with her. I haven't the slightest hesitation in making love to you in my own house.'

When she was staying at his country house she came downstairs in a new white satin dress, and though there was nobody else down, they stood beside each other by the great hearth like strangers. He said, 'That's a new dress, isn't it? Turn round. It's lovely. And it will look

332

its loveliest when I see it tonight as a white shining circle on the floor by your bed.'

'Let me wear it for a moment. I took a lot of trouble over it.'

He gave her a glass of champagne.

'Everything about you is so romantic. You do not belong to my world. You might be a spirit from the woods. All the women look at you with surprise. You don't know any of the things they've worked on all their lives, but you can trump all their aces. They'd be envious if you didn't win them over but it's so plain you aren't out to compete. And all the men wonder what you're like. But are frightened of you. Quite frightened. By God, you weren't the woman to cure Gerard March.'

The mention of Gerard March still hurt her. 'What do you mean?' she said. 'If there is a woman who could cure him, why shouldn't it be me?'

'I notice that you'd like the idea of curing him though I am your lover and you're faithful,' he said. 'We're none of us entirely monogamists. But of course you're frightening. You're intractable. You shot into my life and into my bed, and you might shoot out again. But I don't think you will, for reasons that they won't ever know, quite private to ourselves.'

'Do you mean', she said in sudden shame, 'that they all know that you're my lover?'

'Oh, no, they don't know that,' he said. 'We've both been so discreet. They just consider you as someone wonderful who might be loved. Drink that champagne. I know you don't like it. But you should drink it.'

'Why should I do that?' she asked as she obeyed. 'I don't like it.'

'Because you'll blush less easily if you do. You won't care so much,' he said. 'There's Carrière and his wife coming downstairs now. Start talking to me about dogs. Then she can join in.'

'Just any dogs?' she asked, laughing against the bubbles of champagne.

'I can't remember which breed it is she's interested in,' he said, 'but one dog leads to another.'

The day he made love to her in the afternoon, and a fog fell so that they spent the night together in his apartment. He telephoned to his home. 'I wish I had my dogs here.' The wood fire. The lights. Naked she went near the fire, and he called her away, 'You'll get burned far quicker than you think.' They read, they ate, they listened to a concert on the radio, they made love again, they got hungry, they went to the kitchen and got food, they went to bed and slept all night, they had not done that since the first time they were lovers. His hand round her breast.

'Your breast is hard and yet it's soft. It has the feeling of being something folded upon itself. It might unfurl and be a wing. A torturing thought.'

'Why torturing?'

'To an engineer quite torturing. A couple of wings just there would make a hopelessly unstable unit.'

The telephone rang and he did not answer it. 'I want nobody to be able to imagine that we are together in this room. I won't give them the slightest clue, even the knowledge that I am in this room.' It was true that there was immense joy in the secrecy of their companionship. When he took her throat so that her chin rested on the span between his finger and thumb and looked down on her face while she looked up at the eyes shining light out of his darkness, they could contemplate each other as if they were the only people who had ever been on earth.

She asks him, 'What good is the square root of minus one?' He begins to explain, then bursts into laughter, 'It's too absurd. Anybody who knows about us, or anybody who suspects what we are to each other, knowing we were alone, would imagine us as locked in lust, transported in passion. And how much of the time you spend cramming me with caramelles, with walnut fondants, with macaroons, out of God knows what evil intentions, no doubt so that I will grow enormously fat and you needn't be jealous, and how much of the rest of the time you spend treating me as an encyclopaedia, to fill up the gaps in your deplorable education, it's simply prodigious, you do it again and again, you have a passion for knowledge at the most odd moments, and God knows where it will lead you. When I was a little boy I picked up a copy of *La Vie Parisienne* and on the cover was a drawing of a man fully dressed coming into his wife's bedroom inflamed with rage, and his wife, all pink, jumping out of bed, and a man, all pink, staying in bed, and the wife saying "One moment! I can explain everything!" I wasn't so little that I hadn't a rough idea what was going on but young as I was I couldn't see how she could explain it. But I shall be that man one day and I shall come in one day, and I shall find you in bed with another man, and you will get up and you will say, "One moment! I can explain everything! Just about an hour ago, I felt an overwhelming curiosity about the third law of thermodynamics and this gentleman" – Oh, darling, your fidelity to me hangs on a thread. I may lose you any moment to a man who's better at exposition than I am. I may as well enjoy the privileges I may lose just whenever you get in touch with a man who has a science degree. Sweetheart, sweetheart, open your arms to me, but first brush back that strand of hair, it's the loveliest hair but I don't like finding it in my mouth.'

In the morning the fog had cleared. He was sorry.

He said (some other time), 'I don't make love to you in the morning. One could make love to anybody in the morning. There's nothing personal in that. You and I go to bed because it's the intensest way we have of thinking of each other.'

'You went to — ? Why?'

'Because you did your military service there.'

'Just for that?'

'Why not? I liked to see where you once were.'

'When I was young. Imagine you doing that. What did you do in the town?'

'I stood in the street and stared at the barracks. Then I went into the public park and sat by the bandstand. Then I had lunch. And then I went and walked along the river, under those trees. Down that tributary that comes in after the bridge, where the trees are bleached. And then I went back to Paris.'

'Did that really amuse you? It's nothing of a town.'

'But it was amusing to think of you, and imagine what you were like.'

He was disconcerted. 'You spent the whole day just doing that? But how sweet of you! I can't bear it. Oh, damn it all. It isn't half an hour from Paris, it's two hours. You must have got up in the early morning. You can't have got back until the early evening. And you were at the theatre.'

'Why, how did you know that?'

'Someone mentioned it when they were telephoning this morning. Some man.'

'I didn't see anybody I knew. Except Solange Guidener.'

'If we had money [*during military service*] we had our own girls.'

'Did you have a girl?'

'Of course I had a girl. Girls are what I have.'

'Ah, don't laugh at me! I'd like to be all the women you have ever made love to.'

'Darling, I implore you to give up the idea. Please forget it. I'm really alarmed. It seems so possible that that will show you some wonderful new scientific way of turning yourself into all my mistresses – then you'll say to me, "Wait a moment. This explains everything". Oh, it would take quite a long time and it would be so boring for me to have to do all that a second time.' They were rolled up against each other by their laughter. 'And this girl, oh, I'd hate you to become her. She was thin as an umbrella and pale as phosphorus. She had to be. You see, I was a Socialist then and I chose my girls like that because they were downtrodden victims of the capitalist class and looked it. They had to be skin and bones and livid pale. Like Picasso, I had my blue period. Only like him I'd say by constant experimentation with new ideas I have reached the present stage of my art. O sweetheart, don't, don't take me back to my blue period. What a nightmare,' he said with sudden seriousness, 'if your eyes looked up at me out of someone else's face. Oh, come close. Establish your identity, prove to me that all of you is you.'

'You've made love to me so well that if you meant nothing at all to me, I should be grateful for ever, but, of course, if you were the worst lover in the world I shouldn't mind.'

'Why not, I'd like to know?'

'Well, it would be you.'

He lit a cigarette and she saw that, as on the first time they had made love, his hands were trembling. With his other hand he covered the dark vein on his forehead. 'I have said the wrong thing,' she thought. But how can he expect that I should go on and on being his mistress unless I felt an emotion for him which would make me happy just to be with him? How could he think I can see so much of him without taking him as himself rather than as a purveyor of pleasure?

'The trouble is that there is a physical connection between love-making and having children, though there isn't any mental connection. A man can have children by a woman he doesn't love and be perfectly satisfied with them, and if a man adores a woman he'll probably think of having a child by her. It's a brutal thing to do to a woman who's fragile and pretty and who is being charming to one, to say, "In nine months from now you'll suffer pain, and most of those nine months will be disagreeable."'

'I hate virginity,' he said, 'I think it's the nastiest arrangement of nature.'

'I would have thought you could have avoided it.'

'I have. I've only had one virgin in my life, and as you know the facts of my life you will understand I loathed it. It's a horrible thing for a young man to have to do to a young girl he likes and doesn't love. But all the same I sometimes wish I could have been your first man.'

She had often wished it.

'You make love so beautifully, so intelligently, I sometimes think afterwards, "She knows so many things someone else taught her."'

'Oh God, you are a thundering ass! I don't make love like that.'

'Your skin is different from anyone else's.'

'What's the difference?'

'I'm not sure. My skin knows but won't tell.'

*Nicholas speaks*:

'I distrust any account of a love affair which describes lovers as sleeping in each other's arms. The only comfortable way a man and woman can sleep together is either for the man to sleep with his back to the woman, and she lies with her arm like a little fin through the crook of his elbow, something marine, something seal-like, or for her to sleep with her back to him, which is very pleasant, he can wake her up by kissing the nape of her neck. Face to face may be advisable for conversations of the mind, and love-making is partly that, but it's no particular help for the conversations of the body, and sleeping with you is a heavenly physical conversation. I wake feeling we have come nearer to an understanding of all sorts of things.'

'The real reason against promiscuity for women is that most men have nothing to give any woman, while most women have something to give any man. I mean of course inside the circle of people who have organs that are not merely generative but sexual. However casual an affair is, however commonplace the woman is, there can be something that's charming. Suppose a man's lying on his back on the bed, his arms behind his neck, and a woman's sitting on the edge beside him, and they've made love and it's all calm, she can do something so delightful, simply putting out her arm and caressing him, the way she bends her head, even if she's quite plain, it'll be memorable. What likelihood is there that most men will do that?'

'I'm bored by your body,' Leonora said. 'It makes an inconvenient third. It's as if just because we liked to eat saddle of mutton sometimes we had to live with a sheep as our constant companion.'

'I count it a supreme triumph that I can get a woman who can say such awful things to go to bed with me and like it. Go on and make some more remarks like that. My complacence will get richer and richer. And by the way my sexual being can't be compared with a sheep.

'Why do you goad at sex? It works out pretty well for you. I've never known anybody who likes making love more than you do. You

338

say nothing, you practise reserves which are almost comic, but how your eyes shine, and often you're the most deliberate of artists.'

'What on earth is he talking about?' she thought. 'And is it better for me that he should think I am a deliberate artist, whatever that means, or know that I'm not?'

People guessed they were in love. Sometimes he came over to London. He borrowed a house once on the Wiltshire downs. A shire house on a ledge. Moonlight.

She sometimes, when she was in England, wondered why he should love her and whether he would not tire of her quite soon, but he took pains to make it clear that whether that might happen or not, it had not happened yet. He sent her notes all the time, a telegram just before she came to him.

*Nicholas asks who made a comment which Leonora has repeated to him.*

'A very pretty woman with chestnut hair called Solange Guidener who mentioned Yolande.'

'Who gave this party?'

'Someone called Pauline de Mercier. Do you know her?'

'Yes,' he said, 'but I haven't seen her for years. I'd forgotten she existed. She evidently does.' He went and filled the goblet with wine, came back and put his arm round her waist, and drew her down on the sofa, and made her drink out of the goblet, and then drank himself. 'Léo,' he said, 'you must come and live in Paris. Really you must.'

'I can't, I can't,' she said. 'I must stay with the children at their grandfather's.'

'What can that matter? They can see their grandparents quite often. But you must come over here. And live here all the time. You must. You must.'

'No,' she said.

'You understand that I am asking something terribly important to me.'

'Yes,' she said, 'but it's terribly important for my children that I go on seeing their grandparents.'

'If it's a matter of money I'll give you money. I've always got my women disgracefully cheap. It's time I paid. I'll give you quite a lot of money.'

'But this particular money is the money my children ought to have,' she said, 'and there is the house. And I am sorry for my husband's parents, they are old. It is my duty to be there most of the time. This is the kind of thing you'd make me do, if I were your wife or your sister or your daughter.'

He was silent, and they went on drinking the wine in alternate draughts, till the glass was empty. 'It's ill luck that I've got a moral being for my mistress. But can't it be more than just one week in four? Oh, please, my darling.'

'I'll try,' she said, 'but it's so difficult.'

'Why can't you take money from me?'

'I don't need it.'

'Your husband didn't leave so very much. I had his estate looked up at Somerset House by our London Branch.'

'That isn't all I have. My father left me something too.'

'That wasn't much either. I had that looked up too. I wish we could marry. It would be so much more convenient.'

'No,' she cried, 'no.' A vision of his country house. The roof off, Yolande, the plain daughter, the two sons, sitting exposed to the weather.

'You wouldn't like it?' he asked.

'Not at that price,' she said.

'It's odd, marriage which isn't a marriage because it's incestuous is harder to break than a real marriage,' he said. 'My sons and my daughter are my second cousins.'

'I couldn't bring up my children in your house in Paris if your family was round the corner. You wouldn't like living with my two little girls in a household. We couldn't make love. This is the only way. It has to be secret. You don't know how intimate I am with my children. We couldn't sit and drink out of the same glass.'

'I'd lose you that way too. The fact is, you and I are childless and we want the relationship of childless lovers, but both of us have children. No, there's nothing for it but to go on as we're going.'

'Why do you mind so much tonight?'

'I'm troubled sometimes,' he said, 'by slight apprehensions.'

'But how irrelevant marriage would be to what we've got. How people would interrupt us. We'd have to make love by night. It would get confused with our need for sleep. Now our relationship is perfectly pure, it's unmixed by the slightest taint of anything outside itself.'

'You have some magnificent possessions. There are your eyes. When you came to luncheon at Deauville I was so wildly excited by them. I'd never seen eyes that spoke of such an immense capacity for pleasure. I don't mean just love-making. I hate those dirty old men who say that a woman with three ginger hairs in her left eyebrow is the thing to go for. I mean you enjoy everything, food, spring, me, rivers. I can make you do anything by showing you a river. It's all shining in your eyes, that greed which is so generous, it isn't greed, it thanks so nicely for what it takes. And you have the softest hair, like my daughter's when she was quite a little girl. She was very pretty then. She isn't now. I dare say she will be later, though I had a very plain grandmother. And you have the quickest reaction time of any human being I've ever known. You see every field in a landscape, you see every detail of a tympanum over a church door as soon as you've lifted those deep eyelids of yours. You should never use eyeshadow, your lids are the right colour, they're naturally a shadowy grey. And you can add up a column of figures like a flash!'

'Grey eyelids and mental arithmetic,' she said, 'who would have thought those two would have made a man kiss one from the collarbone to the ear.'

'You think so quickly, you move so quickly, I feel as if I were looking out of a window and watching a swift flying round the house. And there's your mouth. It's quite without form of its own. Then when you feel or think anything, your lips writhe like little serpents and you make yourself a new mouth that's appropriate. When I say to you, "Do you remember that time when we went to the village in the forest near Autun," your lips are blank and then they waver, and

341

there's the memory of where we were and what we did. There's much more to you than that but now tell me why you like me.'

'I like everything about you,' she said.

'You can't. I wonder you like anything about me. Oh, perhaps you don't.'

'Your eyes,' she said.

'They're in bad taste like a loud tie,' he said. 'Find something else.'

'Your high cheekbones,' she said.

'A touch of Albanian blood, we rather suspect,' he said.

'I like your thick hair that looks sleek and isn't, it's rough like a dog's when you touch it,' she said.

'Am I supposed to think that flattering?' he said.

'And I like the way your muscles are like a map over your body,' she said. 'Incontinent continents.'

'And I like the odd way your hip-bones don't lie quite the way one expects, but more delicately, a little bit of Chinese carving,' he said, 'but let's go to bed, let's take an inventory of all the other things we like.'

'I particularly like those queer muscles above your ribs,' she said, 'I've seen them on statues before.'

'As to what I like in you, my taste is less recondite and austere,' he said. 'My dear, you are so sweet today I'll give you a special treat. I won't make you walk along that passage. You won't have to face the fact that you want to be loved and bruised and turned into a quivering little animal and then have to be brought all the way back to being a serene and dignified human being again all by nothing in the least like magic. I'll carry you along that passage so that you can pretend you're being raped. Up you go.'

He set her down on her feet in the bedroom, and unzipped her dress, and kissed her down her spine, while she took off her shoes and stockings. Nowadays she wore no girdle, no brassiere, in case they made a pattern on her skin, only some ribbon suspenders. They were very pretty. She spread them out and wound them round her hand so as not to crease them, and her eyes fell on the reflections of their heads in the wide mirror over the chimneypiece. She saw him smiling, but it was a sad man who was smiling. He was, when she came to think of it, always sad. She turned round to face him, meaning to ask him why he was sad, but he picked her up in his arms and laid her on his bed.

'When you say "hurt me" you are so sweet. You don't really want to be hurt. Your mouth tells me you have to steel yourself to say it. You only like to be hurt the least little bit, there's almost no perversity in you. But you know I like to hurt you that little bit, so you think I might like to hurt you still more, and you want to give me that pleasure. Sometimes I think of that, I can hear you saying, "hurt me", and my eyes are wet. But I have to confess to you that I would hate to hurt you really, pain isn't what I want to give you.'

'Oh, God, oh, God, let this last for ever.'

*In the synopsis Rebecca West writes that Leonora and Nicholas* 'are together in his flat on the quay, when Avril [Waters] comes and calls on him, to get him to pay her hotel bills. [. . .] He is infuriated. Avril [Waters] has never been his mistress but she has for some years been in the habit of expecting him to pay her hotel bills. In a rage he goes in and writes her a cheque and throws it at her. The scene is brutal. When she goes Leonora and Nicholas have a talk and suddenly Leonora realizes he is thinking, "She realizes that Avril is not my mistress, how awful it would be if she guessed the truth." She guesses that when she goes back to England he goes back to the woman who was his mistress when he first met her.'

'She's not my mistress. I don't think she's ever been anybody's mistress. It's not her line.'
'After the last two years you couldn't say that of me.'
'Leonora, you must not talk like that. Of us.'
'Why not? The thing that you do with a whore is what you do with me.'
'Yes. That is the most horrible thing in the world, that the

343

most exquisite luxury should be the same as the most brutal necessity.'

'I cannot bear to be thought of as either a luxury or a necessity.'

'But everything that exists is either a luxury or a necessity if it isn't worthless.'

She was suddenly ashamed of her nakedness, and he perceived it, and picked up her peignoir and slipped it on her. 'How hard you're breathing,' he said. 'This has been a hideous shock. Lie down, lie down.' When she did not move he lifted her off her feet and laid her on the bed, and pulled the sheet over her, and sat down on the end of the bed and lit a cigarette. She thought how many women had probably lain in among these pillows. 'My God, what has this damned woman done to us?'

She went back to London and telephoned to the two men who wanted to marry her. One was out, so it was the second whom she married. She told him that she had been in love with another man, but he did not mind. She never showed the benefits of the experience she had acquired with Nicholas except fitfully, when she was pretending it was Nicholas. Then she was hideously jarred because of his delight which took her out of her fantasy. The violence of her second husband's making love at first surprised her. But he was famined. Nicholas had never made love out of famine. She supposed he had never let himself get even very hungry.

Sex was not a universal function. It was a lottery. Everyone knew that there were some huge prizes of delight and that among them were those which matured into lasting happiness. Hence there was no woman but hoped that she would derive from her relationship with her husband or her love[r] such pleasure as she herself had been given by Nicholas. Yet she believed, and had some basis of experience for that belief, that Nicholas was a genius as a lover, and that genius in this field was as rare as any other. She was further fortunate, she suspected, in that she had some share of sexual genius herself, or rather that her sexual being was of a sort on which Nicholas's genius could work happily. She was in the happy position of a singer whose voice is specially suited to the operatic music of Mozart, and who meets the perfect Mozart producer. Such a destiny as hers could not fall to many women. That the singer was enjoying unusual good fortune would be generally admitted; women who cannot sing usually know it. But her own destiny must have seemed to most women within their reach, if only among the men they met was a man like Nicholas; and certainly genius does not exist in such numbers.

When Leonora thought of what differences there were between Nicholas and other men it seemed to her that other men's kisses had no weight to them. She remembered Nicholas's mouth as pressing down on hers so heavily that it was painful. This was perhaps not purely physical, it was perhaps a trick of her memory that made material *something* which was spiritual. Every time that Nicholas had kissed her she committed herself to *something* she could not name. To a sort of obedience. But obedience was not the word. She would not have performed any act which she believed to be wrong simply because he told her to do it; he would not have asked her to do anything about which she was capable of making a decision. For a woman to obey a man is horrible, to surrender her will, her sense of right and wrong, it is the sort of thing a prostitute does to curry favour with a man. That obligation which Nicholas laid upon her and which she accepted was to go with him out of life, to the place where they went when they made love: to accept their illicit relationship as a means to this discovery.

*Leonora and her second husband spend some years in Africa before returning to London. Ten years after her love affair with Nicholas in Paris, she goes, evidently alone, to Vienna and discovers that Nicholas is staying there too.* 'They have a long dialogue and spend the night together and then part.'

Nicholas says about the future, 'Nothing matters. The flag is torn!'
  'What flag?'
  'The flag. Any flag. All flags.'

He says as he goes about Leonora's room, 'One can see you have been loved. That is what strikes me as so sad about my daughter. Every now and then when she is ill I go into her room and there's nothing lying about that shows she's been successful at convincing anybody she is a woman. You know, the little jars, the unnecessary things. Everything for use. Sensible.'

'I come first with you. You needn't say, "What right have you to do that?" I'm not saying that I ought to come first with you. I'm saying that I do, and by no right that can be recognized by logic. Just as you come first with me. Of course you know quite well that I would automatically say that to any woman I found myself with in any circumstances resembling these. But you know just as well that with you I mean it. And you know that this too I would say to any woman. I am prevented from telling you the truth so that you'll believe it. It's a sort of prison . . .'

'All you wanted, when you asked me to come over to live in Paris, was that it should be more easy for you to desert Solange. Wasn't it?'

'I didn't know you knew about Solange, though I knew that Solange knew about you.'

'How did she know about me?'

'I didn't tell her. I told nobody, though of course it was understood between Yolande and me. But as it turned out everybody knew. One of my sons spoke of you casually the other day, he didn't say anything indiscreet but I realized he'd always known. Yet I tried hard never ever to look at you when we were in the same room. I suppose we were obviously so damned happy that people guessed. You used to sit and glow. I suppose I did too in my murky way. Oh, what you threw away, what you destroyed!'

'The first time we ever made love when I took you to—. We made love so wonderfully that afternoon, but it was not then that I knew that you belonged to me. Do you remember how I slept in the little salon, because you were frightened by it all? I was very stupid with you, even brutal. It was a compliment to you. I was so agitated about you that I could not work things out, and I woke up and thought of the afternoon we'd spent and I was staggered by it all, and went and knelt by the window and looked out at the street, and the river was beyond, and you came in and stood beside me, and we talked a little, and I turned my head and kissed your breast through your nightgown, and you shuddered. Not much. A little *frisson*, that was all. I admired you so much. You'd brought such courage to bed with you. This extraordinary thing happened to me, and you let it happen to you. You might have refused: women sometimes refuse even when what they're getting is the ordinary thing. They're passive. But you came with me, you inexperienced, deliberately limited little creature. But I knew you were horrified because you had gone to the end of the world and back with a naked stranger. So I pretended you were cold. And I carried you back to bed, and then you stretched out your arms to me and told me I could come in beside you. I don't remember what you said but you were very funny. You really felt it was awful of you to make me sleep on the sofa in the other room, from a social point of view, you were just like a nicely brought up woman saying to a weatherbound guest at her house in the country, "Oh, but you must stay to dinner", and at the same time you were agonized lest I thought you were asking me to make love to you again. But your good breeding pushed you on, you just had to tell me that I could come into your bed. It was so funny and so pretty, that I had to make love to you again, and then you were so so sweet, and so – I don't know how to name it, that I found myself thinking, "I must keep her, I must keep her my own for ever".'

When they were making love their other bodies declared themselves, which felt an immense hunger but were not gross, they were joined in chastity.

Making love was not a fury, a madness, or an obsession, it had nothing to do with all that, it belonged to the reasonable side of life.

Again she awoke and it was still dark. He was awake too, and when she stirred he spoke to her.

'Tell me. It's not the sort of thing I should ask you. It's not the sort of thing you should tell me. But tell me. Our case is a special one, so tell me. Were you happy with other men?'

'No. Never. It wasn't their fault. It wasn't what I have always been with you.' Her voice died, she stroked his face through the darkness.

'I know,' he said. 'I know. I never had anything like it.'

They lay close together as if it were a grief they were sharing, and slept again.

When she awoke in the morning she was lying with his left arm behind her head. She put down her head against his ribs to hear his heart beating and brushed his flesh with her lips. At that he stirred, opened his eyes, stretched his right arm across his body and ran his fingers through her hair and pulled it hard. Then he chuckled and said, '*O, toi!*' and with his left arm jerked her up so that his head was on her shoulder, and they laughed into each other's faces. It seemed to her that nothing as beautiful as this had ever happened between two human beings.

But he was not her lover now, he was her friend, and one could not betray one's friends – and indeed friends did not betray one as lovers did. Morton was better value for her than Nicholas. She gave up this puzzle of accountancy. It was the immensity of her love for Nicholas which made the barrier between them. She would not dare go back to him even if Lionel were dead.

'There's nothing we can do,' she said.

'Nothing?' he said.

'No,' she said. 'For one thing, if there is a war, Lionel will have to go back to the Army.'

'Yes, in that case it wouldn't do, of course,' he said. That argument was for him, as she knew it would be, quite final. He got up. 'When war comes I hope you'll be all right. You've got somewhere to go outside of London? Your husband's good at looking after things like that?' He looked at her face, put out his hand and tousled her hair so that it covered her eyes, and said, '*O, les sales Boches,*' and sighed, and went into the bathroom.

'How long did you stay with Solange Guidener?'

348

'How did you know it was Solange? I thought I had been so very careful.'

'Somehow or other after Avril Waters did that abominable thing I knew all about you. I remembered things. I wonder why that should have been. What she did had nothing to do with all that.'

'If an act's abominable enough it explodes. It no longer hits like a thrown stone, it bursts like a bomb. And everything falls in ruins.'

'But did you stay long with Solange?'

'No. A year or so. She was very good to me after you left. She told me she knew and that I didn't need to pretend. But it all petered out. She's all right, however. She married an American and lives in New York. Really, she's perfectly all right. She likes New York.'

'She likes New York because she had suffered here, she hadn't been able to stand sharing you with me, she was brutalized by suffering, and so you left her, or wanted to leave her, and she saw it and went. And now you say, she's quite all right. She likes New York.'

'You don't understand. Solange was a pretty woman, and a nice woman, and I will always be grateful to her but she is not the same sort of animal as you. Not for one moment, not for a second, did she come first with me.'

'It's you who do not understand. She knew that one week out of every four you didn't come to see her, and that you went to bed with me as you went to bed with her, you were naked with me as you were naked with her, you were deep in me as you were deep in her. She could not bear it any more than I can bear the reverse side. Would you have shared me with another man?'

'I've never shared a woman who meant anything to me with another man.'

'That is not what I asked. Would you have shared me with another man?'

He stared at her. 'You. Let's think. Yes. If that had been the only way of getting you. Or keeping you. Or getting you back. What's the good of talking about this? I'd have taken you away from any other man. After that first time you'd have left any man for me. And you didn't leave me for another man. You went to another man, but he wasn't why you left me. Nor, for another thing, would you have ever

349

consented to be shared by any two men, whoever they were. You're too scrupulous. Also you are too cruel. You wouldn't recognize any peculiar situation.'

'That's true. Can't you understand that if I wouldn't have consented to be shared I couldn't consent to share you with another woman?' she asked.

'But you did and you were happy. I don't believe you have ever been so happy since you left me,' he answered.

'How could I help it? You wouldn't come and live in France.'

'I couldn't come and live in France, and you couldn't help being unfaithful to me. And I couldn't help leaving you.'

'But I was doing my best,' he said. 'When you were there I never looked at anyone else.'

'What would you have said if every time I had gone back to England I'd had a lover there?'

'I'd have called you a slut,' he said, 'but it's not the same thing and you know it. When you went back to England you didn't want to be unfaithful to me. Never. I know you. I was faithful to you with my mind, but my body wouldn't hear of it. So I slept with another woman, and I got out of bed the minute I could, and waited for you.'

'That is the arrangement which didn't please me,' she said.

'It did, you thought it oughtn't to and so you pretended it didn't but it did,' he said. 'Ask yourself if we weren't happy. I never was so good a lover in my life. What more did you want? We lived in paradise.'

'I suppose it's hard for you to imagine,' she said.

She realized that he knew something about her but not all, and that he wanted to know whether she had had any [more] children. She saw that though it was possible that at any moment he might say across the room something about her body which would be like a blow across her face, he could not bring himself to ask this question. She stood up by the hearth and faced his form while she lit a cigarette. 'Why should I tell him? Why should I be kind to his jealousy? What did he do to mine? What right has he to disapprove of what I do?' But the childish sullenness of his mouth made her tell him. 'No, I've not had another child.' She went on to think, looking at his mouth which was not sullen for a moment and then was sullen again, 'Now he's wondering whether I chose to or if it's by accident. I will not tell him that. To think he wants to know!'

He said in English, 'My dear love, my dear, true love,' but she was not sure if his English were good enough for him to understand how that sounded to her ear.

The kind of love they had had for each other was bound to end in tragedy: but it alone would give that revelation. Nicholas would not have esteemed it so highly if it had been only pleasure. There was some knowledge and wisdom derived from the discussion of their bodies.

He had never believed that their relationship could have any other ending but pain; and he had never rebelled against this belief. He would be faithful to a woman for a time, and never be happier than during such a time, but his faith would be based on an acute perception of sexual values which would lead him to breach of faith. The god had to be served wherever destiny had built an altar; and Communion had left the last celebrant clairvoyant, so that she would know of the new novitiate. How could this sequence be broken? She had a persuasion that it could be ended by a surrender to love. But if he had been unfaithful to her and had gone on living with her she would have known it in agony; and he would have known her agony; by that he would have been brutalized, for he could not have stopped betraying her, and if he had left her and she had waited for him to come back to her their relationship would not create itself again. She would have been brutalized by suffering. Their bodies would have been connected by another link than pleasure, which would not have served the religion of sex. If she had been married to him and had children she could have endured it. She could see herself annulling sex, making him priest of an inferior religion to her own, by going to him on some night when he slept at home and getting into his bed and saying to him, 'Give me another child,' and lying, unresponsive to his skill and indifferent to his magic, while he did, what was for her, just that, a way to get another child, and again he would have known it, his body knew everything. But she could not have married him; and what a thing it would have been to do to him, who was a priest of that other religion by birth, who should not be insulted for what he could not help. 'Not after we had begun that way. I could not have gone on the other way,' she said to herself. 'And we could not have begun any other way,' for she remembered how she had felt like the sound of a trumpet, day in day out, before he became her lover, nothing of her left but an anguished vibration. There was no other possible relationship between them except the one which had been.

She would never be as useful to any human being as she was to him, no other human being could be as useful as he was to her. It was true but it was in defiance of fact and logic. With Lionel she had known physical ordeals of courage under heat and fear in Africa, and the wild beauty; with Philip she had known all the resources of the civilized world. She had known infinite kindness from both. With Nicholas she had done nothing but perform again and again and again the simple ballet that two bodies can compose together. Yet somehow she had realized a wider range of her potentialities with him, somehow he had disclosed many more qualities than Lionel or Philip. How could that be? To what god was he making sacrifice when he poured his spirit into her through his mouth and his loins? A god, he had always known, without kindness. A god who had to be worshipped simply because he existed. All his fineness had been wasted in the service of this cruel god – there was occasion for such sorrow as simple people feel when they hear of a promising man become a monk, only Nicholas's vows had been of wealth and unchastity.

'I couldn't meet you as a friend,' he said. 'I was your lover, and I can't be anything else. I may be a resentful and hating lover, but I am still your lover. You can't think of a resentful and hating friend, and no more can you think of a friend giving you pleasure that turns your body into something better than your body and floods your mind with light. If we were friends and met and never went to bed, it would be as if one of us had said to the other, "I don't want you any more!" That's not for us.'

'But isn't that what you would have said to me, sooner or later,' she asked, 'if I had stayed with you?'

He was silent. 'No,' he said at last. But he went on thinking about it. She could follow what he was thinking. He was remembering some recent love affair, which had been important to him, though not as important as theirs, and wondering whether he could have brought himself to abnegate the pleasure it had promised if she had still been his mistress. He said, 'I would never have said, "I don't want you any more," because I would always have wanted you. I might have lied to you and deceived you sometimes. But I would have always come back to you. What is between us is the absolute.'

'But you made love to other women.'

'You hadn't any reason to fear them. You must have known you had a unique value for me.'

She paused before the question, because she knew he would never answer it by saying he loved her, but in the end her curiosity forced her. She asked him. 'Why, what was that?'

He told her curtly, and she stared at him in astonishment. She could not see why so slight a physical thing should have mattered so much to him. She said, 'You never told me.'

'Greek cunning,' he said gloomily, 'it often overreaches itself,' and laughed. 'No, it wasn't that. It was my secret, my own joke. It sent me to heaven. It was so amusing that you who were a prude had this marvellous gift and didn't know you were doing anything wonderful.'

She thought: 'He must be using the word prude in a comparative sense', and he burst out suddenly with black hatred, 'Has nobody else mentioned it to you?'

'I'd forgotten what a brute you are,' she said, but he would not say that he was sorry. After a long pause she said, 'I never tried to do it. My body did it because I liked you. So with other people it did not happen.' She paused. 'Was that why you would have shared me with another man? That thing I did.'

'No!' he said. But he would not say, 'I loved you.'

His last words to her: 'You were abominable to leave me.'

353

*Leonora Morton, remembering all this, is still standing in the octagonal hall, preparing to join her friend's party.*

The lovers women remember are usually older than themselves, and women live longer than men; so it happens when they are old that they find themselves thinking with passion of a face or a body which is no longer anywhere in all the world, which has as completely vanished from existence as if it had never really existed, as if it had belonged to an imaginary personage invented by a painter or a writer.

Nicholas had died of rage. The dark vein on his forehead had killed him. He had been in Paris at the time of the German invasion, and had been called to see Laval, and in the course of an interview concerned with the future of the works had broken into shouting and had fallen dead. He had said earlier to his nephew, 'I have a terrible pain in my arm'. His sons had been deportees, and only one had returned to France at the end of the war. Yolande had been in prison but was released.

She felt that it would have been better if she had not left him, if she had gone on and faced betrayal in full consciousness, brutalization, even desertion. Indeed, to have him go from her while she was still unquestioning in her acceptance of him would have been like being abandoned on the burning dunes without water. Yet she did not believe he would ever have deserted her. It would not have been *quite like that.* In Vienna she had seen that what he had esteemed in her was both that she had left him and that what was between them was so strong that she could not really leave him. She had to go back to what was the truth about their relationship. She would have liked to spend the whole of eternity trying out the relationships possible to them. She would have liked to be his wife; the first woman he ever made love to, the girl he kept when he was in military service; she would have liked to be Solange Guidener, she would have liked to be a woman who was only his friend, the mistress he had when he was old, whom he would have clasped to him chiefly for comfort. But there was no such woman, for he had never grown old. That he should have been cut off when he was still strong, that he should have missed some joy, that he should never have had white hair, this brought tears to her eyes.

But it was then that she was pierced by a sensation painful as pain but without site. It inconvenienced the whole of her, but was not present in any part, though she was aware that if it affected her she would be sick for the first time since she was a child. She knew she should walk to a chair and sit down, but she could not move. It struck her as a miracle that she should ever have moved. She could not think how muscles worked. It would be all right if somehow she could get to the man at the front door, which was only thirty yards away, through the main door of the hall, and down the steps. If she tried she could perhaps stagger over to the door, and he would see her. But she heard the front door open on some guests who were even later than herself. They might think if they saw her rocking across the room that she was drunk or drugged, and would be less disapproving but more frightened, perhaps more disgusted, if they recognized that she was, as she supposed she was, dying. So she stood still, and was pleased to find that she could support herself. The latecomers came in, two married couples, and the men halted at the drawing-room door, and the women walked past her to the cloakroom. She had hoped she might know them, know them well, so that if words came out of her mouth as strangely as she feared they would, they would be brave and not show their fear when she asked them to call the butler because she was ill. But they were strangers and she simply fumbled with her bag as if she had stopped to find something. This meant such effort that she panted and had to clench her teeth and check the outflow of her breath lest the panting turn into groaning. She found herself remembering a ballet seen half a century before, which ended with a girl in a white dress standing in just such a house as this in the foreground of a bright gathering like the party in the drawing-room which she doubted she would ever see. The girl had slowly keeled over from the vertical to the oblique, while the man beside her as slowly fell to his knees, so that her head came to rest on his ruffled shirtfront, as the music became fatally sweet, sad like the Russian champions' skating, and the curtain fell. 'The timing of life is all wrong,' thought Leonora. 'How lovely the girl was, with that little oval face all ballerinas had then, like the back of a teaspoon, and her blue lids closed over her eyes. How dead she looked and how pathetic. But when I die and close my eyes my wrinkles will make such a noise about life nobody will be worrying about the pathos of death. Only the young can die beautifully, but the profession is manned by the old.'

For an instant it seemed that she was feeling better. Then the pain found its lodging at last, in her arm, and became an assault, an assassination. Till then she had thought she was going to die, but now she knew it. The body was trying to evict her, to throw her out into the air without a stitch. 'Yes, life is unendurable,' she told herself, 'but it will not have to be endured for long.' Something had gone wrong with her sight. The hall was lit by sconces set halfway up the high walls, leaning forward and spreading their gilded branches towards each other. Now the lights made a continuous yellow band round the room. A mist was swirling round the house, and she wondered if fog had fallen, but when more latecomers arrived, the women's dresses looked as if they were veiled, and all their faces featureless, they might have been spendthrift burglars wearing the finest stockings as masks. She mounted above appearances and suspected everything she saw as a sign of death.

The pain was cutting through her like a kitchen knife, separating her body from her mind, and hurting both. This was too much for her to bear. Ever since she was born she had had to bite off more than she could chew, and this was the last savage excess of exigence. And not to be evaded, not to be trumped by some other resource. One could stop doing things by an act of will, one could not stop being. 'A gasman, a dustman, a postman,' she thought, 'they can lay down tools and refuse to work, soldiers can resign their commission, there are those things MPs apply for, the Chiltern Hundreds, whatever they are,' – what a lot of things she had not time to find out. What had Toc H been? – 'but as human beings we can't say no, we have to go on and on being human, even to frightful this.'

Several people were standing not too far from her, two men waiting for their wives to come out of the cloakroom, a couple who seemed to be impatiently waiting for someone to join them, looking back at the front door as it opened and closed. When she could trust her dry tongue and quivering lips she would ask one of these faceless figures to find the butler. Not the butler belonging to the house, there probably was none, the caterers' butler. She had seen him when she came in, not to be mistaken, the wire-haired terrier type of Scotsman, like Sir Alec Douglas-Home, the butler she always asked Willowes-Aumbrie to send her when she had people to lunch or dinner. He would do what was necessary, take her to a room where she could lie down, and telephone for a doctor and an ambulance, and he would know too that it was just as necessary that it should be done quietly, that she must not spoil Patricia's party.

She said, 'I have a terrible pain in my arm.' She was weeping because the pain in her arm was really terrible. She was smiling because she was saying the same words he had once spoken.

The pain was gone from her arm. It was as if a magnet had lifted it out.

He said, 'I'm bringing you some brandy. I remember you don't partake –' He came to a pause, and gave an embarrassed smile. 'I should say, you don't drink. But I thought it might be what you needed.'

She said, 'How kind,' but looked up into his face, raising her eyebrows. He put her into a chair.

He explained carefully, 'I noticed you were very pale when you came here! Mrs Rhodes came to me and said you were standing here looking very white.'

'Mrs Rhodes? Do I know her?'

He took a canny look at her and waited a moment before answering, 'She's been at your house three times when I've been waiting at table.'

The forgetfulness of old age was not the gentle thing people thought. Old age was a kind of madness. There was nothing to be done about it. But usually one was able to make the connection. As she drank the brandy he said, 'It would be good for you to go home. Your car is still here.'

The chauffeur said, 'Who is your doctor, madam? I'd better ring him.'

'What, send for a doctor in the middle of the night?' said Leonora. 'I would never think of such a thing. So vulgar, I always thought. My daughters were both born at six o'clock in the afternoon. It gave the doctor time to go home and have a bath and a drink before dinner. One must stick to routine. Ring the doctor in the morning at half-past eight. We will be there in five minutes.'

But she had not got five minutes. By an effort of will she recalled that by a foolish mistake she had put all that sort of thing in the transparent plastic purse which she had meant to throw away because it had split at the bottom, but had left it on the dressing-table. It was now empty – everything had fallen out of it through this split. It followed that she would never reach the hospital. But it did not matter any more.